"I gave you my vow not to escape."

He nodded agreeably. "And that, combined with my constant surveillance, should keep you honest. I must warn you also that I've locked the bath chamber door from the other side."

She didn't throw anything at him, though it was tempting. "And you call yourself a nobleman," she said.

"Aye, I do, lass."

"With high ideals and lofty aspirations."

"I believe you may be thinking of the pope."

She preened him a smile. "I shan't confuse the two of you again. Will you at least leave while I don the gown?"

"No."

She paced again, glancing over her shoulder at him as she did so. "On the other hand," she said, "I might mistake you for Satan."

Other **AVON ROMANCES**

LOIS GREIMAN

The PRINCESS MASQUERADE

AVON BOOKS

An Imprint of HarperCollinsPublishers

This is a work of fiction. Names, characters, places, and incidents are products of the author's imagination or are used fictitiously and are not to be construed as real. Any resemblance to actual events, locales, organizations, or persons, living or dead, is entirely coincidental.

AVON BOOKS
An Imprint of HarperCollins*Publishers*
10 East 53rd Street
New York, New York 10022-5299

Copyright © 2004 by Lois Greiman
ISBN: 0-06-057145-4
www.avonromance.com

First Avon Books paperback printing: April 2004

Avon Trademark Reg. U.S. Pat. Off. and in Other Countries, Marca Registrada, Hecho en U.S.A.
HarperCollins® is a registered trademark of HarperCollins Publishers Inc.

Printed in the U.S.A.

10 9 8 7 6 5 4 3 2 1

To all the readers who continue to believe in romance.
Thanks for sharing your time with me
and the countless people who live in my head
and insist that I tell their stories.

Prologue

The Isle of Teleere
In the year of our Lord 1817

A wisp of feminine laughter capered on the spring breeze. Nicolas Argyle, fifth viscount of Newburn, turned, intrigued by the sound.

"Surely you know of a decent inn, Cole," drawled Lord Bentor, better known as Cask by those who drank with him. "Even Teleerians must need libations and a bit of sport from time to time."

Nicol scanned the crowds. Market day was winding down in Portshaven, but the rough-cobbled streets were still bustling with activity. He skimmed his gaze past a farmer, a miller, a rickety dray pulled by a spavined chestnut. And there, just beyond the leather wright's stand, he saw her. She was leaning over a cloth merchant's counter. Her back was narrow, her waist tiny, her hands delicate, and though he couldn't see her face, there was something about her ...

1

Something almost familiar, but not quite. Was it her laughter? Her movements? The curve of her breasts when she turned just so?

"Cole?" said Cask, drawing his attention from his silver flask, which was, by the by, nearly empty.

"Hmm," observed William Enton, baron of Landow. "She doesn't look to be his usual fare."

"Who's that?" asked Cask, glancing blurrily about.

"I believe it's the maid in the straw bonnet who has whetted the good viscount's interest," said the baron.

"Where—Ahh," Cask sighed as he caught sight of the girl. She stood in profile now, with her face gently shadowed by the well-worn brim of her hat. "Not his type?" He drank the last drop from his decanter and gave his friend a rheumy glance. "You must not have noticed her bosoms, lad."

"As a matter of fact, I have." William Enton, third baron of Landow, was bored and inebriated, though perhaps neither so bored nor so inebriated as Cask. "But if you can drag your eyes out of her cleavage for a moment, you'll see that she doesn't resemble a bitch of any sort."

"Umm," said Cask, scowling thoughtfully. "Baroness Delafont did look something like a saluki if you saw her in a certain light."

"Panting to your face, but snarling at your back."

"And the tawny-haired one . . ."

"Exactly like a whippet."

"Lady whose her name . . . The one with the ungodly sad eyes?"

"A spaniel."

"Needy," agreed Cask. "But in a grasping sort of way. Do you suppose he chooses them for their money?"

"Cole?" Will asked, still not glancing at their enraptured companion. Of the three of them, Nicol was the least intoxicated, but he carried their nearly depleted bottle of wine, therefore having a modicum of control over the two who gossiped nearby. "No. He chooses them on the basis of their willingness to see him gone when the time comes."

Perhaps Nicol should have objected at this point, for he heard his companions' every word, but the girl was fascinating somehow—entrancing.

"So what do you think of this maid?" asked Cask.

William watched the girl haggle with a nearby cloth merchant. She wore a simple, mint green gown. It was tied high above her waist and was a couple inches short, even for her modest height. Her frayed, straw bonnet gave her a youthful appearance, and no jewels adorned her slim hands. "I would say she is neither wealthy nor grasping."

"But Cole has had something of a dry spell since . . . What was that last one's name?"

"Amelia."

"That's it. There's been a bit of a dearth since she's found herself a rich husband"

"Six months at least."

"Perhaps he's losing his charm," suggested Cask, but in that moment the viscount began to wend his way through the crowd toward the girl.

Will watched him go and wondered dimly if he himself would ever care enough to pursue a woman again. Grimly taking a drink from his mug, he turned toward Cask. "What now?"

"Well, old chap, we could find ourselves some female companionship."

"You're too drunk for female companionship."

"And you're too morose. But how 'bout we give it a go just . . ."

Their voices faded off, but Nicol barely noticed. Somewhere to his left a pig complained vociferously about its lot in life, while behind him a man roared about the size of his nuts, but the noise of the outdoor market did nothing to break his concentration, for the maid was very close now. She stood stroking a scrap of pink velvet and speaking softly to a merchant who disagreed emphatically.

When she tilted her head much of her face remained hidden, but her plump lips were entirely visible. They were as bright as spring berries and just as lush. But that was not what intrigued him most. There was something entirely familiar about her. Something that drew him on, and in that moment the girl smiled. He had seen that expression a hundred times though he couldn't say where.

Thus he pressed on, making his way through the crush until he could hear her voice. It was husky and soft as she concentrated on the stout merchant on the far side of the counter.

"I'm sure it *is* a costly piece," she said. "But there's so little of it. Hardly enough to stitch into a bonnet."

The merchant scoffed. He was dark and balding, with a short man's bravado. " 'Tis the originality of it that enhances its value, girl. You'll not find another piece with its richness and—" But his words stopped short as he noticed Nicol's presence. "Good sir," he said, his tone rising happily with financial hope. "What might I do for you this fine day?"

It was difficult for Nicol to wrest his gaze from the girl. So difficult, in fact, that he failed to try.

"It would be a good choice for you," he said instead, still watching her.

She glanced up from under the brim of her hat, but her face remained shadowed, her features hidden.

"The color would suit," he added.

Her lips twitched the slightest amount. From this close proximity he could see that her gown was faded and her hands rough. Will was right, she was hardly his usual fare, but there was that niggling familiarity. Or perhaps it was the fact that he had drunk his weight in red wine on the voyage from Sedonia. Of course, it might be the soft rise of her breasts beneath the pastel gown that fascinated him the most.

"Are y' flirting with me?" she asked, her tone blunt and cool.

"Me?" Nicol tried to sound affronted. "Nay. I was merely stating a fact. The velvet would complement your hair." It curled out from beneath her hat in flaxen waves and lapped merrily down her narrow back.

"Um," she said, and he couldn't help but admire how her plump lips curved tantalizingly up at the corners.

"Four anglas," said the merchant, still beaming. "A bargain at twice the cost, and surely the lass would be grateful should you purchase it for her, good sir."

"Would she?" asked Nicol, not turning toward the shopkeeper but keeping his attention steady on the girl.

She shook her head, but her smile widened slightly. "I am never grateful for less than a full yard."

"Truly?" He couldn't help but be charmed by her. There was an honesty about her, a simple earthiness that differed nicely with her cool confidence. "Then I suspect there is little purpose for me to purchase—"

"Ah look!" crowed the merchant, straightening from rummaging beneath the counter. "I've found a bolt of it."

She turned. "Y' said there was no more velvet to be 'ad."

" 'Twas what I believed myself," said the merchant, grinning sheepishly and striking his shiny pate with the flat of his hand. "But your beauty must have driven the cloth straight from my memory. Would she not look fetching dressed all in pink velvet?" he asked, turning like a harried sheepdog from her to Nicol.

"She would indeed," he agreed, "but I'd hate to see her dressed identically to the very next maid who happened to wander past."

"Ach!" scoffed the merchant, shaking his head. " 'Twill never happen. Such quality is only for the most discerning lady."

"Perhaps," agreed Nicol, "but I believe I saw a bit of lavender just down the way a piece, and now that I think on it, I believe that color might suit her better still."

"Lavender! Nay!" The merchant was shaking his head vehemently, his hangdog eyes mournful. "A lady of such obvious delicacy should be dressed in pink."

Nicol shook his head thoughtfully. "I fear I'd have to disagree."

The bolt disappeared like a shot beneath the counter as the small scrap was resurrected. "Two anglas," he said, lifting the small bit of velvet. "'Tis robbery, but it suits you, lass." There was the slight tone of panic in his voice.

"Done," she said, and reached for her reticule, but Nicol was faster. Dropping two coins onto the counter, he picked up the velvet and handed it to her with a shallow bow.

She took it without a word and turned from beneath the wooden awning into the fading sunlight.

They walked side by side in silence for several moments before she slanted a glance up at him. "Shall I assume y' are unusually generous or that y' still 'ope for me gratitude?"

He smiled at her. Contrary to Cask's belief, Nicol had not had a dry spell, for women were attracted to him. He knew it as surely as he knew his name. They were drawn to his noble title, intrigued by his dark gypsy features, lured by his jaded demeanor. Perhaps a few even liked him a bit. But he was always careful that they knew the truth. He had no plans for a future with any of them, for he was neither a man who suffered the pangs of love, nor one who needed an advantageous marriage to improve his bank account. On the other hand, he did, often enough, need someone to share his bed.

And this lass would fill the bill very nicely, for she was comely and quick-witted and had that faintly familiar allure of mystery.

"I've been called many things, but generous . . ." He shook

his head and raised the bottle of wine. It was made of heavy, green glass, nearly empty and stoppered with a cork. "Would you like a bit?"

She took it but didn't drink. "I should probably tell y' that the rumors about me aren't true."

"Rumors." He raised his brows. It was a glorious spring evening. The weather in Sedonia had been dark and drear, but here on the isle of Teleere the sun shone with bright optimism. "I like the sound of this. To what rumors do you refer, lass?"

The top of her bonnet barely reached the level of his nose, but even against the hard-packed turf, he could hear the click of her heels and realized her height was somewhat enhanced. She was a tiny thing.

"You 'aven't 'eard rumors?" she asked. Her accent was that of the working class, burred and slightly lilting, but in his present state it did nothing but tantalize him.

He shook his head. Off to his left, two dogs quarreled over a lop-eared, grinning female. "I'm new to your fair city."

"Ahh, well . . ." she said, and shrugged a little. "Then there *are* no rumors."

He glanced at her. Even from beneath her bonnet, he could see the lovely slant of her smile. "I've spent a rough voyage with two drunken companions. Surely you wouldn't deprive me of a few juicy stories."

He saw her lips quirk and couldn't help but wonder what it would be like to kiss them, to feel them curve beneath his own. In fact, he couldn't stop himself from thinking of other things, just as soft and plumper still.

"Surely y' know what they say about rumors," she said. "They are oft more interesting than they are true."

"Ahh, and more's the pity."

"But y' don't even know what the rumors are."

"That's because you refuse to tell me, and me a guest to Portshaven." He shook his head as if sadly disappointed. "I must say, thus far I'm not overimpressed with your city's hospitality."

She laughed. The sound was husky and curled into his system like woodsmoke on a cool night. "And I suppose y' think I should make amends for our lack of courtesy."

"Or at least tell me the rumors."

She glanced off to the side, where the dogs' quarrel was growing louder. "I'm employed at the Cup and Loaf."

It seemed to be a complete thought, and it took him a moment to read her meaning, but finally he understood. "Ahh, you're a barmaid."

She nodded.

"And therefore the rumors."

"Goodness knows one cannot be a barmaid and be virtuous at the same time."

He remained silent for a moment.

"'Ave you nothing to say to that?" she asked.

"If I knew whether or not you were being facetious, I could agree or disagree as seems most advantageous." He shrugged. "But as it stands—"

"That is *other* people's opinion of barmaids," she said. "Men's opinion."

"Oh!" he said, faking chagrin. "Of course. And they are absolutely wrong."

She laughed, then silence settled in again.

"Aren't they?" he asked.

She arched a brow at him. "I can understand why your companions thought it best to get drunk."

"I but jest," he assured her.

She stepped into the lee of a corner booth. Canvas covered the side of the merchant's stall, leaving them nothing to see but a green sweep of Teleere's renowned hillocks.

"Do y'?" she asked. There was laughter in her voice, but there was, maybe, a deeper emotion.

He refused to acknowledge it. His sojourn to Teleere was bound to be a boring one. He would take his pleasure where he would, and here seemed a wonderfully likely place. "Of course," he said, and gave her a truncated bow. "My apologies. I am often told that I do not appreciate the gravity of the situation."

"Are you?" she asked, and, sweeping her bonnet from her head, wiped away a droplet of sweat with her knuckles. "By whom?"

"By—God's bones!"

She started back, her eyes going wide. "What is it?"

"You—" He shook his head, but the movement did nothing to clear his mind. Standing before him was the spitting image of Anna. "Nothing," he said. "Nothing. You just . . . remind me of someone."

"Who?"

Her eyes were as wide and green as the Teleerian hills. He wondered momentarily if there was fear in them, but he put the thought away. Neither she nor her counterpart seemed the type to fear, but damn they looked similar, though Anna's hair was a shade darker and her skin not so fair.

"Who do I remind you of?" she asked again.

He stared at her for one more breathless moment, then smiled and forced a shrug. "A princess."

Her eyes narrowed slightly. It did nothing to distract either from her stunning good looks or her resemblance to Sedonia's sovereign ruler, Princess Tatiana Octavia Linnet Rocheneau. It was uncanny really. Shocking.

She cleared her throat and moved restlessly away, but he grabbed her arm, and she started, her expression going sober.

"My apologies again," he said and released her abruptly. "It's simply . . . It's surprising."

"My resemblance to a princess."

He grinned, hoping it looked sheepish and harmless. Her

similarity to Tatiana did not make her less desirable. Hardly that. For there were those who thought him in love with her.

"Dine with me," he insisted, though he had not meant to speak.

She raised her brows at him.

"At the Cup and Loaf," he suggested.

"Have y' a wish to die young?" she asked.

He shook his head, still a bit bewildered by her appearance.

"Then I suggest y' eat elsewhere," she continued, and he couldn't help but watch her lips move. Couldn't help but think of what it would be like to hold her in his arms, to feel her bare skin against his.

"And what of their accommodations?"

"Not quite as 'igh-quality as the food."

He smiled. She was, without a doubt, the most interesting woman he had met for some time, for while her face and figure reminded him of Anna, her bold demeanor and earthy charm were entirely her own. Like the flip side of the princess she was, touchable and seductive and lovely. He took a step toward her. "And what of you, lass? Will you be there?"

She had to tilt her head back to meet his gaze, but there was no longer fear in her expression. "I 'ave a small room at the Cup."

She was drawing him into her eyes, into her cleavage, into her world. "Is there room for two?" he asked, and, bending slightly, kissed her lips. They were full and soft and hopelessly alluring, but she drew back abruptly.

"I told you the rumors was false," she murmured, breathless now.

Reaching up, he skimmed his knuckles along the sharp line of her jaw. She was amazing, incredible. So like Anna, and yet not. "Do you know how beautiful you are?"

Her back was braced against the canvas wall. "Like a princess?" she asked, skepticism heavy in her tone.

"Yes." Perhaps it would be wise to deny it, to tell her she was unique and special, but the blood was rushing to his head and other places, and he wasn't thinking as clearly as he might. "Beautiful yet touchable."

"Unlike a princess."

"Yes." He was mildly surprised by her insight, but not surprised enough to refrain from kissing her again.

Placing a hand against his chest, she pushed him gently away. "I 'ave to go."

"No. Please." He caught her arm. It was dim and cool in the shelter of the merchant's stall. "Spend the night with me." He was surprised by his own words. After all, he was no bumbling boy, hot-cheeked with the thought of his first woman, but she did things to him. Seductive, darkling things.

Her expression was tense now, her eyes sharply focused on his face. "Because she won't."

"What?"

"Your princess," she said. "She won't sleep with you. But of course I will, since I'm not 'ighborn."

He skimmed his fingers down the fine slope of her throat. "Believe me, lass, I am hardly in a position to look down upon those of your station."

"Truly?" Did she bat her eyes at him? " 'Tis good of y', sir." Was there sarcasm in her tone? For a moment he wished he had not drunk quite so much, that he was just a bit more discerning. "And you a . . . what?"

Her skin was as soft as a dream.

"Pardon?"

"Your title," she said. "What is it?"

"Viscount." Perhaps he made the statement with some pride, but at times it was still an amazement to him, the second son of a penniless baron who had come into wealth and power. "Come with me, lass," he urged.

She shook her head and scooted sideways, but he skimmed

his fingers around the back of her neck, stopping her movement. Her hair felt heavy and warm against his knuckles. Luxurious and soft and erotic. "You'll not regret it," he said.

"Because you're a viscount or because you're rich?"

He grinned, then kissed her again and felt her weaken. "There might be other reasons."

She pressed her palm to his chest again. Her hand felt ridiculously right there.

"So you're not offering me coin?" Perhaps there was tension in her voice, but he was past caring.

"Is that what it would take, lass?"

She definitely stiffened now. "Being a commoner don't make me a 'ore."

"I didn't say it did, lass. I simply . . ." Her bosom was rising and falling only inches from his face, distracting him. "Tell me what you want, and I will give it to you. We can both win."

"Really?" she breathed.

He slipped his hand down her arm to her waist and very gently kissed the high portion of her breast. "Yes."

She jerked away, and in that moment he saw the wine bottle swing toward his head. Indeed, he almost had time to duck, but it caught him just above the ear. He stumbled sideways. The world spun crazily. Her pretty face tilted, then he hit the earth with a muffled thud, spilling darkness around him.

"Sorry, Govner," she said. "Looks like I'm the only winner 'ere today."

Chapter 1

Somershire, nestled in the southern hills of Teleere

Megan was tired. Her fingers ached as she tucked them into the opposite sleeves of her tattered coat, and her blackened eye still felt tender. She'd never been overly fond of stitchery. It was tedious, and she had to travel through a rough side of Somershire to deliver the garments, but it was a job, and she took any honest work she could find. She also took a good deal of dishonest work. It wasn't something she was proud of, but she could live with her lack of pride. She couldn't live on an empty stomach. And she would live. That's what she did. She survived. A tough 'un. That's what Mum had called her. *"You'll be all right,"* she'd rasped into the darkness of their tumbledown cottage. *"You'll be all right, love, 'cause, you're a tough 'un."* Her voice had cracked. *"My little acorn. So strong. So smart. Like your da."* She'd touched Meg's face. There were tears in her eyes. Even in the pre-death blackness, Megan could see them glisten in some errant shaft of light that had found its way onto her face. *"You'll be all right,"* she'd said again, then she had died, quietly and without complaint, just as she had lived.

Megan cleared her throat. She'd best hurry or she'd be late for work at the inn. Hard work. Time on her feet, which already ached from her hurried trip across town. The cobbles echoed softly beneath her footfalls. Her breath curled smoky fronds in the winter air, and her belly rumbled ominously, but she ignored both the bite of the season and the pang of her hunger, concentrating instead on the coins she'd earned. Perhaps she shouldn't skip supper. She'd already lost weight since her ribs had been cracked, but if she didn't eat, she could save every one of her lovely new coins. She'd wrapped them in a cloth and shoved them into her shoe, having learned early on not to keep them in a pocket. Pockets could be lost. Or stolen. A few abrasions and a day's lost income had taught her that years ago. But she'd not been more than twelve then and had healed rapidly. Her last run-in hadn't been as pleasant, but at least her tormentors had been better dressed. She glanced nervously sideways and winced. Oh yes, she'd learned that a woman alone could not afford to trust men, be he a prince or be he a pauper. The price of a man's clothing rarely told the state of his soul. But she had nearly reached the Lion's Share, where she worked and kept a room. She had nearly beaten the odds once again.

The back door of the inn groaned open as she scuttled inside. A chill draft of air curled in behind her, clashing with the moist heat of the kitchen.

"'Bout time." Cate glanced up from where she slopped stew into a wooden bowl, her bright eyes hard on Megan's bruised cheek. "You look like 'ell. Apt to scare the customers."

"They'll be too drunk to scare, and it ain't so bright in the common room. We busy?" Megan shed her coat quickly, then donned a stained apron with fingers still numb from the cold.

"Some lordly fellow rode in from Ports'aven."

Megan spared her a quick glance. "Alone?"

Cate barked a laugh. Her face was as round as the soup bowl, her arms as beefy as twin hams. "Them lords ever come alone? Nay. They needs an 'oly army just to 'elp 'em lift their mugs. Fig's near to splittin' a gut."

Megan relaxed a smidgen. She'd left Portshaven six months before, and no one had come looking for her yet. "Is that beef?"

"Mutton with lemon," Cate corrected, then sniffed the concoction and winced. "'Ope I caught it 'fore it turned bad."

A voice raised from the common room.

Cate scowled. "Got some hot pot what's good though."

Someone yelled again, and Cate motioned toward the noise. Megs hurried across the kitchen just as Fig Duevel came through the door.

"Where the hell you been, girl?" He was only a hair taller than she, but he had a mean mouth and a meaner fist. Or so she'd been told, though thus far she'd managed to stay clear of the latter.

She glanced through the open doorway to the common room beyond. "Place is packed tight as a oyster," she said, and fiddled busily with her apron strings, though they were already secured in place. "Last autumn's brew was a right hummer, aye?"

He glared at her, but harrumphed in something akin to good nature. He took pride in his beer, which he made himself. Fig might be as mean as an adder and a skinflint to boot, but he had a way of brewing that kept his patrons coming back. It was one of the reasons Megs had taken this job, for although Fig kept his secrets to himself, she was certain she could learn them. Secrets could only last so long. She knew that as truth. A truth that kept her mobile. Never stay in one place too long. Never be who they think you are.

"Take care of them gents," Fig ordered, and she hurried to do just that.

The common room wasn't as busy as she had implied, but it was crowded enough. She squeezed past a pair of farmers who argued boisterously about the weight of a *gargantuan* boar and found the table with the laughing lords from Portshaven. They were easy enough to spot in the rough room. Like pansies set amidst a field of sweet thistle.

"What'll y' be 'avin' this eve, gents?" she asked.

There were five of them. Dressed to kill in cutaway coats and pantaloons, they turned to her one by one, but they saw what she wanted them to see, and tonight she wanted them to see naught but a much-abused maid in a brown woolen gown, two sizes too large and buttoned up tight to her chin. The garment had gone out of fashion sometime around Attila the Hun's era, and as far as she knew her droopy mobcap had never exactly been the rage. But the costume served her purposes well enough—generally. Just now, however, the gentlemen were eyeing her breasts like hounds might watch mutton chops, though the gown hung like a gunnysack from her shoulders. She couldn't help but wonder how they could even tell if she had breasts. Perhaps they were more imaginative than she'd thought. But she rather doubted it.

"Gentlemen?" she said again.

A gawky fellow with huge ears whispered something to his chum, and they snickered together. She refrained from reaching across the table and knocking their heads together, but she did not refrain from noticing that his vest pocket bulged the slightest amount. Neither did she stop herself from storing that information away for later consideration.

"What's tasty?" asked the fellow nearest her, and flicked an elegant hand in her direction. "Besides you?"

The sniggers grew louder. Apparently they'd tested someone else's brew before coming to the Lion. Either that or they were just irresistibly witty and not averse to haggard women with black eyes.

"The beer's good," she said, then smiled. "And the mutton."

They placed their orders without undue resistance and settled back to their foolish banter, leaving Megan to hurry into the kitchen with their orders. She delivered their meals in a moment and pressed on to the table nearest the door.

The man there was alone. He was dressed in a rough woolen shirt and a smithy's leather apron. One shoulder rested wearily against the wall. A weathered hat shadowed his face, giving little clues to his thoughts, but he had the large, sun-darkened hands of a working man.

Megan offered a smile, not as bright as the one for the gentlemen, but honest. "What'll y' be 'avin' tonight, love?"

He glanced up as if disturbed from his reverie. "'Ow's your Scotch?" His voice was deep and burred. She liked the sound of it. An honest man's voice.

"Watered down," she said. "And overpriced."

Even from beneath the hat, she thought she sensed his surprise. And there was something about the way he moved that little bit that made her wonder if he weren't perhaps, a bit younger than she'd suspected.

"What do you suggest then, lass?"

"The beer. It's fresh, and it's quenchin'."

"I 'eard the mutton's good," he said, and nodded toward where the five gentlemen dined.

"It's gone bad."

She was sure of his surprise now and widened her smile. Aye, she needed the wages Fig doled out with miserly greed, but there was no harm in having a little fun now and again. "They're gonna drink until they vomit anyhow," she said, and shrugged. "The 'ot pot's good though."

Perhaps he wasn't quite sure what to make of her, but he ordered the beef stew finally, and she hurried off with his request.

Despite the work, the night went by quickly. The gentlemen tormented her as best they could, but they were inebriated and slow, both in hand and wit, and she avoided them with ease. The pig farmers settled into sulky agreement over the apparently *middle-sized* boar, and the smithy remained, nursing his second beer and seeming nearly asleep in his chair.

But finally the evening was past and the patrons shambled out. Cate had already left for the night. Megan locked the door and gathered up the crockery. She would wash it in the morning, then deliver Mistress Bea's newly sewn spencer. The little jacket would earn her a few more coins to stash away.

The stairs creaked beneath her feet. When she'd first arrived in Somershire, Fig had offered to share his room with her. In fact, he had been drunk and rather insistent. She, however, had been firm and well armed. Later, as sober and chagrined as an undersized Frenchman can be, he had offered her a chamber in the attic in lieu of half of her pay, but she'd opted for a room in the cellar. It was the approximate size of a dinner plate and boasted only a tiny window, but it had a solid wood floor and it was all but free, putting her that much closer to her goal.

Stepping into her cramped quarters, Megan set her candle on a nearby trunk and straightened.

She felt the intruder's presence immediately. She tried to spin toward the door, but a hand covered her mouth. It pulled her backward. Struggling madly, she opened her mouth to scream, but the sound was muffled against the man's palm. She rolled her eyes, attempting to see behind her, but she was already pulled tight against a solid chest. Her money! Had he found it, hidden away in its hole beneath the floor?

But his grip tightened, cutting off her air and squeezing her thoughts down to nothing but her own survival.

"Don't scream."

His voice was low and quiet. She couldn't place it, but lack of air made thinking difficult.

"If I let you go, do you promise not to scream?"

She nodded, wondering wildly what kind of dolt would be honest in this situation? And what kind of dolt would expect her to be?

Nevertheless, he eased his hand from her mouth, but in a moment it was at her throat, nearly enveloping it. Big hands. Who was he? One of the gentlemen? But no, their hands had been soft and narrow.

"What's your name, girl?"

"My name?" She didn't know if she was stalling. But that might be a clever idea. She wished she could think clearly, could plan.

"Who are you?" he asked again.

Who was *he*? Most rapists she'd met didn't insist on being on a first-name basis. Did that mean he was after her money? And would that be better or worse?

"They call me Sparrow." Her voice only shook the slightest amount.

There was a moment's pause. "What?"

"It's . . ." She felt breathless and slow-witted, and neither characteristic was likely to prolong her life. "Because of me small size," she explained, trying to catch her wind.

"What's your Christian name?"

Who the devil was this bloke? "I don't rightly know," she said, her head still tilted away from the pressure of his hand. "Mum's been gone since I were a wee bairn and Da . . ." She shook her head just to see if she could. His hand eased off her throat the slightest degree. "'E weren't never around what I knew of."

He drew his hand away from her throat, and she refrained from screaming, not certain she could even if she tried. Any-

way, he stood between her and the door, and she had no reason to believe he wouldn't kill her before she'd managed
more than a squeak.

"Go sit down."

There was nowhere but the trunk and the bed, and the bed
was farther from him, so she shuffled toward it, her legs
wooden, her feet heavy. She turned just as stiffly, glanced up,
and gasped.

"You're the smithy," she hissed.

Even from beneath the brim of his leather hat, she could
see his mouth quirk. His hands were still dark and sun-
darkened, but he no longer seemed like the salt of the earth.
Apparently even smithies could be bastards.

"What do y' want?" she asked.

"There's no need to fear. I just have a few questions." He
had lost his brogue. Indeed, he spoke now like a London lord.
Holy damn!

"Questions?" It seemed unlikely. Mostly men didn't force
their way into her room to converse, but life was full of surprises and she was still alive. "What do y' want to know?"

"Take off your cap."

"That's um . . ." She drew an unsteady breath. She didn't
like men to see her face unimpaired, but at least the room
was dim, lit only by that one wavering candle. "That's not a
question."

"Take if off, lass."

She did so slowly, not disturbing a hair. She'd pinned it se-
curely beneath her cap. If hair was greasy enough, it would
stay almost anywhere you put it, and she liked it greasy. It
kept the patrons at bay. Mostly. She dragged the cap forward,
covering her face as long as possible before holding the thing
in both hands on her lap.

He winced when he caught his first full glimpse of her
blackened eye.

She tightened her mouth. "The streets of Somershire ain't 'ardly fit for a lady no more," she said.

She thought she heard him curse, but she wasn't sure. "Who did that to you?" he asked.

She almost smiled. She'd thought her eye was looking better. Barely purple at all, and her ribs were healing fine. When she could afford her own inn she was going to hire herself a full-time bodyguard. He'd follow her about like a wolfhound on a string and growl at anyone who dared glance her way.

"Some blokes come on me sudden-like," she said. "When I was 'eadin' 'cross the river."

This time she was certain he cursed, and he was a fair hand at it. One fist tightened against the battered leather of his apron, but his voice was steady when next he spoke. "What do you do across the river?"

"A bit of mendin'. Some sewin'. Nothin' too fancy. But the folks on the other side pays good."

"You live here?"

The answer seemed obvious and harmless enough. "Aye, sir. 'Ave for some months now."

"Have you ever been to Larkscote?"

"Larkscote?" She liked to think she was not slow-witted. But she was having difficulty following his line of thought. But then, perhaps he was mad. Some were. Like old Willy down by the crossing. He'd take you in and give you a meal if you needed one, but you'd best be cautious cuz there was times he might mistake you for a wolf or some such beast and try to beat the living tar out of you. Life was unpredictable.

"How about Inglewood? Have you ever been there?"

She shook her head.

"Ever left the country?"

"Why are y' asking me these things?"

"It's a simple question, lass."

And he was a strange fellow, and scary. Why was he here? How had he gotten in?

He took a step forward. She snapped her mind back into place.

"No," she said, hoping the quick answer would keep him at bay. "No, I ain't never left the isle."

He was silent for a moment, watching her from beneath the brim of his weather-beaten hat. Candlelight flickered across his face, momentarily illuminating his lean cheeks and casting an orange glow to his shadowed eyes. It made her hair stand on end. Like the devil he looked. Like the devil come to make her pay for her sins. And she had a few of them. Mum had said it was sinful to take what wasn't rightfully gained, but suicide was a sin, too. And trying to live without supplementing her income would be tantamount to suicide. She was only looking to take care of herself—the Lord's temple. Speaking of which—a triangular iron lay near the door. It doubled as a pressing tool and a doorstop. If she struck him with it, might she have a chance to escape?

"Were you born here?"

She brought her attention back to his questions with a guilty start. "Born 'ere?" She made her accent very strong. For this moment she was Sparrow, a dowdy but good-hearted barmaid who didn't ask much from life. She shrugged, adding to the act. "I don't know 'xactly where I was born. Seems I always been 'ere."

"You've never left the village?"

She considered lying. She had no aversion to fibbing now and again. In fact, she was quite certain a little judicious fabrication had saved her life on more than one occasion, for while she was not the magician some thought her to be, she had managed a few feats that kept her firmly planted somewhere between the pearly gates and hell's fiery depths. But she had a strict rule about sticking to the truth whenever possible. Lies were difficult. The truth was simple. Besides, he might ask around, and anyone would tell him, Fig included, that she hadn't been in Somershire for more than a few months.

She grinned a little. "'Course I've left the village," she said. "Who wouldn't?"

"Where have you been?"

She shrugged again. "'Ere and there mostly."

"Have you ever been to Portshaven?"

Curiosity dimmed as fear upped its power. Six months ago she had had a bit of a run-in with a viscount in Portshaven. He'd been drunk and arrogant, but she hadn't meant him any harm. Not until he'd become pushy. Even then she hadn't planned to rob him. But the good book said the Lord would provide, and when He did, it would sure be a sin not to take Him up on his generosity. Still, she'd been surprised at the amount of ready cash the gent had carried on his person. And the pocket watch had been a rare find. Gold-plated and smooth to the touch. It had brought a fair penny. Sometimes the Lord did better than other times. Right now He wasn't doing so grand.

"Answer me," he ordered.

She swallowed her fear, trying to peer up under his hat. "Who are y'?" she asked.

The ghost of a smile lifted his lips. "I'm a blacksmith," he said, and took a full step toward her, arms outspread. "Can't you tell?"

She rose to her feet, but there was barely room to stand, much less escape.

"Just like you're a barmaid."

They were inches apart.

"Listen, I don't have no money if that's what you're after."

"It is not."

His words were flat in the shifting darkness and made her

blood run chill. There was nothing she liked better than the shine of coin, but when push came to shove it could be there were more important things. And she was trapped here. Trapped and alone with a man who didn't appear to be easily duped or readily smitten. Not some foolish dandy with nothing better to do than find a likely bedmate, but a no-nonsense workingman with large hands and an attitude that suggested they had met before. An attitude that suggested he had come for revenge.

He took another step toward her. She sidled to the left. There was a knife behind her trunk, a butcher's blade the length of her forearm. If she had her druthers, she would use wit before violence every time, but options seemed in short supply here. Still, the thought of using the knife gave her a pang somewhere between nausea and hope. There was also a walking stick inside the trunk and though it would be more difficult to reach, the idea of wielding it was not quite so horrifying.

"What is it y' want then?" she asked.

He watched her carefully, breathlessly, as if she were naked before him, as if he could see into her very soul.

"I think I want you," he said.

She shook her head slowly. Her limbs felt stiff and her chest tight. "I'm not what y' think I am."

Silence again, so deep she could hear her heart beat.

"I think you are a liar," he said finally. "And a thief."

"Lord help me." The words escaped on their own. She shook her head more vehemently and sidled faster. Her fingers trembled against the wall behind her. "Just cuz . . . Just cuz I'm a barmaid don't mean . . ." She was almost there. Almost to the trunk. She only had to bend and grab—and then stab him, of course. Her stomach twisted. "That don't mean I'm easy. I . . . The rumors ain't true. I—"

"Rumors," he said and suddenly he laughed. His teeth

shone white in the candlelight. White and demonic. "You are a clever lass."

She stared at him. His laughter sounded insane. But damn, he was bigger than Mad Willy, and so terribly close.

"Don't you remember me, lass?"

She swallowed hard. "Listen, I don't want no trouble 'ere. I'm a 'ard working girl, I am, and—"

But in that moment he swept off his hat. The world jerked to halt. She hadn't thought she'd remember him so clearly. But suddenly she did, like it was yesterday, like it was a dream.

It was the viscount she'd robbed. It was the viscount, come for revenge.

Chapter 2

Nicol watched the truth dawn on her face, watched her
eyes widen. They were the same eyes he'd dreamt of
for the past six months, the same eyes he'd obsessed about.
He spread his arms slightly.

"It looks like *I* win," he said.

"Win?" She looked as if she might faint. "Win what?"

"You're a difficult woman to find," he said.

She swallowed. Even in that high-necked gown, he could
see her slim, pale throat convulse. God's bones, that was the
ugliest garment he had ever seen, he thought, and remembered how she had looked on that bright spring day—the
spitting image of Anna. She would look that way again, but
even more.

Right now she was as pale as a shade. He would have
laughed again, but he could almost see the thoughts spinning
in her head and waited in anticipatory silence.

"Find?" If her eyes got any wider, they would swallow her

face. "I don't know what you're talkin' 'bout. Why would you want to find *me*?"

He smiled, willing to play her game, to let her fight the hook, to watch her wriggle. "Because you knocked me unconscious," he said. "And stole my pocket watch."

She shook her head wildly. Not a hair strayed out of place. What the devil had she done to it? It had been so beautiful, long and fair, gleaming in the springtime sun. Not that she would be able to keep it as it was anyway. But she couldn't keep it like this either. No woman with any self-respect at all should keep her hair like *this*.

"I don't know what you're talkin' about," she repeated. "You've mistook me for someone else. I told you, I've only been 'ere in Somershire for a few months."

He gave her a nod for her performance. She was as quick as a whip, as sharp as a dagger. But then—so was he.

"It didn't happen in Somershire, lass, as you very well know."

"It . . ." She looked shocked and bewildered. Her hands were splayed out against the wall behind her. They were long-fingered and curled against the cracking plaster like a sparrow's claws. She was too thin. But that should be easily remedied. "It didn't 'appen a'tall," she vowed. "Not with me."

He ignored the lie, though it was executed with some panache. If he looked close, he might be able to believe there were tears in her eyes. "What did you do with my watch?"

"I don't got no watch."

"Did you sell it?"

She didn't answer, and in the silence he glanced about him. She lived in a hole barely big enough for a dwarfed rat. "You were cheated, lass."

"I don't know what you're talking about."

"The watch was worth a good deal. Enough to afford you a better room."

"I'm a good girl, Govner. I didn't steal no watch. I swear it on—"

He raised a hand. "Don't swear it, lass. Haven't you heard that lying is a sin?"

"Of course I 'ave. I know all the commandments. I even got me a Bible."

"Can you read?"

Something crossed her face. Some emotion he couldn't quite phantom. "There ain't much reason for a girl like me to read," she said.

"So you don't care to learn?" he asked.

Her eyes narrowed for a fraction of a second. "Like I says, there ain't much purpose."

He watched her for a moment, trying to decipher her thoughts, but there was little hope of that, so he plunged forward. Foolishly perhaps. "I have a proposition for you."

"A what?"

"A deal. A business deal."

She canted her head slightly. Her lips were pursed, but if there was one thing about her that hadn't changed, it was those lips. They were the only reason he had sat for hours in the common room of the Lion's Share. The only reason he had tolerated the inane conversation of the irritating gentlemen beside him. He had recognized those lips.

"I'm telling y', mister, I ain't the sort o' girl y' think I am."

"Then you're not interested in receiving three good meals a day as well as new clothes and an education?"

Her brows lowered into a scowl. She would have to learn to quit doing that. Anna rarely showed any sort of expression.

"Three meals a day?" she said, and he smiled.

"Yes."

"Would I 'ave to kill anyone I'm fond of?"

"Not even anyone you loathe."

"What would I 'ave to do then?"

He watched her again. Her face looked dull, but her eyes—"Come with me." She opened her mouth to speak, but he held up a hand. "I know it'll be difficult for you to leave this charming place, but I'm afraid you'll have to."

"Why?"

"I can't say just yet." He didn't dare tell her the truth. He hadn't lost his mind completely—despite his current actions, which suggested evidence to the contrary. "You'll come to my home," he said.

"Yer 'ome."

She sounded a bit disbelieving.

"Once there I will tutor you. If things go well, I will employ you for an undetermined amount of time."

"Go well?"

"If she approves of you."

She stiffened and pursed her lush lips. "I don't 'old with none of that weird goings-on."

He stared at her.

"I ain't going to be no . . ." She flapped her hand wildly, her eyes wide. "No plaything for you and your missus. I may spend me nights servin' drinks, but I got me morals same as—"

"God's bones, girl, you've got a mind like a damned wagon spring. I never know where it's going to hop next."

She canted her head. "You're not takin' me 'ome to your wife?"

He almost had to laugh. "I don't have a wife."

"Then what do y' want with me?"

"I want to teach you things."

She opened her mouth to object, but he held up one palm.

"Manners," he explained. "Etiquette."

"I don't need to learn no manners," she said, and wiped the back of her hand across her nose.

"Of course," he agreed. "She'll be thrilled with you just as you are."

"'Oo will be?"

He paused, thinking of Princess Tatiana Rocheneau, so alone, so aloof, so vulnerable. "She's a great lady. That's all you need to know for now."

"What's she got to do with me?"

"She will decide whether or not you have learned your lessons well enough."

She frowned. "And if'n I 'aven't?"

For a moment he remembered the headaches that had followed his first meeting with her. They'd lasted three days and had made him think his brain might just leap out of his skull like a trained circus monkey. As it turned out, he didn't mind overly much if she fretted a little about her continued existence.

"Listen," she said, and offered a tremulous smile. "I ain't done nothin' wrong. I ain't who you think I is. Just let me go, and I won't 'old no grudges."

"You'll be coming to Newburn with me."

"I umm . . ." She cleared her throat and stared at him as if he'd lost a few playing cards from an already shabby deck. "That's a right kind offer, sir. But I can't—"

"You can keep the clothes."

"What's that?"

"The garments I purchase for you. They will be costly and there will be many of them. You may do with them as you will."

"I could sell 'em?"

"If you wish."

Her eyes narrowed. "And you don't expect me to—"

He waited. She didn't finish the thought. Neither did he. Instead, he merely watched her.

She cleared her throat with a scowl deep enough to drown a small pony. "Do you?"

"Do I what?"

She was exasperated now, her plump lips pursed. "Don't be expectin' me to dong your bell, cuz I won't."

He couldn't help laughing now. For the thought of this creature impersonating Princess Tatiana was suddenly the most absurd thing he could imagine. But he'd always appreciated the absurd. His life, for instance, but finally he sobered and subsequently realized she hadn't joined in on the hilarity.

Her mouth was pursed and her back as straight as a royal guard's. "I don't like to be laughed at," she said.

He sobered somewhat, but couldn't quite conquer his grin. "Then you shouldn't be so amusing. Come along now, lass; we're leaving."

For a moment he thought she might refuse, for her lips were still pursed and her eyes still narrowed, but finally she spoke. "You'll give me clothes?"

"Yes."

She shrugged, then, turning toward the nearby trunk, dropped her hands to the hasp. It opened rustily.

"What are you doing?"

"Getting me things."

"You won't be needing them. As I said, I'll buy you new garments when we reach Sedonia." A noise issued from upstairs, reminding him of his mission. "Come along," he ordered, and took a step forward.

She shrugged, then jerked her arm forward and swung toward him. He heard the whoosh of the walking stick before he saw it, and ducked. It missed his head by a fraction of an inch. He felt it breeze through his hair.

There was no time to think. He barreled toward her, but she was as quick as a fox and twisted desperately away. Still, the room was tiny. There was nowhere to go. He caught her about the waist, wrapping her in his arms and thumping the air from her lungs.

She tried to scream, but he loosened one hand and slapped it over her mouth. She almost slipped from his grasp before he held her in both arms again.

"Listen," he ordered, but she didn't. Instead, she struggled madly. He shook her. "Listen to me! You owe me, lass, and you'll pay me whether it's at the gallows or at my manor."

Her struggles slowed.

"I hear your Laird MacTavish is not altogether gentle when delivering justice," he said.

Her movements ceased entirely.

"I see you've heard the same. I'm giving you a chance, lass, a chance to leave this isle alive and whole. Will you take it?"

For a moment he thought she wouldn't answer, but finally she nodded once.

"Good." He was still breathing hard. "I'm going to let go of you now, but I warn you, if you try again to damage me, justice will be swift."

She said nothing, but shifted wild eyes toward him. He eased his hand off her mouth, then slipped his arm from around her ribs. But before she turned around, he grasped her arm.

"Come."

"Wait." She dragged back, her eyes insanely wide. "My clothes."

"I don't mind you being vicious," he said, tugging her along. "But I won't have you poorly dressed."

Chapter 3

Megan sat very still upon the berth, her knees pressed together, her back straight. The cabin was no bigger than her tiny alcove at the inn and rocked rhythmically to the sway of the sea.

"I'll not be sharin' a room with y'."

The gentleman turned from the door, his face expressionless. "We'll be sailing within hours," he said. "You'd best get some sleep while you can. Unless you're accustomed to rough seas."

"Did you 'ear me?" She rose to her feet, but he pressed her back down with a hand to her shoulder.

"Listen!" he snapped, then drew a deep breath and straightened slightly. "I'm tired. Don't test my patience."

She felt her heart rate pick up a beat. Who was this lunatic? And just how dangerous was he? It had taken them more than an hour to reach the docks by carriage, nearly half that to convince the captain to allow them to board at such an unorthodox hour. Megan had prayed the old seaman would refuse to let them board, had, in fact, toyed with the idea of begging him for help, but the viscount had kept a tight grip on her arm the entire time, threatening her with his mood as much as with a steely hand on her biceps.

But now he looked haggard by the light of the smoky candle. In fact, if she had to guess, she would say he'd be asleep within minutes. The idea made her fidgety, but she dare not appear too eager.

Instead, she lifted her chin. "Y' said y' wouldn't compromise me. Y' said y' was just—"

"God's bones," he murmured, and rubbed a hand wearily over his eyes "You think I want to share a room with you?"

She stiffened as if insulted, though nothing could be further from the truth. If she wanted to attract him, she could sure as hell attract him. Just now she'd rather kill him, but that would be unwise. So escape would have to do. "You think you're too good for the likes o' me?" she asked, careful to sound affronted.

"I think I'm tired, and you stink," he murmured.

"What's that?" she asked, though she had heard him clear enough. She had excellent hearing. And her sense of smell wasn't bad either, which informed her she reeked of onion and stale beer and sweat. She almost grinned.

"Lie down," he ordered.

"Just like that?" she snorted. "And only minutes since you vowed not to take me virtue."

"Virtue," he scoffed.

"I got me virtue," she said, narrowing her eyes.

"I'm sure you do," he agreed wearily. "You're probably a pillar of the damn stuff."

"Just cuz I don't 'ave me no fancy title like you don't mean I don't 'ave me morals."

He glanced at her and laughed. Fatigue seemed to lighten for a moment. "Go to sleep, girl."

She shook her head. "I won't be sharin' no bed with y'."

"No. You won't."

Relief flooded her along with surprise. Escape would be as easy as lifting lemons from a blind man if he took another room. But she kept her eyes narrow, careful to play her part.

"Where'll you be sleepin' then?"

"I don't sleep."

She was momentarily caught off guard. "Ever?"

Sighing, he turned and opened the leather-bound trunk that stood near the door. Reaching inside, he pulled out a white garment and tossed it into her lap.

"Put that on. You'll be more comfortable." He glowered at her, his eyes nearly black in the wavering candlelight. "As will I."

The gown felt deliciously soft against her fingers. It was purest white but for the delicate embroidery that graced the ends of the sleeves and the pristine neckline. Sky-blue ribbons curled at the throat. She all but itched to pull it on, but she dare not act eager. "What do you mean you'll be more comfortable?"

"You stink," he reminded her. "I'm hoping it's the clothes. The sooner we're rid of them the better."

"Rid of 'em?"

He shrugged and glanced out the porthole. "Burn them," he suggested. "Toss them into the sea."

She made a sound she hoped affronted his sensibilities. "You ain't burnin' me clothes. They cost me dear."

"I told you I'd buy you new garments."

And of course she was naive enough to believe him. "Well," she said, playing along. "Till y' do, I'll be 'angin' on to me own stuff, thank you just the same."

Turning again, he reached into the trunk and drew out another garment. Holding it up in the wavering candlelight, he let it unfold. It dropped dramatically downward, sweeping in a graceful sigh to the floor.

Her jaw dropped with it. It was a gown of daffodil yellow. Gathered prettily at the neck and sleeves, it was sprigged with tiny lavender posies and adorned with small neat bows at the hem.

"Who's that for?" she asked.

"When you get cleaned up it's yours."

Her mind was spinning. She hated to believe she was jaded, but when men broke into her room and forced her onto a ship, she had a tendency to believe they had less than her best interests at heart. But obviously he had some sort of plan which extended past rape. Apparently, he had left this trunk here for her use, meaning he had not only been terribly sure of his ability to bring her here, but also very aware of her build, if the cut of the daffodil gown was any indication. It was generous in the bodice, narrow at the hip, and not overly long, even by her standards.

She raised her gaze to his. "Who are y'?" she asked.

"Who are you?"

"I told y'. They call me—"

"Sparrow. I remember. Because of your size. What was your given name?"

She shrugged.

"What was your mother's name?"

"I don't remember me mum." She lied, but she did it well. If a job was worth doing . . .

"Surely you knew her name."

She squinted, as if thinking, but she would be damned if she would share her mother's memory with this man. Lowenna O'Shay had been a saint. A fiery-haired angel. But he wouldn't understand that. Wouldn't see the beauty of a common wash-erwoman who worked like a slave to put bread on the table. "Like I says, she died when I was but a wee thing."

"And what of your surname?"

She shrugged. "Don't 'ave much use of one."

He stared at her. "So you don't know where you were born. You don't know your family name, and you don't remember either of your parents."

"Aye," she said. "I suspect that seems strange to a bloke like you what was coddled all 'is life."

It seemed impossible for his eyes to darken any more. But they did. She watched the effects and carefully kept from wincing.

"Yes," he said finally and smiled, but the expression did little more than tilt up the corners of his devilish mouth. "It does."

"So what's your name then?"

"Nicol," he said, and, closing the trunk, took a seat atop it. Resting one ankle across the opposite knee, he leaned back and sighed almost inaudibly. The lid was flat and hard. She hoped it wasn't too uncomfortable for him to fall asleep. "Nicol Argyle." He bowed his head slightly as if they'd met over tea and crumpets at Westheath Castle. "Fifth viscount of Newburn."

She whistled low. "There's a fancy 'andle and no mistake."

He shrugged. Damn, his eyes were as inscrutable as a bull's and still didn't show the slightest signs of drooping closed. Maybe if she gave him a blanket. But she could hardly just hand it over. " 'Ere ye go then, Govner. 'Ave yerself a couple winks. I'll be gone when ye wakes up, but it's been nice knowin' you." On the other hand, perhaps if she pretended to be sleepy herself, he would relax his guard and nod off.

Stifling a make-believe yawn, she pulled the blankets from beneath her and covered her lap as if hoping to get more comfortable. "Your da must a been a fancy one, too, then."

He watched her in silence for a moment, then, "Change your clothes," he said.

Her heart picked up its pace again, but she merely smiled primly. "I suspect you'd like that, Govner, but it wouldn't be seemly."

"I told you, I have no intention of molesting you."

"Intentions come and goes, don't they now?"

"Put on the gown."

There was something in his tone now that urged caution. She glanced toward the door. "Do I 'ave your word as a gentleman that you'll not watch?" she asked.

His low note of laughter surprised her. "You don't know much about gentlemen, do you, lass?"

She felt her hackles rise. She didn't mind a little hard labor, and she had nothing against being underestimated. In fact, she counted on it, but she didn't like to be mocked. "No," she said, and made sure the sarcasm was thick in her tone. "I ain't 'ad the pleasure of being round your sort much."

For a moment she was sure he'd caught her meaning and was less than thrilled by the sarcasm, but he made no comment.

They stared at each other for a full twenty seconds, but she shook her head finally, foolishly nervous under his perusal.

"You'll 'ave to go out in the 'allway."

"If you're afraid I can't resist the sight of you, you needn't worry."

"If y' find me so unappealing, then why am I 'ere?"

"That's an excellent question," he murmured, and dropped his head back to stare at the ceiling. "God's balls, I'll be lucky if she doesn't have me beheaded."

"What's that?" she asked. She put a good deal of offended pride into her tone, though if the truth be told, she wouldn't care less if he found her inferior to a box of toads.

He sighed and closed his eyes for a moment, as if weary beyond words, and she wondered hopefully if one could die of fatigue. "Change your damned clothes, girl."

"They 'ers?"

"What?" He lowered his chin just enough to watch her. His dark hair was freshly trimmed, and his cheeks showed only a slight bristle. She should have noticed his careful grooming when first she'd seen him at the inn. Blacksmiths were not generally known for their fastidious cleanliness after all.

"The great lady what you talked about. They 'er clothes?"

He made a sound of disbelief. "No. They're not hers."

Irritation rippled through her again, and she decided there was no reason not to let it show. "She too good for the likes o' me then?"

He stared at her for several hard seconds, then, "Yes," he said. "She is that."

Rising to her feet, she snapped the sleeping gown into his face. "'Ere you go then," she snarled. "You can take them to your haughty slut. Cuz I—"

But in an instant he was on his feet. His hand felt hard and ungiving against her wrist.

Megan gasped in earnest and leaned away. The room fell silent but for the soft hiss of the candle.

"I've tolerated much from you already," he said finally. "Theft. Attacks on my person. Lies."

She could hear her own breath in the deadly quiet, could feel her heart beating in her chest.

"But you will not insult her."

Megs swallowed hard, barely daring a nod.

"Good. Then change your clothes."

She opened her mouth to object, but he tightened his grip. "Do it. Or I shall do it for you," he said, and handed her the gown.

She took it in silence and turned around. She heard him back away, heard the trunk creak under his weight, and swallowed once as she stared at the wall.

She refused to believe her hands were unsteady as she put them to her buttons. After all, she'd been in tighter spots. As far as she knew, he wasn't even armed. He wasn't a hench-man. Didn't have a noose or anything. And there was only one of him. Magical Megs could eat him for lunch.

Undoing the buttons that marched down her back, she closed her eyes and pulled her arms out of the sleeves. They scratched over her wrists and flopped to the floor. But in an instant she snatched the nightgown over her head. It sighed across her shoulders, but she barely noticed its softness as she thrust her arms through and tied the ribbons to her chin. Tugging down the kindly cotton then, she eased off the woolen and stepped from the fetid circle before turning around.

"There ye are then. 'Appy?" she asked, but it was apparent in an instant that he was asleep.

So! Removing her clothes put men to sleep. Who would have guessed that? Nearly shrugging, she bent, retrieved her gown from the floor, and silently turned toward the door. If he hadn't been sitting on the trunk, she might have been tempted to take a few items in exchange for the trouble he'd caused her, but as it was, she would have to be content with slipping silently into the night.

But at the first step, he spoke. "Where are you going?"

She stopped in her tracks, gritted her teeth, then turned easily and refrained from cursing out loud. A fact that should surely have won her some sort of spot in heaven.

"I was going to be rid of the gown—as ordered."

A corner of his mouth twitched up, then, smooth as a cat, he rose to his feet. He reached for the gown, and she reluc-tantly handed it over.

Opening the door, he tossed it into the narrow hallway and turned back to her.

"So you weren't planning to leave?"

She let her eyes widen slightly. She'd practiced it a few times in a chip of looking glass she'd found and kept in her room at the inn, but she'd learned to act early on, and the skill had not abandoned her. So she remained as she was, watching him before thoughtfully scowling. "You lyin' to me, Govner?"

"Lying to you?" He was standing uncomfortably close, but it wasn't surprising, considering the size of the room. She had little reason to believe she made him randy, especially considering he'd fallen asleep while she was disrobing.

"You said you was going to feed me," she said.

He nodded once. His hair was as dark as ebon and glistened in the candlelight. His eyes were brown and fringed with thick lashes. Dark stubble shone like a shadow forest on his hollowed cheeks. But it didn't look out of place. Even his clothes, all worn wool and scuffed leather, looked strangely elegant on him. Who was this man who spoke like a lord and dressed like a laborer?

"I'd 'ave t' be a fool to leave now," she said.

His mouth quirked again, but he said nothing. Instead, he set his hands to the leather strips that held his apron in place.

She cleared her throat. "Whatcha doin' there, Govner?"

"Getting comfortable," he said, and slipped the apron to the floor before pulling the rough tunic from beneath his waistband. For a moment she caught a glimpse of his dark skin. A narrow band of black hair did nothing to hide the hard muscle that lay in rows across his abdomen.

It made her feel strangely squeamish. She pulled her gaze upward and pinned it to his face. "How comfortable you plannin' on gettin'?"

For a moment his teeth flashed. Were they as ungodly white as they seemed, or was it simply the contrast against his skin, or the candlelight, or the proximity.

"As comfortable as possible," he said, and tugged the shirt over his head.

She didn't mean to step back, but he was now half-naked, and for a gentleman of leisure, he was packed as tight as a damned pig sausage. His chest was mounded with lean muscle and not an ounce of fat showed around the waistband of his low-slung trousers.

"Go to bed," he said.

She stared. "What?"

A crescent of teeth shown again. "To bed."

"Oh." She nodded, goose-stepped to the mattress, and crawled on. But what the devil was she supposed to do now? They were still all of two feet apart. She lay down, stiff as a soup ladle, and pulled the covers up to her chin.

He kicked off his boots and in a moment his hands were on his trouser ties. The strings loosened. His fingers paused, and she realized with a slight start that she was holding her breath.

He shuffled his feet, stilling his fingers.

She yanked her gaze to his.

"The good news," he began, "is that you don't have to watch."

"Oh," she said again, then realized she was still staring and turned with a jerk toward the wall.

She heard him open the trunk, recognized the sigh of fabric against flesh, and imagined the garment dropping over the taut muscles of his chest. Why would a viscount be so fit? If she were going to be abducted, at least it could be by someone she could outrun in a footrace. But judging by his muscle tone, she'd be caught before she launched from the mattress. And if it came to a test of strength, she'd have little chance. Therefore, she'd best think of another way to escape. But at that very moment she heard the trunk slide across the floor to the door.

Damn. She may have to wrestle him for her freedom after

all, she thought, and fell asleep with that disturbing image dancing in her head.

Nicol steadied the wooden tray and closed the door with his shoulder.

She opened her eyes immediately, but sat up more slowly. "Where am I?" she asked, her voice still husky with sleep. God's balls, he envied that.

"I brought breakfast," he said.

"Yeah?" she asked, and propped her back against the wall behind her.

Sometime during the night she had taken the pins out of her hair. It lay spread across her shoulders, and though it desperately needed washing, it softened her face a mite. Maybe his gut instincts were right. Maybe she was the woman he had met on that sunny Teleerian evening. Maybe not. But whatever the case, it was too late to turn back now, for he had made a promise to a princess.

"Yes," he said.

She reached eagerly for the tray. The skin around her left eye had turned an arresting shade of green. He gritted his teeth and pulled the tray toward his chest.

"A few rules," he said. "You do not say, yeah. You say yes."

"Oh, yeah. Sure." She reached again.

He scowled. The maid in Teleere had been rough, true, but there had been something about her, an intelligence, a wit. He had been certain from the first moment that she could perform the task set before them. But her accent had not been so heavy, her hair so greasy, her cheek so *green*. Perhaps he was losing his mind.

"Y' going to give me that food or not?" she asked.

"Not," he said, "until you say the word 'yes.'"

She repeated the word clearly enough, so he handed her the

tray and took a seat on the trunk. He had moved it back against
the wall once they'd pulled anchor and had spent a good deal
of time there since. He hated the damned thing already.

Breakfast consisted of pasty gruel and rancid cider. The
girl ate it as if it were mince pie and heather wine, or as if she
couldn't tell the difference. He watched in amazement.

She glanced up, still spooning in porridge. "'Ow come
you don't sleep?"

"How." Watching her eat made him feel tired. "*How* come
I don't sleep?"

"Don't ask me," she said, speaking around a mouthful of
well-congealed gruel. "I sleep like a baby."

"You sleep like a road mender. A snoring road mender."

"I don't snore." She looked affronted even as she wiped
her mouth with the back of her hand.

"And you talk in your sleep. You will quit both. In a few
short weeks you will learn to be cultured, elegant, and refined."

She shrugged. "Yeah. Sure."

He snatched the cup out of her hand, causing her to stare at
him open mouthed.

"Yes, my lord," he instructed.

So she repeated his words.

"And never . . ." He managed to resist beating his head
against the wall. What the hell had he been thinking? Yes, he
had been inebriated when he'd first met her, but he hadn't
been deranged. Had he? "Never say 'yeah.' "

"'Ow come?" she asked, and he tightened a fist and
knuckled down.

Chapter 4

◦◦◦◦◦

The carriage jolted along, bearing them due north. Megan was careful to note the direction. Since she'd had no chance to escape during the voyage, and since the viscount hadn't left her alone for a moment on the noisy wharves, she'd damned well better make good use of her time now. She stifled a scowl.

"'Ow long does it take to get to your 'ouse?"

He pulled his gaze back to her, his expression dark, as though he'd been thinking things that did nothing to lighten his mood. Or maybe he was about to strangle her. He really didn't like it when she dropped her aitches. Mum's speech had been quite proper, but it had done her little good in the long run.

"Several hours," he said. "Go to sleep."

"Sleep," she scoffed. "I 'ad me enough sleep to last me a month of nevers." She hadn't actually slept all that well. During the days on the ship he had drilled her endlessly about proper speech and etiquette. Apparently ladies were not supposed to curse or get soup in their hair or spit or take stairs two at a time, or do a hundred other perfectly normal things. The list of rules had kept the days busy. She had spent the nights planning. Once they'd set sail, he had ceased worrying about her escape. Perhaps he knew she had never learned to swim. Perhaps he knew much more than she realized. Or maybe he was only guessing. Guessing and doubting his suppositions. Surely he must think her as thick as muddy water by now, because no matter how many times he corrected her, she always dropped her aitches. She nearly smiled at the thought, especially when she noticed the dark hollows under his eyes.

"Got yourself a big 'ouse do y'?" she asked.

He glanced at her. His arms were crossed against his chest. He wore the brown woolen shirt again and the same faded trousers. Although he hadn't donned the leather apron, he'd pulled the hat low over his face when they'd been at the docks. Why? Perhaps he wasn't a nobleman at all. Perhaps, he was a criminal of some sort. Which brought her back to the original question. What did he want with her?

His mouth was pulled into a hard line, but he didn't correct her speech. He couldn't be giving up already, could he?

"Newburn Hall is large by some standards." He glanced out the window again.

"Got servants and all I suspect."

He turned slowly back to her. "I'm offering you a chance to better yourself." He paused. Outside the rattling carriage, the wheels grated noisily against the hard-packed earth. The horses' cadenced hoofbeats could barely be heard above the rumble. His driver had met them at the docks with his carriage. She had hoped for a moment to appeal to him for help, but he had flicked the door open and whisked away a moment later. She hadn't even caught a glimpse of his face. "Why do you refuse to take it?"

She blinked owlishly. She'd been perfecting that, too, and hoped it looked as daft as it felt. He'd taken her woolen gown and given her a pink muslin to replace it. It was a simple garment with elemental lines and a high bodice, but it was still a far cry from the sheer ugliness of the woolen. And that put her at a disadvantage. Luckily, she'd had no opportunity to wash her hair yet. "I ain't refusin'—"

He gritted his teeth at her phrasing, then relaxed against the upholstered seat and watched her. "Would you rather I turn you over to Teleerian authorities. Tell them you robbed me?"

She made her eyes go big and round. "I didn't rob you, Govner. I swear it. I never laid eyes on you before the other night."

Was there a flicker of doubt in his eyes? If so, this was surely the time to fan the flames of uncertainty.

"But you come sneakin' into me room, grabbin' me." She made a jerky motion as if to seize him. "Sayin' I took things I never took. Scared me 'alf-witted, you did. But then you says you want to take care of me, to feed me three squares and teach me stuff . . ." She shrugged as if she were wounded but forgiving. "I goes along with it. Does me best to—"

His expression darkened. Interesting. She hadn't actually thought it was possible.

"I does me best," she repeated, letting her voice warble a little for effect. "But nothin's good enough."

"Are you saying you are incapable of saying 'how'?"

"I can say ' 'ow' good as the next person."

For a moment she thought he might reach across the carriage and throttle her. But finally he chuckled. "Damnation," he said, and rubbed his forehead with slow, firm strokes.

"You got a 'eadache?" she asked.

He didn't respond.

"Probably cuz you don't get no sleep. 'Ow come is that? You got yourself a guilty conscience or somethin' cuz I knew a fella once. Name was George. 'E worked in the mill. 'E used to sleep like a babe, then one day, on 'is way 'ome 'e finds a purse alongside the road. 'E picks it up and inside there's a bundle of money." She nodded, eyes wide. "Someone musta lost it whilst walkin' along. So George, well 'e keeps it. Couldn't do much else seein's as 'ow 'e doesn't know whose it is nor nothin'. But ever since that day 'e doesn't sleep a—"

"I'll pay you."

She stopped talking. "What's that?"

"I'll give you a sentron if you can speak to my satisfaction by the end of the week."

"A sentron? Just to talk good?" Her mind buzzed along. If she agreed, he would surely be more likely to trust her, and there was no reason she couldn't simply disappear if things took a turn for the worse. And if he wanted to pay her to talk, she was willing to take his money as long as he offered it.

"You got yourself a deal, Govner," she said. "I'll try even 'arder than I 'ave been."

His eyebrow twitched, but he kept his arms crossed against his torso and his gaze steady. "And you'll not try to escape?"

She considered acting shocked, but maybe they had a bit too much history for him to believe that act, so she blew out a careful breath and slowly shook her head.

"Listen, I don't mean to 'urt your feelings, cuz maybe your intentions is honorable, but I don't want to go makin' no vow what I'll 'ave to be breakin'."

"And why would you have to break it?"

She raised a brow and pointed to her eye. She'd seen it in the tiny mirror that hung above the berth in the barque. The skin had taken on a sickish green color that spread well past her cheekbone. She rather liked it. "I didn't get this from no natural catastrophe," she said. "I got it from a fella I'd not met before. Now I'd like to believe you're different, Govner, but I's been around a while, and I—"

"I'll not raise a hand to you, and I'll feed you well. You needn't pocket your crackers."

So he had seen that, had he? They'd served some sort of dry wafer aboard ship and since she'd been full enough after a meal of barley soup and dark bread, she'd stowed the crackers in her pocket with her weighted dice and the piece of colored glass she'd found at the wharves. "Well." She hadn't meant for him to recognize her propensity for hoarding and wondered if he was watching her even more closely than she knew. "A girl never knows when she might get peckish."

"Do you promise?" he asked.

"Very well then, Govner, you got yourself a deal," she vowed just as the carriage began to slow. She glanced out the window. "What's 'appening?" she asked, but he ignored her as he rose to his feet, head bent to accommodate the low ceiling.

The door opened as if on its own, and he stepped down, reaching for her hand.

She came forward with a scowl, noticing the driver had already disappeared. "I thought you said it took some time to reach your 'ouse. We ain't been travelin' for more than an hour. And—"

"We're not going to Newburn."

"Why not?" He gave her hand a little tug as she stepped down, turning her gaze from side to side. "Where's the city?"

"There isn't one."

"How 'bout a village."

"None of those either." Was there laughter in his voice? Was he laughing at her?

She narrowed her eyes a little, squinting against the sun on the fresh-fallen snow and not quite seeing the creature that ambled up until it had nuzzled her leg. She jerked back a step, crowding against the carriage.

"What's that?" she asked.

He scowled down at the thing. "That seems to be a pig."

"What's it doing here?" she asked, but she knew what it was doing. It was rutting around under her skirts, smacking her bare skin. "Holy damn!" she swore, and leapt back onto the carriage step, but at that moment she found that he was laughing at her.

"You won't think it's so all-fired funny when he ruins the fancy clothes you give me."

"I can get you another gown, lass," he said, still chuckling as he glanced to his left. She followed his gaze.

A boy of ten or twelve years was racing across the snow toward them, his battered coat flapping with his speed, but he skidded to a halt not five feet away, breathing hard and gazing up at them as if they'd just arrived from the moon.

"Is this your pig?" Nicol asked.

The lad nodded, then bent and snatched up the animal. It squealed as if bitten and scrambled wildly, but he pulled it to his chest with it squirming like an eel.

"What's your name, lad?"

"Brady," he said. "Master Brady Barnes." He cut his round eyes toward Megan, and she gave him a smile. There was something about his unruly cowlick and smudged cheeks that made him look impishly innocent.

"Well, Brady, perhaps you should inform your mother that we have arrived," Nicol said.

The boy nodded once, backed away a few steps, and sped for the house. Megan watched him go, craning her neck to see past the carriage, over the livestock fences, and on to the house beyond. It was an old wattle-and-daub cottage, boasting a thatched roof and square-paned windows. Megan slid her gaze away, over the snow-white hills and barren trees to the horizon. She licked her lips and remained calm. "What are we doing 'ere?" she asked.

"I didn't think we needed the distractions of Newburn Hall

just now. We will begin your lessons here where we'll have more privacy."

Damn right they'd have privacy. Privacy for him to perform all kinds of atrocities if he had a mind to. She'd just have to keep an open mind about that escaping idea, but she shrugged, not sharing her thoughts. "I ain't never been on a farm before."

She thought he would correct her grammar, but he didn't. Instead, he had a word with the nearly invisible driver, then ushered her toward the house. The door opened long before they reached it, and a woman emerged. She was plump, middle-aged, and homey.

"My lord," she greeted, reddened hands busy drying in her apron. "Welcome to Woodlea."

They stepped onto the single stone stair and through the arched doorway. Kitchen smells tickled Megan's nostrils. Roast goose and sugared yams. No. Wait. There was a tangy scent to the air. She closed her eyes to ascertain the source, but there were too many evocative smells to sort them all out. Her taste buds ached.

"You must be Mistress Barnes," the viscount said, and Megan dragged her attention back to the woman. Her round cheeks were dimpled and nearly as red as her hands.

"I am that, my lord, and this . . ." She motioned to the left and a young woman sidled shyly up to her side. "This is me daughter Deirdre." The girl was not more than sixteen years of age, dark of hair, clear of eye, and as bonny as a spring morning. Megan almost smiled. If this girl couldn't distract the viscount, no one could. "She'll be helping her ladyship with her hair and all."

It took a moment for Megan to realize the woman was referring to herself, a moment longer to understand that she was still rambling off names and duties.

"And me wee lad is round about somewheres," she added, glancing over their heads. "He'll be fetchin' your firewood and helpin' out where he can. Come in now," she said, and waved a dimpled hand as she led the way into the house's interior.

Megan glanced about. She had seen bigger houses in Portshaven. In fact, she had been in a few—mostly at night and generally uninvited. But what this house lacked in size, it more than made up for in mouthwatering aromas. Through a narrow doorway, a bright fire crackled above a stone hearth, and from her left she heard children giggling together.

"Shall I send Brady to fetch your trunks, my lord?"

"That won't be necessary," he said, ushering Megan up the bare wooden steps. "My driver will bring them after he sees to the horses."

"He'll be needing a place to sleep then?"

"No. That won't be necessary."

"Very well then, my lord," she agreed uncertainly.

"We don't mean to be a bother, Mistress."

"Don't be silly," she said, and, glancing up at him, blushed lightly and giggled like a schoolgirl. Megan watched with sheer pleasure. By the looks of things, *she* might be the one to distract the viscount. Or at least she might hope to be. Megan almost giggled herself. A full sentron, a few hearty meals, and the viscount occupied elsewhere. "Lord Landow hasn't been here since his wife and baby died. Poor things." She shook her head and clucked. "It'll be good for us to have someone to look after. Keeps us in our slippers so to speak," she said, and swung open a heavy-paneled door. The room was tidy, but it was more. It was cozy and snug and inviting. "This is to be your bedchamber, my lord, if it suits."

He barely glanced inside. "It suits very well," he assured her.

Her blush deepened, and she scurried away, as if too flustered to stay in one place for long. "And your ladyship . . ." she began, then stopped before the next door. "My apologies," she said, glancing at Megan. "Lord Landow didn't give me your name."

Megan opened her mouth, but Nicol spoke first. "Elizabeth," he said.

"Lady Elizabeth." She bobbed agreement, then swung the door open. Megan scanned the room. Two long, narrow windows graced the chamber, but neither of them could be opened. "If you need anything, you've but to ring the bell near your bed. We'll hear it in our quarters downstairs and come up straightaway. The same with you of course, my lord."

"Thank you, Mistress."

"Might you have any questions or requests before I go about my business?"

"Is there a bathing room, Mistress?" he asked.

"Silly me. Of course," she said, and ambled quickly down the hall, pointing to rooms farther down as she went. "My lord's sitting room. The nursery. His lady's study. She was a scientist of sorts."

"Yes," Nicol said. "I know."

"Sad." Mrs. Barnes shook her head again. "The world's a poorer place without her. But here you are." She swung a door open.

It was a pretty chamber, small but homey, graced with a marble floor, and linen wall fabric. A brass tub stood off to the right. But it was the heavy-paned windows that intrigued Megan the most. Iron latches kept them closed. And iron latches would open them. It would not be a difficult climb to the ground.

"It adjoins the lady's quarters through there. Shall I have Deirdre draw a bath before dinner?" Mistress Barnes asked.

"Yes," Nicol said, and wrapped his arm around Megan's shoulders. She started and glanced up only to find his gaze burning into hers. "I believe my bride would enjoy that."

Chapter 5

Nicol ushered the girl back down the hall to her bedroom. Once there, he hurried her inside and closed the door.

She turned and raised one brow at him. "Bride?"

Her voice was low, too soft to be heard above the water that already ran in the adjoining room.

He watched her. Now that the brown woolen gown was gone, and she was dressed decently, he could almost believe she was the woman he had met some months before. Could almost believe she was the one who had sparked his imagination—so long as she didn't speak.

"We'll be spending a great deal of time together," he said. "I thought it best for the good widow to believe we are wed."

She pulled her arm slowly from his grasp. "I disagree," she said, and in that moment there was a spark of the lady in green. A shade of a woman with breeding.

He shrugged, intrigued but careful to appear nonchalant. "I wouldn't think one more lie would make you so nervous, lass."

"I won't be your whore," she said, and suddenly angels seemed to sing in the heavens. Whore. She'd said the word perfectly, and he laughed.

Her expression was cool, and he sobered quickly.

"Tell me, lass, what happened to the hideous accent?"

She blinked. "What?"

"Your speech," he said. "It improves greatly when you're angry."

She stared at him for a moment, then shrugged. "Good then. 'And over me money, and I'll be on me way."

"What game are you playing, girl?"

She watched him carefully, like a hare might watch a fox. "I'm not playin' at nothing, Govner. I'm just trying to earn a bit o' cash. But I won't be your whore. Not for any amount."

"Why not?"

Curiosity crossed her face, but she didn't speak.

"You're not above a little theft," he reminded her. "And you're certainly not opposed to doing me bodily damage. Why draw the line at prostitution?"

Did she blush? He wasn't certain, but the idea intrigued him.

"I told you, I got me morals."

He reached out and touched her cheek with his knuckles again. "I've got *my* morals. Do you want help removing your gown?"

Her eyes widened, and an unspoken question rounded her lips.

"In preparation for your bath," he explained, though he loved the look of surprise, the lush plumpness of her mouth.

"No. Thank you. I can manage."

"Very well," he said, and turned away. It was only a few short strides to the bed. Seating himself there, he pulled off one boot, then glanced up. She stood exactly where he had left her. "Did you change your mind?"

She raised her chin slightly. "You'll 'ave to leave the room."

"No," he said. "But if you prove that you can say a proper aitch, I'll allow you to disrobe in the bathing room."

"Very well," she said, speaking succinctly. "You, sir, are a horse's ass."

He laughed until she was out of the room and chuckled as he plumped the pillows behind him. There were times, entire moments, when he thought there might be hope.

Ralph arrived noiselessly with their trunks, which he stored against the wall before leaving just as soundlessly. If one couldn't have a castle ghost, it was, at least, nice to have Ralph, he mused, and removing a few items from the trunk, distractedly laid them on a nearby commode. A moment later a soft rap sounded at the door.

"My lord." The voice from the hall was as quiet as the knock. "Mum said to tell you dinner is ready."

Dinner. Meals. He had seen the girl eat aboard ship. It wasn't a pretty sight. Swinging his feet to the floor, Nicol crossed the room and opened the door. The young girl started as though she'd been slapped.

"I didn't mean to frighten you," he said.

"No. Oh no, my lord," she said, and bobbed her head. She was a pretty child, he supposed. "'Tis my own fault. I— Mum says I'm as flighty as a song thrush."

From the bathing room, he could hear water splashing. He turned his attention back to the girl. "What was your name again?"

"Deirdre, my lord."

"Yes. Of course. Lady Elizabeth is not finished with her bath, Deirdre. Could you bring up trays for us, please."

"Certainly, my lord." She bobbed again, and he turned quickly away. Closing the door behind him, he strode across the room to the bathing chamber, and there she was, just rising from the water, with her towel clasped to her chest and her hair pinned tight atop her head.

"What are you doing?" he asked.

She didn't gasp when she glanced up, but he caught the flare of her nostrils, the sharp widening of her eyes. Good God, was the bruising on her cheek ever going to dissipate?

"I'm gettin' out," she said. "As you can see plain as mornin'."

"Get back in the tub."

She tightened her grip on the towel. It was really pretty amazing how much of herself she could cover with that one piece of humble fabric. Not that he wanted to see more. The girl was as skinny as a willow switch. Had he imagined the lovely breasts of the lady in green? Or had she been another woman altogether?

"I bathed," she countered. "Just like you said to."

"I said to get rid of the stench."

She raised her chin. "I don't stink."

He took a step forward. "Sit," he ordered, but she remained as she was, almost meeting him eye to eye now that she stood in the tub.

He sighed, feeling old again. "I'll give you a cantet if you sit down."

Her brows dipped, but she finally sat back down, taking the towel with her. It dripped into the water, but she drew up her knees and managed to keep most everything covered. Amazing. He approached carefully, and she titled her head back, watching him draw near, but in a moment, he was out of her range of vision. He set his fingers to the first pin, and she turned quickly toward him. "What are you doin'?"

"Washing your hair."

"It don't need—" she began, but he allowed one of the pins to poke her skull before he pulled it free.

"Ow."

"Speak correctly or don't speak at all. Dinner will arrive in a moment, and I daren't let you wait any longer lest you begin devouring the furniture."

"Dinner? What are we 'aving?"

He let a pin snag her hair. She glared up at him. "Having," she corrected.

"Don't scowl."

"Don't pull me hair."

He paused, threateningly holding a few strands that had snarled around a pin.

She corrected her speech promptly and he continued with his task. The soap Deirdre had left was scented with lavender, but the odor of her hair masked everything else. It stank like rancid lard and old smoke. He pulled out the final pin and spread her tresses over her shoulders.

"Dunk."

"Not with you in 'ere, I won't."

"Rinse," he commanded, and pushed her under.

She came up sputtering and blinking. "'Ey! What the bloody 'ell—"

He had no compunction against pushing her back down. Her arms started flailing, and the towel, set free from her clawed hands, floated upward to cling sloppily to her breasts.

He let go of her head. Water streamed down her face. "You bloody—"

"A lady does not curse," he warned.

"You—" she began, but when he thumped his palm atop her head again, she fell silent.

"Better," he said, and turned toward the tray of toiletries that stood beside the tub. "Which do you prefer? More lavender or—" He sniffed a nondescript ball of soap. "Roses."

She was glaring at him, but he merely raised a brow, and she settled her hands back on the towel and pursed her lips.

With her face clean and her hair swept sharply back, each facial feature stood out in sharp relief, and it was at that moment that he realized she had the bone structure of a goddess—or a princess. That knowledge was not only surprising but strangely disconcerting.

"Choose," he ordered.

She lifted her chin the slightest degree. It was small and sharp, with a shadow of a cleft in the center. "I am certain you can choose for me, my lord," she said.

Her enunciation was perfect, her demeanor the same. He remembered not to gape. Instead, he rubbed the soap beneath the water before massaging it onto her scalp. Washing around her ears, he managed to work up a pitiful lather. Her head had dropped forward slightly by the time he admitted defeat.

"Rinse," he ordered.

It took her a moment to do so, but finally she slipped under the water. He swished her hair around in the slapping waves, and she emerged again, dripping. Rubbing the soap vigorously, he scrubbed again, concentrating on the ends, which tended to escape. Lather finally formed, and he scooped some off her neck and shoulders, bearing it rigorously back to her hair.

He couldn't help but notice that her eyes had fallen closed. The left lid was the color of a morning sunrise, the cheek still a putrid green. He scowled, then reached for a nearby bowl and moved toward the end of the tub. Her eyes snapped open and her heels scooted against her bottom, but the water was rife with bubbles now and little could be seen even if he tried, which he did not. God knew he had enough troubles already.

Turning both brass handles, he filled the bowl with warm water and retraced his steps. She tilted her head back on command and he rinsed her hair. One water-darkened curl slipped over her ivory shoulder and onto the towel. He scooped it back with its mates and returned to the tap for more water. But a knock on the door interrupted him.

"Here. Finish this," he ordered, and thrust the bowl toward her. She took it with a bobble of hesitation, allowing him to dry his hands and hurry from the room.

In the hallway once again, Deirdre bobbed a curtsy. The tray she carried was filled to overflowing. A steaming tureen was wedged between a pair of empty bowls and a round loaf of oat bread. A crusty pork pie nuzzled a crock of red currant jelly. "Mum said to bring this up first, then fetch mugs and the rest of the lot."

Taking the tray, Nicol set it on the nearby armoire and proceeded to ladle out the soup. By the time he was finished, Deirdre had returned with glasses, a bottle of wine, and two bowls of tansy pudding.

He set the new tray aside, thanked her for her time, and sent her away.

"Dinner is served," he called. There was no answer. "Dinner," he began again, but in that instant panic flared in his gut. Pivoting toward the bathing chamber, he rushed into the room, grabbing the doorjamb as he did so.

The girl was there, clasping her gown to her chest and staring at him as if he'd gone mad.

"I need a minute to dress," she said.

Relief sluiced through him like spring rain, but he loosened his grip on the jamb and made certain his tone was level.

"There's no need to dress."

Her brows rose, and he wondered vaguely if she were holding her breath.

"It's nearly time for bed," he said, and, turning toward the trunk, drew out a robe. It was the color of a midnight sky and made of sheerest satin. "Put this on," he ordered, handing over the garment and retracing his steps into the bedchamber.

Emptying one tray, he set the steaming soup bowls on it, added two glasses of wine, and carried it to the bed.

"Hurry—" he began, but in that moment she entered the room. Wet and disheveled, her hair slipped over her shoulders in waves of burnished gold.

She cleared her throat, tugged the edges of the robe together at her neck, and glanced toward the tray. "The food's 'ere then?"

He continued to stare at her.

She raised a brow. "Mayhap we should eat it."

"Oh, yes." He straightened abruptly. "We shall, if you can do so like a lady."

"But of course," she said, and inclined her head, her raspberry lips slightly pursed. "What are we dining on this eve, my lord?"

"You may call me Nicol."

She gave him a regal look that barely raised one brow. Very good.

"I 'ardly . . ."

He stared. She cleared her throat and tried again.

"I hardly think that would be fitting, my lord."

"I insist," he said, and motioned for her to sit in the nearby chair. "What shall I call you?" A small, round table stood near the window, boasting nothing more than a basket of dried heather. He moved the flowers and carried the table toward the chair. But she had already snatched up the bread and was bearing it to her mouth. He stopped midstride, set the table aside, and stared at her.

It took a moment for her to raise her eyes, longer still to set the bread back on the plate.

"Have I been starving you?" he asked. She opened her mouth to speak, but he held up a hand. "I have not, and I shall not. In fact, I will feed you well and regularly so long as you keep up your end of the bargain."

She straightened her back, eyed the bread longingly, and raised her gaze back to his. Then she took a seat in the upholstered chair and clasped her hands in her lap. Her fingernails, he noticed, were chipped and still remarkably dirty.

Placing the table in front of the chair, he retrieved a bowl of soup and set it beside the bread. She gazed at it with obvious greed.

"When I was searching for you I heard there was a Teleerian thief called Magical Megs."

"Really." She eyed the meal.

He nodded. "I shall call you Megs."

Her gaze never left the steaming tray, but she shrugged. "You can call me Bouzer if you like, just give me some supper."

He wanted to question her, longed to learn the truth. Which was strange, because there was no reason he should care about her past. His only real concern was the final product, after all. It made no difference if she was Magical Megs or the pope or no one at all.

"This is soup," he said, finally turning his thoughts aside and indicating a bowl of the steaming chowder.

She tilted her head and stared at him wordlessly.

"It is not to be slurped like ale nor sopped up like hog swill."

Her lips pursed in disapproval. Her hands were still clasped.

"And this"—he raised the appropriate utensil—"is a spoon."

She looked truly peeved now, and for an instant, for just one second in time, he was stunned by the similarity between her and his Anna, regardless of the bruised eye and wet hair.

"Do you know how to use a spoon?"

The spark in her eyes suggested evil thoughts, but when she spoke, her words were soft and cadenced. "Indeed I do . . . my lord."

He almost smiled, but instead, he handed her the spoon.

"Begin," he said, but before the word was fully loosed, she had wrapped her fist around the spoon like an angry ditchdigger.

"God's balls!" he cursed, and stepped rapidly forward. It was not a simple task to pry her fingers from the metal and realign her grip.

"Hold your utensils thus," he said.

She scowled at their hands. "This ain't no way to 'old—"

"Lass . . ." he warned.

She fell silent, squirmed a little in the chair, eyed the soup, and looked up at him again. He waited.

"God almighty," she said finally. "What now?"

"Now you may begin," he said. She moved to shovel again, but he spoke before her spoon touched the soup. "But if you fail this test, this will be your last course until morning."

She looked past him toward the food that waited on the armoire. Then, nodding once, she dipped her spoon gently into the chowder and took a minuscule sip.

Forty-five minutes later, she patted her mouth with a linen napkin and leaned back in her chair.

Nicol watched her with some amusement. "Sated already?" he asked. She had eaten all her portions and most of his, but she had done it slowly.

Perhaps a shadow of guilt crossed her gamine features. "Widow Barnes be—*is* a fine cook."

"Yes." He rose to his feet. Sometime during the tutelage he had managed to finish off what was left of his own meal. "Will assured me she ran a tight ship."

"Will?"

Striding to the fireplace, he squatted and added a pair of faggots to the flame.

"William Enton," he explained. "Baron of Landow. Perhaps you saw me with him when first we met."

"You were alone the whole while at the inn."

He straightened. "I am referring to the time we spent together in Teleere."

Pushing the table aside, she rose briskly to her feet. "I fear you've mistaken me for someone else . . . again."

"Tell me, lass, did you have the whole thing planned, or was I simply a lucky happenstance?"

"I don't know what you're talkin' about."

He watched her carefully. She was small of stature, but her back was as straight as a pin and her expression serene, if one could disregard the blackened eye. "If you said the very same thing without bastardizing the language one might actually believe you," he said.

"Would one?" she asked, and he wondered momentarily if she was mocking him.

"As it is," he said, "I simply wonder why you chose me. I had done you no harm, meant you no ill will."

She paced toward the trunk, glancing over her shoulder as she did so. And in profile, with her bruised eye hidden, she looked shockingly regal. "So you had never met this thief before?" she asked.

For a moment he had thought she might fall into his trap, might feel a need to defend herself. After all, his motives had hardly been above reproach. But she strictly maintained her innocence. A niggle of doubt irked him. He pushed it aside.

"No, I'd never met you before," he said. "I'm certain I would have remembered."

She fluttered a hand to her chest. "Should I be flattered, my lord?"

"Aye, you should," he said. "I've rarely seen a better actress. Not for a moment did I suspect you planned to rob me."

She shrugged and bent over the trunk. " 'Tis good to know. If one is to be taken for a thief, at least she should be good at the task."

"Accomplished," he said.

She glanced up at him, a question on her face, her hands on the nightgown she'd worn on the ship.

"Anna has an extensive vocabulary," he explained.

"Anna. The great lady," she guessed.

"Yes."

"And why would I wish to be like 'er."

"Surely you're not averse to bettering yourself."

"You think some noble title makes 'er better than me?"

He began to correct her, but her back was up now.

"Wealth don't make her superior," she said.

"What of the fact that she doesn't steal from innocent bystanders?"

Her chin was still high. "Is that what you were?" she asked. "An innocent bystander?" She had turned toward him and kept the gown clasped to her chest. "Cuz from where I'm standing you don't seem so innocent, Govner."

He watched her for a moment, then grinned. "No. Innocent I am not," he said, and took a step toward her. "And what of you, lass? Are you innocent?"

He thought she might step back, put distance between them, but she held her ground. "I am innocent of theft, if that's what you mean."

"But not innocent overall?"

"Do we not all fall short of the glory of God?"

He shook his head, baffled. "When did you have access to scripture?"

She shrugged. "'Tis common sense to believe we are all flawed, is it not?" she asked.

"Some more than others."

"Of course," she agreed. "But who is more imperfect, the one who has much but fails to share, or the one who takes what is needed to survive?"

"Is that what you do, lass? Take only enough to survive?"

"Is that what you have, viscount? Too little to share?"

He opened his mouth to answer, but no worthwhile argument came to mind. "I believe I was asking about your innocence," he said.

She shrugged, her gaze steady. "I don't remember you telling me of your own morality, Govner."

Nor would he, and it was hardly her place to ask. Still, the question rubbed him wrong. "Don't shrug," he said, knowing his tone was irritable. "A lady keeps her movements to a bare minimum."

"You're funnin' me," she said.

"Don your nightgown," he ordered. "It will be a long day tomorrow."

She raised her chin slightly. "I'll wait until you leave the room."

He shook his head. "No, lass," he said. "We'll be sharing this chamber."

Her mouth pursed in anger, and he almost laughed. Give him his medallion—he'd won another round.

Chapter 6

Megan refrained from glancing toward her waiting escape route. "'Elp me understand," she said, careful to retain her cool demeanor as she paced her borrowed bedchamber. She fought the speech lessons in an ongoing effort to make life difficult for him, but she enjoyed the steely expressions and chilly attitudes associated with royalty. They were a shield of sorts. And a girl could never have too many shields. "You want me to act like a lady."

He said nothing.

"Regal. Well educated. Pure."

He nodded.

"But you plan to spend the night in my chamber."

He crossed his arms against his chest and his mouth quirked up slightly at the corner as he leaned his shoulder against the nearby wall. "Circumstances are often not as they seem," he said. "But I am sure you already realize that."

She didn't deign to respond, but paced the room, past the trunk and the commode where he'd set out his personal items—a small mirror, a hairbrush, and a razor. "There are other bedrooms in this house," she said. "Any of which you could choose for your own."

He canted his head as if in concession. "Forgive me if I do not trust you implicitly."

"We are leagues from the nearest village," she said. "What do you think I might do?"

That grin again. He was the picture of cocky elegance. It mattered little that he still wore a smithy's worn work clothes. He was a viscount clear through to the bone. And she hated him for that.

"Will loaned me his country house in good faith," he said. "To help me get some rest in this peaceful environment. I've no wish to see it destroyed."

"Destroyed?"

He shrugged. "Or burglarized."

"I am not who you think I am," she repeated.

"It's bound to be true," he agreed, "since I've no idea who you are. Go to bed now. I'm tired."

"And what of my innocence?"

He watched her in silence for several seconds, then, "Whatever innocence you have left is safe with me, lass."

"That I doubt," she snapped, then softened her tone and forced herself to relax, to adopt his irritating insouciance. "After all, you've threatened and abducted me."

"And you've done nothing against me."

"No I 'aven't."

"Keep your voice down. Or at least shout with proper diction."

"I didn't steal nothin' from you."

He smiled and came away from the wall, his movements as smooth as glass. "And whom do you think they're likely to believe, lass? A grubby-faced urchin with a penchant for dropping her aitches or the viscount of Newburn?"

Anger flooded her, heating her system, steeling her spine. For if she knew anything, she knew he was right. Only a fool would believe otherwise, and she was not a fool.

"I gave you me vow not to escape."

He nodded agreeably. "And that . . . combined with my constant surveillance should keep you honest. I must warn you also that I've locked the bath chamber door from the other side."

She didn't throw anything at him, though it was tempting. She didn't even curse. Instead, she consoled herself with thoughts of vindication. Lovely, comforting thoughts that she kept carefully to herself.

"And you call yourself a nobleman," she said.

"Aye, I do, lass."

"With high ideals and lofty aspirations."

"I believe you may be thinking of the pope."

She gave him a tight smile. "I shan't confuse the two of you again. Will you, at least, leave while I don the gown?"

"No."

"On the other hand." She paced again, glancing over her shoulder as she strode past the commode. "I might mistake you for Satan."

He laughed out loud, and in that instant, with his teeth flashing against his dusky skin, he did indeed look like the devil. Cunning and manipulative but with a darkling allure. "Trust me, girl, your virtue is safe with me," he said, reaching into the nearby trunk and pulling out a trio of books. "I have no interest in you."

"Truly? Then I would appreciate a ride back to Portshaven."

His grin dimmed the smallest amount. "Let me amend," he said. "I have no interest beyond your education."

"Have you ever considered the fact that you might be mad?"

He laughed again, then settled into one upholstered chair, books in hand. "Sleep," he said. "The real lessons begin tomorrow."

There was little she could do but comply. Turning on her heel, she gathered up her nightgown, and although she spared one longing glance toward the bathing chamber, she remained where she was, slipping the robe off her shoulders before yanking the nightgown over her head. Then, stepping out of the ring of fabric, she pattered back across the floor and climbed under the covers. The mattress was soft, the blankets plentiful. She yawned. Vindication would have to wait. Except for the razor she'd taken from the commode of course.

A rude hand shook Megan awake. She moaned and tried to ignore it.

" 'Tis time to arise."

She sat up only to find herself blinking owlishly into the viscount's glare.

"Did you sleep well?"

She made a face. "Not so good really. I got a ache—"

"Very well. Thank you for asking."

She scowled.

"It's the proper response," he said, rising smoothly. "You sleep like the dead."

"Innocent," she grumbled irritably.

"I didn't accuse you of any crime. Not this morning at any rate."

"I sleep like the *innocent*," she explained, and stared groggily in his direction. He was dressed impeccably in tight pantaloons, silver waistcoat, and a midnight blue cutaway coat. His starched cravat was tied just so, but there was, she noticed, trying to push back the wild mass of hair that exploded from her head, a stubble of beard shadowing his perfect jaw.

And she thought there might be a loose thread on one of his waistcoat buttons. "You been awake all night?"

He ignored her question and eyed her carefully. "Have you seen my razor?"

She yawned. "I can't even see me own hands yet."

"I could have sworn I set it on the commode."

"What's a commode?"

He scowled, but turned away. "Deirdre brought breakfast. Are you hungry?"

She scooted up in bed, the pleasure of the moment almost drowned in the thought of a meal. "I'm starvin'."

He stared at her for an elongated moment as if aching to correct her, then exhaled softly. "You're going to learn to read today."

She blinked at him, certain she hadn't heard him correctly. "You're joshin'."

"And for every successful attempt you will receive"— he paused, then swept his hand sideways to indicate the breakfast—"one bite."

Breakfast looked lovely, like a dream really, with boiled eggs, toasted white bread, a small crock of marmalade, golden brown sausages cooked to perfection, and chilled cider in crystal glasses. But it was the bowl of sugared almonds in his hand that made her mouth ache in anticipation.

She reached for the nuts, but he drew them slowly away, making her scowl and lean back against the headboard. "Bring on them books."

"Get dressed first."

She shook her head.

"A lady sees to her personal appearance before all else," he said, and, reaching down, snatched the blankets away.

She gasped as she yanked her tangled nightgown over her legs and grudgingly dropped her feet to the floor. "Ladies," she said, realizing with amazement that the floor was warm from the crackling fire, "must not 'ave a 'ell of a lot to do."

"True ladies such as Anna," he said, and reached into the bowl, "entertain themselves with games of skill and intellect such as chess." Picking up one almond, he dropped it into his own mouth.

It actually hurt her to see him chew it. "I prefer a rousin' game of hazard meself. Got me dice right 'ere if you—"

"I shall teach you to play chess," he interrupted, and dropped another nut into his mouth.

Her fists tightened. "I thought them was for me."

He ate another, then closed his eyes as if in ecstasy. "If you continue speaking as you are, lass, I'm likely to be sated before breakfast begins."

Megan opened her mouth to retaliate, but he picked up another almond and held it like a threat. She considered tackling him and wrenching the almond from his hand, but realized in a fog of almond envy that he might think her undignified. So she turned like a militiaman and marched into the bathing room to don the muslin gown she'd worn the day before. Within seconds she was pattering back into the bedchamber and plopping herself into the cushioned chair.

"Shoes," he said, eating another nut. "Anna would not dine without being properly shod."

"Well Anna probably ain't—"

He munched, and she rose with a jerk to tie on her shoes. She was soon back beside the chair.

He was scowling at a book and munching on his toast. "What about your hair?" He didn't bother to look up.

"What's wrong with me—*my* hair," she corrected, and noticed again the silver-plated button with the loose thread. He should be more careful. It might come off at any moment—if there were a thief in the house.

"You will wear your hair up."

"As you wish," she said, almost smiling at the button as she strode past in search of her pins.

He scowled and caught her arm as she swept past. The ends of her hair brushed his fingers, and he reached out to touch the feathery tresses with his free hand. "It will be a shame to cut it, but I fear we shall have to."

She shrugged.

"But it can wait for now," he said. "You may leave it down. We'll see if Deirdre has any skill later."

His fingers tangled in her wild locks, and she raised her gaze to his, feeling a sizzle of emotion. Hatred, she thought. It must be hatred, but when he released her, she felt strangely unsettled.

Their gazes held for a moment before he shifted his away and cleared his throat. "Sit down," he ordered, and she did so, feeling her nerves tangle at his nearness. "This is the alphabet," he said, indicating two rows of letters printed large and dark upon the page. "You shall learn it first."

"Very well." Her heart still felt odd and her hands unsteady. So she was that much more careful to keep her voice coolly aloof. "What does it say?"

Chapter 7

She read the primer with slow, childish caution. But she read.

Nicol prowled the room again. Eight days had passed since their arrival at Woodlea Farm. In that time she had slaughtered the King's English, learned to walk with passing grace, and nearly managed to best him at chess. In short, they had barely left the damned chamber.

He felt as dishevled as a battered hound, plus he was losing his mind along with half his possessions. He'd finally been forced to borrow a razor from Mrs. Barnes and had recently implored her to replace his mysteriously missing button with something that didn't quite match the row of silver spheres on his favorite waistcoat. The irregularity made him feel strangely off-balance . . . and old. And tired, painfully tired. There was a bed right there, soft, yielding, seductive, and yet he had hardly slept more than an hour at a time. While she . . . He glanced at his student. She was bent over a book, her eyes narrowed in concentration, and in that moment she looked as young as a child. But then she slept like a corpse. Why would she not look young and rested. Maybe she was right. Maybe it was the sleep of the innocent. And maybe his was the insomnia of the guilty. He turned away, almost laughing at such ridiculous notions. Guilt. It wasn't in his nature to feel guilt. He was a viscount after all. Perhaps some years ago, before his uncle's death. Before his father's death, he could have felt some shame. But no more. Wasn't that what money was for? To buy absolution. Money he had plenty of. Sleep, on the other hand, was in short supply. And buttons! Dammit! There was one missing from his jacket! He scowled at it and realized suddenly that the reading had ceased.

He glanced up. Megan was watching him expectantly. He wondered darkly if he'd been staring at his jacket like a brainless oaf, but he clasped his hands behind his back and paced, refusing to blanch.

"Continue," he said instead.

"I've finished."

God's bones! Where was his head? He stopped his pacing and stared at her. "And did you understand the message?"

She returned his level perusal. "I believe it meant that the dog sat, and the cat sat, then the dog ran and the cat ran."

Damn her facetious little soul. She was mocking him, and he deserved to be mocked; he'd lost his buttons, his razor, his concentration, and his mind all in one fell swoop, but that didn't mean he enjoyed being mocked.

"So you think you're ready for something more difficult?"

"That would be entirely up to you, my lord," she said. She had been strangely docile for the last several days. She had also eaten her weight in sugared almonds. "What is your wish?"

She had the most amazing lips. Phenomenally full and as bright as red wine.

"My lord?"

He snapped his mind back into place. "Nicol," he said.

"Call me Nicol." He'd corrected her a million times in the week past, but for reasons unknown, this one mistake bothered more than all the others combined.

She nodded succinctly, and there was something about that simple, elegant motion that moved him, that made him want to reach out and touch her face, to feel her skin, to make certain she was still earthy and touchable and—

"Chess!" he said.

"What say you, my lord?"

"Let's forget the books for a time and relax with a round of chess."

"Very well, my lord."

He ignored her refusal to call him by name as he placed the wooden forms in their appropriate places. His were stained dark, hers were honey-hued. She watched with some interest.

"These pieces," she said, picking up the rough-hewn knight. "Did you whittle them yourself?"

"No," he said, setting his pawns in a row.

"But they're yours."

"Yes. And one of the few things I've not yet misplaced since arriving at Woodlea," he said, and eyed her for a moment.

She didn't seem to notice. "You travel with them?"

He took a seat and motioned for her to do the same. "Do you remember how to begin?"

She perched on the edge of her chair but refused to answer. "Did your father make them?"

"They're simple chess pieces, lass," he said, and gestured for her to begin. "Not so very interesting."

"But that is precisely why I am interested," she countered, raising a regal brow. "Because they are simple. I would expect a man of your position to have a more costly board."

Perhaps he was surprised by her elegant expression, or perhaps it was her insight that made him answer. "They were my mother's."

"Did she make them?"

"Do we begin, or do we return to the books?"

Perhaps she was as tired of reading of cats and dogs as he was, for she focused on the game for the next forty-five minutes. But in the end he won and took her pale king from the board with more than a little satisfaction. She was not an easy woman to best.

Palming the king, he suddenly remembered his mother's face. She was smiling down at him, her face shining with love.

"She was a fine whittler," Megan said.

"Yes." The memories were softened for a moment. Perhaps he kept the pieces with him because of those memories, to reach out and hold them in his palm from time to time. "A simple woman with a good—" He stopped himself and scowled at her. "If you concentrated on the game more, you would do better."

"But I wouldn't be as likely to trip you up," she said, and smiled a little. "Why did you take my king?"

"Because I won."

"It seems to me the queen is more valuable."

"How so?"

"She has all the power. The king does nothing but hide behind his subjects."

"An interesting perspective," he said, and pocketed the piece.

She watched him, looking half-peeved and half-arrogant. "When I win I shall take your queen."

"Lass," he said and shook his head. "No one bests me at chess."

Her smile was full-blown now, bright and pretty and as insolent as hell. "Good," she said. "That will make it all that much more enjoyable."

*   *   *

"God's balls!" Nicol gritted, and jerked to his feet. "The word is 'saint.' The two vowels together make an 'a' sound. Is that so very difficult to remember?"

The girl remained seated but pursed her luscious mouth and turned her wide eyes up toward him. "My mistake, my lord." Her words were apologetic, but her jaw, small and peaked, spoke of treason. Her lips, on the other hand, always spoke of pleasures too seductive to contemplate.

"I am not your lord!" he snapped, and in that moment she jerked up beside him.

"I have been reading since dawn, *my lord.*" Her eyes flashed like dark emeralds. "I can barely see the damn book."

"Ladies—" he snarled, leaning close, "do not curse."

"And gentlemen"—she, too, leaned in—"don't abduct young women and 'ide them away like . . ." She motioned wildly. "Rotting mackerel."

He was about to argue, about to rave at her, but it would do no good. Nothing would do any good, except a full night's sleep and maybe . . . He yanked his gaze away from her lips and massaged his brow. "Rotting mackerel, lass?"

She didn't respond and when he dared turn his attention back to her he saw that her lips were pursed and her brows slightly lowered, though he'd told her a hundred times to keep her forehead smooth.

"You hide me away as if I'm something to be ashamed of," she accused.

He didn't respond, for there was wounded pride in her tone. He had hurt her, and if the truth be told, he had no idea how to right that wrong.

"I've done everything you've asked," she said. "I'm read-ing." She indicated the pile of books with a sweep of her hand. Her fingernails were no longer rimed with black, but they were not exactly clear either. He would have to ask Mrs. Barnes for some lemon to whiten them. "I eat with all due elegance, and I have ceased to drop my aitches."

"And I suppose you think you deserve a respite?" he growled. Prolonged confinement was never good for his disposition. Sleeplessness was hard on his constitution, and celibacy was a downright bitch.

"I think I deserve a barge of sugared almonds and a week abed," she growled back.

A barrage of arguments flooded to the fore, but her delicate hands were formed into fists like a tiny pugilist's and he couldn't help but grin. "We're out of almonds and you've already slept more than any living soul, but . . ." Reaching for the door, he swung it open and bowed, sweeping a hand in front of him. "After you, my lady."

She looked stunned, almost frightened. Like a canary too long confined. "Where are we going?"

"To get some air. Stretch our legs. I've been neglecting your physical needs. Go ahead," he said, but as she brushed past him he caught a whiff of her scent. Lavender and femininity. And he knew it was his own needs that were going unmet.

It took only a moment for him to don his redingote, a bit longer to help her with her cape. He draped it across her shoulders. His thumbs brushed her collarbones and for reasons unknown his fingers fumbled, making it difficult to tie the ribbons. And when the task was done, his hands seemed strangely unwilling to draw away.

"It's almost dark," she said, and somehow her words cleared his head. He pulled his hands stiffly to his sides and managed to open the door. Her dark woolen cape brushed his leg as she strode past, and he gritted his teeth as he followed.

Outside, the air was chill, but there was no wind. Giant snowflakes fell like angel dreams from a darkening sky. Up ahead, the widow's old carriage horse flicked his long ears and whickered hopefully over the uneven timbers of the fence. An owl called mournfully from the woods.

Megan glanced toward the forest. "Where are we exactly?" she asked.

"We are at Woodlea Farm, Lord Landow's country manor," he said.

"And where is that?"

He turned toward her, wondering why she wished to know, wondering about her plans. Her eyes shone like living gems in the eve's last light, and snowflakes melted languidly on her hair. It was the color of autumn wheat and was pulled back with a single blue ribbon, but a few wayward tendrils had escaped, hinting perhaps that while she might be tamed, she would never be broken.

"Here," he said, and, reaching toward her, pulled the hood over the crown of her head. His wrists brushed her hair, and for a moment, he was almost tempted to run his fingers under the flaxen mass of curls. Their gazes met and caught. "I don't want you getting sick," he added, and drew his hands slowly away.

She blinked, then turned and started toward the stables again. The world was silent but for the crunch of their soles on the hard-packed snow. "Are those your horses?"

"The chestnuts are mine." Behind the split-rail fencing, all three steeds watched their progress.

She searched the paddock. "Are you referring to the red ones?"

Her diction was flawless, but he kept his expression nonchalant. It would hardly do to fawn all over her every time she said something correctly. Time was running short. The test was soon to come. "They're called chestnuts . . . or sorrels . . . when their manes and tails are flaxen." He glanced at her. "It's not so different from the color of your own hair."

"Oh?" She glanced their way. "I hadn't noticed."

"Do you like horses, lass?"

She shrugged. "I've had little to do with them."

"We'll have to change that."

They had reached the fence and strolled along the line of it toward the barn. The latch caught under Nicol's fist, but he pulled it up and motioned her in. She went with some misgivings.

It was dim inside and smelled of sweet clover and freshly split oak. From the corner of the barn, the Barnes lad glanced up, startled, the wooden prongs of his fork lying lax on the hay for a moment. His wide gaze moved from Nicol to the girl, then remained steady. Had he quit breathing as he stared at her? Nicol wondered. Were even young boys entranced by her? But who would not be? She had changed a great deal since her arrival there.

"My wife needed a bit of fresh air," he explained, perhaps simply to see if he could break the lad's concentration. "I thought I'd introduce her to the horses."

"I could do that if you like, Govner," said the boy breathlessly. "If you've no wish to soil your fancy shoes." He stood very straight now, and in that moment Nicol realized the lad was older than he seemed. A boy on the cusp of manhood.

"My thanks," he said, and quieted the odd knot of resentment that twisted in his gut. The boy hadn't yet reached puberty. "But my wife is unaccustomed to horses. I think I will acquaint her myself."

"Right then," he said, stabbing the fork expertly into the fodder and hurrying outside with his load.

Lifting his hand to Megan's back, Nicol ushered her to the far end of the barn. Once there, he took some ear corn from a pile and lifted the gate latch to step into the horses' paddock. The girl remained where she was, looking doubtfully into the enclosure.

"Come along," he urged.

"I am accustomed to the city, my lord."

He canted his head, amused and more than a little amazed. She could bash him on the head and steal his watch quick as a thought or face a room full of drunken men without batting an eye. But put her in a barnyard, and suddenly she was as timid as a parlormaid.

"Surely you're not afraid," he said.

She raised her chin but remained where she was. "I've no wish to ruin my frock."

He laughed at such an obvious ploy. Behind her, the lad reentered the barn, watched them for an instant, then hurried back to the hay.

"Come along, lass," Nicol chided, and, slipping his arm around her waist, ushered her into the horse pen.

Her brow was slightly furrowed, her steps slow, and somehow her uncertainty made him want to wrap her in his arms and promise his protection. But that was foolishness. She needed protection like a warthog needed ale.

The chestnuts trotted forward, eager to see what he offered. Megan shifted back a half step, but Nicol tightened his arm around her waist and held out the corn. The gelding snuffled at the bright kernels, but the mare hung back, then stretched her neck over her companion's rump to see what transpired. Beneath her thick, wayward forelock, her blaze looked bright and narrow, matching the gelding's to perfection.

"Are they twins?" Megan asked.

He turned in amazement, but his surprise was unjustified. Just because she now spoke like a lady did not mean she would know much about the things the gentry found so fascinating. Horses were just another animal to her and not the showpieces behind which every preening debutante could be seen parading about Fallcome Gardens.

"Horses rarely give birth to twins," he said.

She didn't respond, neither moving closer nor backing away.

"Croft was my mount years before the mare was given to me," he said, and straightened the gelding's forelock.

Megan shifted her gaze from the horses to him. "Mare?"

He was honestly surprised, and that didn't often happen, not until he'd met a gamine lass on the streets of Portshaven at least. "The female," he said.

She nodded. "Then geldings are . . ." She searched for a moment. "Males."

For a barmaid and a thief she seemed strangely squeamish discussing simple gender differences. But perhaps it was all a ploy. He would be wise to remember the headaches that had followed the loss of his watch. But it was difficult sometimes, when she looked like she did now. Small and refined and strangely in need of protection. Luckily, he was worn and jaded, and not easily taken in by either size or refinement.

Breaking off a few inches of the cob, he offered it to Croft. "Geldings are male," he said. "In a manner of speaking."

Her gaze was on him again. He could feel it in the gathering darkness and turned to look at her.

"But they can't . . ." It was his turn to search for words, because, surprisingly, he found he had no wish to offend her. Her eyes looked wide and innocent, her face young and delicate. The bruise on her cheek had faded, but it was still discernible, and the sight of it made him feel strangely . . . inadequate. "Geldings can't reproduce," he said.

"Oh? Oh," she said, and cleared her throat. "I see."

He wanted to chuckle, but she looked enchantingly embarrassed, so he fought his glee down to a grin. "It makes them less aggressive. More dependable."

She was watching the pair with obvious interest. Breaking off another bit of corn, he picked up her hand and placed the cob in her palm.

"Go ahead," he urged.

She lifted her hand tentatively, and Nicol carefully straightened her fingers away from the treat.

"He'll try not to bite you," he assured her, "but you'd be wise to do your part."

Croft picked the corn off her hand with a prehensile upper lip, then stepped back a pace to munch it. The mare stretched her neck past the gelding's cocked hip, wanting her share but uncertain of the reception.

"Now Baroness," Nicol said, reaching a hand toward the mare, "is a bit more skittish."

"How old is she?"

"Six."

"Is that young?"

He shrugged and broke off another piece. "Young enough to be wary." Placing the cob in Megan's hand again, he smiled into her eyes. "Female enough to be dangerous."

Croft abandoned the cob on the ground and lipped the offering from the girl's hand.

"Is that an insult, my lord?" she asked.

They were standing extremely close. He could smell the hint of lavender in her hair. "Why do you insist on calling me that?"

Their eyes met, but she pulled her gaze away in a moment. "They want more."

And so did he. Suddenly, inexplicably, he wanted to reach out to her, to touch her, to feel her skin beneath his fingertips. He raised his hand, but in that moment good sense smote him and he drew away. "I'll get another ear."

Steadying himself, he stepped into the barn. What the hell was he thinking? She was a thief and very possibly worse. Didn't he have the scar on his skull to prove it? Besides, he had made a promise, a vow, and that vow could not easily be broken. Not even if he wished to, which he—

He heard her gasp and turned just as hoofbeats pounded in the paddock. Cursing, he leapt through the gate. Crowded from behind, Croft had lunged forward. His shoulder struck Megan. She fell backward and in that same instant the gray bit Baroness again. She plunged blindly ahead. Nicol leapt forward, throwing himself at the mare, and the chestnut, frightened from all directions, veered wildly to the right, jumping straight at Megan before disappearing around the barn.

Nicol rushed forward and dropped to his knees.

"Lass." He touched her face. It was cold and pale. "Dammit, lass, wake up," he said, but she remained as she was, unmoving on the scattered snow.

Chapter 8

"Is she dead?" Brady's tone sounded wobbly from the doorway.

"Fetch a lantern," Nicol ordered, his own heart beating hard against his ribs.

The boy's footfalls rushed away, but in that moment the girl moaned and sat up unsteadily.

Nicol supported her back with his arm and leaned close. "Lass," he breathed, relief sluicing through him. "Are you well?"

She said nothing, but glanced dazedly to the left as if uncertain of her whereabouts.

"Can you talk?" he asked.

Raising an arm carefully, she touched her fingers to her skull. "Aye," she said. "But I don't think I like 'orses much."

Flooded with relief, Nicol slipped his arms beneath her back and legs and rose rapidly to his feet.

Brady rushed out of the barn, lanternlight crazily sweeping the snow as he ran, but Nicol brushed past him, barely noticing the lad's pale expression.

"Shut the gate, boy," he said, and bore her rapidly up the hill to the house.

Her head lay against the hard beat of his heart, but she had wrapped her arms around his neck, and he could see no blood. God's bones! Please let there be no blood.

"I'm certain I can walk." Her words startled him, but he hurried on, barely glancing at her face.

"If you'll put me down—"

"Be still," he said, and, opening the door with some difficulty, strode through the foyer and up the stairs, taking them two at a time.

The hardwood floor rapped beneath his heels. The feather mattress sighed under her weight, and he drew his arms slowly away, careful not to jar her.

Someone had lit a trio of candles and placed them on the armoire beside the bed. The light flickered across her face. It looked pale, except beneath her left eye, where the skin was still a weak, greenish yellow.

"You've soiled your shirt," she said, her tone implying that nothing could be more shocking, and he glanced down to find a minuscule smudge of dirt on his right sleeve.

What the hell had he become? "Where do you hurt?" he asked.

She was leaning back on her elbows and shifted to sit.

"Lie back," he ordered. "Did you hit your head?"

"I think . . ." She looked slightly disoriented and refused to lie flat. Pulling a candle from its holder, Nicol held it close to her face. Her eyes looked immensely wide, but they remained clear and bright. His heartbeat slowed a little. "My head is fine."

"She didn't strike you?"

"Maybe . . ." She tried to move her legs and winced. "She may have stepped on me."

He swore in silence. "Stay there," he said, shifting toward the foot of the bed and sitting down on the mattress to push up her skirt.

She immediately yanked her legs away, then gritted her teeth against the pain.

He swore out loud now, wanting to strike something. "I said to lie still."

"Is she well?"

Nicol turned toward the doorway. Brady stood there, his hat in his hands, his face as pale as the girl's.

"Tell your mother to draw a bath and bring up a hot brandy," Nicol ordered and turned back toward Megan.

"I need you to relax," he said. "I'm going to have a look at your legs."

"Me legs are fine."

"Hopefully better than your speech." Worry tended to make him mean-spirited. "We made a bargain, lass," he said. "I expect you to remain alive long enough—"

Megan shifted her gaze to the door, and Nicol realized the reason a moment too late. Brady remained there, his mouth pursed tight and his hat wrung hard in his grubby hands.

"Are you well, my lady?" he asked.

"I am whole. But you are kind to ask," she said.

A look of relief crossed the boy's face, and in that moment Nicol realized this lad would eventually become the kind of man little Megs would marry. An honest lad with a strong back and heart-bending adoration. Not a hardened cad who would use her for his own ends and complain when she was injured by his horse.

"If you're sure, my lady."

"I am quite sure," she said, and the boy nodded and hurried downstairs.

Nicol returned his attention to the girl. A raw medley of unwanted emotions churned in his belly. "Do you affect all males that way?"

For a moment, the girl's lively face showed wide-eyed surprise. It did nothing to dispense the bile in his gut. But in a moment her eyes narrowed, evidencing anger and easing his mood. He had little use for innocence.

"Are you accusing me of something, my lord?"

He refrained from grinding his teeth at the nomenclature. "Of course not, my lady," he said, and put his fingers to the laces of her right shoe. "I am merely surprised how fast you have learned the ways of the upper class." Catching her shoe behind the heel, he glanced at her face.

"Why thank you, my—" She cut her words off with a hiss of pain when he eased off her shoe.

"Where does it hurt?"

"It doesn't," she said, speaking between her teeth. "You needn't look so hopeful."

"Dammit girl—"

"My poor dear." Widow Barnes rushed into the room, her cheeks flushed and her brow furrowed. "Whatever happened?"

" 'Twas nothing," Megan said, and laughed, but the sound was forced. Damnation. The pain must be great indeed if it could impede her acting ability. "The horses bolted and frightened me. I fell. Nothing more."

"Oh! Thank the heavens." The widow sighed. "By the look on Brady's face I feared you were about to leave us. But you seem bright enough." She smiled. "Still, it's a shame, it is." She tutted, standing arms akimbo. "But nothing that a warm bath and a hot toddy won't set right aye?" Scurrying to the bathing room door, she set her hand to the latch. "Now that's strange."

Nicol watched the girl's face. Color had returned to her cheeks, and her eyes looked alert.

"The door's locked," said the widow.

Nicol turned, stamping down his impatience. "My wife is a modest woman," he said. "I fear she locked it from the other side."

"Of course," Mrs. Barnes said, and, chuckling at the idea, hustled from the room. In a moment they heard water running.

"You lie well," Megan said.

Nicol canted his head as if accepting praise. "I can only hope to match your expertise, but I've had many years at court to practice. What of you?" Perhaps he was trying to distract her as he untied the other shoe, or perhaps she just set him off. He wouldn't have to lock the damn door if he could trust her.

She made no reaction as he eased off her left shoe and dropped it to the floor. Her stocking followed.

"Me mum said to bring up something 'ot to drink." Deirdre was in the doorway, bobbing a curtsy, careful not to spill the mugs she held.

"You may put them on the table," Nicol ordered.

She scurried forward to do his bidding and bob another curtsy. "Are you well, my lady?"

"I am fine. No need to worry."

"Is there anything else I might fetch you? Mum stewed pears for dessert."

Megan's eyes brightened.

"Bring up a bowl when you have a minute, will you, lass?" Nicol requested.

"Certainly, my lord. And you will ring if you need anything else?"

He assured her he would, and she disappeared as quickly as she had come.

The room fell into silence.

"You have a gift for winning allies," he said, and eased her skirt up her legs.

She scowled at his progress, and he did the same, though in truth there was little with which to find fault. Her ankles were delicate, her calves lean and shapely. Malcontent stirred low in his gut.

"What are you talking about?" she asked.

"The servants," he said, prying his attention from her calves to her evergreen eyes. "You won them over quickly.

She caught his gaze. "Perhaps it is because I do not glare at them."

"I don't glare," he said, and did nothing to soften his expression as he shifted her gown above the sharpness of her knees. His hand skimmed upward, and he shifted, trying to ease his hardening discomfort and concentrate on her injuries.

The hoofprint on her inner thigh was not perfectly defined, but it was nearly so. The flesh was already swollen in the approximate shape of a horseshoe and turning the color of a ripening eggplant. He touched the edge of it, and she flinched, causing him to swear out loud.

"So gentlemen are allowed to curse but ladies are not?" she asked, her voice prim.

He shifted his gaze to her face. It had gone pale again.

"Gentlemen are allowed to do anything they wish," he said. "So long as they have adequate funds."

"How fortunate for you."

She said the words softly, like a lady, and he settled back, watching her face and trying to relax.

"How much does it hurt?"

"More than a hangnail. Less than decapitation."

"A broad range of knowledge for one who still has her head," he said, looking at the wound again. "I'm going to have to check if it's broken."

"It's—" she began, then gasped as he pressed gently against her leg.

He squeezed her thigh, and she squeaked in pain.

"My lady!" The Barnes lad was back in the doorway like the damned plague, his knuckles white on the bowl of stewed pears as he rushed forward. Nicol swished Megan's skirts back down to her toes, rapidly hiding the slim elegance of her legs. "You are in pain?" he asked, but the girl gave him a tremulous smile.

"It is not so terrible, Brady, really. I am just being silly."

"No, my lady," murmured the child, his expression adoring. "It is not true." He was at a loss for words as he bore the bowl to her bed, then, "I've brought your dessert."

Megan drew the steam happily into her lungs. "That will make everything better, I assure you."

"I would do more to help you, my lady," he said solemnly.

"That will be all, lad," Nicol said.

"But my lady—"

"Will surely summon you if she needs more pears."

"Very well then," Brady said, and left, though his steps seemed a bit slow to the viscount.

Megan scowled. "You were rude," she accused.

He looked at her askance, lifting her skirts again. "I didn't know you wanted him staring at your legs."

Reaching down, she snatched the fabric from his hand and spread it back down to her feet. "I don't," she said. "No more than I want you staring at them."

So that was it then. Despite his grand title and undeniable wealth, she had no more interest in him than she did a ragged farm boy. He would have laughed if he didn't feel like grinding his teeth. Instead, he leaned back and studied her face. She was, after all, nothing more than a political tool. The last thing he needed was for her to become attracted to him. Or vice versa, he thought perversely. "Perhaps I should summon a doctor," he said.

She relaxed a little. "It's not broken," she assured him, and took a tiny spoonful of her dessert. Nicol watched her tongue peek out, watched her lips part. "I'm certain I could walk on it."

"I've seen men walk with leg wounds," he said, tearing his gaze from her mouth. "It doesn't mean they're unbroken."

He considered examining her other leg, but the sight of her bare toes dissuaded him, for even that innocent bit of bare flesh made him feel oddly tight.

"When?"

He lifted his attention reluctantly to her face again. Her tongue swiped her plump lips, lapping up a bit of sauce. "What's that?"

"What men walked with leg wounds?"

"Soldiers," he said, though he was loath to. Hardly had he spent six months searching for her so that he could share his life story. "They'll even run if the motivation is great enough. Broken or unbroken."

"When were you in contact with soldiers?" she asked, and closed her eyes ecstatically as she finished off the dessert with a delicate lap at the underside of the spoon.

"When I was in the army," he said, and realized he had clenched his hands into fists.

"But you're a viscount." She was scowling again. He failed to reprimand her. Funny how a few broken bones made a bloke ease up on a woman. Or perhaps it was the way her lashes brushed the lovely skin of her cheeks, or how he could imagine the feel of her tongue against his—

"How much?" he asked, squeezing her left leg through her skirts and effectively stopping her next words. "Does it hurt?"

Her scowl deepened slightly, but it did nothing to decrease her beauty. "It's hardly unbearable."

He eased his hand up her left leg, over her knee, and onto her thigh. She didn't flinch. He moved slower when he touched the other, probing the outside gently as he worked his way up from the knee. She winced but remained still.

"Perhaps it is just bruised," he said, resting his hand on the outside of her thigh. It was safe, of course, since there were several layers of fabric between them. Yet, even so, it seemed that he could feel the heat of her flesh against his fingers.

"You needn't worry," she said. "I shall be well long before it is time for the test."

Something tangled in his stomach. "Through no fault of mine."

She watched him for a moment. "Aye," she agreed. "You should have known the foolish steed would bite its mate, causing it to career into me at that exact moment."

"Yes," he said. "I should have."

"And that I would fail to get out of the way," she added.

He watched her face. "Are you absolving me of blame, lass?"

"Hardly," she said, and settled back onto her elbows again.

He could not help but rise to plump the pillows behind her back. Neither did he try to resist resettling her so that she rested comfortably against the oaken headboard.

"It is your fault entirely that I am here. Though I doubt . . ." She dropped her gaze to her hands. "It may be that I would never have tasted sugared almonds had it not been for you." She still wore the gloves he had given her and fiddled with them now.

Reaching out, Nicol took her left hand in his and eased off the soft leather one finger at a time.

"And reading . . ." She raised her gaze to his as he removed the second glove. "I've oft wondered about books."

Reaching behind him, he retrieved a mug of hot brandy. "Have you?" he asked and handed her the cup.

She shrugged as she took it, but only wrapped her hand around it, seeming to take comfort in its warmth as she gazed into its depths. "It's something of a miracle. They seem sort of mysterious you know. When you can't read 'em."

He should correct her speech, but he only smiled. "You've done well, lass. No one could learn faster."

"That's the first time you've said so." Her gaze was steady on his for a moment, then fluttered downward. The brandy steamed, sending up a curl of misty warmth to blur her gamine features, and in that moment he wondered if he ever saw her clearly, or if his perception of her was forever hazy. Who was she really?

"Is it?"

"Aye."

He nodded. "Drink your brandy, lass."

"I don't . . ." She searched her phenomenal memory for the proper word. "Imbibe."

Surprise smote him, but not for the first time where she was concerned. "Ever?"

"Spirits," she said, raising the mug slightly, "are quite expensive."

"But you must make a fair amount of money, lass. What with working at the inn and taking in mending. What do you do with your coin?"

"I may not be highborn," she said, "but that doesn't mean I am content to be nothing."

He contemplated that for a moment. "You save it," he guessed, and she shrugged. It was tempting to pry, but he reminded himself there was no point. It didn't matter what she did with her funds, only that she perform the task set before her.

"Drink," he said. "The brandy is free today." She made no move to comply. "And soothing. Please," he added.

She tilted her head slightly, watching him, but finally she bent to taste the hot liquid. "That is also a first," she said, not raising her eyes immediately.

"Your first brandy?"

She sampled it again and didn't seem to find it distasteful

since she swallowed a goodly amount. "The first time you've said please."

He drew a deep breath through his nostrils. "I've an admission to make," he said, and, settling more comfortably upon the bed, watched her carefully. "I come from a long line of bastards."

She laughed. He should tell her that laughter was prohibited. That Anna rarely even smiled, but her face was alight with pleasure, and the sight of her thus made it strangely difficult for him to breathe, much less reprimand.

"Is that so?" she asked, and drank again.

"It's a documented fact."

"Thus, you have no choice but to be a bastard yourself?"

"Just so," he admitted, and watched her drink again. "Are you ready for your bath?"

She looked immediately nervous. "That might be difficult."

"I'm willing to help," he said, and immediately regretted his words, not only for their own foolishness, but for the uncertainty that shone in her eyes. "You needn't worry," he assured her. "I hardly ever molest young women whom my horses have attacked."

"How chivalrous of you. But perhaps I'd best forgo my bath this evening."

"You don't trust me?"

"If I remember correctly, you nearly drowned me last time."

"But as you said, I'm feeling chivalrous tonight."

"Forgive me, my lord," she said, her tone exactly as he'd trained it to be, her expression imperious, "but you must have heard about leopards . . . and their spots?"

Her tone and expression eased his own discomfort, and he laughed. He had been right at the start. She had a sharp wit and a clever tongue, both of which intrigued him no end. "Yes, I believe I have."

"The same goes for viscounts."

"You've learned skepticism quickly,' he said.

"Almost as if I became a skeptic even before I became a lady."

"Almost," he agreed. "Sit up a bit. I'll help you remove your gown," he said, though he knew without a doubt that he shouldn't.

Chapter 9

Megan remained exactly as she was, watching him. She had felt safer when he was a bastard. Safer, steadier. But he was different tonight.

He settled back a little, as if he knew she needed more room. "I'm not going to harm you, lass."

"It's not harm I'm worried about . . . exactly."

He had the devil's own smile. She had never been attracted to noblemen. Had never trusted them enough to get that close, but there was something disturbingly honest about him just now.

"I'm not going to do that either," he said, apparently reading her thoughts.

She neither moved nor answered. Perhaps she looked distrustful.

He sighed. "I've told you, lass, I have made a vow to a friend. A vow I will hold to, and that promise does not allow me to dally with you. Even if we were suited."

But they were not, of course. He was a viscount. She was

the woman who was going to rob him blind. "What vow exactly?" she asked.

He watched her for a moment, saying nothing.

"I've no evil plots in mind. Think of me as an uncle," he suggested.

She raised her brows at him. "I have no uncle," she said. "And if I did, I doubt he would be assisting with me bath."

"*My* bath," he corrected. "Think of me as a kindly aunt then?"

"Perhaps Widow Barnes might better fill that role."

"You're injured," he reminded her. "The widow won't be able to lift you into the tub."

The idea of him carrying her naked to the tub nearly undid her, but she kept her head and her silence.

"I'll not have you putting weight on that leg. Not until you're healed." His gaze felt ridiculously warm on her face. She ducked her head, taking a sip of brandy.

"That's right." She finished her drink and sternly reminded herself of his motives, of his position, of his past actions. "You need me to survive until after the test."

Something shone in his dark eyes, some emotion too unfathomable for her to analyze, but in a moment it was gone. "Did I mention my forefathers?" he asked, retrieving his own cup and trading it for hers.

"They're bastards?" she guessed, and wrapped her hands about this new mug.

"As I've said . . ." He saluted her with the empty mug. "You've a fine memory when you apply yourself."

"Perhaps you could break the trend."

He was watching her closely, but didn't seem to understand her meaning. Things were becoming a little fuzzy to her, too.

"And not be a bastard," she suggested.

"Ahh." He seemed to draw himself from his reverie. "I

doubt it would work. Thick blood and all that. How's the leg?"

"Better."

"Keep drinking," he suggested. "It'll help you sleep through the night."

Would it also help him seduce her? The idea sent a curl of hot emotion steaming into her gut.

"I'll tell you what . . ." He set the empty mug on the trunk and rose to his feet. "I'll go into the hall. You stay here, undress as far as you wish. When you are ready I'll carry you to the tub and let you soak."

He must be out of his mind, or at least he must think she was. But perhaps he read her thoughts, for his mouth quirked. "If I do anything untoward, you can always scream for the widow."

He was hardly a giant of a man, being only eight inches or so taller than her. And he looked neither beefy nor particularly toughened. Indeed, if she saw him on the street, she might have thought him too elegant to be worrisome. But in more than a decade of thievery and subterfuge few had caught her and none had held her. Why him? Why now? "Are you suggesting the widow can save me from your advances?" she asked.

"Did you get a look at her arms, lass? I think she may be able to take me in a tussle."

The mental image of them wrestling made her giggle. God's truth, she giggled, then widened her eyes at the absurdity of it.

He smiled. Perhaps at his own joke or perhaps at her expression. "I'll be in the hall," he repeated. "Don't forget about me."

She wished she could, but he was too unpredictable, too witty, and way too damned close, so she gave a perfunctory nod, and he stepped outside the room.

Her gaze snapped to the windows in the bathing area. The door stood open now, but he would surely hear if she tried to escape that way immediately. Her best bet was to make him trust her, make him think she trusted him.

Her hands shook as she removed her gown. The battered muscles in her thigh complained as she pressed the length of fine fabric past her feet, but she managed it. The white cotton undergarment, however, would remain. He had given the drawers to her. They were the first pair she had ever worn. As soft as a sigh and surprisingly warm, they were suspended from her shoulders by narrow straps, hugging her from breasts to thighs. She hated to get them wet, but she was not about to strip naked, not even to convince him of her trust.

Finding her pins on the nearby night table, she piled her hair atop her head and attempted to secure it there. But, freshly washed and as slippery as wet eels, it kept trying to sneak down past her ears. Finally, however, the majority of it had complied. Flipping the top blanket over the midsection of her body, she closed her eyes for one haunted second, then called his name.

He stepped languidly back into the room. If he had worried that she might try to escape, she couldn't guess as much by his demeanor, and if he desired her even the least amount, she could not read it in his eyes.

"I feared you might have passed out again."

"No." She turned her gaze away. Why did he make her nervous? She had once stolen a brooch from the Laird of Teleere himself and felt not a single butterfly. But that was when she was Magical Megs. Who was she now? "I am well."

"It wasn't unduly painful?" he asked, and nonchalantly tugged the blanket away from her body.

She kept her eyes averted, though the long cotton drawers managed to hide most of her from his view.

He slipped his arms beneath her, and she winced as he lifted her against his chest.

"No, not at all," she assured him.

Their faces were very close. He caught her gaze with his own. "I thought you were a better liar than that, lass."

"You're mistaken," she said. "You are the one with the lying skills."

"True," he agreed, and paced through the doorway.

She felt ridiculously light-headed, and the cotton drawers seemed scandalously tight across her bosom, as if her lungs lacked proper breathing space. A few recalcitrant tendrils escaped her sloppy coiffure and caressed the sharp line of his jaw. Against her breast, his chest felt hard and unyielding.

He stopped beside the tub. "Do you wish to remove your drawers?"

Her gaze flew to his, but if he was jesting, she couldn't tell. "No."

He grinned a little. "Just asking, lass," he said, and, bending carefully, rested her bottom on the edge of the tub.

"Test the water," he ordered, and after one flustered moment, she did so, reaching out to dip her fingers tentatively just beneath the surface.

"Is it satisfactory?"

"It's . . ." She cleared her throat and drew her arm carefully back against her torso. Her left breast had almost escaped the confines of her undergarments, and she felt all but naked against the heat of his chest. "It's fine."

Shifting his gaze slowly from her bosom to her face, he eased her off the ledge and into the water. It slid over her bare feet, greedily devouring her legs and casting tiny bubbles upon her cotton undergarment until she was settled on the bottom.

She cleared her throat. "Thank you, my lord," she said.

He gave her a perfunctory nod and drew his arms slowly away as she leaned against the back of the tub. "My pleasure." His tone was smoky and dark. She snapped her gaze to his, but if there was some deeper meaning in his words, it didn't show on his face. Indeed, he looked as elegant and controlled as ever . . . except for that one disturbing smudge of dirt.

She, on the other hand, felt fidgety and breathless. Past history lent her no idea how to react under his scrutiny, so she tried to match his dignified calm. "Your sleeves are wet," she said, surprised that even water would dare to disturb his perfect grooming.

It took a moment before he pulled his gaze from hers, but finally he glanced at his sodden shirt. "I should change, I suspect, before I get the widow's floor wet. Will you be safe alone for a moment?"

She flickered her gaze to his. His lashes were as lush as sable, shadowing his emotions, but even so there was something about him tonight that spoke of pleasures too dark to consider. She swallowed and pulled her attention away. "Of course."

She felt his gaze linger on her for a second longer, then he half turned toward the bedchamber, but in an instant he stopped and glanced over his shoulder. "Don't do anything foolish," he said. She looked up. His back was broad, and the tendons in his neck were pulled tight, marking a path downward toward the smooth skin of his chest. How would it feel to slip her hand beneath his shirt, to feel his heart beat against her fingertips?

"Foolish?" she whispered, and he grinned a little, stealing her breath.

"Don't sound so surprised. 'Tis not as if you've not been foolish in the past."

She pulled her gaze from him with a hard effort and concentrated on the ripples in the water. "Do you fear I might spring from the tub and escape?"

Humor shone in his darkened eyes. "I feared you might drown," he said. "Are you feeling light-headed?"

"No, my lord," she assured him, but she lied. Her head did indeed feel strange, and she feared he might be the cause. Dear Lord, she'd rather have a concussion.

He delayed a moment, then strode from the room. A thousand rampant thoughts steamed through Megan's mind. None of them were the least bit helpful. From the bedchamber, she heard him add fuel to the fire. Leaning her head against the smooth brass, she closed her eyes against the image of him slipping out of his shirt as the flames flickered light across his chest.

"All's well?" He returned in a moment, startling her from her reverie. His perfectly pressed shirt hung open, leaving several inches of skin exposed down the midline of his body. Dark hair accented the hard planes of his belly, but he seemed unaware of his state of undress, for he was toweling his used shirt dry. Then, reaching up, he hung it on a nearby peg. His shirt gaped open, revealing one flat, dusky nipple.

"Megan?" he said, turning toward her.

She yanked her gaze from his chest to his face, wondering desperately what he had said.

"Are you well?" he repeated.

"Oh. Yeah. Of course."

Drawing a stool close to the tub, he sat down. "You look a bit flushed," he said, and leaned forward to press his palm to her brow.

She hoped quite desperately that she would drown.

He gave her a slanted glance as if to read her mind, then settled back slightly. "Would you like me to read to you?"

Her gaze darted back to him. Was he serious? Did he intend to sit there half-dressed and watch her while her scanty undergarments adhered to her bare skin like the peel of a grape? God help her! "I 'ardly . . . hardly, think that would be proper for a lady of quality," she said.

"But what of a tough little barmaid?"

That was what her mother had called her. Tough. Her tough 'un. Did he know? Was he mocking her? she wondered, but his expression was kind, his eyes soft. "Not for her neither," she said.

He smiled without the expression ever lifting his lips. "If you pass out again, I want to be here."

"I'm not planning to pass out anytime soon."

"So you planned it the first time?"

She shrugged. The movement felt oddly stiff. "I thought highborn ladies was supposed to swoon on a regular basis. It showed their fine breeding."

Leaning forward, he brushed a tendril of hair from her cheek. "There's a difference between swooning and getting kicked in the head by a horse."

"Oh." She swallowed and refused to allow herself to look at him, but he was just as clear in her mind's eye. Handsome and lean and hopelessly elegant. "I'll try to remember."

"You do that. Though sometimes it's difficult when one is intoxicated," he said.

"I'm not—" she began, then stopped abruptly to stare at him. "Am I?"

He didn't answer, but rose languidly to his feet. "I'll fetch a book."

The volume he chose should have been quite boring, for it was the lineage of the royal house of Sedonia. There were a hundred odd names and just as many odd facts, mostly about a princess named Tatiana. The princess was young. Small, like her uncle, the deceased king. She was cool and elegant with a love for horses and an odd, adverse reaction to edible nuts. Nicol's voice flowed on as soothing as the water, even when he spoke of treachery and deceit.

"So the old man was murdered," she said softly.

He glanced up, his gaze sharp. "The king? What makes you say so?"

She scowled. "That Lord Paqual fellow. He was the one what put the girl on the throne after the king's death."

"That is hardly proof of treason."

"No. But 'twas he what said the princess would have to take a husband before she was crowned queen, and 'twas he what hopes to choose that husband." She shrugged, feeling relaxed now, despite her state of undress, despite everything. "Seems to me old Paqual hopes to rule Sedonia through Princess . . ." She paused. There was no reason for him to know she remembered the girl's name. No reason for him to realize she had known about the old man's death for some months.

"Tatiana," he said.

"Yeah. Tatiana Octavia . . ."

"Linnet Rocheneau," he supplied.

"Yeah. Her."

"She was the only one left of the royal family after her uncle's death."

"Was she?"

"Yes." He looked at her strangely and she shrugged, dropping her gaze to the water.

"I suppose she was easier to manipulate than the old man."

"Lord Paqual was his majesty's most trusted advisor."

"Trust," she said, and let her head fall back against the smooth brass of the tub to watch him. His shirt was still open, she noticed, but she felt strangely languid. Warm and fluid and relaxed. "That'll get you every time."

"Is there no one you trust, Megan?" he asked, but before she could answer, a knock sounded at the door.

Setting the book aside, Nicol rose to his feet and disappeared into the next room. There was a murmur of voices and he reappeared, bearing an overloaded tray. Tantalizing scents drifted in Megan's direction. She licked her lips and scooted up an inch.

His gaze dipped to her chest, and her heart seemed to stop beneath the sodden fabric, but she forced herself to think, to be smart.

"Turn your back so I can get out," she ordered, but he shook his head.

"Relax," he said. "I'll feed you there."

She was about to refuse, but Deirdre had brought more stewed pears, and he had already dipped a spoon into them. Steam curled up, spilling the scent of hot cloves and rich port into the room.

She licked her lips and felt herself weaken. "I thought ladies of quality was supposed to eat dessert last."

"That's true except in the case of near-fatal experiences." Sitting with the tray in his lap, he offered her the treat.

Somewhere in her foggy brain, she was certain she should refuse. After all, what she'd said about trust was true. But he was just sitting there waiting with the spoon in his working-man's hand, and there seemed no harm in accepting a few bites. Her mouth closed over the spoon, drawing off the sweetened fruit. He watched her lips move, watched her tongue peek out, and though she supposed she should feel self-conscious, she did not. Instead, she felt strangely flushed.

Exhaling softly, Nicol leaned back, then scowled as he opened a bottle of wine. Pouring a healthy draught into a glass, he touched it to her lips.

She drank. A droplet slipped over the rise of her lower lip, but she caught it on her tongue.

The viscount's nostrils flared slightly as he watched her, and there was something about that expression that made her stomach feel strangely tight.

"I can feed myself."

"Relax," he said, and offered her more wine.

But she dared not relax any more, not when his chest was

bare and so sinfully close. Close enough to lean over and kiss. She cleared her throat and hauled her mind roughly back under control. "It ain't like I'm chopping wood."

"Ladies of quality generally don't," he said, and spooned up more pears and fed them to her. The remainder of the dessert followed, then collared eel, potato pudding, and crusty rye bread. Finally, Nicol settled back in his chair. "Have you had enough?"

Her attention strayed to his chest, but she shifted her gaze sternly away. "Yes. Thank you."

"Is the water getting cold?"

"A bit."

Setting the tray aside, Nicol rose to his feet, retrieved a pair of towels, and disappeared into the bedchamber.

"Come along," he said, reappearing in the doorway. "We'd best get you out of there."

That narrow band of bare chest winked at her again. It had been bad enough being lifted half-naked into the tub, but with his shirt open, exposing his dark skin, sprinkled as it was with a line of black hair . . . Her heart did something funny in her chest. "The water did the trick," she said, hoping she didn't sound breathless. Hoping, in fact, that she sounded perfectly normal. "I feel limber as a kitten. You can go. I'll get out and dry meself off."

"I'll help you," he said, and bent forward. The shirt gaped away from the hard hillocks of his chest. Something like panic twisted in her stomach.

"You're going to get your shirt wet again."

Seeming to see the logic in that, he drew back, then pulled off the garment and tossed it aside.

As sleek as stallions, muscles danced across his torso and down his belly. She pulled her gaze away with an effort, but there seemed nothing she could do to resist as he pulled her back into his arms. Water rushed from her as he raised her from the tub, and there he held her for a moment, letting the stream turn to a rivulet and the rivulet to droplets.

"Ready?"

She nodded, and he carried her through the doorway, past the little table where the chess pieces stood at attention, and on to the stool he'd set on towels before the fire. Leaving her there, he returned to the bathing chamber, then reappeared with more towels.

"How do you feel?"

Flushed and fidgety and strangely . . . heavy. "Good," she said.

"Does your head hurt?" he asked, and stroked a droplet of water from her brow.

"No."

Running the towel over her shoulders, he watched her eyes. Beneath the towel, her strap was dragged downward. She pulled it back up as he dried her arms. "Do you feel light-headed? Dizzy?"

Yes. "No. I'm fine."

"Any tingling in your extremities? Your fingers, toes—"

"No," she said, and refused to mention the butterflies in her belly, the unaccustomed softness between her legs.

"Dry your torso," he said, and handed her the towel. She stared at him.

He smiled the slightest amount. "Your breasts," he explained.

She refused to blush, but industriously dabbed at her chest as he knelt by her feet. Retrieving another towel, he dropped it over her thighs before gently blotting them dry.

"Are you all right?"

She nodded, feeling numb.

He moved lower, past the edge of her drawers and onto her left knee. Once there, he wrapped both hands around the towel and massaged his way downward. The muscles in her calf seemed to sigh like love-smitten puppies beneath his touch.

"Does that hurt?" he asked.

"Not hardly," she said, then realized her mistake and straightened slightly. "No," she corrected. "You needn't worry about me overmuch." He was watching her with embarrassing scrutiny, as if he thought she might faint . . . or spontaneously combust. "I am certain I can finish the task myself."

"You're going to have to get over being embarrassed when people attend you," he said.

"I'm not embarrassed."

"You're blushing."

It was true. She could feel the heat in her cheeks. "'Tis naught but the warmth of the fire."

"Very good, lass," he said, and chuckled. She immediately bristled, but his hands drifted down her leg, easing any frayed nerves as they went. "A lady need never admit the truth."

"Then—" she began, but at that moment he raised her foot onto his knee and massaged her toes with the towel. Indescribable pleasure surged up from her bare digits. Her jaw dropped a mite.

"Feel good?" he asked.

For one foolish moment she almost admitted the truth. Almost told him that in the entirety of her life she had never felt so blissfully pampered. But she had not survived this long by being a fool. "I fear I'm dripping on the floor."

"Others will clean it up. You needn't worry about such things any longer," he said, and moved the towel to her right leg. His progress there was even slower, even more thorough, even more magical as he massaged and eased his way down to her toes. Once again he propped her foot onto the hard muscles of his leg, and once again she felt the heat of his flesh permeate her sole and radiate upward. Every toe was dried individually, as if each digit were precious, as if she indeed were someone to be pampered and nurtured. As if he adored her.

"Time to get out of those clothes," he said.

His sable hair shone in the flickering firelight, and his teeth gleamed against the dark hue of his skin.

"Megan?"

She snapped out of her reverie, trying not to jump. "What?"

"You'd best don your nightgown now, before you catch a chill."

A chill. She felt dangerously warm, as if the fire were inside her very body, but she nodded. Rising to his knees, he put his hands to the laces of her drawers.

Her mind jerked into action just as her fingers caught his wrist. "Nay!" The word was a bit sharper than she'd intended, so she cleared her throat and did her best to calm her jumping nerves. "I'll do that."

His expression was somber, but he drew his hands away, holding her fingers in his own. "I'll not take advantage of you, lass, if that is your fear."

She watched his lips move and wondered with horrific longing what it would feel like to press her mouth to his.

"Lass?"

She swallowed hard and pressed a towel to her chest. "Ladies should surely not allow themselves to be . . ." It was strangely difficult to breathe. "Handled."

"On the contrary," he said, and gently massaged her palm with his thumb. The simple movement felt idiotically wonderful. "Ladies are as pampered and curried as prize steeds." Retrieving a teardrop-shaped bottle from a small table nearby, he poured a few drops of oil onto her palm and smoothed it up her fingers. Pleasure oozed onto her wrist as he massaged circles over her skin. She felt as limp and foolish as a doll of rags, but in a moment he released her hand. She tried to straighten, to regain her senses, but he had already captured her other wrist.

The oil felt cool against her palm, his hands large and strong against her fingers. She shivered.

"Here now," he said, and rose with fluid grace to his feet. "We must get you out of those drawers before you catch your death." His hands were on her laces again, but there was nothing she could do to stop him. Even when he tugged the cotton down over her breasts, she did naught but raise her gaze to his. Their eyes met and for one prolonged moment, all was almost lost, but he rose abruptly to his feet.

"Can you stand?"

She did so without conscious thought, and he peeled the damp fabric downward.

They stood so close it seemed she could feel heat radiating from his bare chest, could feel the very thoughts in his head. His hands stilled on her hips, his eyes seemed to dilate. Tension was wound like a clock in her belly, and there was nothing she could do. Nothing, but close her eyes as he leaned toward her.

But in a moment he drew away. Warmth went with him. Pleasure vanished like hot steam. His footsteps rapped against the hardwood floor. She opened her eyes, blinking like an owlet as she turned to watch him. But in a moment, he turned back to her, nightgown in hand. Scrunching the garment in his fists, he tugged it unceremoniously over her head. She remained unmoving, staring at him.

"Lift your arms."

She only blinked.

"Megan," he said, but there was a strange note in his voice. "For God's sake lift your arms."

She raised her arms like one in a trance, and he drew the garment down over her body.

For a moment he remained where he was, then he stepped abruptly backward. "Get into bed," he said, and turned toward the bathing chamber. "I'll return in a moment."

He closed the door behind him. The lock dropped into place, and with that noise, her mind clicked into gear.

She had fallen into his trap, had fallen under his spell. Aye, she wanted him, longed for his touch, and he knew it. Indeed, he had most certainly planned it. After all, she was naught but a poor barmaid, unaccustomed to the attentions of the highborn. Surely she would be swept off her feet by his charms. Surely she would do his bidding.

But he was wrong. Regardless of the promised coins, she could not remain here. The cost was too dear, for when one lost her heart one lost everything.

Pulling a hank of horsehair from the pocket of her gown, she gazed at the flaxen locks. It wasn't too late. Indeed, it was just the right time.

Chapter 10

~~~~~GQ~~~~~

Nicol stepped back into the bedchamber. The fire had died down to naught but embers, casting the room into near darkness. But it was no darker than his mood. He'd wanted to saddle Croft and ride, to feel the bite of the wind against his skin and drive away his own idiotic desires, but that was out of the question, for he had work to do. So he had remained in the hallway, pacing silently, willing the urgency to ebb from his system as he waited for her to fall asleep, waited for the return of his own self-control. He thought he had recaptured that control, but already he felt tense and awkward, as fidgety as an untried lad as he glanced at the bed.

Lying on her side, facing the opposite wall, she barely made a bulge beneath the covers. But the fact that he could not see her made little difference, for he could remember each delicate curve, had memorized every inch of satiny skin. Now, however, there was nothing to see but a lock of golden hair that curled across the pillow. Perhaps he should tuck it in with its gleaming mates. Perhaps he should make certain she was well. Perhaps he should kiss her . . . He fisted his hands and strode to the opposite side of the room.

It took him only a moment to make certain the bathing chamber remained locked, only a second more to move his chair into its nocturnal position in front of the door.

Settling himself into it, he closed his eyes and refused to see the girl in his mind. Refused to see her ready smile. Refused to recognize her charming awe as she read aloud. Refused to feel her skin, soft as moonlight beneath his hands.

Damnation, he thought, and closed his eyes. Since he'd met her he'd spent every night in purgatory, but tonight he'd reside in hell.

When dawn came after an eternity or so, Nicol rose to his feet. He felt stiff and old and out of sorts, but things were clearer this morning. Time was fleeting. Regardless of the girl's injuries, they would have to accelerate her lessons. She had a quick mind and a clever tongue, but proper speech was hardly ingrained. After only a few mild drinks she had been talking like a fishwife. Anna could drink her weight in hard whisky and not slur a single syllable. And she would never become tongue-tied as Megan had. Never would she allow a man to touch her as he had, to feel the warmth of her skin beneath his fingers. Never would she gaze at him with those lush field-green eyes or let him think there was nothing she wanted more than to kiss him.

Well-worn memories of the night before stormed through his mind. Her parted lips, her velvet skin, her—

Dammit! He stormed around the bed to awaken her.

But he knew the moment he touched the coverlet. She was gone. He threw back the blankets, but found nothing more than flaxen locks of horse tails stretched across her pillow. Throwing them aside, he wildly searched the room. But nothing was out of place. Nothing . . . except the rough-hewn chess pieces. He skimmed the board. And sure enough—she'd taken his queen—and won the match.

Megan slipped off the horse's back in the predawn darkness. The gray gelding stood placidly as she dragged her bag of goodies down with her. She would have liked to take one of the viscount's mounts, but after the episode with the hastily cropped tail and the bruised leg, she'd decided to concentrate on a quieter animal. Still, horseback riding had turned out to be quite elemental. Her style might not have been masterful, but once she'd clambered aboard, she had found a means of steering the animal down the snow-covered road and into the nearest village.

She'd forgotten her gloves inside the house and had been far too nervous to go back for them, but what she lacked in handwear she more than made up for in other garments. In fact, she wore so many layers that she had been certain she would never be able to mount the stolid gray. But once that she'd reached her destination, the next order of business was clear. She'd sell the extra garments, make certain the gelding was returned to the kindly inhabitants of Woodlea, and return posthaste to Somershire. Not that she could remain there. No. That city was no longer safe for her, but she must remove her hidden cache before she made herself a new persona and put the viscount of Newburn behind her forever.

The winds had been favorable and the captain kind. Megan told him there was distressing news from her sister in Portshaven and with her elegant, newfound speech and costly cape, he had believed her to be a fair lady in distress. The journey to Teleere had cost her little either in time or in money. She had even managed to tuck a bit of brown bread into her reticule, but as she left the docks, the sun was already setting. She could afford to rent a carriage to take her to the

Lion's Share, but she would not. She would not even take the longer route around the edge of the city. Instead, she would cut straight through. Though the route was more dangerous, she knew how to step light, where to be cautious and where to be bold. This night called for boldness, for she did not know the viscount's whereabouts.

Perhaps he had already forgotten about her. Perhaps he had moved on. But something told her he was searching for her. A shiver ran up her spine. She increased her pace and glanced over her shoulder, but all was well. The inn where she'd worked was just ahead. Most probably old Fig had hired someone new. Perhaps he had even lent out the tiny cubicle she had called home. But it didn't matter. She would find a way in, and she would retrieve her money. It was entirely possible Fig had already sold her clothes, but they were of little value. Only the coins mattered.

The inn was dark when she arrived there, but that was just as well. She could easily find the tiny window of her undersized room, could just as easily slip inside. It was one of the reasons she had insisted on having it for her own. She could fit and few others could.

Pressing her back up against the rough plaster of the inn, she waited, listening to the darkness. Somewhere far off a dog barked, ending in a plaintive howl, but when the noise died down no other sound could be heard. Dropping to her knees, she slunk forward and peered through the window. The moon was bright and shone helpfully through the narrow pane. By the silvery light she could see that the bed was unmade. The blankets were thrown back, revealing the stark white of her bedsheets.

She breathed a sigh of relief and set to work. It only took her a few minutes to pry the window open, less time still to slip, silent as a wraith, into the room. Her feet made barely a whisper when they touched the floor. Even in the darkness it was simple enough for her to slip under the bed to the loose floorboard. Easing it up, she groped breathlessly inside the hole. Her fingers touched cold earth, rough wood, empty air.

She patted more rapidly, her heart rate bumping up. No. It couldn't be gone. It couldn't!

Scrambling backward, she rose to her feet and prepared to push the bed aside, but in that moment a shadow rose from the darkness.

"Magical Megs," said the viscount.

She croaked something, her throat too constricted to manage more, and in the darkness she saw him grin.

"I've missed you," he said.

"What the 'ell are ye doing 'ere?" she rasped, and his smile brightened.

"I've come to retrieve my queen."

Although they traveled on a different ship, the journey seemed much the same as the first one they'd shared. Megan faced the viscount across the narrow cabin. He had barely spoken a word up to this point, and she hadn't missed the dialogue. Judging by the dark silence, she guessed his mood to be less than jovial.

"We made a bargain, Megan," he said.

She said nothing. She didn't like the way he was looking at her. His manner was still refined, his clothing still elegant, but there was something dangerous in his expression.

She shrugged, remembering he'd told her not to do so. Remembering exactly how he'd told her to speak. It gave her a glowing satisfaction to do the opposite. "Could be I didn't like the terms none."

"The terms!" He tightened a fist, then loosened it and took a deep breath. "You didn't like being treated like a princess? Didn't like—"

"I didn't like being . . ." She searched rather frantically for the right words. His hands had felt like magic against her skin. Like bewitching, bewildering magic and she knew far better than to trust to such sleight of hand. "Abused!" she said, but he scoffed.

"I am the one who has been abused."

"You—"

"Lied to. Stolen from, wounded," he said, snarling the words into her face.

She licked her lips. He watched the movement, then leaned back, seeming to fight his own emotions.

"The chimney."

"What?"

"You went up the chimney, didn't you?"

She said nothing.

Reaching out, he grabbed her wrist. She tried to yank it away, but he held tight, then turned it over to glare at the palm. "You burned your hands."

"Just a bit."

He stared at her for several seconds, then dropped her hand and turned away with a curse. She watched his back, her own emotions tumbling like storm clouds.

"And the hair on your pillow—it was from Croft's tail. You *stole* Croft's tail."

Again, she kept silent, and in the stillness she heard him draw another slow breath.

"Did I hurt you, Megan?" he asked, not quite looking over his shoulder.

A shock of dark hair fell across his brow, making him look strangely vulnerable. For just a moment she was almost tempted to smooth it aside, to apologize, to take him in her arms, but she was not so foolish as she been some nights ago. Nor so drunk.

"Did I?" he asked.

She shook her head.

"Did I starve you?"

"Nay."

"Nay," he repeated and turned toward her. "I kept you carefully and fed you well. I trained you . . ." He paused for a moment as if unable to go on. "I taught you to read and—"

"Why?" Her own voice was low, her emotions wild, making her forget her rough accent. "Why did you do those things? So that I could become like your precious Anna? So that you could look at me and pretend I was she. So I could be a poor substitute?"

He had opened his mouth to speak, but now he closed it. Rarely had she seen surprise on his face, but there was surprise there now.

"Is that what you believe?"

She stared at him, speechless for a moment before throwing up her hands. "How the hell would I know what to believe? You tell me nothing. You abduct me. You threaten me. You—"

"I need you to impersonate the princess of Sedonia."

The world went absolutely silent. She blinked, tried to formulate a question, and blinked again. "What?"

"Princess Tatiana Octavia Linnet Rocheneau."

She waited for more as her mind stormed along at breakneck speed. "The princess," she breathed. The irony of the situation was not lost on her. The princess of Sedonia needed a nameless thief's help. The old king's rightful heiress needed . . . Megan almost laughed. "She's your Anna?"

He nodded once. "Yes. She needs to leave the country, but she cannot abandon her throne."

Megan drew a deep breath, thoughts racing wildly. "Because of Paqual."

He cocked one brow at her, as if in concession to her quick realization, but didn't respond.

"Where's she going?" she asked.

"That is none of your concern."

She scowled, her mind racing. "You expect me to leave my homeland, to endure your tutelage, to risk my very life, and you think 'tis none of me own concern!"

The world went quiet again, then, "She will be sailing for Teleere."

"Here? Why?"

"She wishes to speak to the laird of the isle."

"Laird MacTavish?" she asked, but he shook his head.

"I've told you too much al—"

"For a husband," she said, understanding dawning with clarity. "She wants him to be her husband."

"What makes you think so?" he asked.

She grinned. "Because he's the man I'd marry."

His eyebrow jerked abruptly. "Really?"

"He's not some pampered lord afraid to get his hands dirty." He gave her a look that seemed to assume she was referring to him. "They say he was a pirate before he became laird." She hadn't known that when she'd stolen his brooch. She had thought, in fact, that he was simply another spoiled nobleman. The truth had caused her some consternation. Enough, in fact, that she had kept the brooch hidden away until she decided what to do about it. She didn't normally steal from commoners. "They say he's a bastard." Perhaps it was that bond between Teleere's laird and herself that had kept her from fencing the brooch. But perhaps there were other reasons. She had seen the man's face, after all.

"You think the fact that he's a bastard makes it likely that the princess would wish to wed him?"

There was a strange intensity to his expression. An intensity she could not understand. So she shrugged.

"That," she said, "and the fact that he's the handsomest man in all Christendom."

He was silent for a moment as he settled his shoulder against the cabin wall. "So you've seen them all?"

She cocked a brow at his odd tone. "I've seen enough to know the good from the bad."

"I hate to disappoint you," he said, "but Princess Tatiana puts little stock in physical appearances.

"Then maybe she's interested in him because she thinks he's the one who can stand up to Paqual and his friends. Though there are some who aren't thrilled that he rules Teleere," she said.

"Such as?"

"I'm told the old laird had a nephew that resents him."

Nicol drew a careful breath through his nostrils, and in that moment Megan was certain this was not news to the viscount. "I wouldn't have thought you the type to follow politics, lass."

Maybe she had said too much, had given too much away, but she shrugged, hoping to look nonchalant. "Just because I don't have a grand title doesn't mean I'm ignorant."

" 'Tis good to know," he said, and that cool expression was back. She scowled a little, wondering what was brewing in his head.

"I'm right, aren't I?" she asked. "She hopes to marry Mac-Tavish and form a bond between her country and his."

His eyes were half-closed. "If I say yes, will you help her?"

She stared at him as thoughts rampaged through her mind. Memories of years on the street, of scraping for a living, of her mother's broken heart and tired face. And all the while Tatiana Octavia Linnet Rocheneau had lived like a princess. "Sure," she said, and shrugged with careful casualness. "Why not?"

"Good." He nodded once. "I just have one question then."

She waited, breath held.

"Why would you steal my stocking?"

Chapter 11

The carriage bumped over the rutted snow of the half-cobbled byway. Megan had no idea how Ralph had known where to find them, but the viscount's highly polished vehicle had appeared at the Sedonian port, its driver as silent and sober as a henchman behind the chestnut team.

"Why now?" Lord Argyle asked. Once again, there was not a hair out of place, not a whisker to be seen on his sharp-cut chin, as if he had spent the night at the opera house instead of dragging her across a choppy stretch of ocean.

"What's that?" she asked, though she had heard him perfectly well.

"I thought we had come to some sort of agreement," he said. "I thought you were beginning to trust me." He watched her in the darkness, seeming to examine her with detached interest. "Was it because I failed to protect you?"

She raised her brows at him, and he must have noticed her expression of surprise because he continued on.

"The horses," he explained. His arms were crossed against

his chest. And though the carriage jostled and bumped, he looked perfectly unaware of the turbulence, as if he rode above it. "Your injury."

She couldn't help but laugh. "My lord," she said and took delight in the flash of anger that shone in his eyes at the formal way she addressed him, "I've had broken fingernails that were more alarming."

"Then why?"

Against her will she remembered the feel of his fingers on her skin, remembered the deep, intoxicating timbre of his voice as he read to her. There were many dangers to a woman alone, but there was none so deadly as the weakness of a woman in the dark throes of infatuation.

"Was it all a ploy?" he asked.

Try as she might she could not seem to forget how the candlelight had shone on his hair or how his hands had looked as they held the book—strong, yet strangely elegant, sprinkled with dark hairs that swept up the taut muscles of his forearms. She could not forget his gentleness or the warmth of his chest against hers as he'd lifted her from the tub. Could not forget closing her eyes and longing to feel his lips against hers.

Damn him. Damn him and every pampered lord who had ever whiled his way into a maid's tender heart.

"Was it all a trick?" he asked, canting his head slightly. "To make me let down my guard?"

Who would have thought she could be tempted by a nobleman? And not just a nobleman, but a Sedonian. She would have sworn she had learned from her mother's mistakes. Would have sworn she would not mimic them in her own life. And yet here she was, enthralled with a Sedonian lord who had nothing but his own interests in mind, except perhaps the interests of another woman. She almost laughed at the dark irony of the situation. But not quite.

"Yes," she said instead and turned to watch the snow-covered countryside roll into the approaching darkness. "'Twas naught but a trick."

"Who is your eldest lady in waiting?" Nicol asked.

"Lady Evelyn." The girl's tone was firm yet feminine, her back perfectly straight as she stared out the window to the farmstead below. What was she thinking? Was she planning another escape, or had she decided she could tolerate even his presence if enough coin was involved? "An aging baron's only daughter," she continued. "With dark hair and blue eyes. A rare combination."

"And her cousin?"

"Lady Mary," she intoned, her gaze not leaving the scene below. "Who is quite fair by Sedonian standards."

"What is your country's foremost export?"

"We are rich in rubies and other precious gems, and our craftsmen are the best in all of Europe."

"And your chief chancellor?" Nicol asked.

"Lord Paqual." Her face showed no expression, except perhaps a hint of regal disdain, no joy or animation. God's bones, it was frightening what one could learn in a fortnight. Her feet were laced into a pair of nearly flat slippers and aligned just so. Her hands were clasped primly behind her small, round buttocks. Nicol paced again, but she didn't turn to watch his movement. "He is an old man now and was my uncle's most trusted advisor."

"Your personal guards?"

"Roger is tall and dark. Keeves has a scar through his left brow. Combs is a redhead. Allard is always solemn . . . and secretly in love with Lady Mary."

He glanced at her, and she shrugged. "I am guessing as much from what you told me."

Could she be that intuitive? he wondered. And if so, what did she know about *him*? But he pushed the thought away, moving on. "And your father," he said. "What was his name?"

"Edward Rocheneau, Duke of Northrum. Dead these past several years."

"Your uncle?"

She paused as if lost in deep thought, but in a moment she spoke. "My uncle was the old king, who died some months ago and is missed by all."

There was something in her tone or lack thereof that niggled at his curiosity, but he focused on the lessons at hand. She was just a tool. Nothing more. And a tool who would leave him at the first opportunity, he reminded himself. Hardly did he care about her or her nefarious thoughts. But in the back of his mind, he couldn't forget the rushing panic he had felt when he'd found her gone. Damn her and her devious ways.

"Tell me of your mother," he said, making certain his tone was as cool as hers.

"Lady Margarite." She pursed her full lips and turned her head to study him over her shoulder, and in that moment she resembled the princess so perfectly that it all but took his breath away. Surely that should make him happy. He stared at her in silence as his gut clenched, and she raised one brow as if wondering at his reticence. Not a wrinkle creased her perfect forehead. "She was the duchess of Fellway," she said. He still made no comment. "I believe it was she who said that trying is what one does when one is too weak to succeed," she added, and almost smiled. "She was a cold auld bitch by all accounts."

The sharp contrast of her native accent to her acquired speech yanked Nicol from his reverie. He should reprimand her, he supposed, but a spark shone in her bewitching eyes. A glimmer of the maid who had fascinated him in Portshaven months before. A flash of the wit and charm he had admired. Not that he was either charmed or admiring now that he knew her conniving ways, but he had been right. She was amazingly intelligent. Indeed, she had made fantastic progress. Her tone was flawless, her memory astounding. He gave her a curt nod.

"Is your Anna just as cold?" she asked.

Her question jarred him, but he kept his expression stoic and paced to the nearest trunk to pull out a pair of books. "You've got much to learn yet," he said.

"And this is surely something I should know," she reasoned. Her accent was still perfect, but her tone was animated. "How will I impersonate her if I do not know her demeanor?"

He straightened and glanced at her. Her hair was several shades too light though they'd cut it to match Anna's length. He almost winced at the memory of seeing it fall, of wanting to catch it before it hit the floor, but he brought his mind sharply back to the matter at hand. She was, perhaps, just an inch taller than the princess, but the thing that made her unique was the force of her vitality. When she entered the room all else seemed dimmed by comparison. How would he mask that? Perhaps she was right. Perhaps she should know Anna's temperament in order to mimic her.

He drew a deep breath and watched her for a moment as he carefully chose his words. "The Princess Tatiana does not like to be touched."

Her brows raised in earnest, and for a moment he thought she would break out of character, but when she spoke, her tone was impeccable once again. "Ever?"

How could he explain the princess's cool demeanor to this girl who exuded life itself? Perhaps there had been a time when he had thought the Princess Tatiana was feminine perfection. Perhaps there was even a time when he believed she was all that was good, but now . . . "Her mother was a great beauty," he said. She waited patiently for him to continue. He considered how best to phrase it. "The duchess did not like others to draw attention from herself."

Megan narrowed her eyes the slightest degree. The expression made her look like a sly fairy, pondering things best left alone. "Including her daughter?" she asked.

"The duchess of Fellway rarely touched Anna. Rarely spoke to her in fact, but to reprimand her, and I believe she encouraged others to do the same."

"So the lass grew up untouched? Unloved?"

He said nothing. What the devil did he know of love? But perhaps to a woman like Megan one could not love without touching, he thought, and remembered with startling clarity that she had never so much as brushed her hand against his.

She paced the length of one wall, trailing her fingers along an oval picture frame for a moment. "The princess's title did her little good then. Even his bastards—" She stopped abruptly, stilling both her feet and her words. He watched her, wondering.

"Whose bastards?"

Suddenly she looked stiff and strangely fragile, but in a moment she shrugged. It was one of the few idiosyncrasies he could not break her of. "The old king's," she said. "Certainly he had bastards."

He watched her carefully. "Why would you think so?"

She gave him a prim smile, but it did not reach her eyes, and it was leagues from her soul. "He was a nobleman, was he not?"

Thoughts stormed rashly around in his head. "Who are you, lass?"

She laughed now as though she found him vastly entertaining. "Are you imagining that I am some lost princess in my own right?" she asked and laughed again. "You must be a great tutor indeed if you can make yourself believe your own lies."

He forced himself to relax. Perhaps he was going mad. "So you are naught but a thief."

Her eyes looked almost lazy now. "Nay. I am naught but a beleaguered maid who you *believe* is a thief. But it seems I am lucky after all, for my mother was neither cold nor selfish."

"You said you had no mother."

She shifted her eyes to him and away, then turned and paced back toward the window. "I did not say I had no mother, only that I could not remember her well."

"You said you could not remember her at all," Nicol corrected, trying to keep up, trying to decipher a mystery he seemed on the very cusp of understanding.

She glanced over her shoulder at him, and he was immediately distracted, for it was that pose that made her look most like the princess. With the light shining on her profile, as if she were the very center of the universe. "I did not think it necessary to share my memories with you at the time," she said, "since it seemed extremely unlikely that I would ever see you again."

"And now?" Watching her was fascinating, like watching a fine sculpture come to life.

"I have said I would play the part of the princess until she returns to her throne."

"So there is no reason to avoid telling me of your mother."

"It hardly seems necessary for my tutelage."

He almost smiled at her choice of words. "We've worked hard this morning." Indeed, they had worked hard all week. Had done naught but work. Had returned to Will's country home with nearly no explanations for her escape and begun their lessons where they had left off, beginning her studies long before the first cock crowed and ending after the tapers had burned down to nubs. "Perhaps you deserve a reprieve."

"Is that a compliment, my lord?"

"Call me Nicol," he ordered, though he had done so a

score of times without making any impression on the girl. "Anna does."

"Is the princess so informal with all her advisors?"

"I think you're avoiding the issue, lass," he said, and settled a hip onto the desk the farm boy had brought up from the library. "You were about to tell me of your mother."

"Was I?"

"Eager to, in fact."

An imp of a smile played on her lips, but she glanced out the window again. For a moment he was sure she would refuse, would keep her memories to herself, but finally she spoke. "I truly believe she was an angel."

The words seemed strange, unsuited for either Tatiana's cool persona or Megan's tough character. It intrigued him far more than he dared admit. "When did she die?"

"Many years ago."

"How old were you?"

She shrugged, but even in profile he could see the shadow of a tiny smile. So the pain did not outweigh the joy her mother had given her, he realized, and wondered how that could be.

"My age mattered naught," she said finally. "If she had lived to be a hundred, her death would have come too soon." Turning from the window, she found his eyes. "And what of you, my lord? Were you blessed with a title *and* adoring parents?"

Her question jolted him back to reality, but he rose to his feet with careful grace. " 'Tis time to practice your French," he parried.

"Answer my question . . . *s'il vous plait*," she said, and though he intended to refuse, her whimsical expression changed his mind.

"I remember very little of my mother," he said, and set the books' spines upon the table, still holding them.

She canted her head slightly, silently calling him a liar, and he wished he were.

"God's truth," he said. "I can barely remember her face. She fell down a flight of stairs a few years after my birth." He tightened his grip on the books.

"I am sorry," she said, but her tone suggested something besides sympathy. An inkling that he was not telling the entire truth perhaps, but then he shouldn't be surprised. She might be a liar and a thief, but she was no fool.

"Yes," he agreed, and good God, what an actor he was. There was not a hint of emotion in his voice. Nobles truly were amazing. "It was a terrible loss. Everyone said so. I believe even my father regretted it. Afterward . . ." He knew immediately that he had said too much, but she remained silent for some time, letting him hope she was not as astute as she surely was.

"Afterward." Her tone was soft. "Did he . . ." She drew a careful breath. "How did she fall?"

He turned his gaze toward the books. "Your subjects will expect you to speak several different languages. You will not be able to speak them fluently, of course. But you'd best be able to manage a few words," he said, but when he looked her way, he saw that she had not heard him.

"Nicol." His Christian name sounded disturbingly right on her lips. "I am so very sorry."

He nodded dismissively as he stepped toward her.

"Your father. I didn't realize he was . . . dangerous."

His stride hitched, but he forced himself to continue on, pacing across the room as if nothing were amiss. More than anything, he wanted to pretend she had not guessed the truth, had not come to the very conclusion he had reached so many years before. In fact, he considered denying it even now, but there seemed little reason. She was naught but a tool. An intuitive, intelligent, bewitching tool. "I warned you of my heritage," he said.

"And you lived with him throughout your childhood? Even though—" She let the thought hang.

"Until I joined the army."

"But . . ." She scowled a little, atypical of Anna, but so right for a woman like herself. He tried not to stare, to fawn, to drown in her smallest expression. "You were titled."

He shook his head, as though dismissing her words. "The younger son of a minor lord."

"Then how did you become a viscount?"

"My uncle," he explained, "was not a healthy man. But he was wealthy, and he was titled."

"And he had no heirs?"

"None. Not even bastards," he said, trying for levity.

She ignored the gibe. "Then wouldn't your father inherit his property?"

"My father," he agreed, "then my elder brother."

"They both died before you?"

He wondered momentarily if she suspected him of having a hand in their deaths. He wondered, in fact, if she would have been right. After all, he knew of their animosity toward each other. They had been very much alike, his father and his brother—strong, arrogant, bloodthirsty.

"They were both found dead," he said. "In my father's house." He said the words succinctly and with no inflection, watching her expression the whole time.

"Murdered?"

He wanted to say yes. Inexplicably murdered. "My father had been stabbed repeatedly. My brother died with a bullet in his chest." She said nothing. He drew a deep breath and continued, though he told himself to stop. "My uncle had died some weeks before. Ernest believed he should be viscount. Father thought he himself would make a fine lord."

"They killed each other?" Her words were little more than a whisper.

"I believe they may have," he said, but in his heart he was certain. Ernest, in fact, had told Nicol his plans. Had bragged about them in a drunken stupor. But Ernest often bragged, had often been in a drunken stupor, and Nicol had not thought it would really happen. Had not believed. Had he?

Her face was pale, her plump lips somber. "I am sorry."

"You would be amongst the few."

"You weren't?"

"Lass," he said, and shook his head as though disappointed in her behavior. "If you hope to act like royalty, you're going to have to show less interest in others' lives."

She held his gaze, her own eyes intense. "Tell me of your brother."

Her skin looked as smooth as vellum, her eyes as bright as a Sedonian emerald. "He looked very much like my father."

There was a long moment of silence. "Then you must be like your mother," she said.

There was something about the way she said the words that made his throat close up. Him. The cool lord. "No," he countered. "I, too, am like the old man."

Chapter 12

Megan kept her expression unreadable, though butterflies plagued her stomach. Beneath her, the carriage struck a stone, jostling her against the wall. From the opposite seat, Nicol studied her in relaxed silence. She silently damned him for looking so nonchalant.

"Nervous?" he asked.

"Me?" She mercilessly stomped out the butterflies and lifted a gloved hand to her chest. A couple of weeks ago, when she'd first donned this gown, there seemed to have been a bit less cleavage showing, but perhaps that was to be expected considering her current diet of . . . everything. "Whyever would I be nervous?"

A shadow of a grin shifted his lips. "I can think of no reason," he said. "If you can't."

She raised a single brow at him. She'd practiced it in the mirror at Woodlea and knew how it would look. Regal but tolerant. She liked it. It suited the princess's persona but did not match the butterflies that seemed to have been resurrected in her belly. The damned things had even dulled her appetite. But she was not about to admit that. Not to this unflappable viscount. Even talk of his own mother had done nothing to unsettle him.

"How long will it be until we reach the palace?" she asked, trying to match his insouciance.

"Some hours yet."

Hours. In a few mere hours she would be rattling around Malkan Palace, pretending to be the furthest thing from what she was. She suddenly felt truly sick to her stomach.

"Are you quite well, Your Majesty?"

It was the first time he had called her that, and the shock of his words sent the blood pooling to her feet, but she kept her back straight, her expression impassive. "Of course."

He smiled as though he knew what she was thinking. He would forever be better at this game than she. "You should have eaten," he advised.

"As I said . . ." She paced her words, making sure they were cadenced, unhurried, confident. "I am fine."

For a moment a spark of something shone in his eyes, but it was soon gone, replaced by his usual sophistication. "We'll eat soon."

"Do you think that is wise?"

He was watching her again, closely, and she couldn't help but wonder what he saw. She had colored her hair with some pungent concoction Nicol had brought her. Was it, perhaps, a shade too dark? Did she tilt her head at the wrong angle? Were her hands too fidgety? Her stomach tightened up another notch, but she raised her chin and lifted a single brow, feeling slightly better for it. "What if we are seen?"

He was silent for a moment, but if he found some problem in her demeanor, he didn't voice it. "We'll not chance an inn," he said. "Widow Barnes sent a meal for the journey."

She said nothing for a time, but glanced out the window again. Spring was visiting today, offering them a glimpse of hope and warmth. They rolled along in silence but for the steady beat of the horses' hooves until finally the carriage slowed to a halt. They disembarked on the road and made their way through a copse of trees to a hillside, where the snow had lost its hold and given way to short, springy grasses.

Ralph carried a basket and placed it upon a blanket that the viscount spread upon the grass. From the barren branch of a nearby elder tree a brown thrush whistled a tribute to spring. The driver disappeared without a trace, and Nicol extracted the meal from the wicker and distributed it upon metal plates. Filling pewter mugs halfway with wine, he handed over her portion and settled down with his own.

Although the food was cold, Widow Barnes had produced her usual splendor. There was chilled pigeon pie, baked to bubbly perfection, white crusty bread, still fresh from the widow's stone oven, and sharp yellow cheese. Megan's stomach lurched.

Nicol ate, refilled his glass, and glanced at her plate.

"You've barely touched your food, Princess."

Princess. Her stomach pitched even harder. Until today, perhaps until this very moment, it had all seemed like a foolish game. Now it seemed surreal, impossibly and breathlessly dangerous.

"Are you feeling unwell?"

"Nay." The viscount had said the princess tended toward archaic speech, and somehow following that advice made it simpler for her to stay in character. "I am well," she said. "But still sated from breakfast." Far overhead, a falcon swooped over the glen, its wings spread as it screamed at the valley below. The thrush fell immediately silent. A cloud shadowed the bright sunlight, and Megan shuddered.

"Are you cold?"

"Nay. Just . . ." Her breathing felt out of control, her heart overstressed. "Mayhap a bit."

Unbuttoning his tailcoat, Nicol pulled it off and draped it over her shoulders. The warmth of his skin was retained in the fabric, enveloping her. His fingers brushed her collarbones as soft as a breeze. Her breath froze in her throat, but in a moment he drew away.

"It'll not do if the princess of Sedonia faints from hunger," he said.

She was sitting upon the blanket like a waif, with her legs curled under her skirt, but she kept her back perfectly straight and gave him a level stare.

"Or nerves," he added, and retrieving her untouched mug, filled it to the top. She reached out. Although the stains were gone from her nails and her fingers were clean, her palms were still callused, her cuticles still rough. And three weeks ago, she hadn't known she had cuticles. Neither had she owned a pair of yellow kid gloves to hide the evidence of her past labors—gloves so soft they felt like water against her skin.

"You needn't worry on my account, my . . ." His hand froze in midair, and she gave him the smallest of nods. "Nicol," she corrected.

He handed over the wine, and for a moment their fingers brushed, striking up a flutter of emotions that sizzled up her arm.

Memories stormed in. Memories of wine, of a warm bath, of his words soft on her mind, of his hands, tender on her skin. Wine was not her friend. But there was a challenge in his eyes. And she was not the type to turn aside a challenge.

Taking the cup, she lifted it to her lips.

" 'Tis a lovely day," she said, not meeting his eyes.

He didn't respond. She shifted her gaze from the horizon to his face.

"You will do well," he said, his voice quiet in the falling darkness.

She wanted to agree, to raise her chin in regal acceptance and assure him he was right, but in that second she weakened. "What was my aunt's name?"

He sat with one leg bent up and his forearm stretched across his knee. He had removed his cravat. The neck of his shirt was open, showing the dark skin of his throat and chest. He was the very picture of relaxed elegance. She felt like she was going to throw up.

"Don't concern yourself with that just now," he suggested.

But panic was roiling in her stomach. "I can't remember her name."

A ghost of a smile played upon his lips. "Generally, Anna's loyal subjects don't test the princess's knowledge of her heritage."

"But what if they do? What if I don't walk correctly or laugh just so or like the proper foods?" She knew she was being foolish. She reminded herself of Laird MacTavish's stolen brooch. Sometimes she wore it against her skin to remember her ability. But that was when she had been Magical Megs. Who the hell was she now?

"Lass . . ." Reaching out, the viscount brushed his knuckles across her cheek. "You would eat pig hooves if they were served to you."

She dropped her eyes closed and wondered if she truly was going to swoon. "I can't do this. I am no lady."

He slipped his fingers beneath her chin and raised it slightly. "The truth is this," he said, his voice low, his eyes earnest. "You are no barmaid. Indeed, sometimes I believe you are more of a lady than . . ." He paused for a moment, and for that same length of time, she held her breath, waiting.

"Cole!"

They jerked about in unison. Two men strode toward

them. One was thin and handsome though carelessly dressed, the other tall but soft.

"Turn away before they get a good look at you," Nicol hissed, and, rising, strode toward the road.

"Cask," he said, his tone dry as he addressed the paunchy man. "And Will."

"I thought those sorrels were yours," said Cask. "Whose carriage do you drive?" The newcomer was close, within thirty feet of where their blanket was spread on the ground, but Megan refrained from looking at them. She dared not. For she had no idea who she was supposed to be.

Shrugging out of Nicol's coat, she rose to her feet, careful to keep her back to them.

"I am just now returning to Skilan from Woodlea." Nicol said. "Thank you, by the way, for allowing me to stay, Will."

"It was no trouble," said William, his voice a slow drawl, but in that instant the other spoke up again.

She could feel Cask's attention on the back of her head. "Tell me, Cole, was the lady also in need of a restful few weeks in the country?"

"As a matter of fact she was."

"I didn't think you would abandon your friends for a bit of fluff."

Nicol's voice was lower, but still clear enough. "As you well know, Cask, I would abandon you for much less."

"I'm wounded. Truly."

"Perhaps you could be wounded elsewhere."

The other grinned. "But surely you'll want to introduce me. After all, the lady will certainly need a shoulder to cry on when you've tired of her."

This time Nicol's words were too soft to hear.

Cask chuckled, then, "Well, at the least you could admire

my latest purchase. I've bought a new gelding and Will, as usual, hasn't been nearly appreciative enough. Come along. I'll show you."

Megan heard them retreat, heard their boots rattle through last autumn's leaves as they headed back toward the road. Turning slightly, she chanced a glimpse at them from behind a tree. Nicol was in the lead. His friends followed along behind, talking as they went.

The viscount's answers barely disturbed the silence, and Megan headed into the woods, intent on taking advantage of this bit of privacy. But she'd barely turned about when she heard footsteps running up from behind.

A lifetime of self-preservation swelled up inside her. She swung about, ready to scream or strike or flee. But before she could do anything, the man called Cask skidded to a halt in front of her. For one wild moment they stared at each other in absolute speechlessness, then he dropped to one knee like a drunken squire, his head bowed.

"Your Majesty. Forgive the intrusion. I had no idea—I didn't know—"

She tried to think, to rally, but the world had turned topsy-turvy, and in that second, Nicol joined them. "My apologies, Your Highness," he said, nodding a bow. "You remember Cask, the baron of Bentor."

She had no idea what was expected of her, so she kept her back impossibly stiff and linked her hands in front of her trembling skirts. "Does he always jump out of the bushes at unsuspecting travelers?"

The viscount's lips smirked. "Only when he is inebriated. So . . . yes . . . Your Majesty, I believe he—"

"I didn't mean to startle you, Your Majesty. I simply thought . . ." The drunken baron's words wound to a halt, and he raised his head.

Perhaps she should flee or cover her face or faint dead away, but she did none of those things, though she realized she was holding her breath.

Behind him, the man called Will remained perfectly silent, his gaze sharp on her face.

"What is it you were thinking, my lord?" she asked.

"I assumed Cole . . . the viscount . . . was simply dallying . . ." His words trailed off. His skin was pale, his eyes bright. "Not that you are the kind to dally, Your Majesty."

She nearly laughed. Indeed, if she hadn't felt like hurling, she might have. "And what of the viscount, my lord? Is he the sort to dally?"

She could almost see his mind spinning, trying to work out the situation—why was she alone in this remote glen with the viscount? Why had she not acknowledged their guests immediately? The moment he came to a conclusion, she could see it in his eyes; Nicol was having an affair with the princess. That was what he believed, but Will's expression remained absolutely guarded.

"Of course not, Your Majesty," Cask lied. "Cole is not the sort to dally."

She raised her gaze to Nicol's. "You've a true friend here, my lord," she said, but the viscount's expression was one of bland amusement. "You may rise, Lord Bentor."

He did so, though a bit shakily. "You are overkind, Your Majesty."

"Perhaps," she said dismissively. His eyes were still wide and steady on her face.

She stared back, keeping her spine perfectly straight while her heart pounded like a galloping stallion in her chest.

"Cask, old friend," Nicol said, "we were just about to return to Skilan."

The baron delayed a second, then bowed nervously. "Of

course. My apologies. 'Tis my greatest honor to see you, Your Majesty."

She nodded graciously, and he turned away, heading back toward the road. As for Megan, she stepped into the cover of the underbrush and stopped, trying to hear above the thunder of her heart.

For a moment the men were absolutely silent, but finally the baron of Bentor spoke, his voice barely above a hissed whisper.

"Goddammit, Cole," he said. "Do you happen to know the penalty for debauching a princess?"

Chapter 13

The carriage rumbled along again. Megan wrapped the cloak closer about her. She looked small and pale against the tufted black upholstery.

"We'll be there in a matter of minutes," Nicol assured her. He was hoping to help her relax, but her face looked strained in the flickering light of the square-paned lantern that swayed languidly beside the door. She didn't turn toward him immediately but continued to stare out the window where the fog lay cool and heavy across the rolling landscape.

She drew a deep breath. They had been all but silent since their meal in the woods, but she turned toward him now, her green eyes solemn in the flickering light. "What if they tell?"

Nicol didn't pretend to misunderstand her meaning. "What if they tell others they have seen me alone with the princess?"

"Yes."

"They won't."

"So they are so trustworthy that they would keep even this silent?"

He shrugged but kept his shoulder pressed against the firm cushion of the door. "Will has secrets of his own."

"And the other fellow?" she asked, though Cole was certain she remembered his name.

"Will shall make certain Cask keeps the news to himself," he assured her, but the worry remained on her regal features. "In truth," he said. "I've been alone with the princess many times. I am, after all, her trusted—"

"In the woods?" she asked, her voice charged with emotion. "With no chaperone, sitting close together in the failing light?"

Perhaps it was a good thing his friends came along when they did, for they *had* been sitting close together. He remembered the feel of her skin beneath his fingertips. Remembered the soft look in her eyes. What a fool he would be to fall for this girl.

"You could view this as a roaring success," he said,

"Could I?" The emotion was suddenly drained from her voice, replaced by perfect inflection, as if she were a bit curious, yet just short of disdain.

"Cask has met Tatiana many times and never for a moment doubted that you were she."

"Perhaps. But he has probably not met her in two places at once."

He nodded in concession. "True, but they are not likely to gallop back and check her private chambers. They believe you were with me and will have no reason to doubt the fact."

He could almost see the thoughts racing through her mind. "And you are often in the woods with young, unescorted women?"

Her tone was stiff, but he could not tell the reason. Had she so completely taken on the role of Tatiana, or was she truly miffed? "Not often in the woods," he said.

Her nostrils flared slightly. "You, my lord, are a—" she began, but at that moment the carriage slowed.

"We're here, lass," he said and rose to his feet. The door swung open as if on its own, but she remained exactly as she was, except, perhaps, for a slight widening of her eyes.

" 'Tis only my home, lass. Not the palace."

"What of the servants?"

"They are not expecting us and will surely be abed, but even if they should see you, they'll think nothing of it. They would not recognize you, lass, even if you were the princess."

"So who will they think I am?"

He shrugged. "A friend."

"Your paramour."

"Better that than a thief, don't you suppose?"

"No," she said, her gaze level. "I do not."

He grinned, liking the stiff condescension in her voice, and stepped outside to reach for her hand. After a moment's hesitation, she took it. "If I were not such a heartless man I might be insulted," he informed her.

She gave him a glance from the corner of her eye and stepped regally into the misty night.

"If you were not such a heartless man, I would yet be safely back at the Lion's Share," she said. They were inches apart. He could smell the scent of lavender on her skin.

"It is lucky then," he said, and pulled up her hood, "that I am so callous." His thumbs brushed her cheeks. In the cool spring darkness, her face was no more than a blush of pale color in the night. Like an ivory statuette, as cool as marble, as untouchable as the mist. And for a moment he missed the woman she had been, the unpredictable scrapper he had discovered at a cloth merchant's stall. But of course that was foolish. Pulling his hands away, he bowed and motioned toward his front door.

Not another word was spoken as he followed her into the house.

"My lord." Mrs. Melrose strode down the hall toward him. Her hollow cheeks were as pale as birch bark and her hair perfectly aligned beneath the starched mobcap. "I didn't realize you were coming home tonight, sir. Had you sent word, I would have seen that supper was hot and your bedsheets freshened."

"We ate earlier," Nicol said. "And I wasn't certain when we would arrive. My apologies for awakening you at this late hour." He said the words dismissively and nodded as he did so, but Melrose pursed her narrow lips and watched him carefully.

" 'Tis late for you to be out and about, my lord."

He straightened his back slightly and managed not to shuffle his feet like a recalcitrant boy. " 'Tis nothing to concern yourself with, Mrs. Melrose. You may return to your bed."

She raised a brow at him, reminding him that she slept even less than he. Indeed, as far as he knew she simply stood in a corner like a silent sentry until dawn, but she ran his household like a seaworthy frigate. Not a fork unpolished or a dust mote to be found. If he never returned to Newburn again, it would be run with fluid efficiency until the day Mrs. Melrose was put in the ground. If, indeed, that eventually ever occurred.

"And who might this be?" she asked, her chin impossibly high. She stood slightly taller than Nicol himself. In fact, he'd once considered commissioning boots with higher heels just to even the score, but he had reminded himself he was a viscount and well above such childish antics. He regretted that decision just now.

"You needn't bother yourself, Mrs. Melrose," he said, and just managed to stifle the word "please."

"It is no bother," she said, turning her head like an automaton. "What is your name, girl?"

Perhaps there was a slight rasp of surprise from inside the

hood. Nicol rushed to help her. "This is Lady Joanna, baroness of Kirksway and my cousin, twice removed, Mrs. Melrose."

The widow gave him a narrow look, but he continued on, keeping up his rhythm.

"She just arrived in our fair city and needed accommodations during her sojourn. I thought it best if she wasn't forced to hire a room."

"Hire a room." She all but growled the words, and Nicol almost sighed with relief as she turned her potent attentions on the girl. "Certainly not." She paused. "Give me your wrap, and I shall show you to your room," she said, and reached for the girl.

Megan stepped cautiously backward. "I'll keep my cloak if you don't mind, Mrs. Melrose."

"You should not have been out so late in this chill weather." After one accusatory glance at Nicol, she pivoted on her heel like a well-trained soldier. "Come along," she ordered, "I shall show you to your room while Margaret . . ." A harried abigail appeared instantaneously as if conjured out of thin air. ". . . fetches your tea."

"That is unnecessary. As I said—" Nicol began, but Mrs. Melrose cut him off.

"I assume your driver will be bringing up her trunks?"

"Yes." He had inherited Mrs. Melrose with the house after his uncle's death and had never quite managed to feel like an adult in her presence.

"I shall see that he doesn't dawdle. Here then," Swinging a door inward, she indicated the chamber with a pragmatic sweep of her hand. "I hope you'll find everything to your liking."

Megan scanned the room, lighting on the four-poster bed, the delicately scrolled desk, the flowered carpet, the linen wall covering. "Everything is perfect."

Mrs. Melrose stared at her a moment, then, against all

odds, she almost seemed to smile before nodding sharply. "I shall send Becky up to help you with your garments."

"There's no need for that," Nicol said. "I'm sure Joanna—"

"I'll not have it said that the welcome at Newburn is lacking," Mrs. Melrose insisted, her fingers entwined in front of her stiffly starched skirt.

"The welcome is most gracious," Megan said. "But I am quite tired. Perhaps Becky could see to my clothes on the morrow."

The older woman delayed a moment before acquiescing. "As you wish," she said simply. "I shall see that your fire is lit and your bed turned down."

For a moment Nicol thought Megan might refuse. Worried this might cause an all-out war, he stepped into the chasm. "Thank you, Mrs. Melrose. And please have Becky bring up a tray for the lady's breakfast in the morning."

"Yes, Lord Newburn," she said, and, with the slightest inclination of her head, strode away.

They were left alone in the hallway, staring at each other like a pair of mindless fools.

"I would suggest you get into bed before the maid arrives, lass," he said. "She'll not disturb you."

Megan nodded and turned away.

Once in his own chambers, Nicol poured himself a bit of port, swirled it about in its round bowl, and stared into the fire. All was going well thus far. From two doors down the hall, he heard Becky knock at Megan's door and pricked his ears to hear. Her voice was a soft murmur of sound, and in a moment the maid was inside. He heard the bump of wood in the grate, another murmur of voices, and finally the sound of Becky exiting.

Yes, everything was going well. They were almost there. And they would succeed, for even his friends had been fooled. Aye, they had been a bit intoxicated, but so was half of Europe. If they could fool the barons, they could fool anyone.

And tomorrow . . . tomorrow the girl would be in the palace. Then the most difficult piece of the puzzle would be in place, for once she was there none would suspect her of being what she was. People saw what they expected to see. It was a well-known fact. He was, after all, accepted as a viscount, instead of the scruffy second son of a murderous bastard. Loosening his grip on the glass, Nicol turned his mind back to the girl. She would surely be accepted as a princess. All he had to do was get her safely to Hewton Theater on the following evening. It would be simple enough so long as—

A scrape of sound issued from somewhere down the hall. His blood froze. Surely she wouldn't try to escape now. Not when they were so close. He was in the hallway in an instant, shoving her door open in a second.

Megan stood facing him, her back to the fire. Her face was alternately shadowed and illumined by the flickering light, and her glorious hair was a dark, wild mane, gilded by the living flame. Her eyes looked as bright and sharp as midnight stars, and her nightgown had become diaphanous, limning each angelic curve in golden light.

A noise sounded from somewhere downstairs, dragging Nicol back to reality. Stepping inside, he closed the door quietly behind him.

"All is well?" he asked.

She raised a single brow at him. "Of course, my lord," she murmured. "What could be amiss?"

He crossed the floor and forced himself into the cushioned chair that stood farthest from the fire, farthest from the glowing temptation.

"I thought you might be worrying about tomorrow."

"Worrying?" A fleeting smile crossed her face. Her teeth

gleamed for a moment in the fire, then disappeared behind her entrancing lips. "Worry not for the morrow," she said. "For the morrow will surely have troubles of its own."

"Such as meeting the princess?"

Her nostrils flared and her eyes narrowed and in that moment she looked like a wild vixen ready to flee. God's bones, she was beautiful. Far prettier than the princess, if the truth be known, but her unusual beauty was something others wouldn't see. He hoped.

"Have you ever considered that this may be madness?" she asked.

"Madness?" He found to some surprise that he had carried his port in with him and took a sip now, hoping to loosen the tension that had cranked tight in his midsection. "Surely not, lass."

She shook her head, and though the movement was sedate, he sensed her worry, and somehow that worry soothed him. "I will only be impersonating a princess," she said, and turned to pace the room.

The fire was beside her now, casting light across her back and the lovely curve of her buttocks. Even through her gown, he could see the crease between her cheeks. Good God, he wasn't nearly drunk enough for this.

". . . fool those who know her best."

He realized she'd been talking just as she turned back toward him and threw the dramatic curve of her breasts into sharp relief. Good God. A saint wouldn't be drunk enough for this.

"Have you nothing to say?" she asked.

He searched his mind and steadied his hand as he drank again. "'Tis for a good cause, lass," he said, and marveled at the insouciance in his tone. Maybe he was truly a nobleman after all.

"You think some silly tryst is a good cause?" She shook

her head, casting her sable locks about the proud thrust of her shoulders. Perhaps he should have made Deirdre cut it shorter, but the act had already seemed like a mortal sin. Even so, a stray curl brushed an upthrust nipple. His body jerked. He took another drink in some desperation and found the glass empty.

"'Tis . . ." he began, but his voice squeaked, actually squeaked, and for two seconds he considered hiding under the bed, for the next five he thought about pulling her into his arms and doing the only thing that would make any possible sense. "'Tis a bit more than a tryst, lass," he said, and gave her a sleepy look. His glass shook, so he set it aside and gripped the other arm of the chair as if it might blast into space at any given moment. "Sedonia's future depends on this match."

She turned fully toward him. Light from the fireplace glowed around her body, casting a halo atop her head, illuminating her arms, glowing like sunrise between her slim, shapely legs.

His body actually ached at the sight.

"Sedonia's future," she said.

He tightened his grip on the chair. "Yes."

"So you're willing to sacrifice her for your country."

He kept his gaze steadfast on her face, but he couldn't forget the silhouette of those flawless legs, couldn't turn his mind from the image of them wrapped about his own. He was beginning to sweat. "On the contrary, lass, I'm hoping to save her."

She watched him in silence. Her hair gleamed as bright as her eyes in the flickering light. "Then I am the only one to be sacrificed."

God yes. The virginal sacrifice. For at that moment she looked as untouched as an angel, yet as touchable as a golden paramour.

"If they discover your true identity, I shall be as compromised as you," he reminded her, but she laughed and strode across the carpet to confront him at close proximity.

"You?"

He nodded, though it jarred ever tight sinew in his body.

"The viscount of Newburn? Even if they learn that you had a hand in this subterfuge, you think they will punish a lord of the realm as they would punish a simple maid?"

Simple? She was anything but that. She was magic personified, she was light in the darkness. But she was silent just now, waiting for a response, and he shifted slightly, trying to ease the discomfort and remember her words.

"You needn't fret, lass. All will be—"

"Do not tell me that all will be well." Her full mouth was pursed and her eyes snapped, shining like emeralds in the firelight. They were close now. So close that he could smell her scent. So close that her gown slipped across his knees. He couldn't take much more. "You do not know if it will be well or if it will be horrendous or if I shall die at the end of a rope because of your blind lust for your foolish princess."

"It will be . . ." he began, but in that moment he realized what she had said. "I don't lust for her," he insisted, but she laughed. "I don't," he said, amazed that she didn't believe him. "I lust—" he began, but stopped himself by the barest margin.

She scowled. "For who then?"

Her breasts were nearly in his face as she leaned down toward him. Her succulent lips were parted, and her hair swept over her shoulders to caress his thighs.

He gritted his teeth and closed his eyes for a moment. "Whom," he said.

She glared at him. "What?"

"The correct word is 'whom.' "

She shook her head. Her hair danced erotically across his

legs, sending lightning racing through his body in every direction. "Why are you doing this?"

He shrugged, trying to remember to breathe. "Perhaps I was merely bored. I am, after all, a lord of the realm. Wealthy and frivolous."

"Are you hoping to gain her gratitude?"

"Why would I do that?"

"I could offer some guesses." She shook her head. Her breasts bobbled beneath the lucky fabric of the nightgown. He dragged his gaze resolutely up to her face.

"Back to the lust theory are we?" he asked, but the words sounded croaked to his own ears.

She nodded.

"Do you think that if I wanted her for myself, I would send her to another man?"

She watched him closely. "Yes," she said. "If she is as remote as you say she is."

He watched her, reminding himself to inhale and, for God's sake, to refrain from dropping his gaze below her neck. No, not her neck. Below her chin. But no, not that either, for that would include her lips, which were undeniably irresistible.

"The laird of Teleere is a pirate," she continued. "Bold, impetuous, rough. The last man the ice princess would choose as a mate."

"Maybe you don't know women as well as I do."

She didn't try to hide her anger. "And maybe you don't care if I am hanged because you are bored."

"If you did not wish to hang, lass, you should not have turned to thievery."

She straightened slowly, until she stood absolutely straight, each curve shown to shadowed perfection against the firelight behind her. "Your Majesty," she said.

"What?"

"From here on you will refer to me as Your Majesty."

God's bones, he would call her Aphrodite if it would help, if he could lay her on the bed behind her and . . . But no. He shook his head, trying to rid it of the scandalous thoughts.

"Lass—"

"Your Majesty," she repeated. "Now get out of my room. I wish to be alone."

And he wished for unspeakable things that kept him riveted to the chair.

"Get out," she repeated, "or I shall call Mrs. Melrose."

The girl knew how to deliver a threat. He would give her that. There was little he could do but straighten painfully and make his way into his own frigid chambers.

Chapter 14

Megan heard the rap on her door but did nothing to answer it. Instead, she stood at her window, looking out. Fog had rolled in, muffling the world outside. Nearly twenty-four hours had passed. In that time she paced and fretted and called herself a dozen kinds of fool, but now she stood fully dressed and waiting.

The knock sounded again, then the door opened rapidly. She didn't turn around, but heard the viscount's footsteps stop.

"Some respond when there is a rap on the door," he said, closing the portal and striding across the floor toward her.

"Some are not the crown princess of Sedonia," she said, and turned. The ivory gown swished across her slippered feet.

He stopped where he was, then bowed very slowly. "Your Majesty," he said, and straightened just as slowly.

His gaze was steady and dark, making her nervous. She longed to look away, to clear her throat, to shuffle her feet, but she made none of those peasant gestures.

"I was unsure what to do with my hair," she said instead. Becky had pulled it up, exposing her neck and ears.

"It looks . . . quite lovely."

"A compliment, my lord?"

"Nicol," he corrected, and drew his gaze away, though for an instant, it almost seemed difficult for him. But why would it not be? Apparently she looked exactly like his beloved princess. "And you should become accustomed to compliments. Your public is a fawning lot."

She watched him cross the floor again.

"Surely someone will notice if my hair is not exactly like hers."

"She will be wearing it up. Under a bonnet."

"I don't have a bonnet."

He lifted a hooded cloak from a nearby trunk. "You will be wearing this."

She felt faint again. "And we will exchange garments in the water closet?"

"You will take her bonnet, and she will take your cloak. Your gowns are exactly the same."

She nodded, struggling for some kind of normalcy.

"You're not going to swoon, are you?"

"I have never swooned."

"Perhaps you have never been a princess before."

"Is it required of them?"

"Merely recommended," he said, and settled the cape around her shoulders. It was made of royal blue satin, piped gold at the seams and around the slits through which she slipped her hands. "Are you ready?"

"I haven't swooned yet."

"Later perhaps," he said, and, pulling up her hood, laid an arm across her back. Her slippers rapped down the stairs, then across the marble foyer. Outside, the fog rose to meet her, and she longed with all her heart to slip into it, to disappear. But instead, she mounted the waiting carriage. It was different than the one they had brought here, more ornate, more polished. She settled onto a crimson cushion and arranged her cape around her.

The viscount sat across from her, rapped the side of the carriage, and pulled a watch from his coat pocket.

"I had to purchase a new one."

She brought her attention back to the present.

"The watch," he explained. "My other was stolen."

"Was it?" She tried to play along, to breathe.

"Yes. While I visited Portshaven."

"Really? I've never been to Portshaven."

"You should go there sometime. The countryside is charming and the pickpockets quite lovely."

She thought it would be best if she could continue the charade, but she could not. "How long do I have?"

He closed the watch and slipped it back into his pocket. "You sound as if it's an execution."

"I fear my death will neither be that quick nor that painless."

His lips quirked upward. But he sobered in a moment. "We will be fashionably late for the play. *Macbeth* may already have ended. But we will slip in before Aladdin finds his lamp."

Macbeth. Aladdin. She was far past her depth and sinking fast.

"Aladdin?" she asked.

"The second play. A farcical performance."

"Of course."

"There will be a good deal of banter amongst the audience, but Anna isn't the frivolous sort. You needn't feel that you must exchange niceties."

"Good."

"I will escort you into the theater. You will step into the closet where Anna will be. She always insists on going alone.

There will be no one waiting there. You will exchange costumes. She will leave first."

"Yes."

"I will escort her to my carriage and return for you. Count to one hundred, then exit the privy."

She managed not to beg him to remain by her side. Managed, in fact, to act nonchalant.

"We will proceed to your customary box."

"Simple," she said.

"Afterward I will accompany you home."

"To Malkan Palace."

He nodded. "Do you remember the floor plan for the palace?"

"Yes."

"Good." He shrugged and drew a cheroot from his breast pocket. A match flared, illuminating his face in its sharp light for a moment. Olive skin, seductive mouth, inscrutable eyes. "All should go smoothly."

"Yes," she said. "There is just one thing."

"What's that?"

"I think I'm going to be sick."

He held his cigar out the window and allowed her a grin. "Ladies of quality do not—"

"Nicol!" she said and there must have been something in her tone, because he gave the outside of the carriage two quick raps. It came to an immediate halt, but he was swinging the door open before the wheels had stopped turning. She tried to hustle past him, to escape outside, but her stomach was already roiling and before she had set a foot to the ground she was bent outward, spewing her supper onto the road.

"The lady is feeling a bit unwell, Ralph," Nicol said, though the driver was nowhere to be seen. She hoped desperately that she was hidden behind the highly polished door.

"Shall I turn back, my lord?" The voice seemed to come from nowhere, and Megan wondered vaguely if Ralph was, perhaps, nothing more than a figment of her imagination.

Nicol drew a handkerchief out of his pocket and handed it over. "Feel better?" he asked quietly.

She closed her eyes, wiped her mouth, and shivered. "That depends if you are referring to my stomach or my pride."

He laughed out loud, seeming immensely jolly. "The lady wishes to continue on," he said to the driver. "Though she may have to leave early. Wait by the door for fifteen minutes or so before parking the phaeton."

Taking her arm, Nicol eased her back into the rocking vehicle and settled her solicitously onto her seat. "Clever of you," he said. "A perfect excuse to have him wait for Anna."

She noticed he had tossed out his cheroot. "I do what I can," she managed, but her voice was weak.

The remainder of the journey was a blur. Fog roiled. Carriages passed. They turned a corner and drew to a halt. Her stomach lurched.

"You look a bit pale."

"I can't imagine why."

He laughed again and checked his watch. The phaeton's door swung open as if on command. Fresh air wafted into the carriage, and Megan drew in a few bracing breaths.

He didn't rush her, didn't question, but merely sat across the vehicle, watching her in silence.

"Thank you," she murmured finally, feeling somewhat stronger.

His grin flashed in the darkness. "No need for gratitude," he said. "We're three minutes ahead of schedule."

"In that case, congratulations. You must have figured my weak stomach into your calculations."

He felt for his cheroots again, then seemed to think better

of it and settled his arm across the back of the seat behind him. "I think there is nothing weak about you, lass."

The lanternlight flickered, casting his right side into shadows and glowing on his left. His hair shone blue-black in the fickle light, and his grin was disarming.

Weakness. One never knew where it would grab you.

"You're smarter than all of them, little Sparrow. Don't forget that," he said.

"I fear intellect may not count for much here."

"Intellect always counts," he said. "Especially here, where it comes at such a premium."

"What if I forget—"

"Everyone forgets. Even Anna."

"Her own name?" she asked.

"You are the princess," he murmured, leaning close and taking her hand between both of his. "All will be forgiven. Ladies swoon at the sight of you. Gentlemen scribble poems as you pass. Your only real concern is Paqual. Be careful of him. Time is up. Are you ready?"

"No."

"You don't seem the type to underestimate yourself," he said, and giving her hand a squeeze, rose to his feet, and stepped outside.

She followed him unsteadily.

"If we don't return soon, you may assume the lady is well and park the phaeton until the end of the play."

"Yes my lord." She could only assume it was Ralph who answered, though she never saw him.

A smattering of people littered the lawn, but Megan barely noticed them. Off to the right, she heard someone hacking his meal into the bushes.

"You see," Nicol said, bending close. " 'Tis the thing to do when one visits the theater. Though most empty their stomachs because of an excess of wine."

She cursed quietly at him, and he laughed as he guided her up the stairs. In a moment he had presented his tickets and a blurry second after that they were standing in front of the water closet.

Two women, dressed to the nines and gossiping behind their fans, strolled past.

"I'm certain you will feel better in a moment," Nicol said, pretending she was sick and needing attention. "But I'll wait for you here, just in case."

She almost considered begging him to take her back, to set her free. But instead she gave him a shallow nod inside her hood and opened the door.

It was a strange moment, for the first thing she realized was that privies smelled pretty much the same no matter one's station. Her second realization was that she was in the presence of a princess. Tatiana Octavia Linnet Rocheneau stood with her back straight, her hands clasped before her. She wore a pale blue bonnet tied at her throat. A veil was draped across the front, shielding her face. Megan closed the door behind her. They stood facing each other from mere inches, saying nothing. The world spun slowly on its axis, then Tatiana nodded once and removed the hat.

Megan couldn't stop the hiss of air down her throat, couldn't quite prevent the widening of her eyes, for there, before her now, was her twin, or the twin of the woman she had become. Did she look like the deceased king? Did they both?

"I am in your debt."

It took Megan a moment to realize the princess had spoken, for she didn't look like a living being, but more like the priceless glass doll she'd once seen displayed in a Skilan market. Cool and beautiful and untouchable.

"I . . . What?" Megs breathed.

"Nicol said you would be perfect, that you were the only

woman to perform this task." Tatiana's expression was regal, though she nodded in agreement. "I shall not forget this favor."

And then Sedonia's future queen was handing over her bonnet. Megan took it in fingers that bumbled with nerves.

As for the princess, she didn't hesitate a moment, but untied the cape from Megan's neck and swung it smoothly over her own shoulders. Megan just managed to settle the hat onto her head, but her hands seemed to have forgotten how to function. Pushing them silently aside, Tatiana slipped the wide ribbon around the back of her neck before tying it in front. Megan blinked through the fine mesh of the veil. It was like seeing a goddess through the mist. One moment she was there, the next she was gone, leaving the room empty but for a frazzled thief who blinked owlishly through the fog of the veil.

"Still feeling unwell?" Nicol's voice was clear from outside the closet, Tatiana's a mere murmur as they paced away.

For several seconds Megan's mind went blank, but somehow she remembered to count, starting the numbers in her head with a jolt and rattling them off too fast. She slowed the rhythm, trying to do the same with her heart rate, but thoughts buzzed like angry hornets in her head.

Voices murmured outside the privy, becoming clearer.

"Of course not," Nicol said through the muzz of Megan's jangled nerves. "I wouldn't miss one of Kern's performances."

"At least not the part where Mrs. Ballum tears her bodice."

"Just so," Nicol agreed, and with that Megan forced herself out the door.

Nicol stopped where he was. "Your Majesty," he said, and bowed. Perhaps there was the perfect inflection of surprise in his tone. She couldn't be sure.

"Nicol." She gave him a nod as he straightened. The world felt strangely fuzzy. "Are you just now arriving?"

"Only just. But I beat Will here by a good three seconds."

She turned slowly, her mind working at the laborious speed of a lumber wagon straining uphill. The man from the woods stood beside the viscount. He was as thin as she remembered, with the same world-weary expression, the same casual demeanor he'd displayed at their first meeting. Will was his name. Lord . . .

"Your Majesty," he said, bowing low.

"Lord Landow." The name came to her despite the world's fuzziness. "You and the viscount must keep the same unorthodox schedule."

The baron nodded soberly. "He has been a bad influence on me, Your Majesty."

"That I believe."

Nicol bowed again. There was some unfathomable emotion in his eyes. If she didn't know better, she would almost think it was pride. "May I escort you back to your box, Your Majesty?"

She gave him a shallow nod and took his arm.

From near the wall, three guards hurried up behind. Two women followed them. One was dark, the other fair.

"Mary and Evelyn?" she murmured, not glancing at her escort. "And the guards—Allard, Combs, and . . . Roger?"

"Excellent," he said, looking directly at her.

She wasn't sure what he referred to, but the compliment surprised her, adding to her disorientation. She glanced at him through the veil. His smile was full-blown.

"Her Majesty has an amazing memory."

She couldn't seem to respond.

"Are you enjoying the performance this evening?"

She had no idea how he could expect her to answer, to carry on as if all was well, and yet she did. "Mr. Kern is a favorite of mine."

Off to the right a bevy of ladies curtsied and murmured a greeting. She nodded in return.

"Even more so than Lowry?"

Panic struck her like high tide. Through her veil she could see that he was still smiling at her. "Lowry?" she murmured in terror, but he laughed and squeezed her arm.

"Perhaps you haven't heard of him. As I said before, Your Majesty, you should have more leisure time."

She felt faint. He was teasing her? She was going to kill him. But not just now because he was holding her upright and nodding to a group of gentlemen who rose from their seats and bowed as she entered.

"Your Majesty," they murmured, but their greetings to each other were more bland.

"Lord Glenco. Lord Paqual," Nicol answered back.

She tried not to gawk at her surroundings, but everything here was new and bright, including her circumstances, which made her heart race like a runaway cart horse.

The audience seemed to have no compunction about talking during the performance and kept up a steady stream of conversation though the actors were still at work. From the stage someone screamed. She started, and Nicol tightened his grip imperceptibly on her arm.

"I hope your business went well." Paqual said. He was not more than a few inches taller than Megan herself. Skinny and balding, he seated himself a moment after Nicol handed her into a chair near the railing. The old man's eyes remained on her an instant longer. They were as bright and hungry as a hound's.

"What business is that?" Nicol asked.

"I heard you were in Teleere."

"To visit family."

"You have relatives on the isle?"

"My mother's kin."

"Ahh. How nice that you have time for such things."

Nicol's gaze lingered on the old man a moment longer, and in that instant she felt the aged chancellor's animosity.

"My apologies," Megan said.

They turned to her as one.

"I beg your pardon, Your Majesty," Paqual said.

"My apologies," she repeated. "I depend on you too greatly, my lord, or you, too, could spend time with your kindred."

The old man preened even as he bowed from his seat. "I live to serve, Your Majesty."

She nodded.

Nicol bowed. "I will take my leave then—"

"Nay." Had she said it too quickly? "There is an empty seat," she said, and indicated the chair with a gloved hand. "Join us."

He delayed an instant, then, "Thank you," he said. "I fear my companion had to miss the performance, so I am here alone."

"And who was the lucky woman tonight?" asked Paqual.

Angry voices rose from the stage. Megan managed to ignore them, as seemed the custom.

"My cousin," Nicol said. "Visiting from Portshaven."

"How nice," drawled Paqual, though he managed to convey the idea that there was somehow something distasteful about the viscount's lifestyle.

"Yes," Nicol agreed, and drew the chair closer to Megan's.

Her heart settled down a notch.

Raucous weeping issued from the stage, and finally all eyes turned toward the actors.

Megan watched, too. She had never seen a play, had never been in a theater, not even to pick pockets, but now that she was here, she found it impossible to concentrate.

"Relax," Nicol said, and, leaning toward her, pointed to the stage as if commenting on the performance. "The worst is over."

"Truly?" There was no way any of the others would overhear their conversation. Not above the heaving sobs that issued from the stage. "And what if I vomit again?"

He shrugged, still watching the performance. "Try projecting toward Paqual," he said, and, against all logical odds, she laughed.

Chapter 15

Megan awoke to a shallow clicking sound. Her mind shifted from her dreams, trying groggily to sort fact from fiction. Beneath her, the mattress was soft, and the sheets smelled of rose petals. She definitely wasn't in prison.

She opened one eye and saw that a woman had slipped into the chamber. Lifting her head from the pillow with some effort, Megs watched the girl squat before the fireplace. Ten acres of polished marble lay between the bed and the hearth. So none of it had been a dream. Not the silent exchange in the privy, not the conversation with Lord Paqual, not falling asleep during the play, and not Nicol's gentle teasing about her inability to stay awake to save her own life.

She'd awakened with a start, afraid she had compromised that very thing, but people were extremely indulgent with princesses it seemed, for no one else had even mentioned her faux pas.

God help her.

The abigail bent forward, blowing life into the fire before

feeding in kindling. In a moment she had the blaze started anew. What was her name? She had helped Megan remove her gown the night before. Had taken down her hair and scurried unobtrusively from the room.

"Thank you."

The girl jerked about, making Megan wonder if it was the croak in her voice or her gratitude that was startling. Her eyes were wide and dark, her hair all but hidden beneath a white mobcap that very nearly matched her skin tone. Against her cheeks, freckles stood out in stark relief.

"You're most welcome . . . Your Majesty."

Megan very much doubted if she would ever become accustomed to the borrowed title. Would ever connect it to herself. But of course not, she was only to be there for a few days. A week at the most.

Her bladder complained. Did princesses really have to pee?

"Do you know what time it is?" she asked, scanning the room for a place to relieve herself. A dressing screen shielded the corner of the room. A hunt scene was painted in bright colors across the hinged linen, sleek horses behind baying hounds. It seemed like a likely place.

" 'Tis still early. Not yet nine o'clock. I am sorry to have awoken you."

Nine. She almost smiled. Back on Teleere she would have washed the crockery and fenced five watches by now. "Do you know if the viscount has arrived yet?"

The maid scrunched her freckled features as if deep in thought. "Lord Newburn?"

"Yes."

"I believe he stayed in his chambers here in the palace last night, Your Majesty."

He had a room here at the palace? That would have been a good thing to know, she thought testily, though she realized she had barely had time to learn where her own chambers lay. "Of course," she said. "I'm to meet him in the blue room for breakfast."

The girl curtsied again. "Certainly, Your Majesty. Shall I draw a bath, or shall I tend your hair immediately?"

Bath or hair. They seemed better choices than mending a lady's torn chemise by tallow candles or trying to escape an inebriated miller's pinches. Still she felt tense, but so her day began.

When she reached the blue room Nicol was alone at a small table, drinking tea. Except for one wayward curl, his hair was brushed back from his brow and shone in the light from the nearby fireplace. His russet-colored jacket was immaculate, and dark leather gloves lay perfectly aligned on the table beside his saucer. He rose when he saw her and bowed. "Good morning," he said. "I trust you slept well, judging by your nap during the performance last night."

She gave him a glance she hoped would put him in his place, but she was no match for his elegant nonchalance. He only smiled and deepened his bow. Behind her, three ladies-in-waiting veered off to settle themselves on powder blue divans set along the wall. "Did you wish to speak to me about something in particular, Nicol?"

His eyes sparked at the sound of his name. She took a seat directly across from him at the round table.

He leaned across the smooth surface. "Anna usually manages to put a bit of warmth in her voice when she speaks to me," he said.

"Does she?" Megs intoned, raising one brow slightly. His smile changed to something a bit more devilish, but he sipped his tea as if they spoke of nothing more controversial than the weather.

"She is safely aboard the *Melody* with her guard," he said.

Her stomach lurched at the memory of the meeting in the privy. She would never achieve that polished elegance. Never. "I can't do this," she murmured, just managing to refrain from skimming the room like an escaped criminal in the watchman's favorite pub.

"You already have," Nicol countered.

"I fell asleep at the play," she hissed.

From her left, the chambermaid hurried across the room carrying a highly polished walnut tray.

"What the devil is her name?" Megan asked, feeling desperate, but Nicol only shrugged.

The girl set the tray in the exact center of the table and backed away a step. "Is there anything else I might get you just now, Your Majesty?"

Megan scanned the meal. Warm scones, mulled ale, steaming oatmeal with honeycomb and butter. It looked delectable. Her stomach cranked up tight, feeling sick.

"This will do," she said.

The girl bowed, but Nicol raised his cup. "Might I get more tea . . ." He paused. "What was your name again, lass?"

"Bryna, my lord."

"Bryna," he repeated. "Could I get a pot of tea and marmalade for the scones."

"Certainly, my lord," she said, and curtsied her way out of the room.

"How can you eat?" Megan asked.

He grinned at her as he leaned back. "And this from the lass who consumed five oxen before reaching Sedonian shores. Relax," he said. "Paqual leaves nothing for the princess to do but commission a wardrobe and plan parties."

"That is two more things than I can manage."

He widened his grin.

"Your Majesty." She turned at the sound of Paqual's voice. "I heard you were about already. You should be abed. A princess must get plenty of sleep after all. What with the duke's arrival only weeks hence."

She didn't turn to Nicol in a panic as seemed appropriate, but remained looking at Paqual. "And what of you, my lord? Do you not require sleep?"

He bowed stiffly from the waist. "I am forever busy in your glorious service, Your Majesty."

"And I am blessed to have you."

"Your Majesty is too kind," he said, and bowed again before motioning to his contemporaries and striding from the room.

Megan added honey to her porridge and stirred it absently, but she could feel Nicol's eyes on her. "If you've something to say, you might as well do so now," she murmured, glancing up.

He grinned crookedly at her. "A thief *and* a politician," he said, and toasted her with his tea. "Who would have guessed it?"

"As it happens," she countered, sipping her tea. It tasted bitter as did everything these days. "I am neither—"

But a servant approached, stopping her denial. She turned regally.

"Your Majesty." The man bowed. "Edmund Danzig awaits your arrival in the east salon."

Danzig! Panic spewed up anew. The name meant nothing to her.

"He must feel the duke's guest rooms need emergency re-decorating," Nicol said, carelessly feeding her clues. "They cannot wait another minute."

In her mind, Megan cursed like a longshoreman, but she turned back to the servant with regal aplomb. "Tell Mr. Danzig that I will be with him shortly," she said.

The servant bowed and disappeared. Megan took a sip of tea and resisted crashing the cup atop Nicol's head. "So I am redecorating?"

"From what I have heard Danzig makes the decisions.

Anna merely nods now and again. All is well," he said, and rose to his feet.

"Where are you going?" She hadn't meant for the panic to reach her voice, but some things couldn't be helped.

"I can hardly leave Paqual to his own devices," Nicol said. "Or he'll sell Sedonia to the Turks and send us all to Asia."

"Don't leave me alone."

"You won't be alone," he said. "You'll be with Mr. Danzig."

"I don't even know who Mr. Danzig is," she hissed.

"Not to worry. You shall surely figure it out," he said, but in a moment his expression darkened as he retrieved a lone glove from the table top. "Your Majesty." He executed a shallow bow. "Do you, perchance, know what happened to my other glove?"

She tasted her tea again. It seemed sweeter now. Quite satisfying really. "No," she said. "But not to worry. You shall surely figure it out."

As it turned out, the viscount was right. There was little Megan really needed to do. The chambers the duke would be occupying were nothing if not spacious. The windows were high and broad, the walls covered in bright damask. But the duke, being the brother to the king of Denmark and a well-decorated captain in the Danish army, liked to boast his own colors, which happened to be crimson and gold. The wall linen must be changed, the moldings repainted, and the ivory bed hangings and curtains replaced. They would never do. To Megan, the room seemed more than adequate as it was, but it was she, after all, who was the true visitor here, so she nodded and murmured and looked thoughtful as Danzig fluttered about, skinny and flighty as a starved country hen. Contrary to the current men's hairstyles, which were relatively natural, he wore a huge, powdered wig that tended to list to the left when he got nervous, which was most of the time. His clothing was just as outdated and just as interesting. His breeches were mustard yellow and his jacket pea green. But as odd as his appearance was, he had an uncanny gift for whipping his entourage into a good-hearted froth. Workers bustled about like spring bees, leaving Megan fairly tranquil by comparison.

The nooning meal was served in a gargantuan room called the grand hall, and since Megan's stomach had managed to settle a bit, she was able to test the samples of delicacies the royal chef was experimenting with for the coming festivities.

When Nicol found her she was surrounded by a clutter of crockery and wondering if there was any way she could stash away some of the wine sauce for later consumption. Or at least swipe a bowl or two.

The viscount bowed and straightened. As seemed the norm, there was no one close to her. It made Megan wonder if the princess had isolated herself by choice or by chance.

"So you have found your forte?" Nicol asked quietly.

She raised a spoonful of the last sample and nodded toward the chef, who stood some twelve feet away but still managed to hover. "This, Mr. Hunt, is ambrosia."

He blinked as if confused, wrung his hands once and cocked his head. "You approve, Your Majesty?"

"Most definitely."

"Might it need a smidge more lemon."

"No."

"But what of the texture? Should it be a bit thicker? My assistant's mind wanders like a honeybee. Something about the mason's daughter. The lad thinks he wants to lay brick with the girl's father instead of tend the sauce. Children these days never stay the course set—"

"It is perfection," she interrupted.

"But is it—"

"Mr. Hunt," she said, pursing her lips. "If you change the recipe one iota, I fear I shall be forced to have you beheaded."

His eyes got as round as white onions. His jaw dropped. "Yes, Your—"

She was immediately sorry she had said it. Apparently the princess was not prone to such outlandish outbursts. "Mr. Hunt," she said, and rose to quickly take his hand. "I merely jest. Your cooking is divine. You are, undoubtedly, a culinary genius, and I am not such a fool as to interfere with genius."

Mr. Hunt was sixty if he was a day, but he blushed clear to his ears. It was, perhaps, the most charming thing she had ever seen. "Th—thank you, Your Majesty," he breathed, and, bowing nearly to the floor, escaped like a plump hare into the kitchen.

She drew a careful breath and turned to sit down across from Nicol once again. His dark eyes watched her with cynical knowing.

"You'd best be careful, lass, or you'll have every man from butter churner to prince vying for your hand in marriage. You'll make the good duke of Venge jealous before he even arrives to woo you with his royal wit."

Lifting her cup from its saucer, she carefully extended her baby finger above the rim. "Pray tell, my lord, is there not a barmaid somewhere just begging to be threatened and bullied."

He chuckled as he rose to his feet. "As a matter of fact, Your Majesty, I do have important tasks to see to. As do you, I see." Turning on his heel, he left her with that parting.

Perhaps he had meant to wound her with his words, but if that was the case, he would be sadly mistaken. It was not her job to better Sedonia. She would nod and murmur and scamper back to Teleere with coins in her pocket at the first opportunity. And then she would buy her own inn—somewhere quiet where the working class could relax after a hard day's labor and she would never have to lay eyes on a nobleman again.

That thought consoled her as she stumbled through the afternoon and into the evening.

The next day followed much the same course. She was overfed, carefully watched, and minutely considered. Her hair was brushed and coifed, her costume puffed just so. A bevy of lords and ladies rambled about the palace, seeming both eager and loath to venture too near her. But with a few well-chosen words, she was able to draw them into her circle. For the life of her, she couldn't imagine why they were there, for they did little but drink to excess and tell poor jokes. Her own seemed quite stellar by comparison.

Nicol entered the hall just as her entourage burst into riotous laughter.

"Your Majesty," said Lord Kendall. He was a plump young marquis with a round nose and eyes that sparkled like a weasel's. "I did not realize your wit could outshine your beauty."

She gave Kendall a slanted glance and took the tiniest sip of wine. She might be a fool to be here at the outset, but she was not about to become a drunken fool. "And I did not realize you were so astute," she said.

There was a titter of laughter.

"Nicol," she said, turning slowly toward him. "You have finished closeting yourself away with the other advisors."

He bowed. "We are finished for this day, Your Majesty."

"I fear our Lord Newburn has forgotten the glory of being worthless," said Lord Riven. He was young and handsome and fully aware of both, even when inebriated, which seemed to be his usual state.

"Not at all," Nicol countered. "I am just as fond of worthlessness as the next peer of the realm." He took a draught of his wine. "Which, judging by the present company, is quite fond indeed."

The assemblage laughed, adding witticisms and jests and thinking they were much more amusing than they actually were. It was the way with the upper class, of course, Megan thought. Still, they seemed a harmless lot. Almost sad in their ineffectiveness, their need to outshine the next.

"Your Majesty . . ." Nicol inclined his head. "I was wondering if you might join me in the sword room for a game of chess."

"Ahh, so the rivalry between brawn and beauty continues," said Kendall. "There has been none here to challenge our bonny princess since you've been gone, Newburn."

"Then it's time," Nicol said and held out his hand. "Will you do me the honor?"

"Of course," she said, and rose serenely to her feet.

To her surprise, only her ladies-in-waiting followed her into the chamber where weapons hung like trophies on the walls. Once again, the maids wandered off to the side, finding their own diversions as their mistress took a seat across the table from the viscount. A stately chessboard resided there, its onyx-and-ivory pieces rising regally above a board crafted of the same materials.

He moved a pawn and nodded for her to do the same.

"I hope the duke's chambers have been decorated without mishap," Nicol said.

"It was a bit uncertain for a moment or two, but I think we shall win the day," she countered, and slid a pawn forward. "Tell me, my lord, is your Anna always so well occupied."

His gaze sparkled on her. "Remember, she has been princess only since her uncle's death some months ago."

She concentrated hard on the board before moving a scowling bishop. "Paqual must have some power if he could manage to put a girl on the throne."

"And more power still when he chooses her husband."

Pieces shuffled thoughtfully across the board. "So you would choose him instead."

He paused with his fingers on a black knight astride a rearing charger. "Do you think me hungry for power, lass?"

She managed to stifle a shrug even though she was fairly certain her ladies did not watch her. "I do not assume to know where your appetites lie, my lord."

"Don't you?" he asked, and took her pawn.

She glared at the board, refusing to acknowledge any odd nuances in his tone. "The princess is young and inexperienced, completely unprepared to rule this country."

"Have you learned so much already, lass?"

She did shrug now and took his pawn at the same time. "Lord Riven knows that much," she said.

"Perhaps Lord Riven doesn't know Her Majesty so well as he might," he said, and caught her gaze.

"And you do?" she asked, and though she tried to keep her tone level, she feared she might have failed, for his lips quirked. The table was littered with her purloined pieces and his fingers were on his queen as he leaned closer.

"Are you asking if Anna and I have been intimate?"

She felt the heat of her blush and dropped her gaze to the board. "I would neither have any business nor any interest in asking such a thing," she assured him.

"Check," he said, then, "Anna doesn't blush."

She examined the board, not daring to look up, lest he see the emotions in her eyes. "Perhaps she has forgotten how."

She hadn't meant to say such a thing and was just about to retract her words when he laughed.

"Might it be . . ." He paused, but she refused to look up. Instead, she hustled her knight into place and kept her eyes on her queen. "Tell me, lass, are you jealous of her?"

She didn't answer, and the heat of his gaze on her face seemed to burn into her very soul. "'Tis your move," she said.

He remained as he was.

"Do you wish to make them suspicious?" she asked.

He barely glanced at his pieces, before sliding his knight

diagonally and returning his gaze to her face. "Are you?" he asked.

"She is the princess. Who would not be jealous?"

"The lass I met in Portshaven."

"How lucky for her." She moved. He moved. "Did you, perchance, catch her name?"

"No. But I caught the edge of a wine bottle across the side of my skull."

She moved her queen, then nodded his attention toward the board. He glanced, made a move, and caught her gaze again.

"That girl was jealous of no one. She made her own world. Her own luck."

"Unlike your Anna, who is ruled by people she neither likes nor respects?"

"She has a quick mind and a kind heart. She but needs some room in order to rule her own country."

"And so you would find her a husband to help her do so."

"Yes."

"And spoil your own chance of happiness?"

Surprise or something like it crossed his dark features. "You still believe I am in love with her?"

She settled back in her chair and carefully linked her fingers on her lap. They only shook a little. "I never thought you the type to lie about something as mundane as love," she said.

"Perhaps I do love her," he agreed, and although his tone was casual, his gaze was sharp on her face. "Or perhaps I only love what she could be."

She dragged her gaze from his and made her final move. "Either way," she said. "The princess will marry, and you shall be alone." Rising to her feet, she strode from the room, leaving Nicol to stare after her.

He scowled after her until she was well out of sight, then dropped his gaze to the board.

Damn, he mused, and, propping his elbows on the table, steeped his fingers and almost laughed.

She'd won the game and taken his queen. Again.

Chapter 16

The palace was quiet. Nicol could hear the guards' conversation drift up from the bottom of the steps. But other than that the world seemed entirely silent.

The princess's chambers were just down the hall. Anna always slept alone. She would abide no one to accompany her at night. Indeed, she would not even allow another at her door. There were guards surrounding the palace, guards at the stairs, and guards following her every minute of the day, she said—surely that was enough. And none gainsaid her. Perhaps because none would suspect her of immorality. She was too cool for passion—unlike her counterpart, who shone with life, who burst with vitality. Nicol could remember how she felt in his arms, like a living sunbeam against his skin. Like—

He shut his mind down and frowned into the darkness. It was then that he heard a noise, a tiny snick of sound. Hurrying around the corner, he glanced toward her door, and there, at the far end of the hall, he thought he saw a shadow disappear into shadow. Perhaps he was only imagining, but worry niggled at him. Hurrying up to the girl's door, he set a hand to the latch, paused for a moment, then stepped inside. Once there, he scanned the darkened room. Nothing. He must have imagined the noise. Upon the mattress, he could see the small shape of the pretend princess. Her slim form barely made a crease in the blankets. But suddenly he realized he had thought that before. And he had been tricked. His heart jerked with anticipation.

Closing the door silently behind him, he strode across the floor. Upon the pillows, he could see a wild cascade of hair, but was it her hair? Hurrying around the foot of the bed, he gazed down and now the firelight told the truth. She had not left. Had not escaped into the night. Had not lied.

There was no fire in the grate tonight, but a bevy of tapers in a brass candelabra cast the room in a rosy glow, and by their light, the girl's gamine face looked peaceful, neither as cool as the princess's nor as intense as the thief's. But as beautiful as both. God help him. She thought him in love with Tatiana. An icicle of pain shivered through his heart. She would laugh if she knew the truth, for she was not a person who would understand weakness. Not like him. Now for instance. He knew he should leave. Knew he should return to his own sleepless chamber, and yet he lowered himself onto her mattress and watched her slumber.

It was odd, he thought. He was a viscount, wealthy and secure. Yet he could not manage a full night's rest. She was a thief, barely surviving. Yet she slept like a babe.

Or like an angel. He almost laughed at his own sentimentality. She was here because she had robbed and molested him. She was here because she had no other choice. But she looked so right beneath the pristine sheets. So perfect.

Reaching out, he touched her cheek. She sighed, snuggled deeper into her pillow, and raised her hand to his.

He knew the moment she awoke, though it took her a second to open her eyes. When she did, they shone brightly in the flickering light.

He drew back slowly.

"My apologies," he said. "I didn't mean to startle you."

She sat up with a scowl and blinked at him, her hair disheveled and her wide mouth disapproving. "Then you shouldn't sneak into me room in the middle of the night."

There was something about her newly returned accent that made him smile. Which seemed illogical, considering how hard he had worked to be rid of it. "I hope I am the only one who will," he said, and felt his stomach twist at the thought of another being here, of another watching her sleep or touching her skin.

Her scowl deepened, and he caught himself.

"Your language," he said, "has lost a bit of polish."

"Oh." She drew a soft breath and pushed a tangle of sable hair out of her face. "My apologies, my—" But she stopped herself. "What the devil are y' doing in here?"

He grinned. She was no longer afraid or apologetic, if either of those elements had ever truly existed in her, and he hadn't realized he had missed her. The real her.

"I thought I heard a noise," he said.

"Noise?" She cocked her head and again the tiniest scowl bent her eyebrows into an intriguing quirk.

"In the hallway by your door."

"What time is—? What were you doing by me door?"

An excellent question, but not one he cared to answer or even one he wished to contemplate. "You took my queen again. I'd like the pieces back."

Coherence was returning slowly to her eyes. She pulled her knees up under the blankets and hugged them. By the fickle light of the dancing flames, she looked indecently young and breathlessly innocent. Maybe he had only hoped there was a noise, had only longed for a reason to enter her room.

"Why don't you sleep?" she asked.

He watched her in silence. He had consumed two glasses of port not three hours before in an attempt to relax. He regretted them now, for he was not asleep, and yet he was not fully aware. What tiny idiosyncrasy might he notice about her if he were completely sober?

"Tell me, lass," he said. "Do you think it a sin to be wealthy?"

"A sin?" She rested her chin on her knees and gazed at him. "I hope not, for I've no desire to sin. Gaining wealth, on the other hand . . ." She shrugged. Her nightrail slipped a bit, showing a greater patch of the pearlescent skin of her shoulder. He watched that piece of flesh, noticing the softness, the paleness, imagining kissing her just there.

"What are your thoughts on fornication?" he murmured.

"What?" Her tone was sharp with surprise, and he almost cursed aloud at his own foolishness, but he managed to bite his tongue and pull his gaze from her shoulder.

"Life at court," he said, "is less than moral. How are you faring amongst the gentry?"

Her eyes were somewhat narrowed, but her lips looked more plump than ever, pursed as they were and shiny in the fickle light of the lively flames. "The princess seems to have managed to keep herself apart from the corruption. None approach me with improper suggestions."

"No. They would not."

She cocked her head, and he realized his tone had been strange, almost regretful.

"And that is good, of course," he added, "but I fear . . ." Drawing a breath, he decided on the truth. After all, the girl was risking much. Surely she deserved to learn what she could of the princess. "Her subjects do not find her particularly warm. But neither do they think her immoral. Perhaps it is impossible to have both."

"And which do you have?"

She looked so much like Tatiana, and yet . . . she seemed distinctly different. Oddly touchable in the soft light.

"Neither," he said. "While you—" He stopped himself by the barest of margins, drew a deep breath, and stood. "Tomorrow will be a long day. You'd best sleep." He turned to leave, but in that instant she was out of bed and not an arm's length away.

"What were you going to say?"

He kept his arms at his side, kept his hands strictly to himself, though he would have sworn he did not possess the strength. "Go to sleep, lass."

"While I am what?"

"You are tired."

"Did you sleep with her?" Her words were a whisper, her eyes huge, as though she had wondered a hundred times, had warned herself not to ask, but could no longer resist. And he was hopelessly flattered. There was nothing he could do to stop himself from reaching out. Nothing he could do but touch her. Beneath his fingers, her cheek felt as soft as a dream.

"Would you care, lass?" he asked.

Her lips trembled. "I would know," she said, and against every sane judgment, he brushed his thumb across her mouth.

Emotion flared in his gut. "You have . . ." He tried to stop the words, but the touch of her skin tilted his world. "The most seductive mouth."

Her lips parted beneath his thumb. Her tongue darted out, touching his flesh. Something yanked at his innards.

"My mouth," she whispered, "is just like hers."

He shook his head. "'Tis what I thought at first, but your lips are . . ." It was not too late to flee. He was not a fool after all. Too smart to be in the army, his comrades had said, and if that meant he was too intelligent to take orders unnecessarily from a titled colonel who would blithely send his men to their deaths and never himself face the horrors of battle, then it was true. He was known for his intellect, for his ability to survive, but she was so close and so clever and so damnably beautiful that he forgot his reasons for keeping his hands to himself. "Yours," he said, "are extremely kissable." He tried to draw his hand away, but despite his supposed lack of foolishness it did not work. "It may well prove to be a difficulty."

"Difficulty?" The word was no more than a soft draft of air against his hand, and he was melting.

"Anna never had any trouble dissuading the suitors." He steadied himself as thoughts of this angel hellion in another's arms stormed through his head. "But you . . . You will have to use the utmost caution."

"Caution?" she whispered, and her lips remained parted ever so slightly, teasing him, tempting him.

"Not to let them do this," he said and curling his fingers toward his palm, skimmed the flat of his nails along her throat. "Or this." Slipping his hand lower, he traced her collarbone, then caressed the outer curve of her breast.

Her eyes were wide-open. "What else?" she whispered.

And he kissed her. Her lips tasted like heaven beneath his, like exotic, succulent fruit that he could never resist. And she kissed him back, not with the sweet innocence of youth, but with wild, yearning abandon, grasping his shirt and leaning into the embrace.

Still, he had not completely lost his mind and managed just barely to retreat. Her lips remained parted, her teeth pearlescent in the firelight, her breasts rising and falling dramatically beneath her frail nightgown.

He cleared his throat and tried to do the same with his head. "I . . ." he began, but lost his train of thought when she licked her lips. He watched the quick swipe of her tongue and felt it tug at something low in his gut. And though he tried, he could not quite let go of her arm, could not quite release her.

"You didn't answer me question." Her fingers were tangled in his sleeves, but whether she meant to keep him at bay or pull him close was impossible to say. There was something about the dichotomy of her that drew him, the soft feminine scent of lavender set against the strength of her narrow hands. The pristine white of the gown against her husky accent. Her thighs pressed intimately against his while her lovely breasts bent away. The wild sweep of her hair. The erotic curve of her cheek. Damn!

He leaned closer, but she stepped back and pressed her fingers against his lips. The feel of them was hopelessly alluring. He kissed them and watched her mouth move.

"Did you lie with her?"

Dear God, she was stunning. "Who?" he asked.

She scowled as she drew her hand away. "The princess."

He remembered Tatiana with a hard yank of guilt. That was why this lass was here. That was why she risked her life. Indeed, the same could be said of him. Perhaps some would think he had come to Malkan Palace to atone for the sin of becoming what he was never meant to be, to pay for the crime of taking a title others had died for. But he knew better. He had come to court because he could. Because he was a viscount. But if the girl's true identity was discovered, he could very well lose more than his title. Dropping his hands, he backed stiffly away.

"My apologies," he said, and gave her a sharp bow. "It will not happen again." Gritting his teeth, he prepared to turn away, but she caught his shirtfront in a hard grip.

He looked at her fist. It was tiny, a row of sharp knuckles

set in ivory skin. She drew a deep breath, causing his gaze to shift to her chest. Through the fragile white gown he could see the delectable thrust of her nipples.

"You have bullied me and threatened me and questioned me," she said. "But now you will answer a question of me own." He managed to lift his gaze back to her face. Her eyes were as hard as flashing emeralds, but her lips were still damnably soft. "Were you lovers?"

He was the master of concentration, and yet it was difficult to focus on her words, for her lips kept moving, teasing and quirking and begging for a kiss.

"Nicol!" She actually shook him, and with that, he put his hand on hers and carefully released it from his shirt.

"Tatiana is not that kind," he said.

She narrowed her eyes at him. "And what kind is that, my lord?"

The kissable kind, the touchable kind, the kind that drove him past all good sense and into this hard-edged yearning. "She is a lady," he said. "Gently reared and carefully polished."

"And so, of course, she is innocent."

He nodded.

"And what of me?" she asked. The precision had returned to her tone. She dropped her fist from his shirt and paced the room, paralleling the bed where she had lain only moments before. "I was neither gently reared nor precisely polished. What does that make me?"

Beautiful and tough and achingly desirable. He clamped his jaw and watched her pace. With the golden candlelight behind her, he could see the silhouette of her body through her gown. Again! God's bones, didn't she ever stand in the full light of day where he could see her defects—catalog her flaws?

"You are the opposite side of the coin," he murmured. "The perfect woman to take her place for a time."

"Perfect," she said. Her tone was clipped, and she stopped her pacing to face him. "To threaten and use and discard."

She was a sleek, slim hourglass through the mist of her gown.

"Is that it?" she asked and stepped close. Anger snapped in her eyes.

"I may have threatened," he said. "But you are the one who has actually struck. And as for using you . . ." He shrugged, trying to relax, trying to remember his mission. He had failed as Sedonia's soldier, but he would not fail the princess. His renewed determination did no good, however, for every muscle was cranked tight, waiting to be set loose. "'Tis you who will gain a small fortune from this encounter. Not to mention a bevy of mismatched socks and buttons."

She drew herself up. "I am no whore."

He felt surprise raise his brows. "I didn't say you were."

"But you did not bed her."

"What?"

"You did not bed the princess," she hissed. "And 'tis not because you did not wish to. Admit it."

"I—"

"You did not bed her because she is pure. She is nobility. She is all that is good."

"Never did I—"

She raised her hand to stop him. "But I—" She paced again, watching him the whole while. "I am naught but a thief or so you believe. Therefore, I am free for the taking."

Something ground in his stomach, an odd mix of anger and guilt and roaring frustration. "If you recall, lass, I did not take you."

"No." She stopped again. "And why, my lord? Because you respect me? Because I am a lady? Because I am innocent?"

And suddenly he wanted the truth, needed the truth, though the thought of another touching her made him feel strangely uncontrolled and somewhat nauseous. "Are you?" he asked.

She laughed. "Aye, Govner," she said, and tossed her wild hair over her shoulder. "I be as innocent as a babe, that is why you're willing to sacrifice me, is it not?"

He almost reached out. Almost grabbed her and pushed her onto the bed and did all his body screamed for, but he was still a viscount, by God. "You should save such drama for the stage, lass."

"Aye," she said. "Perhaps I will. Actresses and thieves—they are on the same level in your mind. Are they not?"

"I've not harmed you, girl. Indeed, I have given you much."

"Yes," she agreed, and pursed her lips. "And I have lived up to our bargain. But I will give no more, even if you wish to make me a poor substitute for her."

He shook his head. She was miles from the truth. Leagues. He stepped forward, wanting to hold her or shake her or do a thousand things he could neither name nor admit to. But she stepped quickly back.

"Stay out of my chambers," she ordered. "I am not your beloved Tatiana."

Her delicate body was mistily visible through her gossamer gown, her lush hair swept her shoulders like wilding waves, but it was her eyes that held him captive. They snapped with life, with smoldering passion.

"No, you are not," he said, and stepped forward again, but in that instant she snatched a candle from its stand and held it toward him like a lance.

"Get out," she ordered.

"Listen, lass, I did not mean to—"

"Get out," she repeated, "or I shall scream."

Anger and frustration boiled like venom in his gut. "You

would be wise to remember that I have made you what you are."

"No," she said and firelight shone on her sardonic smile. "God and circumstances have made me what I am, *Nicol*, you have made me what you would like me to be."

God's balls, she was beautiful. Like a wildcat protecting her den. Like an innocent maid defending her honor. "You are wrong," he said, and took another step toward her.

She brandished the candlestick, oblivious of the wax that splashed hot droplets onto the carpet. "What would they think of a viscount who forced his way into the princess's royal bedchamber?"

He canted his head and searched for the humor in the situation. He was certain it was there somewhere. "You are not the princess, lass."

"But they don't know that, do they?"

He watched her—the light in her eyes, the passion in her soul. Never in all his life had he seen anything as irresistible. "They must be blind," he murmured.

"What?" She lowered the candle a few inches, casting the light upward to shadow her eyes and the delicate hollows of her cheeks.

"Good night, my lady," he said, and, bowing extravagantly, left the room.

Chapter 17

Megan did her best to avoid Nicol on the following day, and it was damnably easy. He didn't meet her for breakfast, nor did he seek her out during the afternoon. She was left to deal with decorators and tailors, preening lords, and hovering ladies. It was so much easier than avoiding inebriated sailors and lecherous landlords, but still she felt out of sorts, fidgety, and irritable. Thus, she finally sought the privacy of her borrowed bedchambers. Her ladies-in-waiting deposited her there, but Mary didn't leave at once. Instead, she curtsied in the doorway.

"What gown will you wear for the party this evening, Your Majesty?" she asked.

"Party?" Megan repeated. She was usually more careful to act informed, more crafty, but she was weary and Mary was easy to talk to.

"Lord Melville's birthday celebration. Surely you remember."

"Yes, of course," Megan said, and she did. There had been

some passing detail about yet another festivity. "He's rented a boat, I believe."

"A yacht, Your Majesty. Everyone shall be there."

She felt tired and strangely worn. "Then I hope 'tis a big yacht."

Mary laughed, but it was impossible to tell, even with her, if her humor was faked or real. Being a princess was a tricky business. Everyone wished to be in your presence, but how many wished to be your friend?

"Lord Melville is very wealthy," Mary said, retrieving a pair of discarded slippers. "You'll wish to look your best."

"Aye, unlike if he were poor."

Mary looked at her askance, her fair brow troubled. "Is something amiss, Your Majesty?"

"No," she said, and allowed herself a sigh. " 'Tis just. . . . Do you ever feel as if you are naught but a pet lamb?"

"A lamb, Your Majesty?" She was already drawing a gown from a nearby trunk and turned to glance over her shoulder.

"Yes, coddled and stroked until the day before the feast."

Shock crossed her plump face. "Your Majesty, all of your realm adores you."

Megan found her feet and paced. "All of my realm does not know me, Mary."

"But they adore you still."

"Nay," she corrected. "But perhaps they adore an image of me."

"You are the height of femininity and beauty, the epitome of breeding and good taste."

"Yes." She caught a glimpse of herself in a gilded mirror and stopped to stare in fascination. "That I am." But should a princess not be more? Did Tatiana give them more?

"Come, Your Majesty," Mary said, and motioned to a stool set before a small table. "Sit down. I will dress your hair. It will make you feel better."

So Megan sat down, and it did make her feel better. Is that what nobles did then? Did they diddle their time away, knowing they could do some good, knowing they could make a change? Did they merely drown their minds until the urge to *do* went away?

By the time Megan stepped out into the open air of the courtyard it was well into the afternoon. She was handed into a carriage by Lord Riven, who bowed and smiled at her thanks. The vehicle was polished to an ebony sheen and carried by a quartet of white steeds that gleamed in the spring sunlight. Her ladies, dressed in a fashionable array of pastels, arranged themselves around her as her guards took their stations outside.

The afternoon air felt soft and delectable, even a bit warm for the long, tight sleeves of her gown. The neckline was laced and starched. The slim skirt started just below her breasts and fell in an elegant drape to her slippers. A floor-length pleat bisected the apricot satin of the gown and boasted two long lines of miniature pearls. Even her headdress, a small, sharp cap of the same fabric, was emboldened with a host of ivory-colored sea jewels. But it was the necklace that took Megan's breath away. Crafted of gold links, it was hung with an emerald the size of her thumb and could alone, easily pay for the inn she had coveted for so long.

The ride to the docks was smooth but slow, for it seemed she was hardly the only one journeying to the sea. Indeed, nearly a dozen vehicles rolled along behind hers and a bevy of horses joined the throng. Through the phaeton's narrow window, she searched the assemblage until she realized she was looking for a certain viscount, at which time she settled back, wishing she had a book, but finally entertaining herself by tallying the value of the gems on her person. The ladies beside her tittered on, then exclaimed in soft voices when they pulled to a halt.

Outside the carriage, rows of shops and pavilions lined the thoroughfare. Megan glanced at them, then turned to look at the seafront. It was still a good half mile away, but when she commented she was reminded that she always shopped at Hollyfaire when traveling to the docks.

A liveried servant opened the door and bowed with a flourish. Lord Riven rushed forward for the honor of helping her dismount, and the afternoon commenced. She could hardly complain. After all, she was the princess, beautiful and wealthy and adored.

Her entourage surrounded her, entertaining her with their wit and complimenting her taste. She could do nothing wrong, but out of the corner of her eye she saw Nicol. Still mounted on his burnished chestnut, he was watching her from the far side of the street.

She stiffened and turned toward him. He gave her a nod, and she swiveled away, trying to be sucked back into the pleasure of the facade, but it was not so easy, not when she continued to feel his gaze on her long after she knew he was gone.

The merchants, on the other hand, were giddy with pleasure. It was not every day that dozens of nobles milled in their midst, not every day that scores of wealthy lords and ladies came with naught to do with their fortunes but spend it foolishly and often. Even Lord Paqual had accompanied the entourage, but perhaps that wasn't surprising. After all, Lord Melville was reputedly wealthy, and by all accounts Paqual hoped to secure a financially favorable match for Sedonia's maiden princess. But she had only Nicol's word to make her suspect the man's intentions were less than honorable. It was hardly a crime to try to better the country's outlook by finding Tatiana a good match. In fact, there was probably not a royal family in all of Europe who did not do the same. Perhaps it was Nicol whose intentions were suspect. Perhaps it was he who did not have Tatiana's best interests in mind. Maybe he had sent her to Teleere in the hopes that she would realize she had left behind the man who loved her. Or maybe he had sent her away in the hopes that she would never return. Megan had no way of knowing. Turning slightly, she scanned the crowd.

Her entourage had fanned out, bargaining and flirting and laughing. And there, some distance away, she saw him again. He was talking to a bonny lass who stood behind the counter of a cloth merchant's stand. The girl's cheeks were flushed and her eyes bright as she looked into his face.

It was the scream that tore Megan's attention aside.

"No! Thief! Stop him!"

Megan searched wildly for the source of the scream. There. An elderly lady who clasped her throat, her eyes wide as saucers, and through the crowd, like a nimble-footed billy, a tattered boy was weaving and bobbing. For one breathless moment he was visible, then he was gone, disappearing behind a china shop.

Megan exhaled sharply. Her personal guards had remained with her and none of her elegant hangers-on were inclined to give chase. The boy was safe. But in that instant she heard a howl of agony. She leapt forward before she thought, before she considered. Wrestling her way through the crowd, she careened around the corner of the china shop only to find the boy pressed facedown against the earth. A city guard's foot was planted on the lad's back while his right arm was stretched out and held by another. A second guard raised his gleaming sword into the air.

"Nay!" She screamed the word, but no one noticed her in the hubbub. The boy writhed. The executioner tightened his grip on his weapon's hilt. And she leapt.

"What the bloody 'ell do you think you're doing?"

The mob went absolutely silent. Not a soul moved, and in

that moment Megan realized with breathless terror that she was hanging like a ripe plum on the guard's upraised arm.

"Your Majesty!" The guard's face was as white as the lad's as he dropped his weapon to his side and bowed in confounded reverence.

"Princess." Lord Paqual hurried through the crowd, his lips drawn back in an indefinable expression. "Are you safe?"

"He was . . ." What exactly had she said? And how had she said it? She licked her lips and scanned the crowd. The expressions were stunned and eager, but if there was sympathy there she could not discern it. "He's just a child," she murmured.

"What goes on here?" Paqual asked, skimming the scene until his gaze landed on the boy.

"My necklace. He stole it. Ripped it right off my throat." The elderly lady's voice bobbled as she slipped through the masses. Her face looked as green as her gown. Beside her, a young woman grasped her elbow as if to keep her from toppling face first into the dirt.

"Search him." Paqual's voice was like gravel.

A guard bent to grasp the boy's left hand, but it was empty. Wrestling him onto his back, he searched the ragged pockets, then straightened with a scowl. "It does not seem to be on him, my lord."

"He took it," warbled the victim.

"Perhaps it was another," Megan suggested. The crowd watched her as if she were some foreign intruder. She swallowed and shrugged, doing her best to appear nonchalant. "There is no shortage of ragged waifs at the docks. 'Tis impossible to tell one from the next."

"Nay . . . Your Majesty," said lady, and curtsied. Catherine. Her name was Lady Catherine. "I saw him clearly. It is he."

"Check the lining of his coat," Paqual ordered.

The guard patted about, slowed his movements, then

straightened. A square-cut ruby dangled on a string of gold from his blunt fingers.

Megan's stomach lurched, and for a moment she thought she might actually vomit. She wanted to hide, to run away. Surely they knew the truth. She was nothing but a lowly thief herself. Nothing but an impostor. The entire assemblage was watching her. She could feel their hungry gazes devouring her. Her knees felt week, her hands clammy, but she straightened her back and raised her chin. "He's only a lad," she repeated.

"That may well be, Your Highness," agreed Paqual, "but he is a thieving lad, and bold." He swept a bony hand in a circle, indicating the company in which they stood. "Not even afraid to steal from the cream of society. Not even afraid of your own esteemed person." He bowed his head perfunctorily. "What if he had harmed you, Your Majesty?" He looked pale at the very thought, but then he always looked pale.

There were murmurs of assent.

The ancient chancellor took a step toward the boy, who tried to scramble away. But the guard still held him by the arm and drew him roughly to his feet.

"The very thought hurts my heart," said Paqual, and put a hand to his chest.

"He did not harm me," Megan said, and hoped to God they could not see her knees quaking through the gown's sheer fabric. "As you can see I am whole and hale."

"But we may not be so lucky next time, Your Majesty. If he goes unpunished, he will only grow bolder. But if his punishment is severe and immediate, he will be an example to others."

Her stomach roiled at the thought. "He will most likely be dead, Lord Paqual."

He shrugged. "Life is sometime harsh, my princess." He used the endearment with a smile. "As you know, Sedonian justice is quick and true. If the boy forfeits a hand, he will be less likely to steal in the future."

"If he loses a hand, he will be less likely to survive for the future."

The old man smiled. "You would be surprised how resilient these young brigands are."

She glanced at the boy again. His cheeks were gaunt and little darker than the enormous whites of his eyes.

"We must uphold our country's standards. I did not make the law. Nor did your uncle, the king. But neither did he see fit to change it," Paqual continued.

The boy struggled again, but there was no hope there. He was outnumbered and outmaneuvered.

Panic swelled inside her, suffocating her. She scanned the crowd. Surely they wouldn't let this happen. Surely. But not a soul moved to forestall it. And who was she? An interloper. An impostor. And if they found out, her fate would be worse than the lad's. Perhaps he would survive the loss of his hand. Perhaps . . . She glanced at him and found that he was staring at her, breathlessly watching in petrified horror.

"Then I shall change it," she said.

Murmurs echoed through the crowd.

"What's that, Your Majesty?"

"Release the boy." She was surprised to hear her own words.

"Release him!" Paqual actually laughed, and with that harsh sound, she felt her back stiffen.

"Do you defy me, my lord?"

"No." He bowed slightly, barely bending his back. "Surely not, Your Majesty, but this is not your decision to make. The Council of the Realm made the law long years ago and—"

"And the sovereign ruler has every right to release one prisoner." The crowd parted as Nicol pressed his way through.

Relief flooded Megan, but when she turned toward the viscount, she saw that the baron of Landow was stepping to the fore, not exactly as if he wished to, but as if he were being silently urged.

"That may be," Paqual said. "But our princess, as beloved as she is, is not yet the sovereign ruler. Not until she weds."

"Which will surely be soon the way you are throwing foppish swains—" Nicol began, but Lord Landow stepped in front of him, interrupting as he did so.

"Why not keep the boy safe until she marries, my lord, then she can decide if she still wishes to give him immunity."

"Keep him safe." Paqual scanned the faces around him. "Where do you have in mind? Devil's Garden? 'Twould be kinder to hang him now. Or do you plan to take him to Landow with you, my lord?"

"Yes." The crowd actually gasped, but no one was more surprised than Megan that Nicol had spoken. "Lord Landow can take the child into his care." She glanced at the baron, but his bored gaze was steady on Nicol. "Landow is certainly large enough to hold one small lad, and close enough to the palace for the princess to check on his progress if she so wishes."

The guard called Allard bowed. "Your Majesty," he began, and his tone was actually pained. "You cannot trust this boy."

"And I do not," she said solemnly. "I trust you to keep me safe from him."

He bowed again, looking pale.

"The princess has spoken," Paqual declared, and turned brusquely toward the baron. "Lord Landow." His smile was almost earnest now. "It seems you will be entertaining a small houseguest."

The nobleman nodded as if it did not matter to him either way. "I will take my young ward then and be on my way," he said, and turned into the crowd.

Paqual motioned toward a city guard. "Take the boy to

Landow," he said, but Allard stepped forward in his stead and took the boy's arm in a firm grip. No one argued.

"I will accompany them," Megan said.

The crowd sounded as if it could not possibly bare another shock.

"Your Majesty!" argued Paqual. "Surely you do not intend to—"

"I will ride in my own coach, of course," she said. "But I no longer feel up to celebrating. Indeed . . ." She forced a rough laugh and held out her hand. It shook without any acting on her part. "I am quite unnerved."

"Then I shall accompany you," said Paqual.

"No. Please." Stepping forward, she laid a gloved hand on his arm and smiled into his face. "I need you to be there in my stead as you so often have."

He was weakening. "But Your Majesty—"

"I know I ask a great deal of you, but we dare not offend Lord . . ." For the briefest moment she could not find his name. Was Paqual looking at her oddly? Panic swelled up in her again. She brightened her smile. "There you see," she said. "I can barely remember Lord Melville's name after such an ordeal. I would be little good there."

His expression softened. "Very well, Your Majesty," he said, and bowed.

"'Tis clear why my uncle valued you so," she said, and, turning away, escaped back to her carriage.

Chapter 18

Will sat his steed in absolute silence.

"It was the right thing to do," Nicol assured him. "I could hardly take the lad to Newburn. Can you imagine Mrs. Melrose rearing a child?" He almost shivered at the thought.

Will said nothing. Indeed, he gave no indication whether he had heard, and Nicol, already out of sorts, chaffed at the silence.

"They were going to cut off the boy's hand, for God's—"

"Who is she?" Will's voice was deep and low, barely audible in the waning light.

"What?" Nicol asked.

Will turned toward him. Perhaps he was drunk, but perhaps it didn't matter. His eyes were steady and dark. "Who is she, Cole?"

"I don't know what you're referring to."

Will turned forward again, watching the businesses fade to houses. "When I first saw her in the woods I believed she was the princess. I believed you had finally lost your mind and taken her as your lover. But it seems even you are not that foolish."

"You're drunk, Will," Nicol said, and the baron sighed.

"Usually," he agreed. "Who is she?"

"Once you get some sleep you'll realize—"

"I stepped forward when you asked," Will said coldly. "I am, it seems, even taking the ragged urchin into my house. The least you could do is tell me the truth."

Their gazes clashed. "Forget what you think you know, Will. 'Tis safer that way."

"Safer," Will said and laughed, but the sound was harsh. "You think I care to be *safe*?"

"It was a long time ago, Will," Nicol said. "Two years. 'Tis time to put their deaths behind you. Forget—"

But in that second the baron reached out and grabbed Nicol by his lapel. "Do not suggest that I forget."

Nicol watched his face, watched the pain and regret chase like demons through his eyes, but the baron finally dropped his hand and his gaze.

"The princess is safe," Nicol said. "That is all I can tell you."

Will remained silent as he pulled his mount to a halt. Up ahead, Landow House loomed high above shabby gardens. Behind them the guard dismounted, dragging a tattered boy with him, and behind that the princess's carriage rolled to a halt.

Will turned his gaze back to Nicol and swung down from his saddle. "I hope you know what you're doing."

"As do I."

Striding to the carriage, Nicol bowed as Megan was handed out of the conveyance, but she gazed past him toward Will. "My lord Landow," she said, "where do you plan to keep the child?"

She held her gown just so, ignoring Nicol entirely, acting

as if he weren't even there. He had taught her that cool disdain, had taught her how to walk, how to talk.

"Indeed, Your Majesty," said Will, and bowed, "I fear I've had little time to formulate a plan, but I shall find him a room."

She gave him an approving nod and motioned to the guard. "Bring the boy to the house," she said, and, pacing past Nicol, made her way up the footpath toward Will's door.

Perhaps it was her high-handedness that incensed Nicol, or perhaps it was the thought of her risking her identity in front of Paqual, risking everything. He fell in beside her, his strides long, his ire burning. "What the devil do you think you're doing?" he asked.

If she felt the least bit of consternation for his tone, it didn't show in her expression. "I am not exactly sure, my lord," she said, "but some might say I am saving a life."

"By risking your own?"

"Is it my life you worry about, my lord?" she asked. "Or hers?"

He knew she meant Tatiana's.

"Yours would be the first forfeit," he said.

"Or yours," she countered

"I hope that's not a good enough reason to sacrifice your own."

"They were about to cut off his hand," she hissed.

"He's a thief."

"So, you condone their behavior?"

She stopped dead in her tracks. He forced a smile and bowed as if they exchanged some witty bit of repartee. "No," he said, and, daring to take her elbow, turned her back toward the house. "I do not condone it, but you might have been found out." The source of his anger burst out finally. "Dammit, girl, this is no fine game we play for your entertainment. This—"

"You think I believe this a game?" She jerked her head to the rear, eyes blazing. "You think *he* believes this a game?"

He tried to formulate an answer, but she was still enraged.

"The boy is starving. Do you know what that's like, Viscount?" She said his title with sharp disdain, silencing him. "Have you felt the bite of hunger? Do you know what you would do to be rid of the pain?"

Anger burned through him, but it was washed with guilt now, with chagrin. He reached for her elbow again. For a moment he thought she would jerk away, but she allowed him to usher her down the walkway in silence.

Will passed them, swinging the door open and bowing them in.

"My—" An elderly woman stopped in her tracks, her eyes as round as her face.

"Your Majesty," Will said, "may I present Mrs. Angler, the keeper of my house?"

The plump little woman looked as if she might keel over backward. Instead, she sank into a curtsy from which she had difficulty recovering. Behind her, a half dozen other servants were piling up like bent lettuce leaves.

"We will be having a guest, Mrs. Angler."

It didn't appear as if the good woman's eyes could go any wider, but Nicol had learned sometime ago that appearances could be deceiving.

"Not her— Not—" Angler stuttered.

"No. Not Her Majesty," Will said, and, bowing to Megan, motioned her toward a chair in the nearby morning room.

She brushed past them, wafting lavender scent and an air of dismissal, but she did not take the seat indicated. "Mrs. Angler," she said, and inclined her head ever so little, "there will be a child staying here at Landow House with you."

"A—A—"

"A young boy," she said. "Can you care for a young boy?"

"Yes, Your Majesty. It will be my pleasure, Your Majesty."

"He will need a place to sleep. New clothes, and . . ." She glanced at Nicol. Beneath the elegant gown, her back was actually arched in regal demeanor. Perhaps he had seen her angry before, but now her eyes were afire. "And a tutor I think. Lord Newburn will pay for these things."

"Yes, Your—"

"Your Highness," Will interrupted and bowed. "If I am to be the boy's guardian, I should be the one to pay the bills."

She stared at him. "Thank you, my lord, but that is not necessary. Lord Newburn will be happy to see to those costs."

Lord Landow inclined his head, but did not smile.

Megan shifted her gaze back to the housekeeper. "The lad will require a meal immediately."

"Yes. Yes, Your Majesty," stuttered Mrs. Angler, and, turning breathlessly to the servants behind her, sent them scurrying off in a dozen different directions.

"Lord Landow." She turned to the baron, her expression as cool as etched glass. Nicol watched in fascination. When he created a monster, he sure as hell did so with panache. "Might you have somewhere we could speak to the boy?"

"My wife had a tea-room," he informed her, and led the way down the hall.

"My ladies," she said, speaking to the wide-eyed duo behind her. "You may remain here. I shall return shortly. "Allard, take the boy to the tea-room."

Stern-faced and silent, the guard herded his unwilling ward down the hallway after Will. Megan followed, and Nicol followed her. The boy shuffled stiffly inside. His pants, Nicol noticed, were several inches too short, showing pale bony ankles and amazingly filthy feet. Pulled away from his shoulders by the guard's fist, his misplaced coat revealed a tattered tunic and collarbones sharp enough to cut glass.

The boy stilled as Brigitte entered the room. She walked to

the far side and turned to face him, and he squirmed a little under her gaze.

"What is your name, lad?" she asked.

A myriad of emotions charged across the boy's dirt-streaked face. There was not a single one Nicol could identify, but in a moment the lad dropped his head toward the floor and squeezed his eyes shut.

"I'm sorry." The words were the tiniest whisper. He went limp and hung suddenly from Allard's fist like a shriveled winter pear. Caught unawares, the guard tried to catch his balance and pull the boy back onto his feet, but the lad twisted about, covering his face with grimy hands. "Don't 'it me. Please don't 'it me."

Megan was silent for a moment, then, "Release him, Allard."

"But—"

"Release him," she repeated, and the guard did so, letting the boy spill to the floor. "You may retire to the hallway and shut the door, but keep watch there until I join you."

"Your Highness, please, I do not think—"

And then she smiled. Perhaps Allard had never seen the princess smile, and perhaps one should be prepared for such a shock, for he seemed stunned by its brilliance.

"I appreciate your loyalty," she said. "Indeed, it means more to me than I can say, but I am certain I will be safe so long as you guard the far side of that door."

It took the poor fellow a moment to regroup, longer still to nod and retreat, but soon the room was empty except for the four of them, an interesting quartet of miscreants. A whimpering thief, a drunken baron, a princess who was not, and himself—perhaps the biggest fraud of them all.

Megan turned her attention to Will, then snapped her gaze to Nicol, and he knew immediately what she considered.

Nodding once, he didn't bother to glance at the baron.

"You can trust him," he said simply. "With your life and more."

She turned back to the boy. He was half-sprawled on the floor, his skinny legs curled under him, his hands splay-fingered in front.

"Stand up, lad."

"Please, Your Majesty . . ." he pleaded, and managed to get himself even lower, but she cut him off before he'd finished the thought.

"Who do you work for?"

His head came up with a snap. "Work for?"

"Yes." She was still the princess, her bearing regal, her tone precise, and yet there was something a bit different about her, elegance with an edge.

"I don't work for no one, m' lady. I wouldn't never steal, not if I could make honest coin."

"So you steal ruby necklaces on your own? Who sells your goods for you then?"

His mouth opened. "I don't know what you mean, m' lady."

"So you intended to keep a bauble worth a thousand sentrons for yourself?"

"A thousand!" His tone was awed. "God's teeth, I didn't 'ave no way a knowin' it was worth such a fortune. A thousand sentrons. I could buy me old da a decent room for that. I could . . ." A single tear wended its way down his cheek, leaving a trail through the grime. "I could afford 'is medicine and get 'is job back at the—"

"Oh for God's sake, cease!" she demanded, and rose rapidly to her feet.

The boy's jaw dropped again.

"Stand up," she ordered.

He did so and though his expression was still woeful, there was a glint of caution in his eyes.

"What's your name?" she asked again.

He paused just a moment. "Some call me Jack."

"What does your master call you?"

"Me master?" He shook his head, scowling as he did so. "I don't 'ave no—"

"Allard," she called.

The door opened with a snap.

"Yes, Your Majesty."

"Take the thief to Lord Paqual. Tell him—"

"Nim!" the boy said.

She turned with cool aplomb back to him. "What say you?"

The boy's gaze darted from face to face, but his back was stiff now, his expression hard. "They call me Nim."

She nodded.

"My apologies, Allard," she said, and turned back toward the guard. "You are excused once again."

He looked momentarily confused and less than happy, but he retreated, closing the door behind him.

The room was absolutely silent.

"Sit down," she ordered.

The boy didn't move, but watched her narrowly as she took a seat near the window. It was then that Nicol wondered about her position. Had she placed herself there on the off chance that the lad would try to escape in that direction? Did she plan to stop him herself? Moving across the room, Nicol took a seat not far from hers.

They watched the boy in silence. He remained as he was, staring at them, his jaw set. It was a strange vision, what with that one tear track down his cheek.

"Why Nim?" she asked.

"What are yer plans fer me?" he countered.

"Where are your parents?"

He glanced toward the window, seeming to calculate his odds before answering. "I ain't got no parents."

"Where do you sleep?"

"Wherever I wants to."

"What percent does your master give you?"

His gaze darted again. "I don't know what you're talkin' about."

"He should be giving you half. When you see him demand fifty percent."

"Fifty!" he scoffed. "Poke'd kill me if—" He stopped short. Silence fell into the room again. The boy went paler still.

"What difference does it make?" Her voice was very soft, and suddenly her face was the same. "If Poke doesn't kill you, someone else will, lad."

He jerked up his chin. "I ain't called Nimble Jack fer nothin'."

"And what if they called you One Hand Jack?"

He swallowed, pulled his gaze from hers, and hugged his arm unconsciously against his narrow chest. "They didn't 'ave me yet." There was bravado in his voice, but there was also the dead edge of fear.

"A one-handed thief would not be of much use to a man like Poke."

"I'm better with one 'and than most is with two. 'E knows that."

"You might have to start whoring."

The boy's eyes went absolutely flat as he slipped his gaze from hers to the men's. "What kind o' queen is she?"

Nicol shook his head. "A princess," he corrected. "Perhaps you should listen to her."

The lad's eyes skipped back to her. His pale lips were pursed, but in a moment, he nodded solemnly. "What do y' want?"

She watched him for several seconds. "I would like you to grow to manhood."

He narrowed his eyes even more. "I ain't that kind," he said. "Not even for a princess."

Her face was solemn, her eyes sad. "How long have you been on the streets?"

"Long enough to know to keep meself to meself," he said, and took a step toward the window.

Nicol shook his head. "Don't try it, lad. She'll toss you across the room before you could wrench it open."

"I ain't 'orin' for no one!" said the boy.

"I thought you had been around, Nim." Her voice was soft, but her expression was not.

He flashed his gaze back to Megan. "I been."

She stared at him in silence for a long moment. "Then you should be a better judge of people."

"What do y' mean?"

"I'm not going to harm you."

The room fell silent, then, "Why not?"

It was the strangest question Nicol had ever heard, an odd reverse of the norm.

"Have you never heard of mercy?"

"I 'eard of it," he said. "But I 'eard of Father Christmas, too, and 'e ain't done me much good either."

She almost smiled. "Maybe he's been busy elsewhere."

"Yeah. With them rich kids what live in Oakland Square."

"Do you think you could learn to read?"

"Why would I want to?"

"So you could learn. So you could live to reach . . ." Her eyes flared with emotion. Perhaps she was remembering his aversion to the word "manhood" or perhaps the irony of the situation was not lost on her. After all, she had been in the same situation not so long before. "Adulthood," she said. "So you could become gainfully employed. So you could learn a skill. Maybe become a miller or a silversmith."

"And make jewelry." He laughed. "Me?"

She watched him in silence. "Stranger things have happened, have they not, Lord Nicol?"

"They have," he agreed.

She turned toward him. A spark of a smile lit her verdant eyes. "We shall call it poetic justice," she said, and Nicol realized in that moment that if she asked him to walk on water, he would take a deep breath and step off the dock.

"What makes you think the lad will stay here?" Will asked, his voice low.

She thought for a moment, then called for the guard. It took him no longer to respond than the first time. "Allard." She said his name like an endearment. Where had she learned such a thing? "You will be staying at Landow with the boy."

He looked as if he would object, but he finally nodded. "Yes, Your Majesty." A pause. "May I ask why, Your Majesty?"

She rose to her feet with fairylike grace. "Because the boy is going to be something great someday. He merely needs you to help him find his path."

Nicol escorted her out of the tea-room, down the long hallways, where her slippers sighed against the worn carpet and out into the cool night air. A few droplets of rain sprinkled down on them as they maneuvered the cobbled footpath.

"Will you be accompanying me back to the palace, Nicol?" she asked.

Her ladies followed behind. Her guards were behind them.

"I think it best if I speak to Will for a time," he said.

"He must owe you a great deal," she said. "To be willing to take in Nimble Jack."

There was deep emotion in her voice, and in that foolish moment he wanted nothing more than to take her into his arms and kiss her. "Not this much."

She glanced at him.

"Will's wife and son were killed by highwaymen."

She sobered, and with that change of expression he felt his heart mourn. "I am sorry."

"I shall tell him."

"And I'm sorry if I compromised your plan. It was not my intent."

"Wasn't it?"

She glanced up at him, and the sadness was gone, replaced by a spark of anger that made him feel marginally better. "I did not ask to be a princess," she reminded him.

"No." They were at her carriage, and he turned toward her. In the gathering darkness, her face looked as pale and perfect as an angel's. He bowed, raising her hand to his lips. The sensation sizzled through him, and though he told himself to draw away, he found that he could not immediately manage to free her fingers, could not immediately manage to let her go no matter who looked on. Behind them, her entourage remained absolutely silent. He smiled, and released her hand with stern self-reproach. "You did not ask to be princess," he agreed, and, locking his hands behind his back, took a cautious step to the rear, putting space between them, hoping for strength he was certain he had once possessed. How amusing. "But one cannot fight one's true self."

She scowled at him, but he motioned for her footmen, who handed her inside.

In a moment the door closed behind her, and then she was gone—the princess and the thief and his heart.

Chapter 19

"**Y**our Majesty." The viscount bowed. "I trust you slept well."

Megan nodded, ignoring her breakfast for a moment. She couldn't seem to adjust to either the succulent meals or the late hour at which they were served. Noon had already come and gone.

"Well enough," she said, and motioned to the seat across the table from her. "Sit and tell me of Jack."

"He is well, Your Majesty."

There seemed to be something lacking in his answer, so she raised her gaze. "And Lord Landow's home?"

He shrugged. "Thus far it has survived."

She raised a brow.

"It seems the lad has an aversion to bathing."

"Does he?" She almost laughed.

She set her cup back onto her saucer. The edges of both were gilt and the china itself as delicate as lace. She wondered vaguely if they would fit in her pocket. "But he did not escape?"

"No. But 'twas not for lack of trying."

She looked across the grand hall. Elegant loungers sipped tea and flirted, most of them still inebriated from the previous night. Apparently Melville's party had been a roaring success, offering endless libations, caviar on tiny bits of toast, and a red Indian from the Americas. And meanwhile, across town, one small lad tried desperately to return to a life that would eventually kill him.

"Why?"

She brought her attention back to the viscount. "What say you?"

"Why would he wish to leave?" Nicol asked again, and she sighed.

"Pimps and thieves' masters are not known for their understanding natures." She fell silent as a servant bowed before refilling her gilded cup, then continued. "If the boy doesn't return soon, Poke will assume his star thief has taken his ill-gained goods elsewhere."

"Then would it not be best for the lad to remain at Landow where he is safe?"

"Is there a reason for him to believe he is safe with a nobleman who detests his kind?"

"Just because a man is titled, doesn't necessarily mean he is untrustworthy."

Their gazes met and held. There was something in his voice, almost a plea, but she broke from the trance and cleared her throat as she fiddled with her spoon. She couldn't help but notice it was solid silver.

"Perhaps Lord Landow was not the best choice for the lad's guardian."

"I would have taken the task," he said, "but Paqual already frets over your alliance with me. I didn't wish to make it seem that I would risk my home on a whim for you. He doesn't trust me."

She sipped her tea and said nothing.

"And what of you?" Nicol's voice was low, as if he hadn't meant to speak. "Do you trust me, lass?"

She refused to look at him, for the feelings evoked by his presence were too raw, too foolish. "I trust you to do what is best for your Anna."

Silence stretched out between them. She could feel his gaze on her.

"Tell me, will you be happy when you are no longer the princess?"

"I am not the princess," she murmured. "Pretense does not make it so."

"Doesn't it?"

She found his gaze. His eyes were deep and somber.

"In two days' time I will return to my old life," she said. "And you shall see your princess again.

Heat streaked through his eyes. "And what of you?"

She canted her head the slightest degree, a gesture that had replaced her usual shrug. "The pauper? I will be that much richer."

"Lass—"

From the doorway, a bevy of voices rose in greeting.

"We can hardly afford to let Paqual become suspicious now."

"There are times," he murmured, "when you seem to be the exact replica of Anna, but there are other times . . ." His voice faded. "When I believe there is none in the world like you."

Their eyes met, somber on somber. Paqual's footfalls echoed across the floor and she tilted her mouth up the slightest degree.

"Nicol," she said. "Surely you jest. Two clever rakes such as you and the baron will have no difficulty controlling one small lad."

"Your Majesty," Paqual said, and bowed.

"Don't you agree, my lord?" she asked, turning to the old man.

His lips narrowed. "I fear I must respectfully add my caution once again, Your Majesty," he said. "For while I appreciate your boundless mercy, I myself must think of your protection."

"I don't believe one small boy could possibly harm me here in the splendor of Malkan Palace. 'Tis not as if I am eking out a mean living on the streets of Skilan."

An odd look flashed through Paqual's eyes, but he bowed again, and when he straightened, his expression was all but pained. "Please, my princess, do not speak so flippantly, for life can be unpredictable and hideously short, even for God's chosen one."

"God's chosen one," she repeated.

"Yes, Your Majesty. Surely, you know 'tis true."

For a moment she was tempted almost beyond control to argue, but she could feel Nicol's eyes on her and dropped her gaze to her plate. "Yes, my lord," she agreed. "God and you have been kind."

The dinner dishes were being cleared away as bowls of Cumberland pudding were distributed. Nicol glanced down the dinner table toward Megan. She looked radiant tonight, refined and feminine and too beautiful for words. Sometimes, when he wasn't careful, he almost forgot who she was. Sometimes it almost seemed as if she had been born to this place, had been bred to sit on the throne of queens, and then, without his permission, his mind would slip back to a moment when she was not Tatiana Octavia Linnet Rocheneau, a time when she was but a slip of a girl with a rapier-sharp wit and hands as quick as lightning. Who was she really, a princess or a thief? Or was she the girl with the soft eyes, the girl who had trembled when she ordered all to spare the lad called Nim. She was as complex as a kaleidoscope, as deep as the tide, and she had almost pulled it off. Had almost fooled the lot of them. Even if Paqual suspected some irregularity, as his repeated gaze seemed to suggest, it would be too late to call foul. In two days' time, the switch would be made. Anna would return from Teleere, and Megan would escape back to her own world.

Turning his attention aside, Nicol scanned the assemblage. The peerage glittered in intoxicated glory, laughing and teasing with noble disregard for either propriety or morals. All but Paqual, who attended to his meal, only glancing now and again at the girl at the head of the table.

Did he watch her with increasing interest? Did he suspect something after the spectacle in the market? Was he surprised that the royal princess would save a common thief from mutilation? And what of Anna, Nicol wondered? Would she have done the same in Megan's place? Would she have braved Paqual's wrath to rescue the boy? Would *he*? Or was the wee thief so much superior to their—

But suddenly Nicol's thoughts were torn asunder. Someone gasped. Beside Megan, Lord Riven jumped to his feet. "God's bones, she's choking!"

"She's been poisoned!" someone screamed. "The princess has been poisoned."

Leaping to his feet, Nicol tore the ogling onlookers aside as he rushed toward the princess's cushioned chair. She was slumped over her dessert, gasping for breath, her hand at her throat.

"Fetch the physician!" he ordered. "Give her room. Stand back."

Wrenching her chair away from the table, he lifted her into his arms. Her breath came in labored gasps. Her face was pale. Hugging her to his chest, he rushed through the crowd.

"Send the doctor to her chambers. Mary, come hither. For God's sake, people, get out of my way." They parted reluctantly, and he sprinted up the stairs, taking them two at a time until he reached her bed. Setting her gently upon the mattress, he motioned Mary forward to loosen the throat of her gown.

"Princess! Your Majesty!" Paqual rasped, out of breath and as pale as death as he charged into the room. "Princess, what is it? What has happened?"

Color was returning slowly to her face, and her breathing sounded less laborious. "Almonds!" she rasped. "In the pudding."

"What—" Nicol began, but Paqual drew himself back with a start.

"Send up the chef."

The physician rushed into the room, his face drawn in lines of worry.

"Your Majesty, can you breathe? Does your chest hurt? When did the symptoms begin?" he chattered, but she waved him back.

"I am well. Just a . . ." She opened her mouth, struggling for air. "Just a minor attack."

"Your Majesty," Paqual said, "please let him examine you so that I may rest assured—"

"Give me room," she ordered weakly, and they did, all but Mary, who helped her mistress sit and pressed a glass of water to her lips.

The other ladies-in-waiting fluttered helplessly about by the wall. The doctor scowled. The guards stood at attention by the door, stiff as lances, and in a moment, a dark, squat man rushed into the room.

Paqual turned toward them with the slow venomous grace of a serpent. "Mr. Hunt," he said, facing the master chef, "did you put nuts in the pudding?"

The man's jaw dropped. "Nay. I would never. Nay, Your Majesty," he said, turning frantically toward her. "I know of your aversion to them, and would never—"

"Then the princess has been poisoned," Paqual said.

Hunt dropped to his knees, reaching for Megan's hand as he did so. "No, my princess. I would never betray you. I swear it on my soul."

"Release her," ordered Paqual, and stepped forward, but Megan waved him back.

"If not you, then who?" she asked, sounding stronger.

"No one, Your Majesty, I select the ingredients myself. The flour was freshly ground, the eggs gathered only this—"

But at that moment a lad was ushered into the room. He held a cloth bag in hands that trembled like elder leaves.

Paqual narrowed his eyes at him. "What have you there, boy?"

"I—" The boy's words stuttered to a halt. "I believe— It should be naught but flour."

"What are you saying?"

The boy extended the bag to the chancellor. "It tastes," he said, his voice quavering, "It tastes right. But it has the scent of almonds."

"What nonsense is this?" Paqual demanded.

But the chef rose to his feet. The flush had drained from his face. "Perhaps . . . A few nuts could have been ground with the wheat."

"A few nuts," said the doctor, leaning in.

"Would that be enough to cause the princess such distress?"

The doctor scowled "Her symptoms seem to be lessening. If the nuts were unequally dispersed and she received a large quantity all at once . . ." He shook his head, still scowling.

Paqual turned to the chef, his skin sallow, his eyes intense. "How could this have happened?"

"I know not, my lord. I have served my princess with the utmost care. Just as I have served her uncle, the king. I swear on my life, I—"

"Where did you purchase the flour?" Paqual asked.

"I didn't have— I was so rushed this morning. Breakfast. The duke's arrival— The—"

"Where did you get it?" Paqual repeated.

"'Twas my fault," said the apprentice, his face pale as death. "I fetched the flour."

"Did you not taste it?" rasped Hunt.

"It looked . . . I thought—" the apprentice began, but Hunt interrupted.

"I will leave the palace this very night," he whispered, but the girl raised her chin and watched him in silence for a moment. A tear crept from the corner of his eye, easing its way down his creased cheek. The room went absolutely quiet. The chef shifted his gaze to her and away.

"No," she said finally, "I cannot afford to lose you, Mr. Hunt, not with the duke's upcoming visit. You shall stay at Malkan Palace."

"Yes, Your Majesty." His tears were running in earnest. "Thank you, Your—"

"Your Majesty," Paqual said, "we've no way of knowing if this was some plot against your life. We must at least—"

"A plot?" she said, and managed a brave smile. "I should hope that if my subjects are planning my demise, they will be more clever than to feed me a substance that causes me no more than temporary discomfort."

"Your health is nothing to be laughed about, Your—"

"No, it is not," she said, "and if it will make you feel better you may find a tester to sample my meals."

"I shall do that posthaste, Your Highness, but I must also insist that the apprentice be banned from Skilan."

She scowled as if thinking.

The boy dropped his head.

"From the palace, yes, but not from Skilan," she decided finally.

He didn't even manage a nod as his gaze snapped to hers.

"There is a man in the village who is looking for an apprentice. You shall go there on the morrow and tell him that I sent you."

"A man . . . Y-Your Majesty."

"Yes," she said, "I believe he is a mason."

"Your Majesty, I must insist—" Paqual began, but the girl interrupted him once again.

"If it was poisoning he intended, it will be difficult for him to do so with bricks and mortar," she said.

The ladies tittered nervously, and the boy blinked.

"Thank you," he whispered. "Thank you."

She only nodded.

"Very well. Go now," Paqual ordered, turning toward the cooks. "And do not forget Her Majesty's mercy."

"No, my lord," vowed the aged chef, and disappeared, dragging his erstwhile apprentice behind him.

"Your Majesty . . ." Lord Paqual approached the royal bed slowly, his head slightly bowed. "You are too kind."

She smiled a little. "Perhaps, my lord."

"If word of your compassion spreads, we shall surely be inundated with all manner of rabble ready to take advantage of your generosity." Perhaps it was a smile that lifted his anemic lips.

"Then you shall have no trouble finding someone to test my meals," she suggested.

"Ahh," he said, and, bending, took her hand between his. Her fingers looked as smooth as silk between his gnarled digits. "You gave my old heart a terrible fright, but your levity lifts my spirits."

"And your loyalty lifts mine, Lord Paqual."

"Again, you are too kind."

"I am lucky to have you as my counsel."

"Your uncle would be proud of you."

"I can only hope."

"And now . . ." He patted her hand, then backed regretfully away. "I shall begin my search for a tester."

"Surely it can wait till morning," she argued, but he was already shaking his head.

"Nay, Your Majesty. Nay. I shall not risk you again," he vowed, and departed.

Nicol watched her in silence. His mind was spinning like a dervish. What had made her ill? She couldn't possibly be affected by the same malady as Anna. He had seen her eat her weight in almonds while at Woodlea. So what . . . But in that moment she canted her head and caught his gaze. The truth stormed over him like a tidal wave. She had faked the entire episode. She had remembered his casual mention of Anna's reaction to edible nuts and, when exposed to them, had acted accordingly. God's bones. He was in the presence of a wit greater than his own, and he had no idea if he should be grateful or frightened.

Aye, she had won another match.

Chapter 20

They rode on the following day, and true to simple good fortune, it was Paqual who begged the seemingly recovered princess to ride one of her more docile mounts. After the previous day's terrors, he didn't think his heart could risk another trauma, he said. Thus, Megan acquiesced with royal graciousness, thanking her lucky stars and God that she would not have to mount the devilish gray favored by the princess. Instead, she rode a placid bay, following a pack of hounds at some distance and thrilled to find that she and the aging gelding got on quite well. Lords and ladies dashed past, perched precariously atop four-legged imbeciles, but the bay trotted on at a sedate pace.

Nicol, who had been one of the few to stay behind her, finally rode up on her right.

"'Tis a fine day," he said, eyeing the countryside. It rolled away in awakening signs of spring, bursting with delicate stalks and lacy fronds. The leaves on the hawthorn trees were just peeking out, and high above, on a gnarled, still-bare limb of a wych elm, a warbler sang with heart-wrenching optimism.

"Yes," she agreed, as two young fools galloped past. Nicol's chestnut shook his head and pranced at the restraint, but Megan's remained steady, perfectly content to meander along at its own pace. " 'Tis my own opinion that there is nowhere as lovely as Sedonia in the springtime."

She could feel his attention turn from the impetuous lords, feel him focus on her, feel his mood change. He was a master at hiding his true thoughts.

"A wondrous performance," he said. His voice was casual, unconcerned that they might be overheard, and yet she knew he was referring to the almond incident. So perhaps it was naught but her contrary nature that made her slant him a baffled glance out of the corner of her eye.

"Whatever are you talking about, my lord?"

He gave her a look that suggested he understood her game and was willing to play along. "It seems a bit unlikely that you and Anna share the same aversion to almonds," he said, "especially after consuming a barge of them while at Woodlea."

"Indeed, 'tis strange. Perhaps I ate too many and developed some sort of strange reaction. But it's just as well. Coincidentally, the chef's apprentice wanted to leave the palace anyway. And hiring a tester will give Paqual something to occupy his time," she said, and, seeing a skittish hare poke its head from a nearby hole, drew Nicol's attention to it.

He glanced at the animal without much fascination and turned back to the path before them. "When this first began I didn't expect you to make such a fine politician," he said.

She shrugged. "Perhaps my former occupations have trained me better than you would have suspected."

"So you're admitting you were a thief?"

She gave him a wry glance. "As a *barmaid* I spent a good deal of time pacifying sodden fools and pompous asses."

He flashed a rare smile. Beneath him, his mount pranced

dramatically, but the viscount sat the horse easily. His dark hair gleamed in the sunlight, his capable hands were steady on the reins, and in that moment Megan realized the vast chasm of difference that lay between them. Perhaps to Princess Tatiana he was a lowly underling, but to a bastard lass with no home . . . She turned her face resolutely away.

"Tell me, lass, what will you do when you leave Sedonian shores?"

The thought of her fantasy inn rose mistily in her mind, but she kept the images to herself. He might look like a demigod with the sun in his hair and his sparkling steed prancing beneath him, but he was only a man, and as fallible as any. She would keep her dreams to herself, but suddenly those carefully aged fantasies seemed oddly lacking. "I hope you will not miss me overmuch, my lord," she said, pushing away the disturbing thought.

She felt him turn toward her, felt the warmth of his attention on her face. "Life at court won't be the same without you," he said, and she turned, stunned by the sincerity in his voice.

Their gazes met and melded, but finally he spoke again. "What other irresistible lady is likely to bash me on the head with a wine bottle?"

Irresistible. Her mind twittered, but she kept her expression carefully cool. "I assumed there would be endless applicants, my lord."

The corner of his mouth tilted up the slightest degree. "So you admit you stole my watch, lass?"

"Of course not." Her tone was precisely nonchalant, though in truth, he had caught her unawares. The realization made her feel slightly unbalanced, nervous. She was never unawares. That was how she had survived this long. "Only that I wish to. Strike you, that is."

"Still?" he asked, and there was something in his tone, a seriousness, almost a longing.

But she could afford neither. "More often than not," she assured him.

"I suppose it is just as well then that Anna will be returning tomorrow."

"Tomorrow!" How had she lost track of time? She had been anticipating the princess's return. Indeed, she had been looking forward to it, but now that the time had almost arrived, she felt strangely at odds.

"Aye," he said. "She was to send word if she would be delayed. I've received no message."

Megan turned back to the open countryside. A crofter's cottage sent a silvery stream of smoke wending into the mercurial sky. "Good then," she said. "Our agreement comes to a close."

His gaze remained fixed on her. "You will leave Sedonia quite wealthy."

"Yes," she agreed, and offered no more.

"Perhaps you owe me the courtesy of revealing what you plan to do after leaving the palace."

She shrugged. "Perhaps I will become a princess."

She expected him to laugh, but his tone was serious when he spoke. "The title suits you."

She tried to be flippant, tried to keep her attention on the hills ahead, or on her mount's hirsute crest, or on her own uncertain hands, but finally she skimmed her gaze back to him. "Another compliment, my lord?" she asked.

That smile again, as alluring as a satyr's. "Surely you must have become accustomed to them by now."

"Not from you."

Several furlongs ahead a young buck raced for a fence. The horse maneuvered the obstacle perfectly, but the rider left his mount well before the animal launched from the ground. Nicol seemed entirely nonplussed.

"Would you have me compliment you more, lass?"

She could feel his attention turn back to her, but now did not seem the time to look at him, for she could feel his presence like a tangible object, like a hard force of nature, and try as she might she could think of nothing to say, no witty comeback, no acid set-down. What a poor failure as a noble lady.

"You are incredibly beautiful," he said.

She turned in utter surprise, and the shock must have shown on her face, for he laughed. The low sound rumbled like a stroke of thunder through her belly.

"Surely that cannot surprise you."

"No." She felt breathless and concentrated for a moment on her seat, keeping her back perfectly straight, her legs bent just so. "I suppose it should not, since you went to such pains to make me look exactly like another."

There was a moment's pause, then, "Yes, I did that. I only wonder how I failed so completely."

"Failed?"

"Sometimes . . . now, for instance, you look nothing like Anna."

She wasn't sure why she was angry, but she felt the emotion boil inside her like an evil brew. "I have fooled every one of them."

He canted his head. "Paqual is obviously suspicious of—"

"If I told Paqual I was a turnip, he would prepare the soil and plant me in the kitchen garden," she gritted, and he grinned again, that seductive expression that made her head spin.

"Aye, lass," he agreed finally. His teeth looked ungodly white against the dark skin of his face. "Your beauty is only surpassed by your cleverness. I should have said that *I* see the differences very clearly."

She scowled at him for a moment, feeling her heart pound in her chest, then pulled her gaze carefully from him and concentrated on hauteur. "Be careful, my lord," she said. "I am a surprisingly fragile creature and may very well fall clear from this horse if you startle me with such compliments again."

"Aye," he said, and there was something in his tone that made her turn unwillingly toward him, something that made her chest feel tight. "There have been many surprises, lass. Not the least of which is that I shall miss you when you are gone."

She never knew how she intended to respond, for at that moment a trio of riders galloped up from behind, enveloping them in their group and not allowing her another moment alone with the viscount.

He waited until well past the stroke of two to enter the princess's royal bedchamber. When Anna returned he would have to insist that she keep guards at her door, he thought, and stepped silently into her room.

She slept on her side, facing him, and though he sat upon the mattress for some time watching her serene expression, she did not awaken. Finally, he reached out. Her cheek looked irresistibly soft, but he veered off at the last moment, and touched her shoulder.

"Lass."

She sighed in her sleep.

"Megan," he said, and she awoke with a start.

"No!" she gasped, but he covered her mouth and whispered a reassurance. In a moment he felt her relax and removed his hand.

"Don't you ever sleep?" she asked, and scooted into a sitting position. Her hair was disheveled, her eyes half-closed.

"This will be the last time I wake you," he said.

"Promise?" She sounded more than irritable.

"Anna returns today."

"Yes. I remember." He no longer could guess what her tone implied.

"We'll have to be very careful during the exchange, lest Paqual become suspicious."

"I thought I had resolved that problem."

"He seems mollified now, but he's a suspicious man by nature. I should have foreseen the fact that he would plan a test for you. I'm sure it was no great difficulty planting the almonds in the flour."

She scowled and fiddled with the lace on the bedsheet's edge.

He watched her atypical fidgeting for a moment, then scowled. "What is it?" he asked.

"Perhaps there is something I should tell you."

Nervousness cranked up. "What?"

She cleared her throat. " 'Twas I who put the nuts in the flour."

"You! Why?"

She shrugged, looking defensive and ridiculously small. "Paqual was watching me."

"Watching— You are the princess. Everyone watches you."

"It was different," she argued. "Since the episode with Jack, he never seemed to turn his eyes away."

"So you brought almonds into the palace? What kind of idiotic stunt was that? What if someone found out? How could you—"

She shot to her feet. "I am the princess," she said, stabbing her forefinger toward his nose. "There is nothing I cannot do." And in that moment, even with her hair disheveled and her nightgown askew, none could argue.

So he calmed himself. Regardless of what she had done, all seemed well, though he would watch Paqual more closely.

"Besides," she murmured, "I had brought some from Woodlea."

"So he assumes you must be Anna, since you suffer her unusual malady."

She shrugged.

"And that it was the miller's mistake."

She began pacing. "Or that someone else dislikes me enough to cause me distress."

He shook his head, watching her, assuring himself that she was well. She glanced back at him, seeming nervous under his scrutiny. "'Tis little wonder you were able to survive alone on the streets of Teleere, lass.'

"The isle is not such a dangerous place. Indeed, I found it far safer than Sedonia when first—" She stopped in her tracks, seeming to stumble both physically and mentally.

"You lived here? In Sedonia?"

She glanced over her shoulder at him. In the years to come, when she was long gone, this would be how he would remember her, shrouded in shadow with the firelight dancing on her hair and the curve of her cheek strangely alluring. "I lived here for a time."

"When?"

She exhaled softly. "I was born here."

"Your parents were Sedonian?" It amazed him that even now, after all they had been through, he knew so little about her. For a time it had seemed that he knew all he needed to know. She resembled Tatiana, she was poor, and she was not above a bribe or even blackmail. But now there were a thousand questions that nagged at him. A thousand minute details he wished to know.

She delayed a moment before answering. "I believe my father was a native of this country."

"You said you didn't know your sire."

"I lied."

He rose to his feet. "Didn't your mother tell you that lying is a sin?"

Her expression was all but inscrutable in the shifting light, much like her personality. "She said it was a sin to take one's own life."

He watched her.

"And surely putting my welfare in the hands of others would be tantamount to suicide."

"An interesting theory and one that demonstrates very little trust, lass."

"Trust." She canted her head at him. "I think you will agree that there are those who would use me for their own purposes and discard me out of hand."

He watched her in silence. Silhouetted by the firelight, he could see every delicate curve. She stood with her back absolutely straight, her hands clasped in front of her.

"Is that how you see me?" he asked.

"Forgive me if I don't think you had my best interests in mind when first you arrived at the inn," she said.

Was that guilt that he felt? Guilt? What a worthless emotion and one he thought he had done away with years ago. "I am paying you well for your time, lass."

She nodded. "Else I would not be here."

"As simple as that, is it?"

She shrugged. "As I have said, my mother taught me to care for meself as I am sure the princess's mother taught her. But perhaps we have different methods."

"Actually, you are much alike."

"My lord," she said, and glanced up at him through her lashes. "I am breathlessly flattered."

It was a bit disconcerting that one minute she could seem so sincere and the next so deceptive. "Aye, you are much alike," he said. "Except Anna is not the type to flirt."

"You accuse me of flirting?" She sounded honestly surprised. But who could tell with her?

He smiled as he watched her in the flickering darkness.

"'Tis strange how your varying circumstances have allowed you to be so similar."

"I once met a juggler in Cannaun," she said. "To look at him he could have been your twin."

"Extremely attractive and devastatingly charming?"

"Mildly appealing, and appallingly overbearing," she said, and seated herself in a chair some distance from the fire. The light gilded her, glowing on her face and hair. "And yet I doubt you can juggle a'tall, and he is probably no good at abduction."

He gave her a nod for her acidic words, but felt no need to debate them, not with the firelight caressing her curves through the sheer fabric of the gown. She looked as soft as a kitten, which, perhaps, proved her point very well. "Tell me, lass, do you look like your mother?"

"The juggler," she said, "wasn't so prone to changing the topic without notice."

"He probably wasn't an intellectual phenomenon either."

The hint of a smile touched her breathtaking lips. "But, then, who is?"

He returned the expression. "Was she small like you?"

"Mum?" A shadow of nostalgia flicked across her face, but she shrugged. "She seemed tall to me, but perhaps age skewed my perception. I remember her hair though. I thought it the most amazing color—as red as wine when she brushed it in the firelight."

Images crowded his imagination. Gentleness, warmth, a mother's quiet voice. It almost made him wish he had known those qualities for more than a few short years. "Where did you live, lass?"

"We had a cottage in Glenhollow for a time," she said, and tucked her feet against her bottom. The position did strange things to his equilibrium. She looked like a tiny bundle of desire sitting there wrapped in nothing but one sheer film of white cotton.

"What of your father?" he asked. "He must have been a small man, then, if your mother was tall."

She shrugged. "As I said before, I never met him."

"Then perhaps you resemble him."

"No!" There was a sudden flintiness to her tone now, but she drew an even breath and relaxed a mite. "No," she repeated. "Not in any way that matters."

"Your mother must have told you something about him."

"No. She did not."

"And you never found out who he was? Surely you were curious."

She laughed, but the sound was, perhaps, a bit off. Rising to her feet, she paced to the window. "Perhaps you nobles have time to indulge in idle curiosity," she said, "but we underlings are too often busy surviving."

"But maybe knowing him would have made survival that much easier."

She glanced over her shoulder at him.

"Perhaps he was wealthy," Nicol added.

"Ahh." She nodded. "Yes, and certainly he would have wanted to share that wealth with the misbegotten daughter of a humble washerwoman. 'Tis the nature of the nobleman after all."

"I forget how little admiration you have for the peerage at times."

"Do I have a reason to respect them?"

"Generally not," he admitted, his voice low. Something stabbed his gut again. "I am only saying that it was your father's duty to support you. Perhaps it is not too late to learn his identity."

"And surely he would take me in with open arms. Would be thrilled to see me upon his doorstep."

He watched her in the flickering darkness. She was everything a woman should be: intelligence, beauty, kindness, though sometimes she managed to hide all three behind a steely mask. "Yes," he said. "It may well be that he would be thrilled to call you his daughter."

She remained silent for a moment, and suddenly the room seemed strangely devoid of air. For an instant he thought she would approach him. Would touch his arm again, would give him a smile. Strange. He was known to be something of a rake, and yet the memory of her hand on his skin sent a spur of emotion crackling through him. The idea did nothing to salve his pride. But she turned to pace again. Beneath the pristine hem of her nightrail, her narrow feet silently trod the floor.

"And what of you, my lord?" she asked. "Have you claimed your own offspring?"

Her feet were so very small. They intrigued him somehow, but he drew his gaze from them. "I have been careful," he assured her.

"Perhaps my father could say the same."

"You think he didn't know of your existence?"

"On the contrary." She paced again. Her toes peeked out and disappeared. "I'm certain he did."

"Then who told him?"

She shrugged. "I don't know. Perhaps I am merely too jaded simply to assume he was innocent by way of ignorance."

"If no one told him of your birth, you can hardly blame him for his shortcomings."

The silence was hard for a moment, then, "I think you protest too loudly for a man who has produced no bastards. Is it guilt that makes you defend him, or do you simply side with your own?"

"My own?" he asked, surprise tightening his gut. "Was he highborn?"

She was silent for the slightest moment, then she laughed. "My father, a noble? I greatly doubt it. But I suspect he was a man."

"Forgive me, lass," Nicol said and paced toward her. She drew him, whether he wished to admit it or not. "But I do not consider men 'my own.'"

Her smile lit the night. "You keep avoiding the issue."

"Really, and I thought I was addressing it admirably."

"What of your own bastards?" she asked bluntly, and suddenly he imagined a small girl with emerald eyes and a fire-quick mind. What would it be like to hold such a child in his arms? To hear her giggle with glee. To watch her face light up when she smiled. Strange, he had never been a sentimental man, had never hoped to become a father, not after knowing his own.

"I've sired no children," he said.

"None that you are aware of."

He was close enough now to see the dark specks in her eyes. "I've sired no children," he repeated.

"How can you be so certain?"

"Believe me, the ladies I've known would have informed me."

"And what of your less affluent lovers?"

He raised a brow.

"The chambermaids. The goose girls, the milk—"

"There have been no goose girls."

"Shall I assume there have been milkmaids aplenty then?"

"None of those either."

"Too common for you?"

"Too honest."

"What?" There was surprise in her face, and maybe a spark of something like hope. He could hardly afford that. Indeed, he should dissuade her from believing he had any redeeming reasons for his abstinence. But he found he could not manage to intentionally lower her opinion of him. He had, after all, abducted her. Surely he had done his part to make her hate his kind.

"Rich baronesses, lonely countesses." He shrugged. "They understand the rules of the game."

"So you prefer nobility."

"As it turns out . . ." He reached out, knowing he shouldn't, knowing he should draw back, knowing he should not—whatever else he did—touch her. "I have a weakness for thieves," he said. Her skin felt like a summer cloud against his fingertips. He smoothed his knuckles down her cheek, brushed his thumb along the plump curve of her lips.

"I guess I am safe then," she whispered, but her eyes dropped closed, shadowing her prefect cheeks with her dark lashes. "Since I am neither."

He stroked his hand down her shoulder. "Then what are you, lass?"

She shivered slightly. The tremor quivered to his very soul, jaded though it was. "Naught but a simple maid, my lord," she whispered. "One who—"

But he shushed her with his fingers to her lips. " 'Tis not true."

"Then what am I?"

"You," he said, and tried to stop himself, tried to control his words, tried to think. But he was already leaning in. "Are irresistible."

The first touch of their lips was magic, soft, warm, luring, and there was nothing he could do but wrap his arm about her waist and pull her closer. The hot weight of her breasts crushed against his chest, and suddenly it seemed as if there was nothing between them, no clothing, no mistrust, no barriers.

He touched his tongue to her lips, and they opened to him. Their tongues met and sparred. He swept his hand down from her waist, feeling the firm round curve of her buttocks. Her fingers tangled in his shirt, holding him tight. Against her belly, his arousal was hard and ready, pulsing with need.

But her hands were against his chest now. They felt hot there, and it took him several hard seconds to realize she was trying to press away.

It was horrifically difficult to let her go. But he did, grappling for control, for some sort of unlikely sanity.

"My apologies, lass, I did not mean to force you."

"Force me!" She laughed as if it was the most ludicrous thought in the world, but the sound quivered, and she shook her head as if she, too, was struggling. "Didn't you?"

"No." He tried to relax, but his muscles were cramped up hard. He exhaled and reminded himself to loosen his fists. "Regardless what you think of me, I am not the type to force a woman."

"But you have forced me," she said, breathing hard. "To come here. To pretend to be the princess, to—"

"I will not force you to lie with me."

"Wouldn't you know it," she said, and laughed shakily. "The one thing I—" Her words stopped abruptly, and her eyes went wide.

"What?" he asked, but she had already turned and was pacing away. "What were you about to say?"

She didn't answer, and when he could bear the silence no longer, he took her arm.

She spun toward him, already growling. "I've no wish to share my mother's fate."

"You are right." Nodding, he forced himself to release her, to step back one prudent pace. "Again, my apologies."

Her lips twitched. The motion was reciprocated by a countermovement in his nether parts, but he ignored it.

"Let us plan for tomorrow, and I will leave you be. You'll not have to endure my company again."

She was utterly silent for a moment, then found her tongue and paced away, scowling. "I am to meet her at the theater?"

"Yes."

"After which time I am free to go where I will?"

Free to go. The thought cranked up the knot in his gut. "Tell me, lass, do you think I will stop you?"

She glanced over her shoulder at him. Her full mouth was pursed, her bright eyes narrowed. "No," she said. "I do not."

"Do you think I will withhold your money?"

"No. I believe you will abide by the rules. After all, they are your rules. 'Tis why you only sleep with noblewomen, is it not?"

"There are other reasons."

She waited a long while before speaking. "You think your countesses less likely to be hurt when you leave."

"You make me sound very noble."

"Believe me, my lord, that was not my intent."

He almost smiled, though every muscle was still drawn tight with hopeless anticipation. "So you realize I only abstain because I have no wish to compensate the milkmaid or the chambermaid you mentioned."

"Compensate?"

He shrugged. "It's not unheard of for a woman to conceive a purpose, in an attempt—"

Her expression changed only the slightest degree, and yet it seemed that he could feel her break, could feel emotion slice her like a blade.

"I didn't mean it like that," he said.

"You think Mum meant to trick my father into marrying her?"

He was across the floor in an instant and gripped her arms in his hands. "I swear, lass, the thought never entered my mind. It would make no sense unless he was wealthy, and since she did not even introduce you to him . . ." He shook his head. She stood very still, and so close now he could feel the warmth of her body. "Nobility . . ." He said the word softly. "'Tis a poor word for me and my peers for you have been far more noble . . ." He paused again. It was difficult to think when he touched her. He tried to draw his hands away, but found the best he could do was to slide his fingers down to hers and lift them idly between their bodies. "You have been more than noble in our dealings, lass."

"So you no longer believe I was the woman you met in Portshaven?"

"The one who knocked me unconscious and stole my watch?" he asked, and brushed her knuckles with his thumb.

She nodded. Her hair gleamed in the fickle light, and her hand felt as fragile as a sparrow's wing in his. "You seem far too frail to do such a thing," he said.

"So you believe I am innocent?"

"On the contrary, I am certain it was you," he admitted. "It simply occurs to me that I may have deserved the trouncing. In fact . . ." Bowing slightly, he kissed the back of her hand. Sultry longing shivered through him. "It might well be that I owe you an apology for that day."

He straightened. Their eyes met. Her lips, bright in the dancing firelight, were slightly parted. Desire rumbled like a thunderstorm in his gut. But it was a poignant pain now. She would be gone soon, replaced by a myriad of haunting memories.

"An apology?" she asked.

He cleared his throat and ran his thumb across her knuckles. "For my intentions."

"Which were?"

"Less than honorable I'm afraid."

"Don't tell me you meant to break your own rules."

"The thought crossed my mind."

"But I'm not even a lady. Lonely or otherwise."

"As I have said before, I find you . . . You have a strange allure, lass. I'm sure you know that," he said, and because he couldn't help himself, because she was so damned touchable, so indescribably intoxicating, he kissed her again. Her lips were soft and warm beneath his, her breath as sweet as red wine. But he drew carefully away, willing himself to retain some semblance of control.

Her eyes were wide enough to drown in, then, "I understand," she whispered.

Reaching up, he brushed a tendril of downy hair behind her ear. "What do you understand, lass?" he asked and kissed her throat.

She shivered, and in that moment he realized her hands were clenched to fists. "The rules."

He drew back slowly, careful not to crush her, careful not to frighten her. "What are you saying?"

She swept her tongue over her lips. He watched the movement and felt his mouth go dry.

"Can you promise not to get me with child?"

"Jesus!" The word escaped him.

"Can—"

"No!" Again the single word was released without his permission. If ever there was a time to lie this was it, but he was already shaking his head, already backing away. "There is always a risk. Always . . ." Her emerald eyes sparkled in the firelight. He lost his train of thought. Indeed, he almost lost his entire mind. "I've no desire—"

"Don't you?" Her voice was a low whisper as she stepped closer. Her breasts brushed his chest, like tinder to his flame, or perhaps vice versa. He felt her tremble against him and trembled in return, though he tried to pretend he did not.

"Lass, my title may have come down a much-tarnished trail, but it is mine just the same."

"And?"

"I and my forefathers are not known for our strength of character."

"I am the last person you would need to convince," she said, and laid her hand on his chest.

Every nerve ending jumped at the contact. He scoffed at himself. After all, he was hardly a callow youth. Indeed, he had accompanied a host of bonny debs, had been with his share of elegant ladies. But it had never felt like this. Never felt as though he would die if he couldn't touch her.

"Why?" he asked and found himself unable to form a more coherent question.

"Maybe I have more in common with countesses and baronesses than I realized."

He didn't allow himself to touch her, though it physically hurt to keep that small distance between them. "I doubt it, lass."

She drew a mere inch closer. "And is that an insult or a compliment, viscount?" A small lilt of her accent had returned and shivered through his system like mulled wine.

"I fear I don't have the strength to insult you just now."

She smiled. He watched the curve of her lips and felt his legs weaken. "Because I might change my course?"

"What is your course?"

"I plan to make love to you."

"Why?" Did his voice crack? Please God, don't let his voice crack. And it would certainly be preferable if he didn't swoon dead away.

She shrugged. "I'm naught but a simple maid. Can you blame me for being overwhelmed by your grand title?" she asked, and leaned toward him.

He caught her by the arms, stopping her movement like some demented priest. "Why?" he asked again.

Her face became very sober. "Because I wish to."

But not nearly as much as he wished to. Still, it appeared that he was not completely without scruples, for he spoke again. Against his will, but he spoke. "After tomorrow I shall not see you again."

"Yes," she agreed, and kissed him.

Scruples scurried for cover. Reason fled like river water, drowning him in its wake. He crushed her against himself, and she crushed back, wrapping him in her arms. He grasped her gown in shaking hands, pulling it upward until he felt her skin beneath his fingers. Someone moaned. It may have been him. He told himself to slow down, to take his time, but her hands were on his buttons, tearing them away. He heard them strike the floor. God's bones, he couldn't afford to lose more buttons, he thought muzzily, but in that moment her hands brushed his chest like electrical currents. The feel of her fingers against his skin ignited his very core, burning away every coherent thought. He backed her against the bed and she fell, pulling him alongside her. Frantically, he pulled up her nightgown and just as frantically, she undid his breeches.

But it was wrong, so wrong. She was Magical Megs, not some spoiled debutante. Life had wounded her. Circumstances had been cruel, but she had survived, and now she deserved more than being mauled in the dark—as wondrous as that sounded just now. She deserved tender words and honest promises. She deserved . . . everything.

So he caught her hands in his, kissing her, tasting her, trying to ease their frantic pace. She relaxed a trifle, panting against his mouth, her eyes closed, and he pushed away a mite, taking in her cascading hair, her ripe, parted lips.

He licked his own and steeled himself.

"Lass," he said, employing every ounce of his self-control, "I know I've been less than noble in my dealings with you, but I've no wish to disappoint you in this."

She opened her eyes and squirmed slightly against him. A drop of sweat slid languidly between his shoulder blades, but he remained immobile.

"You think you might disappoint me?" Her voice was husky, her eyes half-closed.

"God's truth, lass, I'd rather be horsewhipped," he rasped, and she smiled.

"That seems a bit extreme," she said. "Since I'm asking for your favors."

"Favors." He tried to laugh. The word seemed absolutely idiotic in this instance, but the noise sounded like nothing more than a croak. "Believe this, lass, there is nothing I want more than . . ." God's truth, she was the most beautiful woman he had ever seen. He throbbed against her thigh, and suddenly he couldn't remember what he had meant to say.

"More than what?" she whispered, and it was those lips that drove him wild. It was those lips that made him forget that he was trying to hold her at bay. It was those lips that made his grip weaken and allowed her hands to break free. They slipped along his ribs. He groaned at the sparkling feelings, and, leaning forward, he kissed her. She kissed him back, hard and heated as her hands slipped downward, over his belly and onto . . .

He froze as she wrapped her fingers around him.

"Lass, I . . ." he began, but in that moment she squeezed. He sucked air between his teeth and tried again. "I would change your opinion of noblemen if I could."

He felt her attention on his face, but could not seem to open his eyes and look at her. It was hard enough just feeling her.

"We should slow down," he suggested. "We should—"

But she kissed him into silence, then trailed her lips down his throat to his chest. A half dozen protests came to mind. None of them came to his lips. Instead, he gritted his teeth as she pressed him onto his side and skimmed hot kisses down the quivering muscles of his abdomen.

And then she arrived.

He held his breath as she touched her lips to his erection. He throbbed as she kissed him there, and when she rolled him onto his back, there was nothing he could do but give in. Perhaps she planned to escape. Perhaps she planned to rob him blind. Perhaps she planned to kill him with his shoe. But for this moment all that mattered were the sensations that throbbed through his system like native drums.

In his defense, he tried one last time to slow the pace, but her hands were suddenly on his hips, pulling him inside.

He growled as he entered her and swore as he tore her hymen, but she never slowed down, and there was nothing he could do. Nothing but race toward satiation and finally, though she gasped on the edge of her own pleasure, he lifted her away to deposit his seed on her belly.

He dropped his head back and gasped for breath, trying to find his bearing, to calm his racing heart, but when he glanced up at her he saw that she was scowling at him.

"Is something amiss?" he asked, striving for innocence, but perhaps it was a bit late for that.

Her scowl deepened a bit, though he would have thought it impossible. "Aye," she said, and eased off him. "I believe this act of coupling has been well overrated."

Chapter 21

The viscount laughed.

"What is so amusing?" Megan asked. Her fists were still wrapped in his shirt, though the buttons were gone and the fabric torn. She wondered vaguely how that had happened.

He propped himself up on his elbow and gazed into her face. "You said you didn't wish to become pregnant, lass. 'Tis the safest way I know."

"If that is the best I can expect from the act, then I know an even better prevention."

"Oh?"

"Aye," she said, and forcing her fingers from his shirt, turned to roll away. He caught her arm and she scowled, ready to reject him, but in that instant, he kissed her.

Desire was resurrected like old Lazarus. She would have liked to refuse him, would have liked to pull away, but her body refused.

His hand was on her throat, cradling her jaw, and his mouth was hot and needy against hers, but he drew away in a moment.

"You didn't tell me you were a virgin."

She licked her lips. They felt bruised and sensitized and longing. Her hands, she found, were once again tangled in his shirt. She heard it tear. One would think a viscount could afford sturdier fabric. "You didn't ask."

"I thought I made it clear that I don't sleep with innocents."

She tried to push him away, but he licked her lips.

A bestial growl echoed in the room. It took a moment to realize the sound was hers, longer still to admit she had rolled him onto his back and was straddling him like a she-wolf might pin her prey.

He stared at her. Then, reaching up, he slipped his hand behind her neck and drew her down. "What else haven't you told me?" he asked and sucked her lower lip.

"What?" Was she panting?

He kissed her again, hard and thorough, then drew back, his hands cupping her buttocks, her nightrail scrunched about her waist. His severed button threads dangled against the dusky nub of his nipple. She licked her lips and lifted her gaze back to his.

"What?" she asked again.

One corner of his mouth lifted slightly. The expression was indescribably cocky, and she wanted nothing more than to wipe that smirk off his face. Except perhaps to feel him inside her again. To douse the fire he had ignited. Still watching his eyes, she lowered her head and lapped her tongue across his nipple. He jerked like a marionette and against her bottom she felt his erection pulse with need.

"God's bones, lady—

"I am not a lady," she said, and, reaching down, wrapped her fist around him. He felt as though he might explode in her hand, but she eased off him a bit and guided him inside.

From then on there were no thoughts. Only needs, only instincts, only pleasure sought and found, given and taken.

They glided together, their bodies melding until she arched on the final stroke and collapsed with a small shriek against his chest.

His heart pounded against her ear. His arms were hard beneath her hands. She rolled to the side, sated and limp. Time eased to a crawl.

"Lass," he said. "You are amazing."

She was still breathing hard. "But no lady."

She saw him grin as he turned to her in the darkness. "I see now that ladies are well overrated," he said, and, easing onto an elbow, kissed the corner of her mouth.

"Are they?"

"Aye," he said and fell silent for a moment. "Where will you go when you leave here?"

"Why do you ask?"

He tugged her nightrail higher. Cool air touched her breasts, but in a moment the garment was replaced by his lips. She gasped and arched against the contact.

"Why do you think I ask?" he said, and suddenly the elegant fluidity was gone from his speech, replaced by a hard intensity.

"I don't know."

"Then you are not as smart as I think you are," he said, and, reaching down, pulled the gown over her head. It slid along her arms, leaving gooseflesh in its wake. She shifted her gaze to his, but his eyes had lowered.

His attention rose with slow heat to her face. His nostrils were flared, his eyes dark as sin. "You are beauty itself."

She watched his face.

"Educated," he added. "Alluring." He curled his hand around her neck and kissed her with slow-burning passion. "There are a host of things you can do to make your living," he said, and never shifting his gaze from her face, slid his hand onto her breast.

She shivered like a child against his touch, but she managed to speak her thoughts. "What are you suggesting?"

"You must not steal again, lass." His tone was raspy with emotion, but she shrugged.

"I'll do what I must."

"What you must," he repeated and eased his finger over her nipple. She closed her eyes and shivered. "What you must do is stay alive. Is that not what your mother taught you?" She tried to nod, but found it impossible to move. "Then you must not steal," he said, and kissed her breast. "Promise me you won't." His chest called to her. Reaching out, she pushed his shirt aside. Another tear had joined the others. "Promise me."

His skin was hot and firm. Leaning forward, she kissed him just above the nipple and watched his eyes fall closed. "I cannot," she whispered.

His teeth were gritted when next he spoke. "Why?"

"Someone told me 'twas wrong to lie," she whispered, and slid her hand from his nipple to his belly. Beneath his misplaced breeches, his desire reared its head again. Her hand brushed it. He quaked at the contact and caught her fingers.

"I could pay you," he gritted.

She caught his gaze as a thousand emotions flitted through her, but she stilled each one and shrugged before slipping her hand up his abdomen to his chest. From there, she eased her palm over his shoulder until the shirt fell away. "So I would be your whore."

"No." He said the word as if he struggled for calm, but it did not matter, for she knew enough of men to realize much might be said in the heat of passion. And there was passion. Despite her innocence and doubts, she knew that much.

Sliding her hand down his arm, she felt the muscles tremble and shift beneath her fingers.

"There have been times," she whispered, barely able to

force out the words for the heat of her own desires, "when all I had was my pride."

He skimmed her with his gaze, and she felt both hot and cold beneath his perusal. His nostrils flared and his eyes grew dark. "You're wrong, lass," he said.

She felt the burn of his nearness, the longing in his touch, but she was what she was. "Then what capacity would I fill? Do you think the ladies of the *ton* might hire me to coddle their children? Or perhaps—"

"I said *I* would pay you. Not some pompous . . ." He had gritted his teeth and took a breath through them now. "I would pay you," he repeated.

"To do what?" she asked, and skimmed a finger along the hard-ridged muscle of his abdomen.

He closed his eyes to the feelings, and though he opened them in a moment, his eyes burned, as if he were doing all he could to keep his hands to himself. To think things through. And the knowledge that she had driven him past his cool self-control was more than satisfying.

"Would you pay me to do nothing?" she asked.

"Many men have . . ."

She skimmed her fingers across his navel.

He winced but finished the sentence, though the word was gritted. "Wards."

She laughed. "So I would be as a child to you."

Since they were naked and sweaty amidst the tangled sheets, perhaps he was too embarrassed to admit verbally that that was exactly what he meant, but he nodded nevertheless.

And she laughed again at the absurdity of the situation.

" 'Tis not a laughing matter, lass," he gritted, as she skimmed her fingers upward.

"No indeed," she agreed. "How could I refuse such an offer?" Indeed, why should she? She had been poor so long, she had lost so much. Surely she should jump at such a chance, and yet, with this man . . . She looked into his eyes again and felt her soul quiver. Somehow she could not bear to take his charity. She would rather scrabble on the streets. Perhaps it was pride, or perhaps it was something she dare not consider, the very thing that had broken her mother.

"I'm offering you a way to better your circumstances," he said. There was frustration in his tone, and she forced a small smile.

" 'Tis very gracious of you, I'm sure, my lord."

"Don't call me that."

"And why not?" She tried to keep the edge out of her tone, tried to remain uncaring, but her mother's haggard face was staring down at her. To love was to lose. Yet the emotions swelled like a wilding tide within her. "I will always be beneath you . . . my lord," she said, but in that moment he grabbed her arms and rolled her atop him.

"I believe we've already disproved that," he gritted, and kissed her with fiery intensity. There was nothing she could do but return the fire. Nothing she could do but cock her bottom against his erection and kick his breeches away.

He slipped inside, and she gasped at the rush of feelings.

"Or . . ." he rasped. "You could pay me. I'm not too proud."

"I don't . . ." she began, and shivered as he tipped in and out. She was panting as she gripped his arms and shoved herself around him. He arched, filling her, and she moaned.

"Don't what?" he asked, and stroked slowly.

She gritted her teeth against the languid pace and pressed against him. "I don't have much money . . . my lord," she said, and pressed faster. Her breathing sounded raspy and her lips felt dry. She swiped her tongue over them and leaned low so that his chest caressed her nipples.

"I might be convinced . . ." His voice was low and guttural as he stroked in and out. "To perform for free."

She moaned and picked up the pace.

"If you'd tell me." He gritted his teeth. His biceps flexed beneath her clawed hands. "Where to find you once you're gone."

She tilted her head back and pressed him in to the hilt, reaching, drawing, sustaining. Their hearts hammered together.

"Lass," he began again, but she kissed him, stilling his words, quieting his worry until they fell together through the bliss and into satiation.

She rolled to her side, feeling languid and strangely soft. Yet, at the same time, something ached inside her chest.

He lay facing her, his expression somber in the firelight from behind. Silence stretched between them. He touched her face with his fingertips. She closed her eyes to the gentle sensations, and he pulled her into his arms. And then, against all odds, he fell asleep. She felt his hard muscles relax, felt his tension drain, and though she knew she should send him back to his room, she couldn't resist the opportunity to watch him as he was now, with no barriers, no cynicism, with his handsome features blissful in slumber.

It was several hours later when she woke him.

"Viscount," she said.

He opened his eyes with a start, glanced around and settled his attention on her.

"Lass." His voice was a rasp, as if he were relieved to find her there. "I dreamt . . ." he began and stopped. Raising himself on one elbow, he watched her in the dying firelight. Outside, the world was still dark. "I have been considering . . ." He paused. "I thought I might purchase a house in the country."

"A house? Such as Woodlea?" She smiled at the memory. She had slept very little, but she did not feel tired. Instead, there was a sort of wistful nostalgia, an aching hopelessness.

"Yes." Silence again. Reaching out, he stroked her cheek with the back of his fingers. "Did you like it there?"

"Mrs. Barnes was kind. And young Brady."

"I could . . ." He sounded strangely tense, almost breathless. "Perhaps I could hire them. Will rarely resides there. Maybe he could find others to replace them."

Her hands begged to touch him, but she kept them curled against the mattress and lowered her eyes. "I cannot," she said simply.

"Then—" he began, but she reached up with harried speed and pressed her fingers to his lips.

"Today will be trying. You'd best find your own chambers."

He watched her in silence for a breathless eternity, then eased away and rose to his feet. "Good-bye then, princess," he said, and, slipping his arms through his tattered sleeves, he pulled on his breeches. As it turned out, they were torn, too.

Nicol paced his bedchamber. The remainder of the night had been restless, the day hideously long, but now it was nearly time to leave, almost time to retrieve the princess and bid the pauper farewell. He ground his teeth. It would be good to have it done, good to know Anna was safe . . . and that Sedonia was safe from Megan. After all, he'd taken a huge risk. But the time was up.

The rules of exchange were exactly as they had been before. The princess would go to the theater, then find her way to the water closet at a precise time. Megan would meet her there. They would change outer clothing, and all would be returned to normal. He should be ecstatic. All had gone well. The princess had been given an opportunity to form her own opinions. The thief had learned a great deal, had earned a great deal, would be able to improve her circumstances. But she had refused his most generous offers. Had turned him aside. Had, in fact, been insulted. Damn her! Couldn't she see he was giving her a chance to better her life?

But in the back of his mind, doubts lingered. Perhaps it

was his life he wished to better. Perhaps he couldn't bear the idea of living without . . .

Tension gripped him. Able to wait no longer, he snatched up his redingote and strode out of his room.

He rode alone to the theater and sat impatiently through a poor performance of *The Merry Wives of Windsor.* From his box he could just catch glimpses of Megan. Lord Riven leaned toward her, whispering something, and she laughed. Although he couldn't hear her, it seemed as if he could, as if the sound shivered through his system like mulled wine.

He hadn't taught her to flirt. She had learned that on her own and had learned it well. Unlike the true princess, she had no qualms about living life to the fullest. And yet he'd been her first. The memory quaked through his soul. He remembered the feel of her skin against his. Remembered the heat of her feverish kiss, the rush of her frantic hands. Wild with desire. Where would she go? How would he find her? He slammed his thoughts to a halt and ground his teeth through the next half hour. The seconds clicked away like a dirge. God's bones! It must be time now. It must be, and still the girl sat and flirted. He stilled his scowl, then checked his watch again, and realized with groaning impatience that only a few minutes had passed.

An eternity dragged by before she rose to her feet. Laughing down at a companion, she made her way from the box. Nicol waited, keeping his gaze on the performance and reminding himself not to fidget. It was over now. Completed. She was leaving Malkan Palace and that was good. All was well. The princess was returning. All he had to do was wait.

But the princess did not return.

It had been agreed that he would not accompany Megan to the water closet. That it would seem less conspicuous if she went alone. But Anna had not returned, so perhaps there was still time to see Megan one last time, to try to convince her . . . But he had already done that, and she had made her wishes clear. She didn't want to see him again. Surely he was man enough to accept that. But where would she go? And how would he survive without seeing her again?

He felt like jerking to his feet, like rushing after her, but instead he rose with careful casualness. He would make certain all was well. That was all. Pacing down the steps, he kept his expression bored, his strides even, but his mind rushed along and his body felt tight with anticipation. He forced himself to pass the closet with steady strides. But when he was nearly past, Megan stepped into his line of vision. His breath caught in his throat, and though he told himself he should be calm, he felt his body tighten at her nearness and just managed to keep from pulling her into his arms.

"You're here," he said. The words sounded marvelously steady, as if someone else had spoken.

"Yes," she said, but her own tone was tense, her expression tight.

"What is it?" Dread shook his soul. "Are you well?"

She scowled at him, then shifted her attention to her waiting ladies and back. "The princess," she whispered. "She didn't come."

And in that moment he realized the truth. The sight of Megan had driven any memory of Anna clean out of his mind. He had forgotten the entire mission. But the implications of the princess's absence came storming in now.

"Where is she?" he rasped.

Behind her, the ladies-in-waiting spoke among themselves, and off to both sides the guards stood at attention, granting them a few minutes alone.

"I don't know." She had managed to smooth out her expression, but her tone proved her worry.

"Dammit!" he swore softly, then saw Mary making her way toward them and managed to soothe his tone and raise his voice slightly. "Good eventide then, Your Majesty. I hope you enjoy the remainder of the entertainment."

"And what of you, Nicol?" she asked. She had almost conquered the tremor in her voice by the time her ladies fluttered up. "Are you leaving so early?"

"I fear I am a bit indisposed," he said.

"Well . . ." The corner of her mouth quirked slightly. Her eyes flirted, her seductive mouth pursed. The consummate actress once again. "Give the mystery lady my regards," she said, but he was not fully appreciative of her performance, for his mind was spinning of control.

He bowed again, trying to keep abreast with the banter, to match her groomed nonchalance. She acted as if all was well. As if they did no more than play a foolish game. Was she such a spectacular actress, or did last night mean nothing to her? And what of Anna's absence? "I am flattered by your faith in me,' he said. "But I assure you, I go to my bed alone."

"And at midnight I convert into a butterfly," she agreed, and, turning smoothly to her ladies, made her way back toward her box.

Nicol turned, too, trying to mimic her insouciance, but there was little hope of that. What had gone wrong? Where was Anna? Why hadn't she arrived?

Once outside, he sped up, pacing down the walkway, searching the night. Off to his right two gentlemen smoked cheroots and talked politics. Catching a glimpse of the flaring hem of a skirt as it swung off the path, Nicol charged after it.

Startling the lady from her lover's embrace, Nicol apologized as he released her arm and hurried away. But Anna was nowhere to be found. There was no sign of her. No clue to her whereabouts. Indeed, he could not even broach a question.

Have you seen the princess dressed as another? Panic

roiled in his stomach, but there was nothing he could do. Nothing but search the grounds until the last carriage had left, then return to the palace alone.

He waited until the small hours of the morning before he dared enter the princess's bedchamber, and when he did, she immediately glanced up and set her book rapidly aside.

"Did you find her?"

He paced silently across the room, restive and taut. What the devil had he done? "You were at the appointed place on time?" he asked.

"You know I was."

Yes, he did. But that was all he knew. "And you saw no sign of her?"

"A sign?" Even in the darkness, he knew she looked at him as if he were crazed.

"A note. A . . ." He paced her room, grasping at proverbial straws. "An article of clothing?"

"No."

"You're sure?" He turned, anger and worry making his tone sharp. "She must have been there. She must—"

Megan came out of bed with a start. " 'Tis not my fault you lost the princess."

Firelight flickered off her smooth skin, casting up memories of the feel of her against his skin. He exhaled carefully, focusing on the problems at hand. "Where do you think she might be?"

She raised a brow at him. "Do you think I abducted her in an attempt to keep my position here?"

He said nothing.

"Well I did not." Her tone was terse. "Indeed, 'tis you who are known to take women against—"

"You and she are much alike." Except that Megan was ir-resistible. So damnably touchable, he ached even now to hold her against him. But he fisted his hands and kept his distance. "Despite your upbringing . . . Despite your manner-isms, you are both clever, both . . ." Words failed him. He should never have lain with her, for now he could concentrate on nothing else. The princess was missing, for God's sake, and all he could think about was the feel of Megan's skin against his. The warmth of her hands, the touch of her . . . God help him! "Where might she be?"

"Nicol." She said his name softly but did not step closer, as if she had no desire to risk what they had shared the night be-fore. As if she had no wish to do what he ached for. "If she is clever, as you say, then she is most likely safe."

He drew a careful breath and turned his mind resolutely back to the princess. "Why would she not send a message?"

She shook her head. "We have no way of knowing. But the fact that we didn't receive one doesn't mean that one wasn't sent. Perhaps the messenger was waylaid."

"The princess's messenger would never allow—" he be-gan, but she interrupted him.

"Her messenger would not know it was a missive from the princess, and therefore he would place no great importance on the success of his mission. Perhaps he took her coin, dis-carded the missive, and departed."

"Perhaps. But—"

"Don't," she said. "Don't look for trouble where there may be none."

He rubbed his eyes. "I should not have let her go."

"She is your princess," she reminded him. "Did you have a choice?"

"I could have tried to dissuade her."

"Would she have listened?"

"She trusts my judgment."

"Then there is probably a reason for that trust."

He moved slightly closer, needing contact, needing flesh against flesh. "And what of you, lass? Do you trust me?"

He could feel the soft sigh of her breath against his cheek and could not help but remember how she had lain against him, how her nipples had brushed his as her breathing accelerated and her legs tightened about him. "No," she said. "But I have my reasons, too."

"Have I been such an ogre?"

Firelight flashed in her eyes, but she lowered them in a moment. "You must search for her."

And leave Megan to her own defenses? Something ached deep in his chest. He couldn't abandon her. He admitted that much to himself though perhaps he could not admit the reason. "I promised Anna I would stay by your side."

"Afraid I will abscond with the crown jewels?"

He had not even considered that. One night in her bed and he had entirely forgotten who she was, where she came from.

"You'll need to stay on," he said, and his voice sounded marvelously rational. "Until she returns."

Megan said nothing, but finally she nodded.

"It will be dangerous."

"Things have gone well enough so far."

Well enough. She said nothing of their night together. As if she had put it easily behind her. "But it has only been a few days. And already Paqual is suspicious."

"I can handle Paqual." She said the words with cool self-assurance. Where was the girl he had taught to use a spoon? Where was the woman who trembled at his touch?

"What of the ball planned for the duke?" he asked.

She shrugged. "I shall welcome him."

He scowled, but surely he was not jealous. Let him have a shred of dignity. "You will be expected to know a host of names."

"As you said, I am the princess. They are underlings."

"There will be dancing and games. Drinking. Anna always—"

"Dancing?" she said, and he scowled.

"Surely you know how to dance."

She shook her head, and she felt relief sluice through him. A reason to be near her. A reason to touch her.

"You'll have to learn before the duke arrives. Come," he said, and took her hand in his. Heat sizzled between them, but if she felt it, she showed no sign. He pulled her close. Her breasts pressed against his chest, sparking a thousand errant emotions. Her waist felt tight and small beneath his arm. Her eyes were lowered, and, as he looked into her face, he felt her nearness like a mischievous spark of flame in his gut.

"Lass—" he began, but she pulled back, putting several inches between them.

"I shall sit out the ball," she declared.

He ached for her, for the intimacy they had shared only hours before. Just the feel of her hand in his made a thousand poignant memories leap in his head. "The princess loves to dance," he said, and spread his fingers across her back. They nearly spanned the width of her. "There is little that would keep her from the waltz."

"Then I shall claim a twisted ankle or a sour stomach."

"We don't know how long it will be until her return." Her hair was loosed about her delicate shoulders. Her skin smelled of lavender and went to his head like a magical potion. "There may well be other balls," he murmured, and pulled her close.

For a moment she relaxed. For a moment, her thigh touched his with sighing intimacy, but in an instant she tore herself from his grip.

"No. I . . ." She was breathing hard. He could see the rise and fall of her bosom through the sheer fabric of her kindly gown. "I am tired."

Tired! How could she be tired? Didn't she feel the sizzling

tension? Didn't she ache? He took a step toward her, but she stepped rapidly away.

"Please. I . . . am feeling unwell."

Something twisted in his stomach. Is this how rejection felt? "Lass, about last night—"

"I won't couple with you again." Her words were sharp, her expression tense in the firelight.

He took a careful breath and watched her. "Was it so hideous?"

She linked her fingers with prim precision, and in that moment she looked like nothing more than the princess he had taught her to be. An ache began down low in his gut, burning hotly.

"I'll not do it again," she repeated.

He waited, catching his wits, calming his body. "I'll not get you with child, lass. If you wish I will find another method. Something to assure you that—"

"I planned never to see you again."

Her eyes gleamed in the flickering light. Her hair was nearly as luminous. He ached to slip his fingers through the silk of it, to run his hand down the curve of her back.

"So that's your way of saying good-bye?"

"I didn't . . . I . . ." She straightened her back. "I think you have nothing to complain about . . . my lord. I've done what you've asked. I've adhered to our bargain. Indeed, I am still here, doing your bidding. But I will not . . ." She paused, and a delicate shiver seemed to shake her. "I will not lie with you again. Not ever."

He almost pleaded. Almost begged like a cur, but he managed to retain a shred of dignity, though he would have thought it impossible.

"As you wish," he said, and bowed. "Your Majesty."

Chapter 22

She didn't sleep well that night, and the following day was long and tedious. Sometime near noon Paqual entered the salon where she sat conversing with Edmund. The scintillating debate about drapery fabric was growing old.

"Your Majesty," Paqual said, and executed a stiff bow. "I do hate to disturb you, but there are a number of documents that require your signature."

"Documents?" Worry cramped her belly. It was not her place to sign documents. She might look like the princess, she might dress like the princess. Indeed, by some miracle, she might even speak like a princess, but there was a vast chasm of differences between Tatiana Octavia Linnet Rocheneau and the girl her mum had called Megs. For instance, Tatiana could probably actually understand said documents. Oh yes, Megan could read, but she was hardly a scholar, especially in the political arena.

Where was Nicol when she needed him? She'd not seen him all morning. Why did Paqual approach her now? Was it mere coincidence that he broached the issue of legal matters now when both Nicol and the baron of Landow were absent?

"I am really quite busy here," she said, and returned her attention to some inane fabric pattern, but Paqual remained where he was, and when she turned back, she saw that he wore a tight smile.

"It will not take long," he said. "Just a few minutes of your time, Your Majesty."

"Oh?" She tried to look regal, but she hardly felt up to making decisions regarding Sedonian politics. "What do these documents involve?"

"Nothing of great import. Laws that have been in effect for years. They simply require a few alterations."

"If they've been effective for years, my Lord Paqual . . ." She gave him a smile and hoped it didn't tremble. "I suspect there is no hurry to change them now.

"Lord Danzig," she said, turning casually away, then almost wincing at her own foolishness. The decorator was not a noble. Indeed, he was naught but the youngest son of an English milliner, but she pressed on as if her mistake was nothing more than a foolish slip of the tongue. "We will need the drapes completed forthwith."

"Yes, Your Majesty."

"Your Majesty." Paqual was still there. "If you will accompany me to the state room, we can have this matter taken care of in but a few minutes. There will be no need—"

"What is it you wish to have taken care of?" Nicol asked as he stepped into the room.

Megan felt her heart cramp at the sight of him and forced herself to breathe around her own idiocy.

Paqual turned his smile on the viscount, but it faded when he saw the boy who entered between Newborn and the baron of Landow. "What is he doing here?"

Nicol canted his head. "Surely you have not forgotten. Young Jack is Lord Landow's ward."

"I'll not have that jackanapes at the palace. Not—"

But Megan rose to her feet. "I asked Lord Newborn to bring him by."

"Your Majesty." Paqual bowed again. "With all due respect, I must remind you, the boy is a thief, a misbegotten—"

"I know exactly what the boy is," she said. Her voice rang in the room, stopping all movement, curtailing all talk. She kept herself from fidgeting, kept her gaze hard on Paqual. "He is my subject," she said, softening her tone. "And as you well know, my lord, as such he deserves my fullest consideration."

The old man's lips were pursed, but finally he bowed. "Yes, Your Majesty. Of course . . ."

"Now . . ." She lightened her tone and hoped she wouldn't pass out. "What documents did you wish me to sign?"

"As you said, Your Majesty . . ." Paqual acquiesced. "The papers can surely wait until preparations for the duke's arrival are complete." Bowing, he turned on spindly legs and left the room.

"Your Majesty," Nicol said, and repeated the old man's bow. "As you can see, we have brought young Jack to visit you."

She shifted her gaze from the viscount to the boy. The lad's expression was dark. Behind him, William Enton took a swig from the silver flask he'd pulled from his vest pocket. He was as raggedly handsome as ever, but there was a yellowish bruise across his brow.

"Mister Danzig," she said, "I would have a minute alone with these gentlemen."

"Of course, Your Majesty," he replied, and, clapping his hands, hustled his frenzied workers from the room.

"So," she began, and turned her attention back to the lad. "How are you faring at Landow House?"

Nimble Jack remained silent. His years on the streets, it seemed, had not made him an effervescent sort of child.

"You are eating well?" she asked.

He stared at her an instant, then, "I 'eard of such places as this," he said.

She raised a brow. "Such places?"

He shifted his eyes toward the guard and back. "Places where they train 'ores."

Nicol straightened abruptly and Will jerked away from the wall, abandoning his usual casualness, but Megan held up a hand. "You think we are training you—"

"'E made me take me clothes off," said the boy, and tossed his head toward Will.

A muscle jumped in the baron's lean jaw as he stared at the lad.

"Lord Landow?" Meg said, calling for a response.

"He reeks," Enton said. "I thought it best if he bathed before visiting the palace."

"'E watched me the 'ole while. I know 'is sort."

"The boy has a penchant for escaping."

"You can't 'old me," rasped the boy.

Will's face was devoid of its usual nonexpression as he stared at Jack. Instead, it was filled now with an indescribable mix of anger and frustration and pain too long dulled with drink, but he turned smoothly back to Megan. "I believe it would be best if you would find another to care for the child, Your Majesty."

"Oh? And why is that, Lord Landow?"

"I am poorly suited to care for children." Something flared in his eyes. "Ask anyone."

"He looks to be hale thus far."

"Thus far." His hand seemed to tighten on his flask, but he loosened it in a moment and grinned that roguish smile for which he was famous. Even Lady Mary spoke of him in dreamy tones. "He has nearly escaped twice, Your Majesty."

"Is that how you obtained the bruise?"

"No, Your Majesty," he said, and paused as if he did not intend to continue. But when the silence stretched out, he finally spoke. "That was my own mistake."

"How did you come by it?"

"I have been told a hundred times to cease drinking," he said, and lifted the flask as if to explain his weakness.

But there was something in his eyes that proved his lie. She straightened her back. "I am tired and I am busy," she said. "Tell me the tale."

He shrugged but she held up a hand. "I do not tolerate lies, Lord Landow."

Will drew a breath and nodded once. "The boy's tutor seemed a bit quick with his switch." He scowled at his flask, seeming to wish there were more.

"What happened?"

"The lad misspelled his name." A muscle jerked in his lean jaw. "It didn't seem a grave offense."

She glanced at Jack, trying to understand the event, but the boy's expression was unchanged. "Did Mr. Friar strike you, Jack?"

He said nothing. The room fell into silence, but Landow spoke quietly into the void.

"Answer the princess, lad," he ordered, and the boy spoke up.

"The old man's as weak as a suckling babe. It didn't hurt me a'tall."

The baron glanced out the window as though he would rather be elsewhere, but finally he brought his attention back to Megan. "Friar left welts, Your Majesty. I know little of children, but—"

"I ain't no child," Jack insisted, and locked eyes with the baron.

"Being a thief doesn't change your age," Lord Landow insisted, his tone evidencing passion she'd never witnessed in him. "Nor does it mean you'll survive should you return—"

"I ask again," Megan interrupted. "How did you sustain the bruise, Lord Landow?"

William's lips quirked as if he fought some inner battle. "Mr. Friar was not happy to lose his switch."

"You took it from him?"

He cleared his throat and glanced away. "Before I threw him out of Landow House."

Megan raised her chin and watched him. For a man who knew nothing of children, he seemed strangely protective and decidedly skittish of the fact.

"I believe he was the tutor my uncle chose for his own sons," Megan said.

"Yes, Your Majesty. I believe he was."

There was something in the baron's tone, as if he were being dragged from his stupor against his will. As though he were being forced to care. "I trust you will find another," she said softly. "Perhaps the very person you would have chosen for your own children."

He looked pale and his fist tightened on his flask. "As I have said, Your Majesty, I fear I am not the best man to undertake—" he began, but she held up her hand for silence and turned to the child.

The boy met her gaze straight on.

"I am sorry," she said simply.

Some emotion crossed the lad's face. She couldn't guess what it was, but his mouth opened, and his brows dropped low over his fire-quick eyes.

"What did Friar teach you?" she asked. "Other than the fact that old men are as weak as suckling babes?"

He shuffled his feet, still scowling, but finally he spoke as if he couldn't quite keep quiet, though he wished to. "Readin'," he said. "It's a fresh 'un it is. Did you know there's a mark for every sound we—"

"Letter," Landow corrected quietly.

The boy nodded. "Yeah. There's a letter for every sound we make."

"It is indeed amazing," she agreed, but his expression immediately returned to one of defiance.

"Not that I need that book learning. It ain't gonna do me no good. I ain't 'ardly in the 'igh life."

"So you cannot learn?"

His mobile face scrunched. "I could learn if I wants to. Same as the next bloke."

"But you do not wish to."

"I got me things to do back on Hack Street."

Yes, he did—things like live hard and die young. She'd seen it happen a hundred times.

"Are you a gambling man, Jack?" she asked.

He blinked as if trying to keep up to the change of topic. "I been known to wager a bit."

"Very well, we shall roll the dice."

"What for?"

"To see whether you will learn or whether you will return to Hack Street."

She thought he might object, but finally he dipped his hand in his pocket and drew out a pair of dice.

"Awright then. I got some 'ere."

She smiled. "I think I shall get another pair. For luck," she added, and raised her voice. "Allard," she said, addressing the guard who stood by the door, "fetch me a pair of playing dice."

"Dice, Your Majesty?"

"If you please. I believe you will find some in the sword

room," she said, then, seating herself by a table, motioned for Jack to do the same.

He did so slowly. His face was clean, she noticed, and his cheeks marginally plumper.

"Do you agree to abide by the results of this match?"

His scowl deepened a bit. "You're gonna let me go if I win?"

"Yes," she said, accepting Allard's dice with her right hand and dropping them onto her lap.

Jack's face was pale and in her mind she knew he wondered whether he hoped to lose or win. Fear of the unknown was only slightly less terrifying than the fear of returning to the street where he had struggled so long to survive.

"And if I lose?" he asked.

"Then you return to Landow House. You do what Lord Landow tells you to do, you learn as much as you can as quickly as you can, and you return here to the palace to report your progress to me."

He blinked.

"Do you agree to the terms?"

His brows bobbled, and his fists clenched. "I ain't no squelcher."

She watched his eyes for a moment, then nodded and tossed the dice. Twelve dots appeared on the ivory pair.

Megan handed over the dice. He tossed. They counted. Sixes also. He rolled again, seeming to hold his breath as he did so. Seven spots shone against the yellowed ivory. Taking the dice, Mcgan blew into her hand and sent the cubes spinning across the table. They rolled on their edges and landed—two sixes.

She caught the boy's gaze. He blinked, narrowed his eyes, and stared at her before rising slowly to his feet.

"You win," he said.

"Yes," she agreed. "I do."

His eyes narrowed slightly. "You're almighty lucky."

"Perhaps it wasn't luck."

He shifted his eyes to Lord Landow as if debating whether he should speak again, but finally curiosity won out. "'Ow then?"

Rising from her chair, Megan retrieved a fat volume that lay on a nearby table. "Do you see this book?" she asked.

He nodded.

"When you can read me the first three pages, I shall share my secrets."

He stared at her for a full twenty seconds, then he turned of his own accord and walked back to the baron. They left together.

She could feel Nicol's gaze on her and when she could no longer avoid his attention, she turned with a scowl.

"What is it?" she asked.

His eyes were dark and intense. Something curled up hard in her stomach. "Where were you when I was in grammar school?" he asked.

She pursed her lips and ignored the knot of emotion in her gut. She was nothing but a tool to him. "I believe I was not yet born, my lord," she said.

He canted his head. "Nicol," he corrected.

"I am the princess," she said. "If I wish to call you Mr. Toad, I shall do so."

His lips quirked slightly and it was the sight of them that twisted the knot up even harder in her stomach, for she could not forget how they had felt against her skin, how he had spoken low and sweet in her ear.

"Of course, Your Majesty," he said, and, bowing, took the few steps that remained between them. "But what of dancing?"

His nearness made it impossible to think. Hot memories steamed in her mind. But she must not let that happen again. She had hoped bedding him would release the tension, would prove she was missing little by resisting him. Or at least that was what she had told herself, but since touching him she could think of nothing else.

"What of dancing?" she asked, feeling weak, feeling lost and forsaken and frightfully alone.

"You need to learn."

"I told you . . ." He was standing too close. She could feel heat radiating from his body. "I will create a fictional malady of some sort."

"Every lady should know how to dance," he said, and though it almost seemed that he tried to keep his hands to himself, he reached up and brushed a coil of hair from her cheek. His knuckles grazed her ear.

She closed her eyes to the hot sensation and refused to press her cheek against his hand. "You forget," she said. "I am no lady."

"If you are not," he murmured, and skimmed his fingers down her throat, "then no one is."

She shivered. "My lord—"

"Nicol," he corrected, but his voice was gritty, as though he fought some battle of his own.

"Nicol." The name sounded far too much like a caress, but there seemed little she could do to correct it. "I cannot do that again."

"What is it you cannot do?"

"What . . ." His eyes were steaming, frying the thoughts from her brain, but she straightened her back with a snap and stepped back a pace. "I cannot sleep with you again."

"I believe I was the only one who slept," he said. "A fact for which I have yet to thank you."

She remembered how he had looked, his lashes soft as a child's, but his bare chest as hard as whittled oak. She had not, until that moment, realized how truly beautiful he was. But beauty meant nothing to her. Survival was everything.

"You did a good thing," he said, and, skimming his hand down her arm, retrieved her hand and kissed her knuckles. "With the lad."

Frizzled sensations sparked up her arm. She licked her lips and tried to focus. "I cannot . . ." she began, but the words were pathetically weak though she tried to strengthen them. "I cannot . . . be with you again."

A muscle jerked in his jaw, but he bowed perfunctorily. "As you wish, Your Majesty."

But she didn't wish. Yet she could not afford to lie with him again, to feel the magic and know his grip tightened around her heart every moment she spent in his arms.

"But you must learn to dance." There was something in his eyes. An intensity yes. A command. But there was more. An uncertainty. Almost a pleading. Or did she imagine it? "Leave your door open for me tonight, lass," he murmured.

She tried to object, but he turned her hand over and kissed her palm. Hot emotions sizzled like wildfire up her arm, and suddenly she could form no coherent words, could think of nothing but the feel of his skin against hers, the heat of his kisses as they trailed down her body.

Still she was about to refuse, about to be strong, but in that moment he turned and left her.

Chapter 23

Megan tried to convince herself to lock her bedroom door, but it was all foolishness. After all, he had made no objections when she refused to lie with him again. Indeed, he had not spent a single breath trying to convince her otherwise. Had she been a disappointment? Not that she cared. Indeed, it would be best if he had no desire ever to see her again, she decided, and, slipping into her nightgown, left the door unlocked as an oversight. Almost.

She was sitting at her desk, reading, much as Tatiana must have down, when she first heard the music begin. It wafted up to her in haunting melodies. A few minutes later Nicol stepped inside.

She turned, feeling breathless and idiotic as he closed the door behind him. He looked delectably rakish. His dark hair curled over his forehead, and his shirt was open at the neck. It was all she could do to keep from rushing across the room and snatching him into her arms, but the memory of his torn shirt made her blush. Perhaps that was what a lady of quality would do differently—allow his clothing to remain intact. Self-conscious under his gaze, she set the book primly aside and rose with a scowl. "Don't you ever knock, my lord?"

"Of course."

"But not with me."

"I feel we're beyond that, lass," he said, and silently crossed the floor. She couldn't help but notice that he wore no shoes. Still, when he stepped up to her, she had to tilt her head back to look into his eyes. They were dark and deep and shone like polished onyx in the firelight.

"And what about you and the princess?" she asked. "Do you knock for her?"

"I knock every time I come to her room in the small hours of the morning."

Her stomach churned. She stepped back a sharp pace, bumping into her chair. The corner of his irresistible mouth quirked up. "Is something amiss, lass?"

"Nay," she said, and actually considered slapping him, but she kept her hands to herself and straightened her back. Her nipples felt strangely sensitive against the soft fabric of her simple gown. "Of course not."

His gaze dropped for an instant, and his nostrils flared, but in a moment he raised his eyes and lifted his hands to shoulder height. "Shall we dance?"

Panic struck her. The bed was so close. He was closer still, and she couldn't seem to get certain images out of her mind. Images of his nipples hard and flat pressed against her naked breasts. Images of their bodies straining together amidst tangled sheets.

"I have been thinking," she said, and paced away. But even with her back turned she could feel his hot gaze. The room was silent except for the haunting strains floating up from below. She turned finally. "I am certain you are wrong. There is no reason for me to learn to dance."

"Lass—"

"I am the princess," she said, pivoting toward him. "If I say I am in no mood to dance, there is no need for me to dance."

"But Anna would say no such thing."

"How do you know?"

"I know her well."

"How well?" she snapped and wished she hadn't spoken, or at the very least had kept her tone as cool as his always seemed to be.

He stepped up to her, his expression quizzical. "Tell me, lass," he said, his voice quiet. "Might you be jealous?"

"Jealous!" She laughed, but the sound was not quite so refined as she had hoped. Indeed, it came out as something of a wild snort.

His lips twisted as he stepped toward her, but she turned stiffly away. "I'll not dance with you."

"You'd make the musicians labor away for no reason? After I told them the princess was having difficulty sleeping and would dearly appreciate their masterful—"

"I never have difficulty sleeping."

"'Tis a strange thing," he murmured. "I've been sleeping better myself of late."

His voice was low. Memories stormed in again. His touch, his eyes, the hard play of muscle beneath his hot skin. She licked her lips.

"Dance with me, lass."

She tried to shake her head, but he was already taking her hand, was already wrapping his arm around her waist, and somehow they were dancing—without conscious thought, without volition. They were simply sweeping across the floor together. If she made any mistakes, she was completely unaware of them. As it turned out, dancing was life set to music. And life was warm, full, pulsing with possibilities.

"Lass." His voice was soft against her cheek. "You must have done this before."

She tried to respond, but he was so close. She could feel the heat of his chest through his shirt, could feel the fluid shift of muscles in his shoulder beneath her hand.

"Tell me the truth," he said.

"I have not."

"Another first then," he murmured against her ear. The sound shivered like a lightning bolt to her heart. "Why?"

She tried to think coherently, forced her lips to move. "I had more important things to occupy my time."

"Such as stealing infatuated men's watches?"

She tripped. He tightened his grip, bearing her back against his chest and watching her face.

"In . . . fatuated?"

"I'm not speaking of myself of course," he said, and drew her marginally closer so that the hardened tips of her nipples brushed against his chest. Dear God. "I'm far too elegant to feel such mundane emotions."

She told herself not to speak, to ignore his words, but she could just as well have commanded herself to stop breathing. "What did you feel?" she whispered.

"When I first saw you at the market?" He spread his fingers across her back. Excitement raced down her spine, tingling off in a thousand directions. She forced a causal nod, but in a moment she realized he had gone silent, realized he was watching her in silent contemplation, and in that instant she knew she had finally failed to see his trap.

She tried to pull from his arms, but he kept dancing, drawing her along with him. "Is everything you do calculated to wring a confession from me?" she demanded.

"I don't resent the loss of the watch." His words were

quiet, his eyes intent. She felt herself falling into their depths, but she yanked herself out of the trance.

"Good!" she snapped. She should be silent, or deny, or plead ignorance, but anger and fidgety frustration drove her beyond those careful precautions. "Because I sold it the very next day."

His lips quirked again as if he were thinking things best left unsaid, but finally he spoke again. "Why me?"

He was so arrogant, so beguiling, so irresistible, and he knew it. The thought made her crazy. "Because you wouldn't leave me be," she gritted.

"So 'tis the men most attracted to you who lose their valuables."

She glanced into his eyes, then snapped her attention away, refusing to be drawn into his snare, refusing to allow her mind to settle on his haunting words. Refusing to care. Maybe he truly was attracted to her. But what difference did it make? Many men were attracted to her. He was no different, chasing every skirt that crossed his path—just like her own father, in fact. "It is only the men who hope to use me who tend to lose their valuables."

"I had no intention of using you, lass, only of becoming acquainted with you."

"Of course."

"You still don't trust me."

"If I don't trust, it is your fault, my lord. After all, I am what you made me."

"I did not make you a seductress, lass."

"I am not—"

"Of course not," he murmured, and kissed her. Desire roared through her. She stumbled again, and he steadied her, drawing her back into the circle of his strength. Her nipples brushed his chest again, like flint on steel. "I would ask a favor of you, lass."

She couldn't pull herself from his gaze.

"When dancing with the duke perhaps you could refrain from pressing your breasts against him."

She jerked back and he shook his head, his eyes entrancing.

"I did not say you should do the same with me."

Snatching her hands away, she glared at him. "Get out of my chambers."

"We've yet to master the quadrille."

"If I mistake a step, I can always resort to blatant seduction," she snarled.

He grinned at her, but there was something in his eyes. "You forget," he said. "The princess is not one to flaunt herself."

"And you forget," she said, leaning in. "I am not really the princess."

"No. I do not," he argued and stepped closer, but she jerked cautiously backward.

"Get out," she repeated, and though somewhere inside her she desperately hoped he would refuse, he kissed her hand with lingering heat, then turned on his heel and departed.

The days creaked by. Nicol tended to state business, doing his best to keep a certain thief out of his mind and keep himself out of her bedchamber.

He had sent three loyal spies to Teleere, telling them to look for a woman named Linet Mulgrave. Word had returned that such a woman had been found in Laird MacTavish's castle. She was safe and healthy, and though he had not yet heard why she remained in Teleere, everything seemed to be going well enough. Why, then, did he feel so fractious, so irritably out of sorts? Rumor had it that the duke of Venge had arrived that morning. It was also said that the princess had welcomed him as though he were God's own messenger. Damn, he had trained her well. She was a diplomatic genius. There was no reason for Nicol even to remain at the palace.

Perhaps he should sail for Teleere and look into Anna's well-being himself. Perhaps he should meet with his spies. Perhaps he should call on an old paramour.

But as he stood before his beveled mirror that evening, he knew he would do none of those things. Instead, he buttoned his silk burgundy waistcoat, yanked on his charcoal-colored tails, and made his way down the endless corridors to the ballroom.

The grand hall was lit with scores of candles, but still the room seem dimly lit, casting a romantic glow over everything. Diaphanous red-and-gold streamers swept like royal banners from hooks high in the beamed ceiling and amidst the endless yards of flowing material, a surprisingly lifelike eagle soared in effigy.

Nicol snagged a glass of champagne from a passing servant and noticed that a river of sorts had been constructed upon the tables that ran the length of the room. The tiny stream wound across the surface, bordered by miniature hillocks festooned with moss and dried flowers. Then, at the eventual end of the watercourse, a golden cascade splashed down to a pool that rippled beside a tiny replica of the duke's tree-shrouded manor. A group of gawkers hovered about, awed by the masterpiece.

"Drink up," Will said, and, leaning forward, dipped his glass into the cascade. It was not until that moment that Nicol realized it was a river of champagne.

"You're here early," Nicol said, and the baron raised his glass.

"No point waiting for a drought."

"How does Jack fare?"

The baron drank. "He's opinionated, perverse, and difficult."

"Like a son then," Nicol said, and winced at his own foolishness. "My apologies."

Will shrugged, but his eyes were dark as he drank again.

"Looks like every poor bugger with a title to his name is already here."

"And not too insulted by the lack of formal introductions."

"You jest." Cask shouldered his way through the crowd. "We are, every last one of us, far too curious to miss the gala. 'Tis said the princess hopes to marry this duke fellow," he added, turning his gaze toward Nicol and falling silent.

Nicol drank again, still eyeing the crowd, and Cask laughed.

"He's always been a close-mouthed bloke. Aye, Will?"

"Aye," Will agreed. "Never a slip-up from Cole."

Nicol shrugged. "I'm not privy to the princess's plans. She will marry whom she will."

"And I suppose it won't matter to you either way," Cask said, but there was sarcasm in his tone.

Nicol turned to stare, and the other shrugged. "Royal princesses are hardly expected to remain loyal to their husbands these days."

"What are you suggesting?"

Cask eyed the crowd. The room was packed with overdressed nobility. The air was charged with a thousand emotions. Cleavage showed pale and high above frilly, pastel bodices. Men boasted, and women flirted. Liaisons were carried on with the barest of subterfuge.

"She's little more than a child. The duke is old and none too well favored by all accounts," Cask added. "She'll be in need of a . . . friend."

"I'm afraid you're mistaken about my relationship with her," Nicol said, his tone cool, and Cask grinned.

"Of course," he said, but before he'd raised his glass in an impromptu toast, a voice rang over the crowd.

"Hear ye one and all." The mob fell into hushed anticipation. The majority of the guests had not yet seen the new princess and waited breathlessly for that opportunity. "Make ready for Her Majesty." The speaker paused, letting the anticipation grow. "Tatiana Octavia Linnet Rocheneau, royal princess of Sedonia, God's chosen one."

The orchestra struck up the royal anthem of the Rocheneaus. The guests bowed their heads and sank into obeisance, then, through a doorway draped in scarlet, Megan entered the room.

For a moment there was absolute silence, then, as the crowd got its first impressions of her, a murmur began.

"Lovely."

"A bit thin."

"Cool."

"So young."

But Nicol found it impossible to speak. Indeed, he was transfixed by the sight of her. She wore a gown of gold satin that stood out among the pastels like the sun in an azure sky. Her pale arms were bare, her expression somber. In her hands, she bore a scepter and upon her head a crown gleamed with a dozen rare gems, but each jewel was dulled by her beauty, and for just a moment the irony of the situation struck him—a thief with a crown—but the thought would not stay. For she seemed so right, so perfect as she made her way between the riven crowd. She held her head high, and now and then she would nod regally to a subject until she ascended the stairs to her waiting dais. Once there, she turned with sober cadence and received the crowd's adoration.

The steward remained silent for several moments, letting the orchestra complete the stirring anthem and the crowd still somewhat. Then a new song began.

"Honoring us from Denmark, our esteemed ally, Sir George Orwall, the duke of Venge."

George Orwall entered a moment later. So this was why the

ballroom was dimly lit, Nicol thought, and absorbed his first impressions of the duke. As far as Cole could tell the royal Dane had no neck. It seemed to have been swallowed up by a row of chins and heavily rounded shoulders. Perhaps he was not an old man, perhaps no more than forty, but he had gone to fat early. His face was masked by heavy side whiskers, and the high portions of his cheeks were ruddy as if he had already drunk too much. He shuffled up the stairs, took the princess's hand, and kissed it. Something clutched in Nicol's stomach. He studiously ignored the grinding knot, and in a moment the duke straightened. Instead of releasing the girl's hand, however, he leaned close and murmured something for her ears alone. She laughed, and the sound tinkled through the crowded hall like silver bells on Easter morning.

"Well," Cask said, as the duke tucked her fingers under his arm and escorted her around the table to the huge chairs set at the very center of the far side. "At least you're giving her up to someone amusing." He drank again. "And rich. It's said he has more property than the old king himself. In fact—"

"Cask," Will interrupted dully.

"Yes?"

"I believe you might be well advised to shut the hell up."

Cask took one look at Nicol's face, then threw his head back and laughed. Nicol watched him for an instant, considered smashing him in the face with a right hook, remembered that was decidedly inelegant, and made his way stiffly through the crowd toward the long rows of dining tables. The seating arrangements were denoted by flowery penmanship on stiff parchment. Almost snarling at the names, Nicol settled gratefully into his chair and glanced at Megan. She and the duke were tilting their heads together, seeming to share a moment.

"My lord."

Nicol turned slowly away, glancing up as he did so. "Lady Delafont," he said, and rose to his feet.

The baroness touched his shoulder. "Please, don't bother, my lord. It's absolutely crushing in here," she said, and took the chair beside him. "I was thrilled to see we were seated together. It has been too long."

"Indeed," he said, and though the lady looked as beautiful as he remembered, he wanted fervently to turn and watch Megan again. Or at least to be mindlessly drunk. "And where is your husband this evening, Baroness?" he asked.

"Baroness?" She laughed as she lifted her drink to her lips. She had painted them bright red. "Please, Nicol, let's dispense with such formality. Call me Melly." She leaned closer. "As you once did."

He raised his brows at her. "You once were unwed, Baroness," he said, and she laughed.

"Marriage, it is such an inconvenience."

"I wouldn't think so," Nicol said. "I hear your husband is richer than the devil himself."

"Oh, not richer than the devil. Perhaps richer than God," she said and smiled as she slipped her hand onto his thigh.

Who, Nicol wondered, had decided on the seating? He hadn't seen the baroness in more than a year. And now she appeared, without her husband, and they just happened to be sitting directly across from the princess's high chair.

"Lord Newburn." Paqual made his way through the crowd. "And Lady Delafont." He managed a slight bow, despite the crush. "I trust you are enjoying the festivities."

"Yes," said Amelia, and smiled. "A wonderful time."

"Good. Good. And surely we'll have many more such fetes once the duke and princess marry. Aye?" said Paqual, and, catching Nicol's gaze, moved on, leaving the other to stare at his retreating back. So the old man was still scheming, Nicol thought. But why would he bother putting the lovely Amelia in his path.

He pondered that question as the first course was served

by waiters dressed like Danish soldiers. Surely this garish opulence wasn't Anna's idea. She had never shown much interest in decorating, and though her advisors seemed to urge her in that direction and away from politics, she tended to be more intrigued by matters of state.

What was she doing now and would Megan be able to hold her own until the princess's return?

"Nicol." Amelia's tone was pouty. "You've barely touched your soup."

He drew his attention from the head table. "I'm afraid I'm not partial to cucumbers."

"You don't like cucumbers?" The baroness sounded aghast as she spread her gloved fingers over her carefully displayed bosom. "But they are unquestionably my favorite vegetable."

"Are they?" He wondered idly why he had ever found her attractive. Aside from her bosom and her lovely face, she had little to recommend her. She was vain and shallow and self-serving. But perhaps that explained everything, even Paqual's reasons for wanting them seated together. It was said the baroness of Delafont could distract a stone.

"Oh absolutely," she said, and gave him a wicked smile. "They have such a marvelous shape."

He took a drink of his champagne and remembered another reason for his attraction to her. She had no compunction against having sex outside of marriage. Unfortunately, or perhaps fortunately, she preferred money to sex. The elderly baron had offered her both. Or perhaps he'd offered her enough money to make sex inconsequential.

"And size," Amelia finished. "The size of a cucumber has much to recommend it."

"You haven't changed," Nicol said, and the baroness laughed.

"I shall take that as a compliment. Here, let me help you

with your soup." Scooping up a spoonful, she leaned close and fed it to him.

He considered suggesting she had prostituted herself for her husband's wealth. He considered telling her to return to the baron forthwith or at least to be silent so that he could try to hear Megan's conversation, but he merely accepted the soup instead.

"There now, isn't that delicious?" Leaning against his arm, she pressed the bulge of her breast against his biceps.

But at that moment Nicol heard the duke laughing and glanced up. Venge leaned toward Megan, staring down her dress. Nicol held his breath, knowing the girl's temperament. For a moment he remembered the pain of being struck by a wine bottle but instead of looking for a weapon, she turned toward the old lord and laughed.

The rest of the meal was just as wonderful. Amelia got drunker by the minute. The duke got louder, and despite all his good intentions, Nicol couldn't seem to become either drunk or loud. Instead, he watched the couple on the dais and felt his stomach cramp with distaste.

He doubted if the fat duke was so irresistible that the girl couldn't spend more than a moment without tittering at his jokes. Indeed, he had thought she was different than the average woman. But she seemed absolutely enamored of Venge, and since it could not be either his looks or his obviously lacking charm, Nicol could only assume it was his title that attracted her. But then what did he expect? If a pampered lady like Amelia would cast everything aside for a title and a fat bank account, how much more would a girl who had once haggled over a scrap of velvet?

With those morose thoughts ringing in his head, Nicol pushed aside his dessert, a serving of loundes pudding which continued the red-and-gold themes in currant jelly and lemon sauce. After an interminable amount of time, they were finally ushered into the ballroom. The decorations there were even more garish than in the dining room. The elite society of Sedonia lined the walls in intoxicated happiness while Megan placed her bejeweled hand atop the duke's and made her way down the carpet to the center of the dance floor. Nicol watched with darkening anticipation. The music began. The duke grasped her about the waist and swung her into a waltz. Gone was the grace she had displayed in her bedchamber, but if any onlookers wondered about her inabilities, it could certainly be blamed on the duke's tottering drunkenness.

Still, the dance seemed to last forever. Finally, however, Megan pulled herself from her guest's embrace, curtsied, and made her way back to the throne placed against the far wall.

She was approached long before she reached that sanctuary, however. Nicol watched her nod, watched her drawn into Lord Riven's embrace, watched her execute another waltz.

As for the duke, he was dancing with Lady Edwina, the youngest daughter of the bishop of Founder. She was all but a pauper, but she was young and widowed, and Venge clasped her to his barrel-like chest as he stumbled about the dance floor. Nicol scowled. The duke of Venge may be wealthy and influential, but even a fool like Paqual couldn't think he would make a match for Sedonia's young princess. Spotting the old chancellor in the crowd, Nicol tried to shift through the mob to speak to him, but just then Amelia snuffled him out to insist on a dance.

The evening droned on. Perfumes mingled with sweat from scores of overheated bodies. Laughter boomed. Amelia clung and giggled and became more annoyingly intoxicated by the moment. Luckily, she was not so inebriated that she would refuse another drink. Nicol made his way through the crush toward the champagne, caught her a draught of liquor, then stood watching Megan as she danced with an unknown lord. Her cheeks were slightly flushed as though she had drunk too much, but her eyes were bright with that sharp wit that was hers alone, and in that moment he was tempted beyond reason to insist on a dance. Why not, after all? He had been the one to teach her. Indeed, he had been the one to find her in the first—

"Nicky," Amelia said, ferreting him out once again. "I am quite disappointed in you." He managed to tear his gaze away from Megan as the baroness ran her fingertips down his arm before retrieving her drink. "You are not nearly so attentive as you once were."

He nodded in concession. "And you are not nearly so unattached."

She laughed. "I don't know why you are so concerned about my marital status. Believe me." She drank again, watching him the whole while through her lashes. "I am not. Indeed, since my wedding I've thought of you often."

"Have you?" Just past Amelia's shoulder, he could see the duke make his lumbering way through the crowd toward the princess.

"Tell me, have you ever thought of me?" she purred.

"How could I not?" Nicol asked, pulling his attention back to the baroness. "You married the baron a week after saying I was the perfect man for you."

"So I hurt your feelings," she pouted. "I was afraid that was the case."

The duke had reached the girl's side, but Lord Kendall whisked her away. Venge swayed slightly and waited. The pair danced past him. He seemed to try to speak to her, but the duo swung away again. It was then that the duke waded through the crowd and grasped Megan's partner by the arm.

There was a moment of conversation, then Kendall bowed stiffly and left Megan to the duke, who dragged her into his arms.

"Nicky, are you listening to—"

"Would you like to dance?" he asked.

Lady Amelia's scowl lightened a little. "Very well."

He led her onto the dance floor, through the crowd to the center. From the corner of his eyes, he could see the duke's broad form shadowing his partner.

Amelia cuddled up against Nicol's chest, and he eased her into the steps, watching the duke as he did so. The big man swung sideways, allowing Nicol a glimpse of the girl for a moment, but soon she was hidden again.

"I missed you."

Nicol lowered his gaze to the baroness's face. "Surely Paris can't be that tiresome."

"Paris," she said and snorted. "But for a handful of times, the closest I get to Paris is my own back door. It was all I could do to convince my husband to allow me to come here," she said, and skimmed her fingertips down the back of his neck. "If I didn't know better, I would think he doesn't trust me."

"I've no idea why that might be," Nicol said.

She chuckled. "Neither do I. Perhaps someone is spreading rumors about me."

"Or the truth," he suggested.

She tsked at the implication. "Nicol. So bitter. I must have truly wounded you."

Nicol caught a glimpse of Megan's face through the crowd, but she turned, showing her slim, regal back clad in shimmery gold. The duke's arm lay heavily across her waist and his hand was spread with indecent intimacy across the girl's buttocks.

Nicol swore, and Amelia drew back with a start.

"*Mon ami*," she said, "I did not know you bore such strong feelings for me."

He tried to keep dancing, to focus on the woman in his arms, but at that moment he saw the duke dip his head toward his partner's bosom, saw the girl jerk to a halt. There was nothing Nicol could do but lunge through the crowd toward them. Perhaps he heard Amelia complain behind him. Perhaps he was a bit rude in his haste to make his way to Megan's side, for people seemed to bobble in his wake, but he couldn't see her face past Venge's broad back, couldn't guess her thoughts. Indeed, all he could hear were tidbits of the duke's harangue.

". . . uppity considering your country's the size of a rotten turnip and . . ."

"My lord," Paqual said, appearing out of nowhere by the duke's side. "Perhaps you should take a bit of a respite. I have a nice bottle of port set aside for the occasion."

The duke turned his head toward the chancellor, seeming to have some difficulty focusing on the narrow man.

"Port, you say."

"Yes. Nearly as old as myself."

"God's balls," expounded the duke. "I didn't know they'd invented port before the birth of Christ." He boomed a laugh at his own wit. "But mayhap I've had enough to drink. There is something I've not had enough of though since coming to this God-forsaken country," he said, and lifted his hand toward Megan's bosom.

Rage burned like venom through Nicol's system. "Venge," he said, nearly at the duke's side. The duke turned his head to glance over his shoulder, but in that moment there was a flash of gold. The duke croaked out a bestial sound. His head jerked back. His body stiffened like a mountain pine, and he crashed to the floor. He shuddered once, groaned, and lay absolutely still.

"Good God!" Paqual wheezed.

Women gasped, the crowd drew back, staring, and Nicol rushed through the opening to Megan's side.

"Are you well?" he rasped.

She lifted her attention from the man on the floor to

Nicol's face and drew a careful breath. "Yes," she said. "I am quite well. Thank you for your concern." Her expression was still somber, her stance perfectly erect, but there was something in her eyes. Something wonderfully alive.

"What happened?" Paqual rose stiffly from the duke's prostrate form.

"I do not know," Megan assured him, shifting her expression to show perplexed concern. "One moment he was speaking to you, and the next he collapsed."

Paqual scowled. "You didn't . . ." He paused, looking bemused. "It almost seemed as if someone struck him."

"Struck him, my lord?" Her tone was a perfect meld of innocence and bafflement. Her gloved hand fluttered to her throat where a dozen rubies shone against her perfect skin. "I assure you that is not possible. I was standing right here. Perhaps he imbibed a bit much and was overcome by the effects."

"Perhaps," said Cask sardonically, and the onlookers laughed.

The duke's retainers had arrived, and, seeming surprisingly unsurprised, were already carrying him from the room.

Paqual watched them cart Venge away, then turned to the princess with a worried expression. "You are well, Your Highness?"

"Yes," she said, but her tone was strained. "I am fine, but I think I shall retire for the evening. It has been a taxing day."

"Perhaps that is wise. I could not bear it if something should happen to you," Paqual said, and, bowing, motioned to her guards. They came, crowding the others back.

"I've learned something," she said quietly so that the words reached no farther than Nicol's ears as she turned toward the door.

"Many things I would guess," Nicol countered, his fists clenched as he watched the duke's feet disappear through the archway ahead of them.

She smiled slightly, just a shadow of joy, undimmed by the remaining spark of anger in her eyes, and in that moment she shone more brightly than every jewel that adorned her, so full of intelligence and life that it was all he could do to refrain from dragging her into his arms. "Dukes fall just as easily as plowmen."

So he had been right. She had kneed the good duke in the groin without ruffling a hair, and Nicol himself had blocked the crowd's view.

"Remind me to raise your pay," he said.

The ladies-in-waiting rushed forward, enveloping her in their presence.

"I'll do that," she said, and, nodding with regal aplomb, disappeared from sight.

Chapter 24

〜◦⌒◦〜

Nicol forced himself to remain in his own bedchamber that night, though his feet strayed toward her door a dozen times. He knew that every time he went into her room he put her at risk. Indeed, every time he spoke to her he took a chance, and he had no intention of compromising her. Yet the temptation gnawed at him like a rabid hound.

By morning, his eyes felt gritty, and his mood the same. Megan had failed to appear at breakfast, and though he tried not to let his gaze stray to the doorway, her absence grated on his nerves. Was she well? And if so, why hadn't she come down for breakfast? There were few things that could keep her from her meals. But despite his preoccupation, he had little enough time to worry about such things. The Council of the Realm, that unique but fractious meld of the house of lords and the order of men, had already gathered in the palace's state room. Thus, he sat in silence, listening to the debate and trying to focus on matters of the state.

"Our coffers are all but empty," Lord Fairfield was saying.

"And why is that?" asked Mr. Grafter. He was a jeweler by profession and more wealthy than most of Sedonia's grand peerage.

"The cost of maintaining the palace is ever increasing."

"Maintaining it!" Grafter scoffed. "You have redecorated it a dozen times in the past score of years. And now the princess takes the throne and decides to remake it again for the duke's visit. Perhaps it is money well spent if a bond is formed between Denmark and Sedonia, but it is money well wasted if naught comes of it. How is their courtship advancing?"

An uneasy silence spread through the room.

"I fear the duke may be a bit . . . boisterous for our princess," Paqual hedged, speaking up for the first time.

"Who the devil cares if he's boisterous? He's richer than the king of England and has his brother's ear."

"We must think of the princess's sensibilities. Give her time—"

"To hell with her sensibilities. If the man can produce an heir and pass down an inheritance, there is no problem."

"As king he will have a good deal of power," argued Lord Riven. "And after his performance last night I fear his intellect, along with his manners, is somewhat suspect."

"What happened last night?" asked a bent old lord in a tilted wig.

"He passed out at the ball," said a lanky commoner.

"Passed out?" Franklin Twyndon was a wainwright by trade and had made a fortune crafting viceroys for those who lived to be seen dashing about Fallcome Gardens. "Is he ill?"

"Perhaps the duke is simply not accustomed to our champagne," Paqual suggested.

Or perhaps he was not used to being kneed in the balls by a woman half his size, Nicol thought, and felt anger swirl like bile amidst worried admiration. It was certainly not the champagne that had felled the duke. In fact, it was not the two quarts of wine he had consumed before that either.

"'Tis sure his lordship is abed with a raging headache about now," someone said.

"I heard there are other problems," Riven said. The entire assemblage fell silent. "I heard there may be trouble with his . . . nether parts."

"What the devil are you talking about?" Grafter roared, still eager for the match.

Riven squirmed like a boy before a steely-faced schoolmaster. "The duke's men called in a surgeon first thing this morning. It seems Venge was complaining about pain in his . . . man parts."

"Christ!" said Grafter.

"'Tis said his nuts are as swelled and purple as eggplants," added the lanky commoner.

"He says she kicked him," said Lord Fellden.

"The princess!" interjected Lord Riven, aghast. "She's barely big enough to wound a fly."

"And mild-mannered."

"She's naught if not sophisticated."

But Fellden shook his head. "He says she kicked him a good one right between the legs, and he's heading back to Denmark just as soon as he can walk."

General chaos broke out, but finally Grafter shot to his feet. "Well, ain't that grand! All the money you spent to woo him, and she goes and maims him before—"

"I assure you," Paqual said, rising stiffly. "Princess Tatiana did not injure the good duke. The idea is ludicrous. You've nothing to worry about. If Venge returns to Denmark, there are certainly others just as wealthy who would be thrilled to take the princess's hand in marriage. The prince of Romnia for one."

"And what if she maims that one?"

"She did not maim—"

"Well, whether she did or nay, the duke is hobbling back to his mum, leaving us taxpayers to foot the bill."

Paqual spread his knobby fingers. "I fear there is naught to be done but shoulder the burden and pass the bills on to—"

"If you raise the wheat tax again, half of Sedonia will starve before spring."

"Then how do you propose that we pay our debts, Mr. Grafter?"

"What about a window tax?"

"'Tis clear you've got but two in your entire house."

"Two is all I need."

"And what of the rest of us? Do you want the majority of Sedonia's peerage to board up their windows as they've done in England?" asked Lord Melville.

"I don't give a good Goddamn if they live in holes and eat mustard seeds," Grafter snapped.

"And I don't care if you don't eat a'tall!" Melville stormed.

"So you'd put the burden squarely on the shoulders of the working class," accused Grafter, jerking to his feet.

Lord Melville rose with him. "The working class is the largest class. Of course they should pay the greatest portion of—"

"It ain't just! 'Tis—"

"No." A woman's voice echoed through the room. Each man turned toward the sound, and there, framed in the doorway, was the princess. She wore a gown of gray and ivory. Her hair was swept atop her head, and her long slim throat was bare.

"Your Majesty."

Chairs scraped, and men shot to their feet, only to bend and bow.

She entered the room like an elegant archangel, her head held high. "No," she repeated. "It is not right that we should burden our people more than they can bear."

"But the debts," Paqual said, and swept his hand sideways to indicate the grandeur of the palace where they met. "They have to be paid. If you could form an alliance with the duke of—"

"I will not marry the duke." She clasped her hands in front of her body. Nicol could not help but notice that her knuckles looked white against the silvery gray skirt. Could not help but notice that though she was nervous, her eyes were sharp and her chin high. Indeed, he could not guess how every man there managed to keep from pulling her into his arms, from touching her face and kissing her lips, her only feature that, even now, looked hopelessly unbusinesslike.

"Your Majesty, this is hardly the place—" Paqual began, but she interrupted him.

"I believe this is exactly the place," she said. "I believe my people deserve to know the truth and the truth is this—the duke of Venge is selfish, crude, and vain. He detests Sedonia and thinks the Danes far superior to my own people. Is that the kind of man you want on your throne?"

No one spoke. She skimmed their faces.

"What would you suggest then, Your Majesty?" asked Fellden softly.

She caught his gaze, then shook her head slowly. "There are surely no simple answers, but it seems fair that each person should pay an equal percentage according to his income."

"But Your Majesty," argued Melville. "That would mean the peerage would pay a disproportionate part of the taxes."

She smiled at him. "I have heard, Lord Melville," she said, "that you are extremely wealthy."

He stuttered something, but she held up her hand to stop his words. "I do not mean to suggest that we tax anyone unfairly, but think of this, good gentlemen, troubles brew like storm clouds against France's royalty. England's working class is rioting. If the same happens here, will any of us profit? Would it not be better to make a more equitable system, to care for our workers, to appease our laymen?"

"Certainly, your ideas seem sound in theory, Your Majesty, but how would we implement such changes? And how would we convince my contemporaries that raising their taxes is a just idea? That is to say, surely they will feel unfairly put upon, especially with the money just spent to renovate the palace. And when they hear that you've no intention to marry the duke after all—"

"You are right," she said and nodded solemnly. "I've no right to spend such exorbitant amounts of money."

Jaws dropped like dice around the room.

"Therefore, I shall cut Malkan's expenses in accordance with the amount of taxes levied against our citizens."

"Your Highness," Paqual began, "you must not be hasty. I know last night was trying for you, but you must not give up on the idea of an advantageous marriage. In fact, there are several extremely suitable young lords who even now—"

"I am not giving up on the idea of a match," she said. "I am merely saying there are other ways to pay the bills without prost—" She stopped and pursed her lush lips. Nicol wondered silently how many others knew she had been about to call them whoremongers. "Until I do wed," she said, "there are other ways to pay the bills."

"Begging your pardon, Your Majesty," Paqual began, and smiled eerily. "But your council has spent endless hours wrestling with this very problem. It is not so simple as you might think."

"Did I say it was simple?" She could look as disdainful as a monk. "No, I did not," she said. "But there are means."

"Again, begging your pardon," Paqual said. "But what would you suggest? Just the bills from last night's fete run upward of ten thousand sentrons. How do you propose that we pay that?"

Nicol saw a moment of astonishment flash through her eyes. Ten thousand sentrons must seem like an insurmountable debt to a woman who hoarded crackers and bits of colored glass, but in an instant she turned with regal aplomb to her assemblage. "I will need help in deciding where costs might be cut. What are your suggestions?"

They were flabbergasted, struck dumb. Nicol almost laughed out loud.

"Your Highness," he said, and rose to his feet with a bow. "If I might be so bold—"

"Speak freely, my lord."

"Your stable in England costs more than 120,000 sentrons per year to keep." If she was surprised to hear she had horses in England, she refrained from saying so. "Perhaps," he continued, "you could sell the stud, and—"

"That was the old king's favorite pastime. Surely—"

"But the old king is dead," said Twyndon, practical to the end. His scraggly, gray brows were pulled low over squinty eyes, but he was gazing at the princess as if seeing her clearly for the first time. "And his niece is on the throne."

She gave him a regal nod and the slightest suggestion of a smile. "And what would you suggest that I sell, Mister Twyndon?" She must have only heard the man's name mentioned once, but she had remembered. Nicol felt his chest swell.

She canvassed the room. At first the suggestions were sparse and careful, but the girl's receptiveness drove them past their wariness until the room was all but spinning with ideas, not only of how to pare down the palace's expenses, but how they might manage their own, how they could approach the average citizen, how they could better their country.

When Megan rose from her chair amidst the company, Nicol rose with the others. His throat felt tight with emotion, but he was careful not to let it show in his expression. The council bowed as a unit, their faces reflecting their feelings, some hopeful, some wary, but all surprised.

The princess, it seemed, was far more than a pretty face and a royal name. She was a woman with a heart.

Chapter 25

"But Your Majesty, the horses at Braeton Stable are amongst the finest in the world." There were actual tears in the horse master's eyes. It seemed he had journeyed from London the moment he had heard there was a possibility of closing the stud. And only two days had passed since that suggestion had first been discussed. Roger Sunderlund was, apparently, a man who kept his ear to the ground. "'Tis said you are a fine judge of horseflesh. Surely you realize how splendid they are."

Megan truly didn't know what to do. She wished, in fact, that she had not agreed to meet with Roger Sunderlund and his eerie attachment to his, or rather, *her own*, horses.

"I understand they are fine stock," she began, but in that moment Nicol interrupted from the doorway.

"Your Majesty," he said and bowed. "May I enter?"

She nodded urgently, hoping for an ally. "Lord Newburn," she said, widening her eyes a bit at Sunderlund's lavish sentiment. "What are your thoughts on Braeton Stable?"

"Fine steeds are housed there," he said "and everyone knows of your love for a good horse, but you've yet to find the time to visit the stud in England."

Oh for heaven's sake! Tatiana owned twoscore of blooded horses that she'd never even seen?

"But if Her Majesty could make the time to visit," pleaded Sunderlund, "she would surely realize that such equine quality must not be lost. And New Mint . . ." His eyes misted over again as he twisted his hat in his hands. "He is the finest stallion in all of England. Perhaps in all of Europe. I could not bear to be parted . . ." He broke down and fell to one knee, grappling at her skirts. She scooted her legs back even as her guards rushed forward.

"Please, Mr. Sunderlund," she said, but he was sobbing onto her slippers.

"Not my Mint," he pleaded.

The nearest guard grasped him by the shoulder and dragged him to his feet, but he was still bent and broken.

"Your Majesty, he is like the son I'll never have. You cannot—"

"This I promise you," Megan said. "I shall not sell the stallion."

He gasped and wrung his hat harder. "But they said the stable—"

"The stable may be sold," she said. "And many of the horses might also have to be—"

He sucked in his breath.

"They might also have to find new homes," she said. "But if New Mint is as good as you say, I shall surely find a place for him here at the palace."

"And . . . me . . . Your Majesty?"

"You shall remain with him."

She thought he probably would have collapsed like so

much loose chaff if the guards hadn't been holding him up, but he remained in an upright position as he was taken from the room, thanking her profusely.

The chamber went quiet, empty but for Nicol and herself.

"Sedonians seem prone to sentimentality," she said.

"Horsemen are overly emotional by nature," he corrected. "The average Sedonian is solid as a rock."

"Really. And are you a Sedonian or a horseman?"

"I am a gentleman and a whip," he said.

"Elegant to the last."

"Certainly," he said, but there was something in his eyes that spoke of passions unleashed. Or was she imagining it to salve her own raw feelings?

"I am surprised you waste your time in council then."

He narrowed his eyes slightly, but she couldn't read his thoughts. "Tell me," he said finally. "If they had rioted against your suggestions instead of rallying to your call, what would you have done?"

She shrugged. "I would have told them I was nothing more than a barmaid from Teleere."

"They would never have believed you."

"The truth is often surprising."

He smiled a little. "Not that surprising, lass."

"Your Majesty."

Megan shifted her attention past Nicol's shoulder. Halfway between him and the door a young boy stood. His back was as straight as a lance, his hair as neat as Sunday, and his face absolutely spotless.

"Master Jack," she said. "You look very handsome."

"And you look as good as a five-course meal."

She laughed and he reddened, so she sobered quickly and motioned him nearer. "Tell me, Nimble Jack," she said, and noticed Lord Landow enter soundlessly behind him. "Do you have business here in the palace?"

"Yes," he said, his face absolutely sober. "I come ta read you a book."

Nicol found them some hours later sitting alone in a private alcove. Their backs were to the door as they hunched together over a small gaming table. He nodded to the guard as he stepped inside.

Dice clattered against wood, then bumped to a stop.

"That's it then," Megan said, gathering the ivory cubes. "You owe me seventy sentrons."

"You told me you'd show me 'ow to cheat."

"And I have."

"You ain't cheatin'." Somehow the boy's words sounded like an accusation.

She laughed. "So you think I'm so very lucky do you?"

Nicol could see the boy's profile. His eyes were wide, his somber mouth pursed.

"You're the princess."

"And so I'm lucky?"

The lad nodded.

"This is the best advice I can give you, as a princess and as a friend," she said and, taking his hand, pressed her own dice onto his palm. "Never trust to luck. It will surely abandon you when you most need it."

He was silent for a moment, staring at her fingers, then lifted his eyes to hers. "Then what do I trust to?"

"God." She closed his fingers, leaving him with the dice. "And yourself. You're a special lad, young Jack. I see it in you."

The boy stared at the table. "Me mum was a whore."

The room went silent in the wake of his abrupt words, but her gaze never wavered, never shifted from his. "Was?"

"Long time ago, seems like another life, she went on a drinkin' binge one night. There was men, and laughing. I wondered where she got the money for all that wine. Then the next day, she took me down to Monroe Street to see Mr. Compton. He wore rouge on 'is face and paint on 'is lips. But 'e 'ad 'im a grand 'ouse. I thought I musta died and gone to 'eaven."

She closed her eyes for a moment and took his hand in hers.

The boy's head bobbled a little as he stared at their fingers, and his mouth pursed harder. "Mum said I should trust 'im to take care of me from then on."

She exhaled carefully. "Sometimes life's a right bitch," she whispered.

He jerked his eyes to hers, and she held his gaze steady. "Even a princess knows that much, Jack."

They watched each other in silence for a long moment, then, "Did you love your mum, princess?"

"Infinitely."

He narrowed his eyes in solemn thought.

"More than I can tell you," she explained. "But she deserved to be loved."

He bit his lip. "And mine . . ." His words frayed to a halt, like a shadow of the angry lad he had been just weeks ago. "She said I 'ad ta love 'er. Cuz she was me mum."

"I don't know a great deal about love," she said. "But this much I can tell you . . . love is not something one can demand. It is freely given or it is not given at all. Your mother was weak and foolish, lad. But you are neither."

The boy swallowed, closed his eyes and opened them to find hers again. "I think I killed 'im," he whispered.

She sat perfectly still, thinking, then, "Mr. Compton," she guessed.

He nodded jerkily. "Mum said 'e liked boys. She said . . ." He swallowed and continued slowly. "But she was wrong."

Nicol tightened his fists and said nothing.

"'E 'ated 'em," Jack said. "'E would come into me room at night and . . ." His voice failed again, but he cleared his throat and continued on. "I struck 'im with a poker. 'It 'im as 'ard as I could. 'E fell. There was blood." His hands were shaking. "And then I run."

She said nothing, and Jack glanced up again. "Will I 'ang for it, princess."

She drew in an unsteady breath. "How long ago was that?"

"Most of five years ago I suppose."

"No one knows?"

He glanced at their hands again, and when he spoke his voice was nearly too quiet to hear. "I ain't told no one but you."

"And I'll not tell, young Jack. You have my word."

The silence seemed physically painful. Jack's Adam's apple bobbed. "How come?"

"Even a princess knows pain when she sees it." He scowled, and she continued. "You didn't deserve to be misused, lad."

"My mum said—"

"It doesn't matter!" Her voice was harsh for the first time, but she soothed it. "Forget what she said, Jack. Please. You are what God made you, not what she made you. You were right not to stay on Monroe Street. You did what you had to do."

"I ain't never seen Mum again."

"I'm sorry."

He jerked his eyes up. "It ain't like I wanted to. She 'ad a quick temper and all, but sometimes at night she'd sing to me. She 'ad a pretty voice did Mum. Even when she was drunk . . ." His voice faltered.

She didn't make him go on. "So Poke finally took you in."

"Yeah. And 'e'd 'it me too. But 'e never . . ."

Perhaps she winced. Nicol wasn't sure.

"Just because he's better than the worst doesn't make him good," she said.

He neither agreed nor disagreed.

"Don't go back to him," she murmured.

His face contorted, but not a single tear dropped from his eyes. Instead, he cleared his throat. "I can't pay you."

She glanced up.

"The bet," he said. "I can't pay you just yet."

She laughed, and the sound seemed strange in the tight emotions of the room. "Lord Landow can see to your debt."

The boy straightened his narrow back. "I pay for me own gambling."

"I'll tell you what, Master Jack," she said. "Promise me you'll not gamble again, and I'll absolve you of your debt."

He scowled at her. "I can't make that promise, Princess, not even to you."

"Then I can wait until the baron gives you enough coin to pay me."

"Lord Landow . . ." He laughed. "Give me money?"

"You *are* his ward."

Emotion flashed through his eyes, something between perplexity and hope. "What does that mean?"

"It means he'll pay for your needs, your food, your education, your housing."

"But 'e don't . . ." He paused." " 'E doesn't even know me. And sometimes I think . . ."

"What?"

"Sometimes I think 'e 'ates me." He winced. "But sometimes I thinks 'e likes me, only 'e don't want to."

"Give him a chance," she said. "Just as he is giving you. You can read now, and write. But there is so much more, Jack. You'll be surprised."

"Am I supposed to trust *'im*, princess?"

She dropped her gaze to their joined hands.

"Try," she murmured. "Lord Newburn tells me he's a good man."

"I never trusted no nobleman before."

"No," she said and glanced up. Her eyes met Nicol's with a hard flash of feeling. Like a lightning bolt straight to his chest. "Me neither," she murmured. "But perhaps it's time."

Chapter 26

They rode the next morning, and although Megan felt a bit more comfortable around horses, she was still more than happy to ride the bay gelding she'd found to be so patient some days earlier. Lord Kendall spent much of his time by her left side, and Lord Riven was oft on her right, and though they were fine companions, she frequently found herself scanning the throng ahead. She had barely spoken to Nicol in days. Which was just as well, of course, but wasn't he supposed to be looking after her?

There was a bit of a flurry over who could help her dismount once they returned to the palace, but Lord Kendall won out, slipping her to the ground, then bowing with a flourish.

In the afternoon she visited an orphanage that had become Anna's pet project, and early evening found her dressing for the opera. Mary chose a gown for her. It was the color of a summer peach and just as soft to the touch. Her hair was pinned up and her neck draped in ivory pearls before she finally stepped into her carriage and rode down the cobbled street to the opera house. Paqual sat across from her, making dull small talk and sitting as stiff as a hairpin.

The opera was, apparently, the place to see and be seen. The glitter of the place was astonishing. The chairs, set in a box at the exact center of the garish stage, were not particularly comfortable. But the astounding volume of the musicians, combined with their bright face paint and revealing costumes gave her much to marvel at. Still, to Megan's frustration, she found she could barely understand a word.

True, she was hardly a connoisseur of language, having studied it for approximately three minutes, but it had been a hard three minutes, and even the viscount had admitted she was an apt student. The thought made her restive, but she dared not fidget, for next to Paqual's stoic demeanor, she always felt as if she were as restless as a red ant.

Intermission came finally. Because of the crush of nobility, exiting her box took all of ten minutes, but finally she found herself sipping punch and scanning the crowd.

"Your Majesty."

Megan glanced at Paqual. He bowed stiffly, then indicated the young stranger who stood to his right. "I would like to present Giovanni Fantino, the marquis of Altura."

The young nobleman bowed from the waist, sweeping his black top hat inches from the floor before straightening and finding her eyes. "Your Majesty, I am most honor to make your acquaintance."

"Lord Altura," she said, and nodded briefly. At last, someone with whom she was not supposed to have had a previous history. "Are you enjoying the show?"

"But of course." He had a strong accent, which she couldn't quite identify, and his eyes sparkled in the uncertain light of the wall sconces. Not much taller than she, even in his high-heeled Hessians, he had a wicked smile that winked like lightning beneath his carefully trimmed mustache.

"Who could not be enjoying a Frenchman in Sedonia doing a poor rendition of an Italian opera."

"A poor rendition?"

He bowed again, and perhaps he tried to look humble, but he didn't quite manage it. "I mean no offense to you or your fabulous country, princess," he said. "But you must be visiting my homeland if you wish to experience true opera."

"Your homeland?"

He looked horrifically surprised. "Italy," he said, sounding aghast that she might not know, and perhaps she should have, but she was a princess and all was easily forgiven.

She gave him a blithe glance. "But where in Italy exactly?" she asked, making it sound, with the briefest of efforts, as if it had been his mistake and not hers at all.

"Ahh, of course." His tone was apologetic. "My home it lie in Florence. The most beautiful city in all of the world. You have been there?"

"Not recently, I fear."

"Then you must come soon. It is . . ." He made a broad motion with his hands. "As heaven in the summer."

"I shall try," she said, and turned smoothly away, but he stepped up beside her.

"And what of you, Your Majesty?" he asked. "Are you enjoy the opera?"

She had almost fallen asleep once her initial shock had worn off. She had almost hoped to later, in fact, but Francois Dubois's high notes were a bit too loud.

The marquis laughed at her reticence. "They are difficult to understand, no?"

"The princess speaks fluent Italian," Lord Kendall argued, falling in step with them.

"Ahh well, I myself speak it quite well," said the marquis, and smiled as he brushed his chest with his fingertips, "and yet I sometimes find myself at a loss. Would you, perhaps . . ." He gave her a truncated bow as they walked along. "Could I be so bold as to offer myself as an interpreter?"

She turned coolly toward him. "You are kind, my lord," she began, but he interrupted with daring speed.

"Not at all, Your Majesty. I would forever be in honor for the opportunity to assist Sedonia's royal jewel. And, too," he said, leaning a bit closer and sharing a conspiratorial grin. "I will make my brothers ache with the envy when I tell them I shared a box with a lady of your unsurpassed beauty."

"I have a need to speak with Lord Dellaire," Paqual said. "The marquis could take my seat."

"Well," Megan said, and, lifting her skirts carefully in one gloved hand, gave the marquis a slanted glance as she climbed the steps to her lofty perch. "I would hate to cause the loss of your siblings' respect."

"You are most gracious," he said, and offered his hand to assist her up the stairs. She took it with slight misgivings. "Since such a stunning lady as yourself has surely not experience such sibling squabbles."

She picked her way through the compliments. "I fear I was not blessed with either brothers or sisters."

He shrugged, his grin ever-present. "They may come in handy when looking for sisterly advise or appropriate footwear," he said, indicating his boots. "But when each one of them is taller than one's self it becomes naught but . . . irritating."

It took her a moment to realize his implications. "Each one?"

He sighed dramatically, looking her straight in the eye. "My sisters they are unreasonable tall."

She couldn't help but smile as a large lord in an old-fashioned powdered wig bowed dramatically. "So many people are," she murmured, nodding pleasantly.

Fantino laughed as he handed her into her chair. "I knew at the first that we were kindred spirit."

The second half of the performance began with new scenery and a handsome woman in blond braids shrieking something inarticulate. Her gown was made of blue velvet, which was laced tight up the front, causing her gigantic bosom to swell up close to her collarbones.

Megan glanced toward her interpreter and he jumped slightly as if he had been transfixed. "My apology," he said and leaned close. "She says her husband is dead and she has nothing for which to live." The words shrieked on. The marquis raised his brows and listened raptly.

"And?" she asked.

"And," he said as the woman began tearing at her clothes with overzealous drama. "I . . . seem to have a mouse in my gown." His brows were up in his hairline as he watched the performance. "Which make me squeak on the high notes."

Megan raised a skeptical brow at her interpreter just as a man strode onto the stage. Already in full roar, he raised his hands toward the heavens as he rambled endlessly on.

"Well?" she asked finally.

"He say . . ." Fantino began, turning from the stage in obvious amazement. "Lucky mouse."

"Really," she said, her tone skeptical.

"*Si.*"

"I fear my speech tutors may have misled me," she quipped, and he laughed.

The rest of the evening went by amicably. The marquis was as clever as he was attentive, and begged her to call him Giovanni. Though he tended to sit a bit close and touch her hand with more frequency than she would have liked, she found his youthful foolishness somewhat refreshing after Paqual's gray stodginess.

But retreating from her box finally, she caught a glimpse of Nicol. He was standing with his back to her. His companion glanced up. She was a tall, elegant beauty with sleepy eyes and dark, flawless skin.

"Your Majesty?" the marquis repeated.

"I beg your pardon?" Megan asked, returning her attention to him.

"I asked if I might accompany you back to the palace."

"'Tis late," she said, and turned her gaze forward again as they made their way down the stairs and through the great, arched doors. "Surely you will wish to find your own bed."

The Italian smiled. "I shall be sleep at the palace tonight, with your permission, of course."

She raised a brow, and he hurried on.

"I have brought a message for your chancellor."

"Ahh." Who was the dark-haired beauty who stood so close to the viscount? An old paramour or a new conquest? She felt her stomach twist.

"And I thought if you would being so gracious, I might take a bit more of your time on the journey to the palace."

They had just reached the royal carriage. Four white stallions champed their bits and tossed plumed heads. Two liverymen mounted the vehicle behind the box while a half dozen guards stood in an arch around her; the extravagance was impressive, the crowd gay, and her companion entertaining. Yet she wanted nothing more than to find herself alone, nothing more than to sit in the darkness with her thoughts and try to unravel the mystery of how she had gotten where she was.

"I fear my carriage is already quite crowded," she said, remembering the current conversation.

"But of course." He gave her another bow and reached for her hand. "I am hardly hope to have you to myself. But I will not take up so very much room." He stroked her hand

with his thumb and straightened. "After all, I am small."
He was standing quite close now. "In some areas," he
added.

She was about to pull her hand away, to mount her carriage
and leave him standing there like an oversexed cockerel, but
it was at that very minute that she saw Nicol exit the opera
house. His companion, her expression seductive and her dark
hair perfectly coifed, was smiling into his face and pressing a
less than subtle breast against his arm.

"Very well," she said, and gave him a portion of the smile
the dark-haired woman had shared with Nicol. "After all, Sedonians are known for their generosity."

"'Tis exactly what I was hope for," he admitted, and
handed her into the swaying carriage.

From the window, Megan watched Nicol and his companion disappear into the crowd. Giovanni introduced himself to
her ladies-in-waiting, and though he subsequently tried to
draw Megan back into conversation, she kept herself to herself.

Thus, he satisfied himself by sharing his flirtations with
Lady Mary and Lady Carolyn who laughed dutifully if a bit
too loudly at his jokes.

By the time they reached the palace, Megan's head was
pounding. With what she hoped was a stately nod, she said
her good nights and made her way up the wide and winding
staircase to her apartments.

Once in her bedchamber, Lady Mary helped her disrobe,
but Megan shooed her away before she could see to her hair.

"Is something amiss, Your Majesty?" she asked.

"Nothing except for this ache in my head," she said, and,
pushing the image of Nicol from her mind, massaged her
brow.

In less than a second Mary had hustled off to find a rem-
edy. Megan sat upon a stool and unwound the string of tiny
pearls from her hair. Her reflection gazed back. An elegant

lady in a pristine nightrail. An adored princess in an opulent palace. A young beauty with a host of suitors.

But it was all a lie. Nothing was hers. Not the identity. Not the clothes, not the suitors. Indeed, the only man who knew the truth was ensconced with another—an ebon-haired beauty with a legitimate title and a fondness for a man who was her equal.

There was a quick rap at the door and Mary hurried in carrying a steaming mug. "Here then, Your Majesty," she said, handing over the offering. "A bit of mulled wine with a pinch of valerian. It will soothe the ache and help you sleep."

Megan sipped the drink, but her melancholy mood remained, haunting her. She wished she could disappear, that she could slip away into the night and leave this all behind. And why could she not? The guards who watched the stairways did not hope to keep people in. Only to keep them out. It would be simple enough to leave. But what of this place? These people? What of the true princess? Megan had vowed to stay until Tatiana returned. But that should have already taken place. She should have already been long gone, returned to her own world. A stab of emotion pricked her, but for the life of her, she couldn't tell what it was. Regret or fear or mere sadness.

"Are you well, Your Majesty?"

She sipped the wine and glanced up. "Do you think . . . In the time I have been here, Mary, have I done any good?"

"Of course, Your Majesty. You needn't ask."

Platitudes. But what had she expected? She nodded. "My apologies," she said. "It must just be the headache."

Mary was silent for a moment, then, "Your mother oft suffered from headaches."

Megan glanced sharply up. "What?"

"I knew the duchess quite well."

"Oh." Megan's mind, lulled by some strange depression,

was playing tricks on her. Or perhaps it was the wine, but for a moment she had thought the other had known her own mother, a red-haired angel with a heart of purest gold. "Did you?"

"Yes." Setting aside a pair of slippers, Mary caught Megan's gaze in the mirror and shyly made her way across the floor. "She was a great beauty. Like yourself."

Sincere kindness. Megan could hear it in the girl's tone. But what she wanted just now, was her own mother. Or at least a memory. Another to remember her goodness.

"I thought," she continued, "when you first came to the palace that you were like her in other ways."

"Such as?"

"She was . . . Forgive me, Your Majesty," she said, and bobbed her head, her cheeks blushed. "I speak out of turn."

"No. Please. Say what you will. Lady Fellway and I were never close." Finally, a sliver of truth.

"No." Mary shook her head. "You wouldn't be. She was . . ." She clasped her hands in front of her mint green skirt. "She was a duchess."

"And I am a princess."

"Yes, but you are more. If you take my meaning."

"I'm not certain I do."

Mary was silent for a moment, then, "I heard about Jack."

"Did you?"

"Lady Catherine said he stole her necklace."

"He tried to steal it. There is a good deal of difference."

"Not to some."

"She resents the fact that I kept the boy from the gallows?"

"She and some others. And they are not happy that you set Lord Landow up as his protector. A baron—taking a back street thief as his ward."

Megan glanced down at her hands, wrapped as they were around her mug. Her head did feel better, and her face felt flushed. She liked wine and wished she had a bit more, for the truth was bitter. She had no more idea how to be a princess than how to soar like a butterfly.

"And what of you, Mary?" she asked. "What do you think?"

"I think . . ." Her voice was soft, but finally she raised her face and spoke with less caution. "Allard said you saved the boy for no reason other than kindness."

"Allard. My guard?" Megan canted her head. "How do you know what Allard says?"

Mary's cheeks brightened again. "He and I . . ." She swallowed and glanced down. "He is a good man, Your Majesty."

"Lady Mary!" She put some scandal into her voice. "What would your father say?"

The girl's eyes went as round as guinea eggs. "You won't tell him."

"No I will not," Megan promised, and laughed. "But a lady and a guard?"

"His prospects are good. Or . . ." She cleared her throat. "They were good until he was pulled from palace duty."

"Oh, I see."

"No. Begging your pardon," she said. "I don't suppose you do. He wanted to come back here, to secure his position. And . . . I wanted him to. But now he says the boy needs him. Lord Landow needs him."

"I'm sorry."

"No. Don't you see what you've done?" Mary asked, and touched her shoulder. "You care, and in so doing, you have taught others to care."

For a moment, she actually feared she might cry. Maybe wine wasn't her friend. Or at least not one to be trusted.

"You're right," Megan said, swallowing her foolish sentiment with the last of the wine. "I'm a saint. Saint Megan."

"What?"

God's knees! For a moment her mind went absolutely blank, but then she smiled and rose to her feet, fighting for calm. "Saint Megan," she said. "Surely you've heard of her."

"No. I'm sorry, I don't believe I have."

"Perhaps the wine is making me imagine things."

"You've only had but one cup. Last Christmastide you drank two bottles yourself and were not the least affected."

"Well . . ." For a moment she could think of nothing, then, "saints aren't supposed to drink a'tall."

Mary stared at her for a moment, then smiled and finally hurried to the bed and pulled back the covers. Megan crawled onto the mattress and let the woman pull the blankets up under her chin.

"Would you like me to remain in the room with you this night, Your Majesty?"

Did she jest? Megan obviously couldn't hold more than a thimbleful of wine. One more word and she'd be blubbering like a baby and spilling the entire truth like a flood from a broken dam.

"No, Mary. That won't be necessary," she said. Holy heavens, she thought as she closed her eyes. What an idiot she'd become. But at least she was safe from her own foolishness for the night. Until morning, until sobriety, she wouldn't have to speak to another living soul.

Chapter 27

~~∞~~

Megan sighed as she stirred from her sleep. The bed was warm and soft. The mattress, freshly plumped and perfectly shaped, smelled of dried heather. She knew immediately where she was and who she was. She was the princess Tatiana and she resided in Malkan Palace. Megan O'Shay, on the other hand, slept on a rotting pallet in a cold dungeon of a room. And no one touched her there. No one turned down her covers or held her in his arms or taught her to waltz. Images of Nicol slipped gently into her mind. The dark intensity of his eyes, the entrancing twist of his lips. She could almost feel him stroking her arm, her cheek, her . . .

Stroking her hair?

She opened her eyes groggily. The fire had burned down to embers, but she could still see him. He sat on the edge of the mattress, watching her, and though she couldn't make out his face, her dreams detailed every irresistible feature.

A dozen emotions smote her, but she was careful to ignore each one.

"So," she said, keeping her tone steady, "you were able to tear yourself from her arms?"

"Of course," he said, and in that instant, she realized her mistake. This man was not Nicol.

Jerking to a sitting position, she stared into the smiling face of the marquis of Altura. "What are you doing here?"

"I am watch you sleep," he said. "You are beautiful beyond word."

"She glanced toward the door, toward the window, the door. "How did you get in?"

He chuckled. "Surely there is nothing that can keep me from such beauty." She could smell the wine on his breath. Apparently, she was not the only one made foolish by alcohol.

"I think you might be wrong there."

"Mere wall cannot keep me away."

"You're drunk."

"And you are irresistible."

She sighed. "I bear you no ill will, Fantino, but if you're found in my chambers, there will be trouble."

"You are worry about me," he said, sounding near tears. "That is beautiful."

Pushing back the covers, she prepared to rise to her feet, but he grabbed her hand.

"Such beautiful fingers," he said, and, lifting them to his lips, kissed the tips.

She pulled her hand away. "Quit that."

"I cannot," he said, and captured her fingers again. "You are too beautiful. My heart it is fill to burst."

"Your head's going to be bursting in the morning. We'd best get you out of here."

"I cannot. Your beauty holds me fast," he said, and kissed her fingers again.

"Listen," she said, feeling irritable as she snatched her hand away for the second time. "As I said, I've nothing against you, but if you say 'beautiful' one more time, I'm going to have to slap you."

He chuckled. "You are fiery. Fiery and beautiful, just as I suspect."

She ground her teeth. "How did you get in here?"

"I climb toward your radiance."

"You climbed the wall? Truly?"

"I am small, but I am wiry, aye, my beauty? We shall fit together like the hand and the glove."

"You will get yourself back down that wall before you get us both in trouble."

"You, my beauty? In the trouble?"

She gave him a look. "Yes," she assured him and managed to gain her feet as she tugged at his arm. "Here in Sedonia, they frown on their princesses being caught in bed with drunken marquises."

"I am more than drunken marquis," he said and staggered to his feet.

She turned him carefully toward the window. "Of course you are."

"I am spy."

"Good."

"I have the important news," he said, not moving from the spot.

"You also have a drinking problem."

"The old king had another . . ." He searched his foggy brain for a moment. "Child," he said, and tottered back onto the mattress, pulling her with him.

"What!" she gasped, tumbling down beside him.

"Yes," he said. "It is truth. There was a bastard born."

"What makes you think so?"

He smiled at her in the darkness, his face inches from hers. "I am a fabulous lover," he said, "but I am also a fabulous spy."

"My uncle had two sons," she said. "They both died years

ago. There were no other children. 'Twas the reason she . . . *I* was put on the throne."

"There was maid in a village to the south that would not agree with you."

"Where did you get this information?"

"I searched. I asked the questions." He tapped his fore-head. "I thought. Why did the old king travel to Glenhollow, I ask myself. Then finally I found one who knew of a maid there. She was the rare beauty, 'tis said. Unfortunately, the *bambino* died while still small."

"Dead?"

He touched her cheek, pressing back her hair. "I could find no evidence that he had survived."

"He?"

The marquis chuckled as if flattered by her disorientation. "The king's son," he explained.

Megan drew a careful breath. "So you believe the old king had an illegitimate son, but he is dead."

"I am sorry, my beauty," he said. "But surely this is the best for you, aye. No . . . contention for the throne."

"I never wanted the throne," she whispered.

He drew back slightly, and she realized she had spoken aloud.

"Never wanted it? But you jest. What woman would not wish to be the princess?"

"One that is not meant to be one."

"Ahh." He stroked her arm. "Conscience and beauty all in the so lovely form."

Her head was reeling, but she focused on the immediate. "You have to leave."

"Now?" He sounded genuinely surprised.

"Yes."

"But no," he argued, and, throwing a leg over hers, pressed her onto the mattress.

Small or not, he was considerably heavier than she. She scowled into his face.

"Get off me."

"I cannot. You have intoxicated me."

"You've intoxicated yourself."

He chuckled. "Let me initiate you into the ways of love."

"No thank you."

He scowled. "You wound me."

"I may."

"I will be gentle."

"Get out before I call the guards."

"Surely you would not."

"Surely I would."

"Admit it. You feel it." He fisted his hand near his chest. "A melding of our souls."

"I feel an ache in my knee. Get off me."

"I cannot," he said, and kissed her.

She growled and pushed at his shoulders and in that moment the door swung open.

"Megan?"

The marquis jerked to the side, still pinning her legs with one of his. She sat up with a start.

By the light from the fire, she could see Nicol's profile limned to perfection. He closed the door with careful precision and crossed the floor with slow, cadenced steps.

"Who are you?" Fantino asked.

Nicol ignored him. His expression was cool. "Bored, lass?" he asked.

She pushed at the Italian's shoulders, finally freeing her legs. "What are you doing here?"

He bowed. "I was passing your door when—"

"In the middle of the night?"

He lifted his watch from his waistcoat pocket and glanced at it. "At a quarter of three to be exact. It seems there is a good deal of activity at a quarter of three. As I said, I was passing your door when I heard a commotion. Thinking you were in distress, I entered."

"Who the devil are you?" Fantino demanded.

"How did he get in?" Nicol asked, still facing Megan.

She stared up at him, anger and frustration and embarrassment all boiling inside her. She considered a million statements, a thousand foolish rejoinders. Instead, she said, "I believe he came through the window."

Nicol raised one brow, turned to the marquis, and asked, "Why?"

The Italian opened his mouth, found his feet with stumbling difficulty, and waved in her vague direction. "Why? She is beauty itself, and you would ask the foolish question?"

Nicol's eyebrow twitched. "She is a princess."

"The princess, she needs love, too. No?"

She never saw it coming. Never saw Nicol move. But suddenly the marquis was lying on his back, and Nicol was standing over him. His fists were clenched, his face alight with fury, but in an instant, he hid the anger carefully away.

"Tell him to get out," he said, his voice low.

Her heart was thumping like a gong against her ribs. "Go on, Fantino."

The Italian found his feet, but he was already shaking his head. "She did not inviting you into her chamber, sir."

"Did she invite you?" Nicol asked, his tone low and deadly, his fists still clenched.

"We share the soul, she and I."

Nicol stepped forward, but Megan scrambled from the bed and stumbled between them. "Stop this, both of you."

"Do not worry for me, *amato*. I am the prized pugilist."

Nicol took another step. She crowded backward, pressing the marquis along with her.

"Leave, Fantino," she insisted. "Now."

"You want me to go? To leave you alone with him?"

"He is my bodyguard," she said.

"But no," he said. "A bodyguard he is not. And he should not be here."

"Neither should you."

"I cannot let him stay."

Nicol stepped around her and grasped the other by the shirtfront. "I hate to spoil Sedonia's relations with Italy by throwing you out the window."

"Do so, and you will—"

But by then Megan had reached her door. It opened with a creak.

They turned in unison. "I am going to fetch the guards," she said evenly. "If you are not gone by the time I count to five, I shall call my guards. It will take them less than ten seconds to ascend the stairs and reach my door."

"My beauty—"

"One."

Nicol released the marquis who stumbled back.

"My love—"

"Two."

"I did not—"

"Three."

"I shall never forget your beauty," vowed Fantino, and slipped like water through the window.

Nicol faced her in the silence. Seconds ticked wistfully by.

"You could have told me if you were in the mood for company," he said.

"And disappoint your current liaison?"

He smiled, but there was no humor in the expression. Indeed, if she had not known better, she would think him enraged.

"At least you could have chosen someone taller than yourself, princess."

She shrugged as she paced the room. She felt cold suddenly and angry. "Tell me, Nicol, what really brought you past my door at this hour?"

"I am but your faithful servant," he said, bringing his hand to his chest.

She forced a laugh. It sounded harsh in the stillness. "Were you afraid I would learn the truth?"

"What?"

"Is he your spy?"

His face showed his surprise. Was that two honest expressions in one night? "What the devil are you talking about?"

"Get out," she ordered.

"Or you will call the guards?"

She nodded.

"Have you no more respect for her than that?"

"Her?" The word gritted out. "You mean your princess? Your paragon?"

"Aye," he said, and suddenly he was directly in front of her, his face intense, his teeth gritted. "She would not have invited some stunted Italian to share—"

"Invited!"

"She is pure."

She could feel the blood drain from her face, could feel the heat disappear from her body. "So was I. Until I met you."

"Lass," he began, and reached for her, but she stepped away from his hand.

"Four," she said.

"I did not mean—"

She stepped into the hall, but he caught her arm.

"I did not intend to come here tonight."

She raised her gaze from his hand to his face. "Then you should not have," she said.

"What should I have done?" he whispered. And emotion

was back, lighting his eyes with frustration. "Leave you here with that randy half-wit?"

"As it happens, my lord, I have spent most of life with randy half-wits."

He glanced toward the window. A muscle jumped in his jaw. "Listen, lass, I cannot—"

"Five," she said.

He shook her arm. "Listen to me," he growled.

"Guards," she yelled.

"God's bones! What do you think you're doing?"

"Saving your paragon's reputation."

Footfalls rushed up the stairs. Nicol stared down at her for an elongated second, swore softly, and slipped out the door and into the dark hall.

The guards appeared in an instant.

She told them she had heard something. Told them she was nervous. Thus, they posted a man at her door and dutifully searched the hallways for no one.

Latching the window, Megan returned to bed and lay in silent wakefulness.

It was time to leave, she thought, before it was too late, and Magical Megs was lost forever.

Chapter 28

Nicol watched her from across the dining hall. She looked untouchable this morning. Ethereal, and strangely sad.

He almost went to her then, almost crossed the floor and fell down on his knees, but he was not yet that weak. Aye, he had not quite been able to keep himself from her door during the night, but who could blame him? She had been with a man! A man! Like some common street wench. Damn! It made his teeth hurt. Him! Lord Nicol. Always cool. Always elegant. God's bones. He was acting like an inebriated blacksmith enamored of a well-endowed fishmonger instead of the princess he had trained her to be.

But what did he expect? He had found her on the street. Still, he had taught her everything. Had given her everything. Had—

He almost swore out loud as he glanced at her, for she was stunning, regal, irresistible. He should leave Malkan Palace. Should ride as far away from this hell as possible. Should leave her alone. But nay, not alone. Worse. She would be here with scores of suitors who groveled at her feet. Remembering the night before, he gritted his teeth, but at least the Italian fool had left shortly after dawn. How many others would be willing to risk their lives for a few minutes of her time?

Rising to his feet, he made his way across the hall. She was conversing with Lord Melville and entirely ignored him as she laughed at some sorry jest. He remained silent, barely managing to keep from yanking Melville away like so much rotten fruit. Instead, he waited quietly, but Melville was already launching into another tale, so Nicol bowed, grappling for his well-renowned insouciance.

"Your Majesty," he said.

She lifted a regal brow and turned to him in mild surprise. "Lord Nicol, I didn't see you there."

He gave her a tight smile. She'd learned those lines from him, those haughty expressions, those tiny dismissive mannerisms. But he could play this game as well as anyone. "I have a matter of some import I must discuss with you, Your Majesty."

"Certainly," she said. "What is it?"

"It is something of a discreet nature," he explained.

"Oh." She paused as if mildly miffed. "Very well then, perhaps I could adjourn to my solar." Rising, she made her way through the hall, stopping now and again to speak to a score of irritating intruders. Behind her, a half dozen denizens followed in her wake. Nicol chafed at the delay, but finally they reached the solar. She took a chair and motioned to another as her entourage occupied themselves about the edges of the room.

Nicol watched her. When had she become so controlled? So serene? He remembered their first days at Woodlea and wondered if he took her back there if she would be the same.

If her eyes would shine with fire and wit. If her face would be full of life and earthy humanity.

"I have a busy schedule, viscount," she said, implying, of course, that she did not have time to wait for him to speak. He was almost tempted to remind her who she truly was, but they were not alone, and sometimes, when he wasn't thinking clearly, like now perhaps, he wondered if he had ever known her true identity.

She made a motion as if to rise, and he spoke more rapidly than he had planned.

"About last night—"

"You said your matter was of some import," she said, her body suddenly stiff and her expression as cool as cut glass.

He wanted to kiss her, to yell at her, to drag her off that damned chair and carry her to bed. Instead, he nodded curtly and fisted his hands lest he reach out and throttle her.

"Very well then," he said. "I shall get to the point."

She waited, seeming not the least bit nervous, not the slightest bit curious.

"Tomorrow is Midsummer's Eve."

The tiniest scowl marred her brow. There! That was entirely wrong. The princess would not look at him like that. He wanted to scream the words, to point, to prove that she was not who she said she was, the very person he proclaimed her to be, the person he had forced her to become. She was a thief. He was sure of it. She'd stolen his razor and his buttons and . . . where was his damned watch? He'd had it just the night before. She must have taken it. But how could she? She hadn't touched him.

He gritted his teeth. No, she hadn't touched him. Of that much he was certain. For he would remember that.

"Did you ask me here to tell me the date, Lord Newburn?" she asked.

He gave her a curt nod and knew without looking that the

others could not hear him, yet they were not so far away that he could yank her into his arms and insist that she felt something for him, that she had reveled in his arms. She had torn his shirt to shreds, for God's sake. And where were his damned stockings?

" 'Tis the day when you shall go to Bartham and choose Sedonia's prize steed."

Her expression changed the slightest amount, as if, perhaps, she was the smallest bit curious.

"Traditionally, the king rode there," he continued. "It was something of an excuse to allow the people to view him. He wore his state robes and crown as a symbol of Sedonia's power and wealth, but if you would be more comfortable, I could find an excuse for you to take a carriage."

"No. I shall go astride."

"Paqual might think it strange if you ride the bay again."

"Then I shall ride the gray."

"The mare can be unpredictable. If—"

"I am certain I will be fine."

He considered arguing, but she looked firm and cool, as distant as a winter cloud. "Very well," he acquiesced.

She waited. "Is there something else, Lord Newburn?"

Yes, why the hell had she been with that Italian? Why the hell did she refuse to see him? Why the hell did she only look at him with that icy veneer?

She shifted as if to rise, and he spoke quickly, saying anything to keep her there.

"I thought you might wish to know that Sunderlund himself has been training the gray, so you needn't worry over much about your choice."

"Mr. Sunderlund, the horse master?"

"Yes."

She nodded and made a motion as if to leave.

"Perhaps I was wrong!" The words spurted out.

She settled back, watching him narrowly. "You, Lord Newburn? Wrong?"

He gritted his teeth. "I didn't mean to imply that you had invited the Italian into your room."

She raised a brow. His stomach curled up tight and he couldn't stop the words.

"Did you?"

"Did I what, Lord Newburn?"

"God damn it, woman! You're driving me mad!"

"You? The elegant whip? Surely not."

"Did you invite him to your chambers or not?"

She shrugged. "I would have called on you, but you seemed preoccupied by another. I believe someone said she was a baroness."

"Listen—"

"Listen to what?" she interrupted smoothly. "Are you about to tell me that I should not have dallied with the marquis because you never touched the lovely baroness?"

"I didn't—"

"Ever?"

"Dammit, girl, you're the princess! Well above—"

"No!" she said, and rose abruptly to her feet. "I am not."

The next day was devoted to feasting and celebrating. A huge breakfast was served in the great hall, but Megan found she had little appetite. She sat, instead, talking with her guests and remembering to smile now and again. Was this what a princess did? Pretend, carry on, smile?

She was tired of it. Sick to death of it, in fact. The hall was packed with gentry. People with nothing more to concern themselves with than whether their gloves matched their jackets.

But then, across the room, she caught a glimpse of Jack as he entered the chamber. The boy wore a high, starched collar beneath a black tailcoat. His posture was stiff and his expression sober, but in that moment Lord Landow and Nicol stepped through the door together. Landow set his hand on the boy's shoulder. The lad glanced up. Nicol spoke a few words, and the boy grinned. It was hardly laughter, hardly unbridled joy, but just a hint of happiness, and with that thin expression Megan felt her heart twist, for she would leave soon. Must leave soon. And this is what she would leave behind. She stared at the unlikely trio, and in that instant Jack caught her eye.

He lifted his hand to point at her. Nicol's attention turned with him. For a moment their gazes caught, then he bowed. The boy did the same, and with that identical motion, her eyes began to sting.

Pursing her lips, she gave them a quick nod and hurried back to her seat. She was more than ready to tangle with the gray's fractious moods.

It seemed to take forever for the royal entourage to be ready to ride. Megan chafed as the ermine robe was placed about her shoulders, but when the crown was settled onto her head, she remained very still, letting Mary steady it into her mass of hair before making her stately way down the wide marble stairs and through the palace doors.

A cheer rose up and she stopped, nearly knocked back a step from the roar of the crowd that flooded from the grounds below her. They roared again, lifting their glasses in a happy toast.

"Smile," Nicol said from beside her. She managed to do so, managed, in fact, to wave before making her way down the arced stairway to the gleaming gray mare that waited in the cobbled courtyard. Her hide shone with health and she rolled her black eyes toward Megan, worrying at the bit as her groom held tight to her bridle.

Nicol was close at her side. "The bay has been readied, if you wish to change your mind."

But she shook her head and allowed him to boost her into the saddle. The crowd cheered again. The gray danced beneath her, muscles twitching like knotted ropes beneath her sleek skin. For a moment Megan almost quailed, almost begged them to take the mare back to the stable and bring out the gelding, but a wild host of Sedonians surrounded her. She nodded to the groom to release the bridle, and the horse pranced forward.

"Relax." Nicol's voice came from directly beside her.

The mare shook her head, fighting for control and tossing a bit of froth from between her clamped teeth and onto the crowd.

"Give her a bit of rein," Nicol said, and though logic told Megan to grip harder, she took his advice. Tossing her head again, the mare relaxed a mite, settling her weight onto her bunched haunches and easing into a rocking, high-stepping trot. Behind her, the royal carriage followed. It was empty but accessible, supposedly at Nicol's request. And behind that scores of highborn Sedonians toasted the crowd as they followed her lead.

Nicol remained silent. The tension cranked up a notch. "The marquis has returned to his home," he said finally.

She didn't respond.

"But I was told he had a meeting with Paqual before he left."

Someone called to her from the crowd. The mob cheered and the mare became more animated.

"Might you know what they spoke of?" Nicol asked.

"How would I know, my lord? We surely did not waste time in idle conversation."

From the corner of her eye, she saw his hands tighten on the chestnut's reins. "I've no wish to fight with you," he said.

"Then perhaps you should ride with another. I believe I

saw your baroness—" she began, but in that instant someone screamed. Nicol yelled her name and spurred his mount ahead of hers. A shot rang out, and she saw the viscount jerk.

"Nicol!" she screamed, whipping around. Trying to see. Trying to make certain he was safe. The gray reared. Megan fought for control, but the crowd was milling madly. The mare shook her head, hit the ground with her forefeet, and reared again. And then Megan was falling, tumbling backward. She struck the earth with a jolt. Above her, Mist pawed the air. Megan covered her face in fear, but suddenly someone threw himself atop her. She struggled to get free, but even through the haze of terror she heard Nicol's voice.

"Anna." The name escaped him on a breath. Disoriented, she thought he spoke to her and tried to reach him, but her captor held her at bay. "Anna," Nicol breathed again. "You are well."

Megan's attacker rose to his feet, pulling her with him, and in that instant she recognized him—the Laird of Teleere— the man from whom she'd stolen an ancestral brooch. She jerked away, but he didn't attempt to grab her as her guards rushed forward.

"Arrest him," she ordered, her voice shaking, but the viscount spoke.

"Hold," he said, yet he failed to glance at her. She turned, and in that moment she knew the reason. A woman stood there. Her hair was disheveled and her gown nondescript, but there was no mistaking royalty. Princess Tatiana had returned.

The truth rushed Megan like a pack of wild hounds. This was it then. It was finished. She was no longer needed. Indeed, for all Nicol knew she was already gone. His gaze had not shifted from the princess for a moment.

Someone yelled, seeming to break him from his spell.

"Inside the carriage," he said. "We'd best get out of sight."

It was then that she saw the crown. It lay on its edge near

her feet. Mud was spread across the golden band, but the sun caught a ruby and shone blood red in the evening light. She bent to pick it up, and then, like one in a trance, she stepped into the carriage.

Her guards were still disoriented but managed to assist her into the rocking vehicle. Turning immediately, they lifted their weapons and set their backs to her as they watched the crowds. And outside, Nicol still faced Anna like a moon-struck calf. So the princess had returned to him, had returned and was just as entrancing as ever. Something twisted in Megan's heart, something tore, and then, without another thought, she slipped off the royal robe and stepped out of the far side of the coach. The guards there were busy watching the crowds, and it was simple, so very simple, to duck beneath the carriage. She froze there, waiting to be discovered. But the mob was fractious and loud, the guards besieged. She felt the carriage tilt as people entered it, heard voices raised at her disappearance. But it was not difficult to find a way to hold to the bottom of the conveyance.

In fact, the biggest problem was finding a place to secure her crown as the carriage lurched into motion.

Chapter 29

Nicol poured himself a generous amount of sherry with his left hand. His right arm was still bound up against his chest. Did she know he'd been wounded? Did she realize he'd spurred his horse ahead of hers without conscious thought? Had she known even as she escaped?

"You have people looking for the girl?"

He turned slowly toward his princess. This was not the first conversation they had had here in the last few days.

"They look," he said. His voice was slightly slurred, he noticed. Perhaps he was already drunk. He hoped so. "But they won't find her."

"You are certain she escaped beneath the carriage?"

He smiled grimly, for he could imagine her there, clinging like a spider monkey with the crown clasped tight in one grubby hand. "I am sure of very little where Megan is concerned." He gazed out the window. "In fact, I did not know her name until yesterday."

Anna shook her head. "Magical Megs. Teleere's premiere thief. On my throne!"

"You look very much alike," he said, and swirled his sherry.

"Apparently the Laird of Teleere agreed. Enough to mistake me for her. Enough to threaten to have me hanged. It seems she stole his brooch once upon a time. I believe he wants it back."

"I'm sorry, Anna," he said.

"Yes." She watched his face. "I can see that you are. But I wonder why. Is it because she is gone, or because I have just spent a good deal of time in . . ." Her voice petered out as memories seemed to assail her.

He turned her way. "In hell?" he asked.

She exhaled and scowled. In all the time he had known her, he had never seen her scowl, and in that moment she looked so much like Megan that his chest hurt. 'Twas strange, for the wound was in his arm.

She turned to stare out the window. "If hell makes one confused and frustrated and . . ." She paused, closing her eyes, and in that moment he understood.

"So you're in love with MacTavish." The Laird of Teleere had entered the carriage with them when Nicol had first been wounded, but the moment he had learned Anna's true identity, he had left, had stepped from the moving vehicle and disappeared into the crowds.

The princess's back straightened a mite, but when she spoke her voice was soft and perfectly controlled. "I would be foolish to be in love with him," she said, "He is rude and overbearing."

"What can you expect? He's a pirate."

She shrugged. Another unexpected mannerism. "I want you to find the thief."

"Megs? Why?"

She raised a regal brow and glanced over her shoulder at him. "She has absconded with half my favorite jewels. Not to mention my crown."

Something twisted in his stomach. It felt strangely like fear. "I believe you have enough problems right here at the palace," he said.

"Problems?" She laughed. "Surely not. We already know who paid to have me assassinated during my supposed ride to Bartham."

"MacTavish?"

" 'Tis what Paqual's spies told him, after all. Surely I cannot doubt Paqual."

"Of course. And you believe, too, that it was the prince of Romnia who happened to come along at that precise minute and shoot your would-be assassin."

"Naturally," she said. "It is pure coincidence that he is the man Paqual currently wishes me to marry."

Nicol lowered his voice. "He has to be stopped."

She nodded grimly. "I learned much of him while I was in Teleere. It seems he knew I was interested in MacTavish. It seems, in fact, that he hired a man named Martinez to implement a plan that would make it appear as if MacTavish was trying to kill me."

"The Pirate Lord would not be easily manipulated if he were to become your husband. Paqual could never accept that."

"True."

"So you're unlikely to marry any man Paqual suggests."

"Also true."

"But how to be rid of Paqual? Despite his treachery, he is powerful."

"Yes. He is that. We shall have to bide our time, wait—

"If we had Laird MacTavish's power behind us, we could—"

She turned abruptly away. "Don't speak to me of Mac-Tavish."

"He's the very reason this entire debacle was set in motion, Anna. You hoped to marry him at one time, remember?"

"That was before."

"Before what?"

"Before I met him."

"So he was not as strong a leader as you thought he would be?"

She paused for a moment before answering, then entwined her fingers and looked him in the eye. "He is strong."

"Then he was cruel?"

She pursed her lips and raised her chin slightly. He refused to remember Megan doing the same. "I do not believe this is any of your concern, Nicol."

"I beg to differ," he argued, feeling unacceptable emotion flooding in. "We all risked much to give you a chance to meet him."

She was silent for a moment before sighing and turning away. "No," she said. "He was not cruel."

"Then perhaps you did not find him attractive."

She snorted. Actually snorted. The princess. It took him a moment to accept the fact.

"What does that mean?" he asked finally.

"You saw him, did you not, Nicol?"

Perhaps he felt a twinge of jealousy. Perhaps even now, after all he had learned, after all he had endured, he still felt an emotion as mundane as jealousy. "He was not painful to look at, I suppose."

"I suppose," she agreed, and he saw her mouth quirk into a whimsical smile.

"Then why—"

"I told you before, I've no wish to talk about him."

"You must marry, Anna. Why not—"

"Enough," she said, and turned back to face him. "I want you to find the girl."

He drew a deep breath. "I do not mean to be disrespectful, Anna, but I believe you owe her for what she has done for you."

"Truly?" She was the princess again, as cool as a winter breeze, as hard as a marble statuette. "And what do I owe her, Nicol? My crown? Because that's what she took."

"She kept your country safe in your absence. She risked her life to—"

"Find her," she ordered. "Or I shall get others to do so."

Morning dawned, though Nicol thought it might not. Anna breakfasted early. He watched her from across the room. Aye, she was beautiful, but there was something missing from the princess that had not been missing a week before. A life, a spark. Though no one else seemed to notice.

It was then, however, that he saw Nimble Jack. He was rushing across the room, his narrow form stiff and his expression somber.

"Your Majesty," he said, and bowed.

It took Nicol a moment to drag himself from his self-pity, a moment longer to realize the catastrophe unfolding. He had not found an opportunity to tell Anna Jack's story. Rising, he, too, hurried to the princess.

"Jack," he said, meeting Anna's eyes over the boy's head. "How did you get here?"

The lad scowled, but he didn't raise his gaze from the princess. "'Tis said there was an attempt on your life, Your Majesty."

Anna hesitated only a moment. "Aye . . . Jack, there was."

The boy's scowl deepened slightly. "You are unhurt?"

"Yes." Her back was perfectly straight, her expression unreadable as she shifted her gaze to Nicol's.

"You should not have come here alone, lad," Nicol chided, laying a hand on the boy's shoulder. "Where is Lord Landow?"

"I feared . . ." Jack paused, narrowed his eyes and continued. "Who was it what tried to kill you, my lady?"

"I am not yet certain."

There was a prolonged moment of silence, then, "So you were lucky yesterday?" the boy asked.

"Aye." Anna tilted her gaze up to Nicol's and down again, searching for answers. "I was lucky."

" 'Tis time to go now, lad," Nicol said.

The boy nodded once and let Nicol usher him from the room. But once past the door, Jack stopped and turned. His eyes were deadly earnest and his mouth pursed.

"Where is she?" he intoned.

Something like premonition stirred in Nicol's gut, but he fought it down. "Where is who, lad?"

"The princess."

"What do you mean, boy? She's there dining."

The lad shook his head.

"Jack." Allard rushed in, his brow furrowed with worry, but Nicol held the boy's gaze, feeling his own pain reflected and wondering how the hell this could happen.

"You must not leave your lord's house without permission," insisted the guard.

"Go home, Jack," Nicol said.

"Will she be back?" murmured the boy, but Nicol had no answers, only questions and an empty hole where his heart had once been.

* * *

Nicol glared out at the rain that beat down on the courtyard below the solar's window. Damn his spies. Why hadn't they returned yet? How hard could it be to find the princess's double? He should have gone himself. Should have searched the first day. But the rightful princess had returned, and he couldn't leave her. Couldn't allow her to fight this battle alone.

"So you're certain Prince Edward did not shoot the assassin as Paqual contends," Tatiana said.

Nicol shrugged. He felt as old as death and tired beyond hope. What would he give to sleep as he had in Megan's arms? "The prince fired a gun," he said. "But I believe it was one of his guards who killed your would-be assassin." At least his spies had learned that much.

Anna sighed, sounding as tired as he felt. "Might the guard be in the market for a bride?"

Nicol turned toward her, forcing his own thoughts behind him. "I haven't asked. But I hear Lord Malborg is."

"Lord Malborg?" She turned her gaze back toward him. "Is he the suitor du jour."

"He waits in the morning room as we speak."

"Well." She gathered her skirts in one delicate hand. "I had best paint on my smile then," she said, and rose to return to her rooms, but Nicol stopped her.

"Tell me," he said, "if you weren't the princess of Sedonia, would you have remained in Teleere?"

He saw her hesitate, saw her weaken, saw the wistful look in her eye, but in a moment she straightened. "It matters little," she said, and turned regally away. "For I *am* the princess."

Her ladies followed her silently to her chambers. Nicol turned back to the rain-drenched courtyard. Where was she now? Did she think of him? Did she miss him or wish him dead?

His mind wandered, and then, like an opium addict, he shifted back through his memories—the lithe sway of her body against his as they danced, the sound of her laughter, the crush of her breasts against his chest. Dear God—

A shout drew him from his reverie. The next shout brought him to his feet, and in an instant he was flying down the hall toward Anna's chambers. Her door stood open. Not a guard was in sight. Nicol sprang into the room and stopped. The chamber was filled to brimming—guards, ladies-in-waiting, and a giant of a man who looked like an ancient Viking. But it was the couple in the center of the room that snagged his attention. For there Anna stood, wrapped in Laird Mac-Tavish's arms.

"Stand back! Release her!" demanded the captain of the guard, but MacTavish turned slowly toward them, not retreating an inch.

"Shoot him!" Paqual shouted, striding into the chamber.

MacTavish turned his gaze slowly toward the chancellor. "Lord Paqual," he said, "how was your visit with Martinez?"

The blood left Paqual's face in a rush. "If you will not shoot him, I will!" he hissed.

Tatiana stepped in front of MacTavish, her arms outstretched. "Shoot my betrothed, and I swear by all that is holy, I will see you hanged this very day if I have to tie the rope myself."

"Your . . ." Paqual stumbled back a pace. "Betrothed!"

"Aye," she said. "You have manipulated and murdered, but you have lost, and Sedonia has won. We will ally ourselves with a great force, with Teleere and her master."

" 'Tis not for you to decide, girl," he hissed, stepping forward. "I have made you what you are, and you'll not ruin my plans by binding yourself to a bastard pirate."

"Better a pirate than a traitor," she said. "I know your plans, Paqual. You hoped to make me believe MacTavish had hired my assassin. You planned for me to fall into the arms of the prince of Romnia. But you are not so clever as you think, and you are naught but a murderer.

"Take him to the dungeon," she said to her guards. "And hold him there until his trial."

They did so, and he went, squawking all the way.

"Your Highness." Lady Mary bowed nervously. "If Lord MacTavish will meet with your advisors, they could discuss the wedding plans."

"I will meet with them shortly," MacTavish said.

"It is surely not proper—"

"Not proper." Tatiana smiled as she shook her head. "Nay, it is not. But it is what I want. He is what I want."

"Your Majesty, you cannot—"

"I can and I shall."

"Get out," MacTavish ordered, then he turned as if they were no longer there, and kissed her.

There were gasps and hisses, but Nicol had heard enough, and so had the others. Gathering up the interlopers, he pushed them toward the door and found that the giant Viking was doing the same. Once on the far side, they gazed at each other as the crowd slowly dissipated.

"The lad calls me Burr," said the giant, nodding toward the room they had just left.

"The lad being the lord of Teleere?"

"Aye."

Nicol nodded. "What do others call you?"

"Whatever I wish them to."

He almost laughed. "Tell me, Burr, will he treat her well?"

The huge man stared off into space for a moment. His legs

were spread. Arms the size of oak trunks bulged from the holes of his fur vest. "I raised him from a bairn."

"MacTavish."

"Aye."

"And?"

"He will treat her well."

Nicol studied him carefully. "I noticed the laird had some bruising."

The Viking shrugged. "Sometimes the lad is foolish."

"Foolish?"

The Viking narrowed his eyes, which were already pretty narrow. "He thought the lady was something she was not and refused to return to Sedonia because of it."

Nicol shook his head, bemused. "He mistook her for the thief called Magical Megs, yes, but—"

Burr looked mildly surprised. "So far as the lad knows Megs is naught but an honest thief. He thought your princess was a lady."

"She is a lady."

"Don't tell the lad," Burr rumbled. "He thinks her a woman with a heart."

Nicol shook his head but returned to the main focus. "You know Megs?"

"I've not met the little scrapper. But I know of her."

"What do you know?"

The Viking squinted. "A good deal."

Hope swelled in Nicol's soul. It was difficult to breathe. Harder yet to think. "Such as?"

Burr shrugged. "She stole the lad's brooch." His lips twitched. It might have been a smile. "He was fit to be hanged." He actually chuckled now, apparently entertained by the thought of his lord's anger.

"What else can you tell me?"

The eyes narrowed again. "Why do you wish to know?"

A thousand thoughts ripped through Nicol's mind, but vanity won out. "She stole the princess's crown."

Their gazes held tight for a long moment, then the Viking shrugged again. "I can't help you, lad."

"Can't or won't."

He smiled, belligerence showing in every hard line. "Won't."

"I'll pay you," Nicol said, and Burr laughed as he tilted his head toward the chamber just exited.

"The lass inside offered me coin, too."

Frustration warred with desperation in Nicol's soul. "The lass inside is the princess of Sedonia."

"Is she now?" said the Viking, his face impassive. "And does that make her more important than the wee thief you're searching for?"

"It does to Sedonia."

"How about to you, lad?"

"I am not a lad, Viking," he said, but suddenly his mind clicked on something spoken minutes before. "You said as far as he knew."

"What's that, laddie?"

"You said, so far as the lad knows, Megs is naught but an honest thief."

"Did I?"

"What did you mean?"

"Things are rarely what they seem."

"What did you mean?" he repeated.

The Viking eyed him up and down. "Seems to me, the wee lass has enough troubles without being hounded by a rich dandy like yourself."

"Dammit!" Nicol swore and temporarily losing his mind, grabbed a hank of the giant's vest. "Tell me what you know."

The door beside them opened, and Anna stepped through, followed by MacTavish.

The Viking nodded, not bothering to remove Nicol's fist from his vest. "Lassie," he greeted, "I hear you're a princess."

She smiled, full force and beaming, not like the princess at all, but like a woman in love. "And I hear you've enraged my unflappable advisor."

He didn't even glance at Nicol. "Aye. I believe I have."

"May I ask how?"

"He wants to know where to find the wee thief."

"Tell me where she is, Goddammit!" Nicol growled.

Burr grinned. "He seemed quite concerned."

"Perhaps you should tell him then."

The Viking shrugged. "I've no way of knowing why he wishes to locate her."

"You could ask him."

"I did, but the next thing I know he's hanging on to me vest like a hungry hound."

"Nicol," Anna said. "Let Burroun go."

He did so slowly, finding his wits and feeling a bit foolish as he did so.

"And tell him the truth," Anna added softly.

"The truth," Nicol said, "is that I was ordered to find the girl since she escaped not only with the royal crown, but a good deal of jewelry. Not to mention my buttons!"

Every soul within hearing turned to stare at him.

Nicol cleared his throat. "She's a thief," he explained lamely.

Anna stared at him for some seconds, her expression serene, then she turned back toward the Viking. "He wants to find her because he's in love with her."

"He didn't say as much."

"Men are sometimes slow to share their feelings. I've seen it happen before."

The Viking drew a hard breath through his nostrils. His half-bare chest expanded like bellows. "Come, lad," he said. "We shall share what we know of life and wee thieves."

Chapter 30

Megan wiped down a table. A drunken tanner reached for her, but it was late, and he was slow. In less than ten minutes she had shooed out the last patron and locked the doors.

Her own inn. Her own property. She had purchased it only a month before. Finding this place, this quiet inn in a little known Teleerian village had been the difficult part. It had taken her most of eight months, but paying for it had been simple, for she had the princess's jewels. The crown she had kept. Even now it was hidden safely away. She didn't know why. Someday she would pry out the gems and sell them, of course. Someday, when she could bear to do such things. But for now she would leave matters as they were. Except clean.

She glanced around the common room. Empty tankards remained on every table. Beer stained the floor. She should clean it now. But she was tired. Weary to the bone.

"Why?"

She shrieked as she spun about and there, standing on the bottom stair was the viscount of Newburn.

"How did you find me?" Her heart was pounding in her chest, making it difficult to breathe. He looked tired and dirty. His boots were caked with mud, and his cloak was stained. His face was whiskered, and his eyes . . . Her heart hitched in her chest, but she hardened it carefully. "Why did you come?"

He pushed away from the wall, heading toward her. "I would have paid you as I promised."

She shrugged, watching him, calming her heart. "We can call it even."

"Even!" He jerked toward her, and she stepped back, putting a table between them. "You think us even?"

"Yes," she said, and lifted her chin, careful to keep her head, to keep her distance, lest she fall too hard to recover. "I do."

"You stole my—" he began, and stopped. His mouth twitched. "You stole Anna's crown."

"And you stole my life." The words hissed out, too close to the surface, too close to the truth.

"Aye, well . . ." He swept his hand sideways, indicating the room in which they stood. "It looks as if you've traded up."

She shrugged. "'Tis hardly a palace. But it is mine, and it—"

"Then why didn't you stay if you wanted a palace?" His voice was rife with frustration.

"Stay?" She snapped off a laugh. "And do what? Pretend to be your Anna's long-lost twin?"

He was silent for a moment. "You could have said goodbye," he said finally. "I think I deserved that much."

"I—"

"Jack deserved that much."

She winced and twisted her hands together. "How is he?"

"He's gone. Disappeared shortly after you did, but at least he had the courtesy to leave a note."

She remained silent, unable to utter the obvious question.

"He said he went to find the princess."

"The princess." Her words were no more than a whisper. "But she was there. At the palace."

Nicol shrugged, but his expression was tight. "He didn't seem to think so. Seemed to think, in fact, that we had all duped him. On the other hand, his penmanship was excellent."

"He's gone," she murmured.

"Will is searching for him, but surely you cannot blame the lad for leaving," he said. "Since you did the same thing."

She said nothing.

"I am told the Barneses mysteriously received a handsome new steed at Woodlea."

"Truly?"

"And that Allard suddenly came into a small fortune."

"How nice."

"He and Lady Mary plan to wed."

"All is going well without me then."

"No." He said and shook his head. "It is not. Why did you go?"

Frustration burned through her. "I left . . ." she began, but she stopped herself before it was too late. Before too much truth was spilled.

"Tell me why."

"You didn't need me anymore. My job was done."

"You're wrong."

There was something about his tone that made her heart twist, but she dared not care. "Leave me be, viscount. I've done all you've asked."

"No," he said and shaking his head, took a step toward her. "You have not."

"Leave off!" she rasped. "For I won't be goin' back with the likes of you. Ye can't make me."

He kept coming. She backed away.

"Get out, or I swear I shall spill the truth to any who wish to 'ear it."

"Oh? And what truth is that, lass?" he asked and rounded the table.

She was backed against the wall and raised her chin. A flash of nostalgia leapt into his eyes, but he kept coming.

"Don't you be coming a step closer."

He did. "What will you tell them, lass? That you are the king's own daughter?"

She felt herself go pale, felt her knees buckle. "What?"

"I've met some interesting people since you left," he said. "Laird MacTavish for one. It seems he mistook Anna for an Irish pickpocket when first she arrived on his shores. It seems he mistook her for you."

She shook her head, though she wasn't sure why.

"But though she looked like a thief, she didn't speak like a thief. She didn't act like a thief. Thus, he began to wonder. So he learned all he could about Teleere's Magical Megs."

"Dear God."

"I fear Laird MacTavish's spies are more adept than my own."

"I don't know what you've heard," she said. "But they're lies."

"I heard that the old king had an illegitimate child."

"I wouldn't know."

"The mother was a washerwoman. A rare beauty, I'm told."

Her throat hurt.

"She gave birth to a baby girl in the spring of 1797. The king never knew he—"

"He knew!" she spat. She realized she should have remained quiet, but the words were spilled, and she did not care.

Nicol narrowed his eyes, watching her closely. "I was told—"

"You were told wrong." She was breathing hard, and her chest ached. "Mum was already sick when she went to him. She loved him, worshipped him, but he couldn't be bothered. He had a son. Two, in fact. What did he care for a skinny urchin of uncertain birth?"

"Lassie. I'm—"

"Leave me alone," she whispered. "I'm nothing to you."

"Nothing?" The word sounded hollow, empty, as if it were devoid of meaning. "I've thought about nothing but you since the day you left. I've spent . . ." He chuckled. The sound was weak. "Nine months. Nine . . . searching in every hovel in every village in every country I could imagine."

Her chest felt cramped. "Because I have the crown."

He watched her, his gaze hot and intent, his mouth unsmiling. "Because you have my heart," he whispered.

"Love hurts, viscount," she rasped. "Love kills. I've seen it happen."

"Love heals, lass. I've seen that. Seen it in Anna's eyes. Seen it—"

"I'm not an heiress, Nicol. No matter what you believe, I will never be princess."

He laughed now, like a man gone mad, like a man set free. Gone was his cool nonchalance. And in its place was a desperate man with budding hopefulness. "Is that what you think? Is that what you believe? That I want a princess?"

Silence again, then, "What do you want?"

"You." The single word fell softly into the silence.

She shook her head, trying to denounce it, but his gaze held her trapped.

"I want the thief who stole my watch. I want the princess who stole the crown." His voice softened to a whisper. "I want the lady who stole my heart."

She tried to escape then, tried to run, but he caught her by the arm.

She twisted away, desperate to be free, to be gone, to keep from believing. "I am no lady, Nicol."

"You are more lady than any I have met."

She jerked out of his grasp. "Well, I don't want to be. Nobility!" She spat the word. "They use and discard and defile."

"So you stole from them."

Her head hurt. "Aye. I stole. Took a little back of what they took from me."

He drew a deep breath. "So now you wish to be a pauper."

"I wish to make my own way. To live honestly. To—"

"Good. Then I shall do the same."

She blinked at him.

"I shall work for you, lass. You can pay me what you see fit."

"That's ridiculous. You're—"

"A lord?" He laughed. "My father was a penniless womanizer. A grubby low-titled bastard without a soul to redeem him. My brother was worse. I knew Ernest planned to kill Father. I knew it, and I did nothing to stop it. Nothing, until it was too late. What does that make me?"

"A viscount?" she said, and he laughed.

"Then you're a princess."

"I'm not—"

"You are in my eyes."

"Nicol—"

"Marry me."

She gasped like a child. "I . . . I can't . . ."

"You must."

"I don't—"

"You do."

"What would I . . ." She was shaken, rattled, breathless. "What would I do with the inn?"

He touched her cheek and moved closer. "I don't care. Sell it. Live here with me. Give it away."

"Give it away!" she gasped, appalled and breathless. "Do you know what I paid for it?"

"A crown?" he guessed. His eyes were smiling. She felt her muscles go weak even before he kissed the corner of her mouth.

"No," she whispered.

"No?"

"I kept the crown."

The smile had reached his lips. He eased his fingers around the back of her neck. "You sentimental fool."

"I missed you a bit."

"Did you?"

She closed her eyes. "But I won't be your lackey."

"Lackey?"

"I'll speak 'owever I like."

"*How*—"

" *'Owever!*"

He grinned. "Whatever you say."

"And we'll tell no one who my father was."

"I didn't even know you had a father."

She paused and shivered. "And we'll sell this hideous inn."

He laughed out loud and swung her into his arms.

"I love you," she whispered.

"You own my soul," he murmured, and kissed her.

She smiled, her heart filled to brimming. "And your watches."

"Yes," he carried her across the floor. "I was wondering if I might have them back."

"I don't think so."

"Can I have my buttons?"

"I've become rather attached to them."

"Can I take you to bed?"

"Anytime," she whispered, and kissed him.

He returned the caress, his lips warm and firm against hers. "Then I win," he murmured, and carried her up the stairs two at a time.

The days may be getting longer, but the nights are definitely getting hotter with these sizzling titles, coming in May from Avon Books.

A DARK CHAMPION by Kinley MacGregor
An Avon Romantic Treasure

Stryder of Blackmoor has never desired the comforts of home and hearth—until he gazed upon the exquisite face of Rowena. He dares not succumb to her sensuous charms, but when treachery and danger threaten, the noble knight must stand as the lady's champion—though it could cost him his honor, his heart . . . and his forbidden dream of happiness.

WHAT MEMORIES REMAIN by Cait London
An Avon Contemporary Romance

Cyd Callahan has no memory of the terrible event of her childhood, and she'd rather the truth remain buried. Ewan Lochlain, however, is determined to unravel the mystery of his parents' deaths—and he's convinced Cyd holds the key. But Ewan realizes too late that his personal investigation may have just cost Cyd her life . . .

ONCE A GENTLEMAN by Candice Hern
An Avon Romance

Nicholas Parrish had no intentions of taking a bride, but when Prudence falls asleep in his townhouse, her irate father demands satisfaction. Being a true gentleman, Nicholas agrees to do the proper thing. But he may need to reconsider his plans for a "marriage in-name-only" when his bride decides to make him fall in love with her!

THE PRINCESS AND THE WOLF by Karen Kay
An Avon Romance

Married by proxy to a European prince she doesn't love, the princess Sierra will not believe her husband died in far-off America—and crosses an ocean to discover the truth. But she will need a scout in this wild land, and puts her life in the hands of High Wolf, the proud Cheyenne brave she once loved . . . and should rightly have wed.

Have you ever dreamed of writing a romance?

*And have you ever wanted
to get a romance published?*

Perhaps you have always wondered how to
become an Avon romance writer?
We are now seeking the best and brightest undiscovered
voices. We invite you to send us your query letter to
avonromance@harpercollins.com

What do you need to do?

Please send no more than two pages telling us
about your book. We'd like to know its setting—is it
contemporary or historical—and a bit about the hero,
heroine, and what happens to them.

Then, if it is right for Avon we'll ask to see part of the
manuscript. Remember, it's important that you have
material to send, in case we want to see your story quickly.

Of course, there are no guarantees of publication,
but you never know unless you try!

*We know there is new talent just waiting
to be found! Don't hesitate . . . send us
your query letter today.*

*The Editors
Avon Romance*

Avon Romantic Treasures

*Unforgettable, enthralling love stories,
sparkling with passion and adventure
from Romance's bestselling authors*